# BECOMING

# BECOMING MRS KUMAR

## HEATHER SAVILLE GUPTA

RANDOM HOUSE INDIA

Published by Random House India in 2013
1

Copyright © Heather Saville Gupta 2013

Random House Publishers India Private Limited
Windsor IT Park, 7th Floor
Tower-B, A-1, Sector-125
Noida 201301, UP

Random House Group Limited
20 Vauxhall Bridge Road
London SW1V 2SA
United Kingdom

978 81 8400 041 2

Typeset in Electra LT Std by R. Ajith Kumar

Printed and bound in India by Replika Press Private Limited

*For Vivek, my own Mr Kumar,*
*who restored my faith in happy endings*

# 1

I was woken from a very deep sleep by the persistent ringing of my alarm clock. I struggled to reach across and grab it, but I was caught up in a complicated arrangement of bedding which bound my arms tight to my sides. Despite the fact that my feet were flapping around in the direct chill of the air conditioning unit, I was sweating profusely, my tongue glued firmly to the roof of my mouth. The alarm clock, programmed to wake even the hardiest sleeper, cranked up its level and pitch as an accompanying throb began somewhere in the recesses of my aching brain. I peered through my eyelids, which were practically glued together, my eyeballs feeling as though I had added a bucket of sand to my contact lens cleaning solution. Everything around me was familiar—the lilac coloured walls with their patches of damp from the previous monsoon season, the bookcases groaning under the weight of their load of trashy novels with a sprinkling of more pretentious titles, the white cotton curtains, which I had been meaning to change for months, fluttering uselessly under the blast of the AC. The sounds were typical of a Mumbai morning—I could make out the insistent call of the chai-wallah, the chorus of horns that indicated the early morning rush hour and the strained engine sounds of the tired old Fiat taxis struggling to make it up the hill. Nothing, including the by now insistent pounding of my head, was any different from any other day of my life in Mumbai—my home for the past two years.

I managed to extricate my arms from under the sheet, which had by now wound itself around me several times, and finally silenced the alarm. It was 8 a.m., time to get up and force myself into some semblance of readiness for the day ahead. Although I generally felt less than my best most mornings, I was aware of a new emotion—a suffocating, stifling feeling that was making me want to cry. I wondered whether I'd switched from my usual vodka to gin the previous night—gin always made me depressed—but no, I had stuck to the vodka-diet cokes as usual. I tried to work out whether I was PMS-ing, but remembered that I'd just finished my period and there was at least a couple of weeks' hiatus until the mood swings began again.

I thought about the events of the previous evening. A big party at one of the fancy five-star hotels in the suburbs, a glamorous fashion show, spotting Bollywood stars, conversations with random strangers, pretending to find everyone interesting, more drinks, which helped everyone seem more interesting, and finally being driven home safely by my endlessly patient driver and the usual 'walk of shame' (though I wasn't actually ashamed) past the doormen who inevitably found it almost impossible not to raise their bushy eyebrows at me. The conversations were indistinct, the people I'd talked to fairly blurry but I know that I would have spent a fair amount of time discussing the latest gossip—who was supposedly sleeping with whom, the guy who got angry and drunk and embarrassed himself and his ex-girlfriend the week before, the new bar that had opened up across town and which was the place to be seen for Mumbai's glittering in-crowd.

This was a typical evening for me, one that I had repeated excessively for the past couple of years, and one that usually left me briefly satiated despite the inevitable headache the next morning. I did try to keep my party nights to the weekend, but typically they spilled over into the week, and I usually joined the majority of the Mumbai party crowd in starting the weekend on a Wednesday or a Thursday night.

I closed my eyes again and tried to work out exactly what was causing the nagging feeling of unease. Everything was completely normal, I was in bed alone, I had plenty of time to get ready for work. I had a fairly relaxed day ahead of me, no deadlines or heavy meetings to get through at the advertising agency I worked for, and it was almost the weekend. I wasn't really prone to being sad or depressed, in fact most people called me the life and soul of the party, and I was famous for being able to bounce back, rally the troops, organize social events and generally behave like the happy, carefree thirty-something that I was. I had little time for moaners, those who wallowed in self-pity, or read endless self-help books, and I saw depression as something to 'get over'. I picked up my phone and scrolled through recent text messages. 'C U soon babe. Thanks for a fab night'. 'Team meeting at 10 a.m. Have sent you agenda'. The latter was from one of my junior team members, Rohit, the former from my friend Maya. Shaking myself from my (hopefully temporary) melancholy, I headed for the bathroom to begin a much needed repair job.

As the ancient geyser warmed the water for my shower, I

scrutinized myself in the mirror, cringing at the dark shadows that looked as though they'd resist even a double layer of my trusty Touche Eclat cover up. My eyes were an even cloudier grey than usual, and my shoulder length wavy hair, which looked sun-kissed on a good day, now looked frizzy and an unappealing shade of mouse. Even my freckles, which I'd been told that Indians found cute, now looked grubby against my wan skin. I wasn't the kind of girl who suffered from huge complexes about my looks, and was generally fairly happy with my lot, despite my tendency to gain weight around my already substantial hips. Today, however, was another story. I looked exhausted, drained, and older than my years.

A couple of hours later, I was on the way to the office. I did the usual metaphorical intake of breath when the driver swung left into the great expanse of Marine Drive, aptly christened 'The Queen's Necklace', the long sweeping shoreline that took you all the way to the southern tip of Mumbai, a great expanse of glittering sea and gorgeous swanky apartments. This morning, the sun was shining from a clear bright blue sky, the usual pollution swept away by the fresh breeze that typified Mumbai's 'winter': the sea looked vaguely blue rather than its usual muddy brownish grey and even the buildings appeared clean and white rather than grubby and discoloured. It felt like my surroundings were conspiring to cheer me up, but I wasn't having any of it. I was still filled with despair, and suddenly it all seemed completely pointless.

Despite a few ups and downs, this was the first time I had felt this disconsolate since arriving in Mumbai two years earlier. I had fallen in love with the city the minute I arrived, and was instantly hooked on its energy, its raw vitality and its chaotic madness,

4

which seemed to border perpetually on insanity. India certainly hadn't been the easiest of places to live, but I'd loved the fact that it was different from the typical expatriate cities, that it required a gritty determination to survive and that its rewards, though often hidden from immediate sight, made life rich and interesting. I'd led the life of a typical single girl — made lots of friends and interesting acquaintances, dated a few (largely inappropriate) men, worked hard at an interesting and challenging job in advertising, and generally focussed on getting the most out of life in a city that had a huge amount to offer the curious foreigner. This sudden feeling of ennui had hit me by surprise, though now I came to think of it, all the signs had been there for a while.

I'd spent two years having a fabulous time, wowing my friends back in cold, dreary England with my flamboyant tales, racking up friends and party invites, sunning myself on golden beaches and spending evenings at swanky apartments, and despite all that, I suddenly felt empty and as though I'd actually done nothing at all with my life.

With a sudden, brutal clarity I realized that the vast majority of my so-called friends here were only interested in the social butterfly that I had become, that my white skin lent me a certain aspirational value, a badge that opened doors and created connections, but that in fact no one except perhaps my Indian friend Maya had even come close to knowing the real me, and that I had successfully managed to bury myself so deeply beneath the superficial trappings of a so-called happy life, that I had lost touch with what was really important.

There, I had finally admitted it to myself. I was lonely, missing my friends and family and yearning to settle down.

I wondered why this moment of sudden clarity had descended upon me on a random Friday morning, after all, there was nothing different about this day, and nothing particularly unusual about the night that preceded it, it wasn't as though some momentous event had shaken me from my reverie, no thunderbolt or godly revelation or vodka overdose or near death experience on Mumbai's lethal roads. Instead, I had just woken up and not liked what I had seen and in fact I was disgusted that I had let this go on for so long, covering up my loneliness and insecurity with a shallow veneer of booze and casual friendships. I ached for my friends and family back home. Maybe I should leave India, go back to England, and find a way to avoid admitting defeat, possibly with a fat, well paid job that would at least allow me to hold my head up high. I had had a crazy, roller-coaster time here but I'd come to a decision point and knew that I couldn't keep running away. It was time to face up to the truth and make some tough choices.

## 2

My arrival had been quite different. I had just turned 30 and hit my own early mid-life crisis. All through my twenties, I had thoroughly enjoyed life as a single girl in London—though I'd had a few brief affairs and a couple of on-off relationships, I figured that I had plenty of time to worry about getting into something serious. I was vaguely expecting to meet the man of my dreams in a few years but I was still young and it really felt like the world was my oyster—my work was the most important thing in my life and I relished the fact that I could work 14-hour days without having to worry about rushing home to anyone. I genuinely didn't feel any pressure to get into a serious relationship.

As my thirties approached, however, the comfortable, relaxed, 'anything goes' feeling I had cultivated throughout my twenties began to be surreptitiously eroded by a set of niggling worries that started keeping me awake at night. I'd done well at work, but had I just been wasting my time when it came to relationships? My friends were starting to settle down, forming cosy domestic twosomes, which left little time for their single friends like me.

Don't get me wrong, I certainly wasn't obsessing about finding Mr Right, but there was certainly a little voice in my head that was getting louder and louder as my thirtieth birthday approached, and it was telling me that it was time to make some serious changes. On my birthday, I had actually gone into a mild depression and started to pick my life to pieces. All of this soul searching resulted in one thing—a clear realization that whatever happened, I definitely didn't want to be fighting my way onto the tube every morning and every evening or spending my days cramped into a tiny cubicle sharing stale air with a hundred co-workers as I fought for recognition and promotion and a few extra pounds in my pay packet every month. In short, I was bored of my future already, and I knew I had to do something about it.

I had developed an obsession with the thought of leaving the UK and heading off to travel the world, but this didn't seem practical or reasonable. I'd been working for a few years, but hadn't managed to save much money as I'd spent most of it on having fun and enjoying myself, paying extortionate rent for my bedroom the size of a broom cupboard in London, and blowing cash on nights out at trendy clubs. I wondered whether I should just buy a one-way ticket to an exotic location half-way around the world and head off into the sunset in search of adventure and perhaps a big fat love affair. I'd always been a complete sucker for romantic novels and now that I'd started introspecting and my priorities seemed to be shifting, I couldn't help wondering if I might meet the man of my dreams in some exotic location, though I tried to avoid fixating on this. Being single and thirty was OK, but turning into some sad Bridget Jones obsessive was not. At the end of the day, however, I was a realist. I'd spent a few years climbing the career ladder and it seemed like a crazy time to throw it all away in search of a romantic dream, which might turn out to be little more than a few anecdotes about diarrhoea and long train journeys.

Call it coincidence, call it fate, but the day my boss called me into his office to talk to me about a job in India felt weirdly and almost ridiculously prescient—as though someone had been taking a sneak peek into my head when I hadn't been paying attention, read my mind and decided to offer me a way out of my existential crisis. I was working as an Account Director at one of the big advertising agencies in London, and had been there all my working life, being promoted slowly but steadily through the ranks after joining the company as a management trainee. I didn't know whether I'd inadvertently let any of my inner turmoil show, or even whether I'd talked about my desire to travel to my co-workers on one of my more drunken nights at the office bar, but when my boss James called me into his office one dreary Monday afternoon, and asked me to consider taking on an assignment working with one of our international clients whose Asian hub was located in Mumbai, India, I was shocked to the core.

Though I didn't want to be labelled as one of those annoyingly pretentious types who wanted to go to India to 'find themselves', I had always been fascinated by this vast and unknown country— imagining it to be a sweet and spiritual place, beset occasionally with floods and droughts depending on the time of year, but largely peaceful and friendly and, of course, hot. Besides, my Indian friends in London were lovely, the curries in Brick Lane's restaurants were awesome, and Indian culture was becoming really trendy in certain parts of the UK, so heading to India felt like a positive and exciting choice and a chance to be a part of something that was genuinely different from all my life experiences so far, with the added security blanket of a job, salary and all mod cons provided for me.

I immediately called an emergency meeting of my closest girlfriends, Lizzie and Annabel, intending to deliver my news and ask their opinion over a few bottles of wine. I'd been friends with both of them since we were together at university in Sheffield, and we'd all ended up together in London—Lizzie on the road to becoming a hotshot lawyer in one of London's biggest legal firms and Annabel shuffling from temping job to bar job while she pursued her dream of becoming an actress. We had been bound together by our experiences as we made the transition together from naïve freshers to experienced women of the world, and I valued their opinion enormously. They both looked expectantly at me as I navigated the busy wine bar with a bottle of chilled Chardonnay under my arm.

'Well, Jules?' demanded Annabel, always the impatient one, tossing her unkempt blonde curls out of her eyes. 'What's up? New man? New job? Won the lottery?'

'Kind of,' I answered a little nervously. 'It is a new job, but with the same company.' I poured us a glass of wine and continued. 'Actually, I've been asked to go and work for the company in Mumbai.'

'Mumbai???' they both chorused in unison, with looks of shock and amazement on their faces and, in Annabel's case, horror.

'Mumbai as in India?' asked Lizzie.

'Is there any other Mumbai?' I replied, smiling.

'But why? Why on earth would you want to go and work in India? It's dirty, and poor and smelly and completely chaotic. At least that's what I've heard,' said Annabel, her usual direct self.

'Well, to be honest, I've heard all those things as well,' I said, trying not to let the disappointment show on my face. 'But I've also heard amazing things about it. You know, the food is incredible, the people are friendly and of course it's hot and the sun shines endlessly.'

'But why India? Do you really want to leave all this behind and go half-way around the world and live in a place that is filthy and unhygienic?' she continued.

I suddenly felt defensive about the country I'd decided to relocate to.

'It's not all dirt and poverty' I said, twisting a lock of my newly highlighted hair, a gesture I made when I was feeling unsettled. 'What about Bollywood? And what about all of those rich Indians and their glamorous weddings? I think the richest and most successful people in the world are Indians actually.'

Lizzie, the more sensitive of my two friends, could see I was getting upset.

'Well, I think it's exciting and a huge adventure. It's just that we'll really miss you, that's all. We've been together forever and it won't be the same without you.'

'I know', I said. 'But I'll be back, it'll only be for a couple of years max, and I'll come back for holidays and you two can come and visit me and we'll have some crazy adventures. Please be happy for me.'

'Well, I have just one thing to say,' declared Annabel. 'Indian men are awful. Seriously. Those moustaches! And that dress sense. Just be prepared to be single for a long time, or develop a new-found love for polyester and cheap shiny suits.'

We laughed and clinked glasses and I was relieved that at least the tension had been broken.

When I broke the news to my family and other friends and work colleagues, a lot of them told me to think very hard before making my decision. They used well-worn phrases like 'look before you leap' and told me that I was too old to make rash decisions based on the fact that I thought India might be an exciting place to go. They warned me that India was crazy, difficult to adjust to. Many people told me that it was a dangerous place to visit, let alone live in, especially given the recent episodes of bombings and terrorist attacks within the city. Logically, they were probably right, but I decided to listen to my heart, not my head. I instinctively felt that there was something appealing about India and that was good enough for me to take the decision to accept the offer, move to Mumbai and start a new life there. The fact that I had been offered a job in a city like Mumbai struck me as an incredible opportunity; I had read about people who had been drawn to India for a variety of reasons, many involving the search for meaning or a desire to do charity or humanitarian work, but I hadn't heard of anyone who had been given the chance to take up a 'proper' paid job there.

Despite my decision and the excitement I felt as the date for leaving England came closer, I couldn't help but feel nervous about giving up the security of being surrounded by the familiar — my friends, my family and even the routine comfort of knowing how things were done in the office. Though I'd been moaning to myself about being bored of a life that stretched monotonously into the future, punctuated only by parties and the occasional holiday, at the end of the day these were the things that had given my life shape and meaning for a long time. My family, my circle of friends and my cushy office were like lifeboats—something to cling to, something comforting and somehow an endorsement of a successful life.

In between my moments of panic, I looked on the bright side. Certainly, the thought of leaving my twenties had become much more palatable. Now I could start to see myself as a free spirit, a wanderer, someone brave enough to move to the other side of the world. I hoped fervently that it would be a gamble that would pay off—my friends, family and the safety net of familiarity in exchange for the possibility of an alternative future.

And so I decided to take the plunge. I packed up my belongings, storing most of my paltry possessions, which seemed to consist of no more than a few boxes of clothes and books, in my parents' small attic at my childhood home in Dorset. I had been born and brought up in the same area, in a small village fifteen miles from the nearest town. My parents had scrimped and saved to send me and my younger sister Louise to a fancy school, a fact that I only came to appreciate after I'd graduated from university and realized how important old school networks were.

Louise was younger than me, she'd just turned twenty-five and was busy planning a family with her long term childhood sweetheart, Matthew. She lived close to my parents and was much more dutiful than I had ever been. We'd always had a bit of a love-hate relationship; there were times when I couldn't stand the sight of her and her lack of ambition always bothered me.

She, on the other hand, seemed to resent the fact that I'd left Dorset and I knew that she thought I looked down on her and the others I'd left behind. She thought everything came easily to me, and I assumed that she was a little jealous of my apparent success. We were very different to look at as well, she was dark, wiry and athletic looking, while I was blondish and curvaceous on a good day, plump on a bad one. The only thing we had in common seemed to be our grey eyes, which were exactly the same shade and luminosity. But she was my sister and of course I loved her.

I told Mum and Dad that I had been offered a fantastic opportunity in India, which came with more money as well as a promotion. My parents were wonderful about the whole thing, supportive as well as excited for me, although it was difficult for them to imagine that anyone would want to leave our sleepy village, let alone leave the country. They had never really been able to work out what I did in London, let alone understand how I could possibly do the same thing in far off India.

'See Mum, Dad, for the past seven years in London I've been doing a similar job. Basically, I have to make sure that the ads that you see on TV get made.'

'So you make up the ideas then, do you Julia?' Mum asked.

'Well, no. Not exactly. I don't write the ads. I ask other people to write them.'

'Why do you need to do that? Can't the people who make the products tell them to write the ads?'

'Well yes, they could. But if they did then the ads wouldn't get made how they should be made.'

'Why not?'

'Well. It's a bit difficult to explain. But I kind of interpret what the client wants and then tell the guy who writes the ads and then I present it back to the client, who is paying for the advertisement in the first place.'

'It all sounds a bit complicated to me. But as long as you're happy love, then we're happy for you.'

This had been Mum's stock response over the years. In many ways, it was very liberating to be supported so blindly and with such faith. There was never any criticism, never a suggestion that perhaps I should think about doing things differently.

'You've always had your own mind,' Mum told me with a smile. 'You'll always end up landing on your feet, it's just the way you are. I don't know where you get that from, mind you. Even your sister is happy with her lot here.' There was nothing holding me back from exploring my bright new future. At the same time, there was no one else to blame if anything went wrong. My parents' perspectives on life were very different from mine and our aspirations so diverse. Mum had told me many times that all she'd ever wanted was a family. Two kids and a house. There was nothing wrong with that; deep down I knew that I wanted to end up in a happy relationship, but I couldn't help feeling that there must be so much more to life. As I hugged them both goodbye, Mum clung on to me, with tears glistening in her eyes.

'You take good care of yourself out there. I wish you weren't going so far away. London was bad enough, let alone India.'

'Mum, I'll be back soon,' I said, feeling guilty that I was leaving my parents behind. They weren't getting any younger, but I knew that I had to do this for myself, or regret it forever.

I spent the month enjoying the small pleasures of Englishness, clinging on to the last remnants of the life that I was leaving behind. The weather was uncharacteristically good for September and I felt like the sunshine was hanging on just for me, in an attempt to send me on my way with a good feeling about my home. Annabel and Lizzie threw a huge farewell party for me at my favourite local bar and gathered all of my friends together. I felt simultaneously sad and excited, I couldn't quite wrap my head around the fact that I was actually leaving all this behind, but at the same time I felt somehow smug, and dare I admit it, a little bit superior, that I had chosen to take a more interesting path in life, even though that path had actually been offered to me on a plate. I figured that the tough part wasn't being offered the job, but actually deciding to take it and I revelled in my bravery and daring. I stocked up on anti-diarrhoea tablets, bought a *Lonely Planet* and headed off for the airport, full of nerves and excitement.

## 3

I landed into a grubby Mumbai night. It was dark when I landed so I wasn't able to make out the endless rows of slum dwellings that lined the airport. Though I didn't realize it at the time, this was in fact one of Mumbai's largest concentrations of human inhabitants, the blue tarpaulin-lined roofs looking deceptively clean and tidy from a few hundred feet up.

After fighting through the crowds, I finally walked out of the cool air-conditioned airport, through the sliding doors and bang into what can only be described as utter chaos. The first assault was on my nostrils—a mixture of diesel and the exotic whiff of curry, underlaid with a faintly sweet tang, which I later came to realize was the smell of human excrement, sloshing its way through the nearby creeks and finally out to sea. And the noise was indescribable—a cacophony of voices all simultaneously yelling in my direction—'madam, hotel', 'madam, money change', 'madam you are coming with me for good sightsee'. A seething mass of humanity stretched as far as the eye could see—all pushing and jostling and elbowing and shoving in an attempt to be the first to reach the poor innocents arriving from presumably more affluent locations. My senses were assaulted from all directions and it took a superhuman effort to keep myself focused and my wits about me. Holding my head high, I marched resolutely through the crowds, searching for the driver who would apparently be there to meet me. Eventually, after several minutes spent frantically searching the rows of identically clad pot-bellied men sporting huge bushy moustaches and holding up signs outside the airport, I found someone bearing a sign with my name on it (or at least an approximation of my name), and my company's name. He was wearing a grubby yellowish uniform that was probably once white. He stared curiously at me, presumably expecting someone looking more corporate, suited and generally more professional—I was wearing a frayed pair of jeans, a T-shirt and a pair of Teva sandals, which I had thought would be both comfortable for the long flight and appropriate for my arrival in the Indian subcontinent. I was utterly relieved to see him, and thankful that I wouldn't have to navigate my way through the apparent chaos alone. I wasn't carrying a mobile phone, and I hadn't made any kind of back-up plan for my arrival, trusting blindly that the corporate gods or at least one of the many Indian gods would provide.

The driver introduced himself as Sanjay, his English heavily-accented but strangely formal. He took my heavy bag from me and insisted on carrying every bit of my luggage. It was too hot to argue, but I felt vaguely guilty that he was laden with all my worldly possessions while I skipped beside him carrying nothing but a bottle of water and a small handbag. He led me across the road, striding out into the oncoming traffic, seemingly oblivious to the cars, which were in turn ignoring what passed for a pedestrian crossing beneath our feet. I nervously dodged the cars, accompanied by a chorus of horns louder and more piercing than any I'd heard before in England.

Eventually we arrived at a battered vehicle that was scratched heavily along one side and had dents all over it. I must have looked a bit nervous, because Sanjay broke into a huge grin, his white teeth gleaming in his brown face. 'Don't worry. All cars in Mumbai like this. This one have good air-conditioning.'

We piled my possessions into the back seat and I sat nervously in the front next to Sanjay. The streets of Mumbai passed by in a blur—all I was able to register during that incredibly bumpy and uncomfortable journey was an unfeasibly large number of people who all seemed to be simply milling around. The roads were packed, traffic was bumper to bumper and crowds thronged the streets. Unlike in London, where people walked purposefully with heads down and eyes fixed to the pavement, everyone here seemed to be ambling around looking everywhere but ahead. Ladies in bright saris were chatting in the street amidst the chaos, men were holding hands with each other and wandering along the road, and mangy looking dogs were meandering through the crowds, dodging the occasional kick—all set against a deafening backdrop of blaring horns. Every car, lorry and bicycle seemed to be doing its best to out-horn the other, and strangely enough, no one seemed to mind. As I stared at the lorry in front of us, I saw the words—'Horn OK please'. Odd, I thought, I wonder why that lorry was inviting others to beep their horn at him. Then I looked at other vehicles. Each and every van and lorry had the same words hand painted on the back in bright colours—many with ornate flourishes and designs. Clearly, this was a country with very different rules from back home, and where the use of the horn was not only welcome but would certainly not incite the kind of road rage associated with over-zealous horn usage in the UK.

We drove for about an hour through tiny streets clogged with cars, bicycles, people, dogs, cats, goats and the occasional cow. Finally, we arrived at my new home—an apartment provided by the company, which turned out to be situated in a shabby building just off a busy intersection. The agency had told me when I accepted the job that they would be providing me with a 'comfortable' apartment in one of the posher areas of Mumbai, Breach Candy. This looked neither comfortable nor posh to me but I told myself to be patient and not to jump to any conclusions. We pulled up outside a shabby building that bore the grand but erroneous name of 'Sea View', despite the fact that the only views from each side were telegraph poles, trailing wires, and neighbouring buildings.

My heart sank. Despite my research, which had told me that India was dirty, polluted and chaotic, I had expected something a little nicer, given that I had relocated here for a job with one of Mumbai's top companies. Sanjay stepped out of the car, opened the door for me and handed me an envelope with my name on it. It was a note from my new boss together with a key to the apartment. I entered the rundown and ramshackle building, stepped into an ancient creaking lift which looked like it hadn't been cleaned for years, and gingerly closed the grating that served as the lift door.

The interior of Flat 301 didn't look much better than the outside of the building. It was furnished simply with a tasteless blend of seventies-inspired brown and yellowish décor: there was an uncomfortable looking three-seater sofa, some dark red curtains that were a pale pinky-red where the sun had hit them, and a decent-sized bedroom with a bed that sagged sadly in the middle. The bathroom was clean enough and the kitchen was equipped with a four-burner gas ring, some basic provisions and a fridge that hummed loudly. All in all, it didn't feel much like home, but it was a start. I forced myself to look on the positive side—I was here in Mumbai, I had a job and a flat and this was the start of my shiny new life. I fell asleep to a chorus of dogs barking, horns beeping and men shouting 'Madam, Madam', and though my sleep was fitful, it didn't take me long to sink into unconsciousness.

I woke the next morning to a blinding bright cerulean sky, cloudless and luminous in its intensity, and surprisingly devoid of the smog that I'd expected and read about. I'd arrived on a Saturday and so I had all of Sunday to recover from the jet lag and prepare myself for the start of the working week. My friends and family couldn't believe that I had landed up here without even coming for an exploratory visit. But I hadn't wanted to come here and then leave again. I had wanted to leave England once and for all. I figured that I could cope with whatever India decided to throw at me and if it was really as bad as some people said, I could always go back home.

I spent that first Sunday wandering the streets of my new neighbourhood, which was characterized by towering apartment blocks and tiny, dusty shops jammed together in rows. Most of the buildings looked absolutely filthy, some were black or covered with bamboo scaffolding, or both. Others looked a little cleaner, but the majority just looked as though they might fall down at any moment. The pavements, where they existed, consisted mainly of a few broken paving stones, and the roads were ridden with potholes. I wondered whether this really was considered one of the nicer parts of Mumbai, as the company had led me to believe, or whether in fact I'd been fobbed off with a cheap and nasty part of the city in a bid to save money. I couldn't really work it out, as there seemed to be plenty of smartly-dressed people ambling along despite the lack of decent pavements, including whole families with pristinely turned-out children who looked as though they had been dressed up in their Sunday best.

I changed some money and bought a few provisions to keep me going—a small loaf of bread, a fat chunk of butter and some jam, some masala flavoured crisps and some Cadbury's chocolate, which looked reassuringly and strangely familiar amongst the piles of dusty jars of curry paste and strange local foodstuffs. I fumbled with the unfamiliar notes, not wanting to reveal my novice status, managing to complete the transaction with no clue as to what I'd actually paid in real terms. I found a small restaurant with a long menu that served vaguely familiar dishes, and ordered an aloo gobi, rice and daal, figuring that I couldn't do myself much harm if I stuck to vegetables and bottled water while my stomach got used to the local food.

During that very first day in Mumbai, I was overwhelmed by the simplest things—by the piles of green 'young' coconuts that lined the streets, by the richness of the coloured sarees worn by women walking proudly along the dirt lined streets, by the noise and the chaos and the dirt and the smells and the delicious cheap food I ate and the gorgeous though neglected buildings. I had arrived in Mumbai in late September, just after the monsoon had ended. The air was heavy with a rich, damp smell faintly reminiscent of cut grass. The city looked incredibly green, I was surprised by the number of trees that lined the chaotic streets, and delighted to discover that Mumbai was not the arid, dusty city that I had imagined it to be. Though I was a complete Asia novice and had no benchmarks to compare my experiences to, I instinctively felt from the very first moment that there was something very special about the country. It had an energy that could literally be felt in the air, a positive spirit that made me feel good about myself, and a dizzying array of new experiences which were mine for the taking. I didn't feel the 'deep spiritual connection' that I had heard other Westerners talking about—those generally clad in grubby, flowing robes with a look of the unwashed about them. Nor was I searching for a guru, Enlightenment or the path to salvation. I was simply enjoying the heady experience of having all of my five senses simultaneously walloped by a massive sensory overload, and after grey, predictable London, I was loving it.

The next morning I woke early, still a little jet-lagged and sweating despite the fan that was trying its best to cool the warm air, to a chorus of dogs barking and the omnipresent sound of beeping horns. I managed to boil some water, made myself a cup of tea, buttered a piece of bread and tried to contain the feelings of excitement as well as nervousness that were bubbling up inside me. I was feeling excited as well as a little scared about starting work. James, my former boss in London, had already told me that I would be the only foreigner in the office—I'd been hired to set up a regional team for one of the agency's biggest clients, who had recently moved their head office to Mumbai from Singapore. I dressed a little smartly that morning, wanting to make a good first impression. I wasn't sure whether I should have tried to find some kind of Indian outfit, but I didn't want to get it wrong or to be seen as though I was trying too hard. Also, my bible, the *Lonely Planet*, had told me that it was important not to bare too much flesh in India, and so I opted for a simple knee-length skirt, smart sandals and a long-sleeved shirt. I'd made an attempt to wash my hair, despite the trickle of warm water that passed for a shower, and pulled it back into what I hoped was a demure ponytail, not wanting to appear too 'obviously blonde' in front of my colleagues.

There was a knock on the door—it was Neil, the Admin Manager from the office, who had come to make sure I got to the office safely. Neil was a smiling, well-built Goan who immediately made me feel comfortable. He talked energetically, without pausing to draw breath as he told me what to expect from the company and its employees. It was nice to see a friendly face, and his cheeriness inspired me, filling me with warm thoughts about the day ahead.

'Your office looks right over the Arabian Sea,' Neil told me with a grin. 'You can see miles and miles of ocean. You'll get bored of it eventually.'

We set off for the office and as we entered the lanes of cars weaving haphazardly across the crowded roads, I lost myself in the contemplation of life in this new city. This was all a far cry from the Mumbai that I'd imagined. While I'd seen some dirty, ugly, overcrowded bits, so far this morning it had just been bright clear skies, tree lined roads and a vast expanse of blue sea. Later that day I sent an e-mail to an Indian friend of mine from university. I described how beautiful Mumbai was and how good it made me feel. She sent me back an amused response, told me I was insane, and that I would soon come to realize that what glittered deceptively on the outside in fact hid nothing but dirt, corruption, and angst.

'Don't worry', she wrote, 'you'll soon learn. Eventually you'll hate it as much as the locals do.'

My first day at the office further enhanced my mood of excitement and optimism. I was introduced to countless people with complicated names, shown into my own office (which did indeed have a wonderful view of the sea) and left alone to settle in. As the only foreigner in the office, it seemed that I was also an object of curiosity. I caught people giving me furtive glances and it was only later that I was told that people were fascinated (and in some cases shocked) by the small tattoo on my right ankle, clearly visible thanks to my knee-length skirt. It was a small and fairly innocuous star design that I'd had done during one drunken hen weekend in Amsterdam. Apparently tattoos were associated with a certain type of girl.

My first day at work passed relatively uneventfully, and when I reached home at the end of the day, dropped back at my new home by the ever helpful Neil, I gave myself a mental pat on the back for having got through the day and starting off my new life as an expat. Even though I had been here for a mere twenty-four hours, I was already starting to miss my friends, particularly Lizzie and Annabel who I would meet up with every week in London without fail for drinks and gossip and a good session of putting the world to rights. I knew that I would need to create a support system for myself here or risk becoming terribly lonely.

## 4

I had one other expat contact in Mumbai, Johann, a friend of a friend back in London, who had e-mailed and offered to show me around and take me to a few parties. I jumped at the suggestion, after all, the *Lonely Planet* would only send me to the more popular tourist haunts and I was dying to get to know the 'real' Mumbai. Johann was a tall German married to a gorgeous Indian girl whom he had met in Mumbai and fallen in love with literally the first week he arrived. He'd been here for a couple of years, and was apparently very well connected with a non-stop flow of invitations to all of the best parties. I immediately warmed to his direct, honest, and very open manner.

'You'll be fine here,' he told me. 'The Indians love the white skin, and you'll soon find that doors open up for you. The trick is to be selective and always keep your wits about you.'

'Well, it would be nice to make some friends' I told him. 'I kind of miss my friends from back home.'

'You'll find the social scene here a lot of fun, but quite superficial,' he said. 'This is a very safe place, you can do what you want, but just don't trust people too quickly. You're not in England now, there are different cultural rules here, so just take it easy.'

I wasn't really sure what he meant, but I decided to keep his words in mind. The last thing I wanted was to be taken advantage of, although my naturally trusting nature made it difficult for me to keep my guard up for long.

Johann took me to Indigo, a popular bar in town that was apparently the place to be for Mumbai's glitterati and social wannabes. The bar was located in an immaculately painted gorgeous two storey house in bustling Colaba—the heart of Mumbai's old town, close to the Taj Hotel, which had recently hit global headlines with the shocking Mumbai terrorist attack. It was bordered by lush, well-maintained trees and bushes, a stark contrast to the more rundown exterior of the neighbouring buildings. The gate was closely guarded by an officious looking uniformed watchman, who was busy scrutinizing the line of people keen to enter. Judging from the people who were waiting in that line, and from the fancy cars that were crawling up and down the road outside, this was a pretty upmarket destination. The girls were all in full bling attire, perched on precariously high heels and wearing incredibly short skirts and backless glittery tops and dresses. They all had long tumbling curls, many had golden highlights and all of them were plastered in immaculately applied makeup—impossibly long lashed and doe eyed, with glossy red mouths and petite figures. The boys were in regulation designer jeans and fitted pastel coloured shirts or tight T-shirts. They all looked incredibly buff, as though they worked out obsessively (they did) and there wasn't a lot of facial hair in sight save for the odd neatly trimmed goatee. They all seemed to have identical collar-length haircuts, and were clearly fans of wet-look hair gel. The entire crowd looked incredibly young, early to mid-twenties, and all of them were frantically checking their mobile phones, sending text messages or shouting loudly into the handsets.

Johann guided me smoothly to the front of the queue and the door immediately opened. He greeted the doorman like a long lost friend; it was clear he was a regular here. The queue jumping actually made me felt less conspicuous amidst all these perfectly groomed twenty-somethings—I might have been older and a little scruffier, but I had the connections that mattered.

The interior was equally stylish: there was a long bar that ran the entire length of the room, tasteful dim lighting, an assortment of low tables and comfortable wicker chairs and some funky, low-level lounge music accompanied by the muted hum of conversation. The crowd was a mixture of pretty, young Indian girls, handsome, hunky Indian guys and foreigners. Without exception, the foreigners looked scruffier than the Indians who appeared to have spent hours perfecting their appearances. I noticed that the clusters of groups seemed to be either white or Indian, there didn't seem to be a lot of mixing going on.

Johann strode to the bar, ordered us drinks and immediately started to introduce me to people. He seemed to know everyone, and he was clearly a guy whom people wanted to be associated with. Within a few minutes we had quite a group surrounding us, and quite a few young Indian girls were casting looks in his direction. It was hardly surprising—he was tall, blond, and handsome in that typical freshly scrubbed, Northern European way. As the evening progressed, I met all kinds of people, from Indian movie-makers to actresses, to expat bankers and foreign embassy staff. The drinks were flowing and I was feeling great— everyone was so friendly and they seemed incredibly interested to know about me and what I was doing here in Mumbai.

I was a few drinks down when I caught the eye of a tall Indian guy leaning against the bar. He was looking at me, and winked in my direction. How cheesy, I thought, secretly flattered by the attention. When I returned from the loo, pushing my way through the crowd which by now filled the room, he suddenly appeared next to me at the bar.

'Hi, I'm Krishna,' he stated in a confident, deep voice, offering me a hand to shake. 'I've been watching you for a while. Is it OK if we chat?'

'Sure,' I replied, surreptitiously checking him out.

Krishna was easy on the eye and it had been ages since anyone had chatted me up in a bar, so I decided to give him the benefit of the doubt. He had those typical Indian dark brown melty eyes, eyebrows that looked suspiciously like they had been plucked, springy hair that curled just below his jawline (I'd always been a sucker for long hair) and particularly well-shaped, plump lips. His cheeks and chin were covered with a light stubble just the right side of unkempt, and his jaw was squarish. His nose was large and a little flat, but it prevented him from looking too chocolate box perfect. A few chest hairs were poking out from his shirt, but happily there was no gold chain in sight. I was sure that he'd even pass the scrutiny of the ever-fussy Annabel back in London.

Krishna asked me how long I'd been in Mumbai and how long I planned to be here (who knew). He also asked me where I lived in the city and I told him that I was staying in a company apartment in Breach Candy, which seemed to impress him, judging by the way his eyebrows moved upwards. I guessed that just as in London, postcodes were an important indication of social status, although it seemed to me that Mumbai's rich and

29

poor were all living cheek by jowl anyway. He told me that he had his own business exporting jewellery from India to the UK and the US, that he was born and brought up in Ahmednagar, a small town about 200 miles from Mumbai, and that he'd been in Mumbai since his college days.

I wondered vaguely how old he was. It was impossible to tell how old Indian men were. Indians lacked the telltale signs of ageing that we Westerners tended to exhibit—the lines, the dull pallor, the greying hair and the sagging chins. Instead, their skin seemed to stay firm and fresh, and the only sign of impending middle age for Indian men was the acquisition of a beer belly. I was very conscious that I had crossed thirty, and whereas in London this wouldn't have bothered me too much, I'd been made to feel older than my years by the abundance of twenty-year-olds in the office and in all the bars and restaurants in the city. I'd heard all the statistics about how young India was as a country, and you only had to set foot in Mumbai to be reminded of this on a daily basis.

I estimated that Krishna was at least in his late twenties, which didn't make me feel too bad; besides, he had impeccable manners, and he seemed genuinely interested in me. He bought me a drink, and then I tried to return the favour. The English concept of buying a round was clearly not something that flew here—Krishna was horrified when I reached for my purse.

'No, no, I cannot allow a lady to buy the drinks. I insist.'

This seemed sweetly old fashioned, and a little disconcerting, but I gave in. Later, I learned that men were always expected to pay for women, and that in groups of people it was always the eldest who paid. The British concept of taking turns to pay seemed much more equitable and progressive, but I kept my mouth shut and politely accepted another drink. Krishna told me more about his family.

'My sister is at university and my parents own a small business making technical products. It's all pretty boring really, they're lovely but I want more for myself. I travel quite often for business, I love to see the world, to experience other cultures and meet people from different countries.'

'I know what you mean,' I told him. 'Home is great, but you don't choose where you're born and if you're lucky enough to travel then you should make the most of it.'

I felt a light pressure on my arm, and turned to see my friend Johann.

'Everything OK, Julia?' he asked, looking directly into my eyes. 'Absolutely fine,' I told him. 'This is Krishna, we just met and got chatting.'

The two men exchanged handshakes, and the conversation moved smoothly onto the topic of travel—Krishna had just returned from a business trip and talked with excitement about his travels through Europe.

Eventually the lights went up, the music stopped and it was clear that the bar was closing. It was midnight already; the time had flown by. Krishna turned to me, and looking slightly awkward and with a covert glance in Johann's direction, asked if I had any plans to go anywhere else now that the bar had closed. Johann was still standing beside me, giving off a slightly protective vibe, but decided diplomatically to visit the loo. During the course of the evening I'd had quite a few drinks, and the bartenders here certainly weren't skimping on the vodka in the cocktails. My head was buzzing pleasantly, I felt energized and super confident, and I didn't felt like calling it a night just yet. I wrestled briefly with a tiny voice in my head telling me to play it cool, to head home and leave any potential flirtation for another night. But I was on a roll, and buoyed up by the cocktails and the ego boosting effect of an attractive man's attention, I decided to ignore the inner advice of a more sober, rational self to see if tonight's magic would last a little longer.

5

'I'm just going on for another couple of drinks,' I told Johann, as we made our way outside the bar.

'Are you sure?' he asked. 'You've had quite a few drinks and you don't know your way around Bombay very well.'

'I'll be fine,' I told him. 'Krishna seems like a really nice guy and I think he's pretty harmless.'

I was aware that I was behaving impetuously, and I didn't care, but at the same time I didn't want Johann, my only friend in Mumbai, to think badly of me.

'Why don't you come along with us?' I asked him.

'I have a lovely wife to get home to.' He smiled. 'She's been working all evening and I really need to get back. Just keep your wits about you and be careful, these Bombay boys have a reputation for wanting white girls either for their money, for sex, or both. They think that white girls are easy, and they also assume they have lots of money.'

'Well, I don't have much money and I'm not going to jump into bed with the guy,' I told him, laughing.

Krishna and I went outside to find a taxi.

'My car is getting serviced,' he told me, slightly sheepishly.

'That's fine,' I said. I loved the rattling, dilapidated old

Mumbai Fiat taxis with their groaning, ancient engines and their religious paraphernalia hanging from the rear-view mirrors. Most of these vehicles were clearly held together by string and a prayer, and certainly none of them would ever have passed an annual MOT test, but these cars were anyway exempt from any testing requirements and so they were driven until they literally fell apart. Though everyone complained about them, the taxis were just another of the things about Mumbai that I found fascinating and endearing.

'We're going to a friend's place,' Krishna told me. 'He's having an after party and we're invited.'

'Sounds good to me,' I said. 'Won't he mind that you're bringing a stranger along?'

With a laugh, Krishna replied, 'No, not at all. This is Mumbai. Anything goes, and the social scene is pretty small, at least for our kind of people, if you know what I mean. Plus, you're a foreigner and everyone loves talking to foreigners, especially Brits. You'll get invited to all the parties in town, just wait and see.'

His words were reminiscent of Johann's earlier claims that the expat crowd got easy access to Mumbai's party scene. It sounded like a lot of fun to me. I'd always loved to party and to be part of the in-crowd, and I'd been missing this feeling of being at the centre of things since leaving London.

During the short taxi ride Krishna was polite and attentive. At one point he slid his arm along the back of the taxi seat, and though it never came into contact with my shoulders, I was aware that it was there.

We arrived at Krishna's friend's place. From the outside the building looked typically jaded and grubby but I'd learned not to take appearances to heart in Mumbai. It seemed that no one here was very interested in the outside of the buildings, they were invariably filthy, with peeling paint, grey or even black mouldy exteriors caused by years of monsoons, and often covered in makeshift bamboo scaffolding. It was what was inside that counted here, and Mumbai's residents poured all of their efforts into creating their own little havens, spaces where they could escape the daily grind of a city that was over populated, polluted and an assault on the senses. The vast majority of Mumbai's inhabitants, excepting the many millions who lived in the ramshackle slums, resided in soaring apartment blocks that towered over the city's skyline. There simply wasn't enough space for Mumbai's vast population to squeeze into its limited land mass unless they were literally living on top of each other. Everyone, except an extremely privileged miniscule set of A-list actors and politicians who lived in sprawling, luxurious bungalows, lived in an apartment where the daily challenge was to maximize often very limited living space.

My assumptions that the tatty exterior would hide an inner charm turned out to be correct, as we stepped out of the lift and into a swanky apartment with stunning views of the sea. The décor was a little too bling for my taste—there was a fair amount of gold paint, a lot of dark brown panelling and old fashioned furniture, but it was a good-sized room and the spacious feeling was heightened by the panoramic view. A dozen or so people were sitting or standing around, chatting and drinking. 'Yo buddy,' said one of them, approaching us and slapping Krishna on the back in the time-honoured gesture of male bonding. 'Long time dude. And who is this?'

Krishna introduced me, omitting to mention that we'd just

met. 'This is Samir, one of my oldest friends. We were at school together.'

'Welcome, welcome,' cried Samir. 'Please come in, make yourself at home. There are plenty of drinks and the party's just started.'

I accepted a drink and clung to it, feeling slightly self-conscious. The crowd was entirely Indian and everyone seemed very close. The term 'dude' was being thrown around a lot in a kind of eighties revival way, which I found amusing though I suspected the guys weren't being ironic. Meanwhile, the girls had formed a separate group and they were busy eyeing the boys through heavily mascaraed eyes.

'Don't worry,' Krishna whispered, sensing my discomfort. 'They're really nice people once you get to know them. Come on, I'll introduce you to everyone.'

The boys were very affable, some even went as far as to kiss my cheek, while others shook my hand, but the girls were a little more reserved. I could feel that they were checking me out, and though they seemed friendly enough, their smiles didn't really reach their eyes and I got the feeling they assumed that I was some kind of threat to them. I made an effort to chat with a couple of them.

'O yaar,' one of them told me. 'I love England. All that shopping, Oxford Street and Selfridges. To die for.'

'Yes, its pretty good,' I told them, 'but expensive.'

Their eyes flickered from Krishna to me and it was clear that they were trying to work out whether we were together. After a while, Krishna and I sat down on one of the uncomfortable, ornate sofas.

'Your friends seem nice,' I said.

'Yes they're a great bunch of guys. We've been partying together since we were kids.'

'The girls seem a bit less friendly though. I'm not sure they like me much.'

'Don't be silly,' he exclaimed. 'Actually, I used to date one of them, the girl in the green dress. We broke up ages ago, though.' Green dress looked stunning, like a model, with endless legs and waves of tumbling curls. I immediately felt uncomfortable, fat and frumpy.

'Don't worry, we're great friends now and I know she wants me to be happy.'

Yeah, right. Krishna, like most men, was obviously not well versed in the ways of the female mind. It was obvious that she was still extremely possessive about him and that explained the slightly chilly reception from the rest of the girls.

'So how does your friend afford the rent on this place?' I asked Krishna. 'Or has he bought it?'

'It's his family's place of course', said Krishna, looking at me as though that should be completely obvious.

'So his parents live here too?'

'Yes, they live here and so does his sister. They're all asleep.'

'You mean the rest of his family are here, in the flat?'

'Yup. It's a big place, four bedrooms, so the rest of the apartment is quite separate from this part.'

I was amazed, I couldn't have imagined living with my parents into my twenties, let alone partying in their house. That explained the old-fashioned furniture and dodgy décor. Later, I discovered that the vast majority of unmarried Indians lived with their parents, sometimes into their forties. Even after marriage, most of them then lived with the boy's parents, and there would often be huge numbers of assorted relatives living under one roof. Though I loved my parents, I had moved out of the quiet family home as soon as I had turned eighteen, and the thought of living with them throughout my twenties and thirties was completely unthinkable.

'So his parents don't mind him bringing random people back to their house, and drinking?'

'Of course not. These are not random people anyway, they're his friends, and his parents have no idea how much we really drink.'

It still all seemed odd, and I kept expecting an angry parent to stride into the room yelling at us to keep the noise down.

By 3 a.m., I had had enough. I could feel the vodka sloshing about inside me, and I was dying for my bed. The party, however, was in full swing, and Krishna and his friends were showing no signs of wanting to call it a night. They were doing shots, and it looked like the night was only just getting warmed up. Krishna's eyes were glittering, and he was talking animatedly when he noticed that I was fading.

'Are you OK?' he asked me. 'Having fun?'

'I'm having a great time,' I reassured him, 'but I'm really tired. I think I should hit the road soon.'

'Shall I take you home?' asked Krishna.

'I don't want to spoil your fun,' I replied, torn between wanting this evening to go on for a bit longer and wanting the comfort of my bed and a deep, vodka-fuelled sleep.

'Don't worry, I can drop you and then come back again. These parties usually go on until the sun rises and then we all sleep all day on Sunday.'

'Well, if you don't mind,' I grudgingly acquiesced, hoping that he wouldn't think I was a complete wimp. 'I could really use my bed right now and I have some stuff to do tomorrow.'

I said goodbye to a couple of people, they were all engrossed in some complicated drinking game, but they waved goodbye. The host came over and hugged me. Krishna hailed a cab from the street—though it was late there was still plenty of traffic on the road.

'Don't worry about dropping me, I'll be fine. My place isn't far off, and I vaguely know the way.'

Krishna seemed torn between wanting to do the gentlemanly thing and wanting to carry on partying. 'Ok, if you're sure. I'll give you a call and maybe we can hang out some time?'

He leant into the taxi to kiss my cheek, I turned my head and his lips brushed mine. I was a bit embarrassed, and hoped he didn't think that I was trying to deliberately kiss him on the mouth, but he brushed it off.

'See you, Julia. Send me a text message when you reach home.'

As the taxi driver headed for my street I thought about the evening. I liked Krishna but was glad I'd left when I did. The party crowd seemed like a fun bunch, but it was exhausting constantly having to make polite conversation and keep my wits about me with a bunch of strangers. I wondered how long it would take for me to call Mumbai home and in fact whether I'd ever really feel like I belonged here. I also wondered whether Krishna would call me again, or whether I was just a useful, exotic accessory for the night. Johann's words about trophy white friends were ringing in my ears, and I knew I'd just have to be patient.

## 6

After my night out and my after-party adventures, I felt a little more confident that I would be able to forge my way alone in this city. I still felt a bit like a fish out of water, and I was missing my friends terribly as well as the comfort of being able to head down to Dorset on the train at weekends when I needed a little parental attention and home cooking. I'd spoken to Annabel and Lizzie regularly on the phone, and tried to remember to call Mum and Dad at least once a week, but I still felt the sharp pain of separation from them. At least now I was able to console myself with the thought that I had at least had a sneak preview of a world that I could hopefully become part of and which, with a bit of luck and effort, would now open up for me.

Three days passed, I threw myself into work and tried to stop wondering whether Krishna would call me again. By Friday I was guessing that I hadn't made that much of an impression, perhaps I'd bored him by running off home mid-party. I told myself that I wasn't particularly bothered by his silence and deleted his number from my phone—I didn't want to be tempted to message him after a few drinks, or to embarrass myself by calling him. The last thing I wanted to do was stalk some perfectly nice guy who wasn't interested in me.

On Friday afternoon, just as I was packing up to leave the office, my phone pinged with the arrival of a text message. 'Fancy meeting tonight? K.'

Though I'd deleted his number, I assumed that this must be Krishna. I debated whether to play hard to get. Though I wasn't fond of dating games, I knew there were certain 'rules' that one should play by in order to keep a potential love interest keen. That said, I didn't have any weekend plans, Johann was out of town, and the thought of sitting alone in my flat wasn't particularly appealing.

'Sure', I texted back. 'What do you have in mind?'

'Let's go for dinner. I'll pick you up at nine. Send me your address.'

I decided to go with the flow of this rather determined approach. 'OK. See you then.'

Typically, I spent ages agonizing over what to wear. My wardrobe was still a work in progress; I'd bought a few smartish items for work but my party outfits were all a bit sad and had an air of grimy backpacker chic about them, which I wasn't sure would go down particularly well with Mumbai's perfectly groomed, seemingly label obsessed fashionistas. Eventually I pulled out a plain but classy looking black top which I knew flattered me, and wore it over jeans with my only smart pair of black heels and a blingy necklace which I hoped would suggest trendy rather than scream attention junkie. I'd washed and conditioned my hair, which hung around my face in what I hoped were sexy waves, and applied some discreet but confidence boosting makeup to accentuate my grey eyes, which I had been told were my best feature.

At 9 p.m. sharp, my doorbell rang. I opened it to find Krishna standing there, with a grin on his face. He was as handsome as ever, he'd shaved the stubble so he no longer looked like a wannabe Bollywood actor and he'd put some kind of gel in his unruly hair to calm it down. He leaned in to kiss my cheek and this time there was no awkward head turning on my part.

'Hey you look great,' he said. 'All set for dinner?'

I was actually a little too nervous to eat, the concept of the dinner date had always been one that left me cold, unless the meal was accompanied by lots of wine to take the edge of the intensity of a one on one conversation.

'Sure. Where are we off to?'

'You'll see. It's a surprise.'

This time he'd brought his car, a fairly standard Honda Civic, which was clean inside and smelled faintly of cigarettes. He took me to a crowded bar called Café Mondegar, which was apparently very popular with both locals and backpackers alike. It was absolutely jam-packed, but he'd managed to reserve a small table in the corner for us.

'I hope this is OK,' he murmured. 'It's not nearly as fancy as Indigo, but it's one of Mumbai's most popular bars and the crowd is really lively. Let's just have a couple of drinks, and then we'll head somewhere else to eat.'

I looked around at my surroundings. The walls were covered with cartoon style murals depicting Mumbai life, there was a jukebox playing soft rock in the corner, and the tables were crammed with groups of people ranging from the typical twenty-somethings to older types with greying hair and comfortable shoes. There was conspicuously less bling here than at Indigo, and I was glad I hadn't dressed up too much, but I was at least different from the clusters of backpackers who dotted the room. I noticed there were a few mixed groups, with Indians and foreigners sharing tables. All in all, though I loved the luxurious ambience of Indigo, I felt right at home here in this mish-mash of styles and unpretentious surroundings. We ordered beers, which came in ice-cold frosted pint glasses, and I felt a sudden nostalgic pang for England. Though this was very far from a typical English pub, the rowdiness and smoky atmosphere reminded me of my local back home. The beers went down easily, there was no air conditioning in the main bar, and the whirring fans only served to stir the warm air and the smoke around the room.

'How was your week?' asked Krishna.

'It was OK,' I said. 'Pretty good actually. I've just hired a couple of people for my team and we're planning a trip to Bangkok to meet with some of the other regional agency people, so it's starting to come together.'

'I love Bangkok,' he said 'Such a fun place.'

A few of my friends had lived there, and I'd heard terrible things about the city from them. 'People have told me that it's a bit sleazy and full of revolting old men, and that the Thai people are difficult to get to know.'

I bit my lip, worried that I'd been too direct with my criticism of a country I hardly knew. He grinned and asked, 'So, what about Indians. Do you find us sleazy? '

'Not at all,' I said, relieved to have my chance to express my love for his country. 'I know I've been here less than a month but everyone I've met has tried really hard to make me felt welcome. Indians seem very hospitable and yes, very friendly. I think maybe there's some age-old connection between Indians and Brits, somehow we seem to understand each other, although there are times when there are cultural clashes.'

'Like when?' he asked.

'Like when I use sarcasm, which people in the office don't understand at all. And I guess there's this whole thing about Westerners finding India fascinating, while Indians generally just want to get out of India.'

'Yaar, I guess that's true,' he replied. 'I can't wait to leave one day, although I love it here. I just think the city is in such a mess, the corruption is so bad and Europe is full of better opportunities, both in terms of money and business. Plus I love the cold weather.'

'Well, I guess we'll just have to disagree on that one,' I laughed. 'I hate the cold, and I don't think I want to return to the UK to live in a hurry. It's not only cold, it's miserable and boring, too. Have you ever lived outside of India?' I asked, interested to know more about his background.

'I've travelled a fair bit, at least since I set the business up a few years ago, but I've never stayed anywhere for more than a month at a time.'

I was intrigued to know how he'd felt arriving in the city that I'd already fallen in love with. 'Well I told you that I'm from a small town in Maharashtra right?' he asked. I nodded in agreement, my mouth full of the cheese biscuits that had been put in front of us in tiny bowls by the waiter. 'Well, I always knew that I wanted to leave that place once I'd finished school. I would have loved to have gone to a boarding school but my parents couldn't afford it. They were pretty poor when I was growing up. Not as poor as many people in India, but there wasn't a lot of spare money lying around. But then my Dad started to do really well in his business, they own a small manufacturing plant, and so he offered to send me to Mumbai to finish my studies.'

'You didn't want to go abroad and study?' I asked. I had worked with Indians for long enough to know that the premium placed on higher education was huge. Back in the UK, we were content to scrape through a university degree, and our time at university was more about having fun, joining clubs and getting drunk than about studying. I knew that Indians generally took their studies much more seriously, and that they tended to pile up post graduation degrees and MBAs, presumably as a way to compete in the highly competitive and crowded workspace.

'I thought about it, after I'd done my graduation, but then I decided it was time to make some money,' he continued. 'Being at university in Mumbai was amazing. Suddenly I found myself bang in the middle of an incredibly hectic but inspiring city. I was so frustrated by my hometown, it was full of people without any real ambition, living on top of each other, going about their menial everyday lives and content with that. Once I came to Mumbai, I met a whole new set of people, and I saw a whole new potential for India. I realized that I could do anything if I put my mind to it, and that my ambition and hopes for the future could be realized, with a lot of hard work and a bit of luck.'

'I know what you mean about Mumbai,' I told him. 'It has an incredible energy. It's as though nothing is impossible here.'

Krishna smiled at me in agreement, and I felt like we were really connecting. 'Most of my friends are people I've met in Mumbai. Apart from my family, I don't really have any ties to Ahmednagar,' he said. 'I mean, I'm not embarrassed that I'm from a small town, but there's nothing to make me want to go back there, especially now that I have my own income and my own business.'

I asked what he did for a living. 'I export gemstones out of India and sell them to wholesale clients in Europe and the US. It's a decent business, and I get to travel, but it's a bit up and down.'

I got the feeling that he wasn't particularly comfortable talking about his work and decided not to push it too far. Maybe he was being modest and was sitting on top of a multi-million dollar business or maybe it wasn't really working out too well for him. Either way, I didn't want him to think I was being nosy, even though I knew that in India, unlike back home, it was perfectly normal to demand information about people's private lives, even down to asking how much they earned. In England, of course, such questions would have been unthinkable.

We carried on chatting, ordered a couple more beers, and suddenly I realized I'd devoured most of the bowl of the cheesy biscuits.

'Hungry?' asked Krishna.

'Starving,' I replied, embarrassed.

'OK, let's go and eat,' he said and gestured for the bill. I reached into my bag to get my purse and caught the warning look in his eye.

'OK, OK,' I said. But at least let me pay next time.'

We stepped outside into the sultry night. It was early October, typically one of the hotter months of the year, the monsoon was over but the air was heavy, charged with static, and at times suffocatingly humid.

'You don't mind the heat?' Krishna asked me.

'No, I love it,' I told him truthfully. I loved to walk out of a cool bar bang into a warm evening, it was a complete reversal of the English scenario and I enjoyed the feeling of my body being warmed right to my core. We walked around the corner towards the Gateway of India and slipped into a side street.

'Prepare yourself for a proper Bombay experience,' Krishna remarked. 'This is one of the most authentic food places in this city, and the food is amazing.'

He had brought me to a small outdoor food joint, with plastic chairs and tables laid out in the street around a makeshift grill billowing out clouds of deliciously fragrant steam.

'This is Bade Miya,' he told me, sounding a bit like a tour guide. 'It's been here for literally decades, it's a part of Bombay culture and all the best people come to eat here. You won't find better kebabs anywhere in the city.'

Almost all the tables were crammed with people chatting, eating and sipping Coke and Thums Up, the Indian equivalent, from old fashioned glass bottles. At either end of the street, fancy looking cars were parked nose to tail, with people eating from plates positioned precariously on top of the car bonnets and roofs. We sat down at one of the few empty tables, and Krishna ordered a few dishes. They came in a matter of minutes—there were a couple of different types of chicken kebabs, succulent and juicy and perfectly spiced. There were mutton kebabs, which we dipped into spicy, tangy mint sauce and ate with raw onions and a squeeze of lemon. There was delicious tardka daal—yellow daal with dried chillies floating on the top, which we mopped up with fluffy naan bread.

'Good?' he asked.

'Absolutely amazing,' I replied, my mouth full of the most incredible flavours and textures. I hadn't eaten food this good anywhere in Bombay, and I was loving it. I was so relaxed in Krishna's company that I forgot to worry about looking ladylike, and instead ate to my heart's content, chomping on raw onions like a local, and even considering the raw chillies, though I stopped short at actually eating one.

'I love to see a girl with an appetite,' he grinned. 'These Bombay party girls never eat, they are all too worried about smudging their lipstick or gaining a kilo.'

I hoped this wasn't a dig at my less than pristine makeup and the additional weight I was carrying around my hips. 'Well, if food is this good then it should be enjoyed,' I said. 'Though I can see it being a bit heavy if you eat it every day. It's kind of difficult to eat healthily in Mumbai, everything seems to be loaded with oil or sugar. Or both.'

'That's true. We Indians are not particularly health conscious and we love our fried food and sweets. Europeans are generally much healthier.'

'Except for our alcohol consumption,' I replied, with a laugh. 'Most British people drink way too much, it's part of our lives from an early age and I don't think we generally handle it very well.'

'Well, you're doing just fine,' he smiled.

We finished eating finally, and I realized that I was totally full. 'I don't think I can ever eat again,' I murmured.

'Let's go walk it off somewhere,' he said, decisively. He paid the bill and took me to Marine Drive.

Though I drove along this sea road everyday, I'd never actually walked along the long expanse of shoreline. He parked the car at the southern most end, and we walked slowly north. It was a beautiful evening, warm and slightly muggy, but the sky was clear and we could see the moon. The pavement was wide and well kept, unlike the majority of Mumbai's so-called walkways, which were generally hazardous, potholed and full of accidents waiting to happen. It was a busy evening—we were surrounded by couples wandering hand in hand, dark figures silhouetted against the sea, clearly embracing, and even a few people marching along wearing salwar kameezes with billowing dupattas, or kurtas and trainers. Though it was late, Mumbai literally never slept, and exercise was generally crammed into the beginning or end of the day, before chores began or once the family was asleep.

Suddenly I felt Krishna's hand in mine. It was firm and dry, possessive without being clingy. I turned and smiled at him, and he grinned back. I felt like I was in some cheesy Bollywood movie, walking against the stunning backdrop of Mumbai's cityscape, hand in hand with a tall, handsome Indian star. All I was missing was a flowing saree and a low cut blouse, and a yearning, dreamy musical melody playing in the background. There were people sitting all along the sea wall, in couples, small groups and even alone. They stared at us as we walked past with huge wide eyes. I was used to being an object of fascination here, and I was accustomed to dealing with the stares which initially seemed overly intrusive especially given the 'it's rude to stare' mantra that had been instilled into me as a child. Now, however, I felt particularly self-conscious, as though I was flouting some local rule conducting respectable behaviour, especially given all the stories I'd heard about the police swooping in to arrest young couples enjoying a romantic encounter in certain parts of Mumbai.

'You OK?' asked Krishna.

'Yep, great. This is so nice and exactly what I needed after all that food', I said. We walked slowly for another fifteen minutes or so, past more couples deep in conversation and enjoying their rare moments of physical contact in a culture that frowned upon sex or even co-habitation before marriage.

I wondered whether Krishna was going to kiss me, and I could feel my palms dampening and my stomach throwing random flip flops at the thought of kissing a virtual stranger while almost completely sober. I'd never kissed a foreigner before, all of my boyfriends and even the occasional flings had been white, middle-class types—and the nearest I'd ever come to an encounter with an exotic nationality was a Spanish guy who tried to seduce me on a school trip when I was eighteen. I'd never really thought about my rather one dimensional romantic experience before but now I did, and I couldn't help but think it was rather boring. I supposed that a kiss was a kiss, regardless of nationality, but I was still curious—perhaps there were cultural variations and techniques here that might take a little getting used to.

The kiss, however, didn't materialize, though we were still walking hand in hand back towards the car.

'Do you fancy going to a club?' asked Krishna as we slid into the stuffy interior.

'I'm not sure I'm really dressed for clubbing,' I said, conscious of my simple attire.

'It's ok, you're white, you can get in wearing anything.' Krishna had slightly misinterpreted the reason for my concern but it made me smile.

We ended up at the appropriately named Insomnia, the

nightclub at the grand old Taj Mahal hotel. As Krishna predicted, we were waved through the velvet rope by the stocky bouncer who didn't give my attire more than a cursory look. The club was full of locals and expats, and as usual the locals were dressed up to the nines in tight, glittering finery while the foreigners managed to look just that bit shabbier. Many were clearly hotel guests, standing alone at the bar looking nervously around them and clutching bottles of Kingfisher. The giant speakers were cranking out earsplitting sounds, a mishmash of popular Bollywood tunes, each of which prompted frantic cheers, whoops and yells from the crowd when the opening chords started up. The dance floor was jam packed with people who were strutting their stuff without the slightest inhibition. I was used to a more reserved version of dance floor activity; in English nightclubs, the girls moved disdainfully around their handbags, pouting and looking bored, and their men shuffled around them, uncoordinated and awkward. Here, the men were the ones throwing the fanciest dance moves, they all looked like mini Shah Rukh Khans with their exaggerated hip movements and jutting crotches, which left little to the imagination. The girls were twirling and whirling, fluttering their eyelashes and looking seductive. Everyone knew the words of the songs, and they were singing along and presumably enacting the love scenes between hero and heroine. The entire place was a seething pit of testosterone, a crowded expanse of unrequited desire and barely veiled lust — in other words, a good club.

I suggested getting a drink before hitting the dance floor, keen to have an excuse to avoid an exhibitionism that felt so alien to my reserved British sensibility. I knew of course that many Brits could fling themselves confidently around the dance floor, but this was only ever after consuming copious amounts of alcohol and usually forgotten the next day. As a nation, we lacked that natural self-confidence and exuberance that Indians just seemed to be born with, and that made me a little sad somehow.

Krishna was looking even sexier in the shadowy lighting, his height differentiated him from most of the other men in the place, and I felt protected, emboldened by his presence and very attracted to him. I was not sure though that an Indian nightclub was the best place to kiss a man, and I certainly didn't want to make the first move. In English nightclubs, men and women invariably paired off and spent the evening sucking each other's faces and even removing clothing. Here, people just seemed generally more well-behaved, there was a greater sense of propriety, which bordered on the virtuous. I later learned that while many Indian girls maintained that they were pure, virginal and wholesome, they in fact did experiment with sex before marriage, claiming to be virgins when they eventually settled down with the boy that their parents had often chosen for them. This smacked of hypocrisy, frankly, but then again who was I to argue with a society that seemed to be riven with contradictions—the papers were full of stories of abuse and worse, often by family members and people in positions of authority, while the entire country seemed to be labouring under the collective delusion that no one had sex, or even met with the opposite sex, especially in stricter communities, until they were married. I was glad that I came from a more permissive society, but at the same time, I thought that my own country had gone too far in terms of underage drinking, sex and permissiveness, so I supposed there was nothing like an ideal equation.

We grabbed a couple of drinks, Krishna met a few people he knew, and I began to feel a bit more relaxed once the vodka had kicked in. After a couple of the barman's infamous 'freepour' cocktails, I felt sufficiently emboldened to be able to venture onto the dance floor. The area was heaving, and I felt myself being pushed closer to Krishna than I'd intended, enjoying the feel of his warm, solid body against mine, but managing to keep an air of propriety as I blamed neighbouring dancers for our up close and personal moves.

'Sorry,' I mouthed as yet another dressed to the nines young girl careered into me, pushing me into his chest. 'It's OK,' he smiled back, looking as though he was enjoying it.

As I pulled away from him, I felt myself toppling backwards on heels that had become steadily more precarious with every drink I'd consumed. Suddenly I could feel myself losing my balance, and visions of falling and landing in an ungainly, drunken heap flashed through my mind. As I closed my eyes and waited for the inevitable, I felt strong arms grab me, and a deep voice in my ear.

'You're OK, I've got you.'

I looked up, directly into a pair of deep brown eyes and a smile that played on full, rather attractive lips. My dance floor saviour was a youngish guy with long, dark, wavy hair pulled back into a pony tail, wearing a white shirt which glowed neon under the lights, covering a set of clearly defined muscles. Despite my embarrassment, my flirtatious brain had clearly kicked into action, and I hastily refocused my attention on getting back to my feet. As I did, I came face to face with two different but equally malevolent faces.

'What the hell?' yelled Krishna, stepping forward as if to grab my rescuer by the scruff of the neck. At the same time, a tall, gorgeous looking girl wearing a minuscule dress with endlessly long legs stepped forward and pulled at the neon white shirt, flashing me a look of possessive anger. I figured that this had to be the girlfriend, and quickly pulled myself upright, yanking down my top as I did so. Krishna looked furious.

'What the hell are you doing with your hands all over my girl?' he shouted, wrapping his arm protectively around my shoulders.

The long haired stranger shrugged, a hint of a smile on his well shaped lips. 'I thought I'd come to her rescue actually, but never mind. No offence meant.'

Krishna looked as though he was ready to throw a punch, and I decided that I needed to intervene.

'It's all fine, actually I fell and…he caught me. Actually, I think its time we headed off anyway, it's almost closing time.'

As I pulled Krishna away in the direction of the exit, I couldn't help but glance back at the handsome stranger whose eyes still seemed to be twinkling at me, or perhaps that was a combination of the flashing lights and the drinks already in my system. I was embarrassed by Krishna's overly possessive reaction, and wasn't sure that I entirely liked being the object of a jealous rage, but I figured that he was probably as intoxicated as I was and decided not to dwell any further on the matter.

He dropped me home, my ears still ringing with Bollywood tunes, and actually got out of the car to open the passenger door. It was a sweet and slightly old-fashioned gesture which I was not at all used to and at odds with his earlier loutish behaviour. I wondered briefly whether to invite him in for coffee, but decided against it.

I wasn't sure that women were supposed to be so forthright here and the last thing I wanted to do was come across as over keen. As I stepped out of the car, Krishna's arms wrapped tightly around me, and he held me in a firm clinch.

'Thanks for a lovely evening,' he said. He kissed me on the cheek, then on the mouth, and then suddenly we were locked in a full-blown passionate embrace. It was slightly awkward, as all first kisses inevitably are, but he had his basics in place and I was relieved to discover that kissing seemed to be a universally consistent activity. The kiss lasted for half a minute or so, then he hugged me tight.

'See you soon. I'll call you.'

I was excited and happy, and relived the kiss endlessly once I was in bed, dissecting the events of the evening and trying not to dwell on the handsome twinkly-eyed stranger, nor get too hopeful about the prospect of a long term and happy relationship with Krishna.

## 7

Now that I had been in the country for a month, I suddenly remembered that I was supposed to have registered myself here as a resident, and received some mysterious 'blue book' which apparently meant I could reside here legally (the visa only allowed me to work, not live in Mumbai). I had completely forgotten about this bureaucratic requirement, and hoped that I wouldn't be penalized for registering late. I checked the stamp in my passport, and discovered that I was supposed to go somewhere called the Foreigners Regional Registration Office, or FRRO. Neil, the admin guy from the office who welcomed me on my first day in the city, offered to come with me.

'It's better if you take a local with you. It can be a bit difficult otherwise, trying to navigate your way through the paperwork.' He told me to make three copies of all of my documents, including my passport, visa and letters of employment from the company.

The FRRO office itself was situated in a winding dusty lane, inside a fairly ramshackle looking low building with an old colonial feel about it. We headed to the third floor and arrived into a sea of chaos—there were people everywhere, crammed up against a desk behind which three ladies in pale blue sarees with immaculately glossy hair and gold nose rings were studiously ignoring the shouts for attention. There was no queue as such, only a seething mass of people fighting for attention.

'Why don't people just stand in line?' I wondered aloud.

'We're not really a nation of queuers,' answered Neil. 'People are far too impatient to wait in line. If you try and queue, you'll never get anywhere.'

Many of the people pushing and shoving for attention were foreigners, so I was a little surprised at this, but then again I figured that it was only the British who were really uptight about forming queues everywhere and brutal in their treatment of queue-jumpers. 'You wait over there,' said Neil. 'I'll get us through this.'

True to his word, he disappeared into the scrum and re-emerged triumphantly a few minutes later.

'OK, I've put your name down in the book. Let's go through.'

We headed into the main waiting area, which was already full of people sitting around listlessly, looking frustrated, bored or both. There were foreign families with small children, foreigners with Indians who were apparently helping them deal with the bureaucracies and a few who looked to be of Indian origin but who could of course have been any nationality. The room was stiflingly hot, there were a couple of fans that seemed to be stuck on the lowest setting, and there was a distinct smell of urine emanating from one of the corners, presumably where the toilet was located. We found ourselves a seat and sat down, prepared for a long wait.

'How will we know when it's our turn?' I asked, feeling stressed by this general absence of systems and worrying that we might end up missing our turn.

'Don't worry, they'll call us.'

An hour passed, more people entered the crowded room,

and some eventually got called in to the adjoining room, where presumably the FRRO officials were sitting. Eventually, I heard my name being called, or at least an approximation of my name. 'Yes, I am here,' I piped up, and was ushered through, without Neil, to the next room.

'Sit,' growled the official before me, a burly man wearing a white shirt stretched tight across his pot belly, with a huge moustache and a frown on his face.

'Passport. Visa,' he barked at me.

I nervously pulled out my passport and showed him the visa, along with the letters of employment and 'indemnification' — basically a document which stated that the company would take responsibility for my actions while I was in India and would repatriate me if I misbehaved.

'Copies. Three copies,' snarled Mr Surly. I handed over my copies, thankful that Neil had had the foresight to do a little research before bringing me here.

'You were late. You were supposed to come two weeks ago.'

'Er, yes,' I mumbled, feeling like a schoolgirl being chastised by a headmaster. 'I forgot and then I was busy.'

'Maybe I don't give permit,' said Surly.

'Oh please,' I panicked, my voice cracking slightly, 'I am so sorry. I really was busy and completely forgot about the formalities.' I wondered at this point whether I was supposed to offer him a bribe, but I didn't want to embarrass myself in case it wasn't the done thing.

'You pay fine. One hundred dollar only.' I figured that that wasn't such a bad deal to at least get myself legal here.

'Go outside. Take this. Pay fine. Come back.' He tucked a

receipt into my passport and waved me away. I was dismissed, at least for the time being. I went outside, and found the lady whom I was supposed to pay, judging from the old-fashioned cash box and receipt book in front of her. She was sitting at a rickety desk, chatting with the man who was presumably responsible for operating the photocopier (which had a large sign above it saying 'Broken. Use downstair'). There were a couple of people ahead of me who were sighing and huffing impatiently. Cashier lady was deep in conversation with copier guy and though I couldn't understand what she was saying, I was able to gather that it was fairly idle chit-chat. I noticed that the red nail polish on each of her nails was half scratched away, and that both her arms were jangling with bright bangles, which moved up and down as she gesticulated to her friend. Finally, and with an air of exasperation, she turned her attention to the foreigners who were waiting to pay for visas and registration booklets. She pulled out an ancient looking receipt book, carefully folded back the top page, inserted a carbon sheet underneath the page and smoothed it down. She took the receipt from the first customer, and began to write, slowly and laboriously. She was deep in concentration, eyes narrowed, her bangles jangling ever so slightly, as she formed the letters and numerals on the page, painstakingly and deliberately.

'This could take all day,' I thought to myself, used to far speedier service in an age where most systems were computerized and where the concept of customer service, though often grumpy, was at least usually efficient. Eventually, the receipt was filled, money exchanged hands and then came her response 'Change?'

'Er, no,' stammered the foreigner. 'I don't have change.'

'Go, get change. Downstairs, shop,' she ordered, and closed the receipt book. 'Next.'

Luckily I had brought plenty of change with me, aided once again by the ever-prepared Neil, who must have spent at least part of his childhood as a boy scout. I counted out the money for my late fine, one hundred dollars, which was about four and a half thousand rupees—a small fortune to many, but for me a small price to get out of this hellhole. I was a bit confused about why they asked for payments in dollars and then took rupees. It was as though they imagined that all foreigners used the dollar currency, and that the dollar to rupee conversion would be obvious. I could only just work out how many pounds there were to the rupee, and I was totally confused by the additional complication of the dollar rate, so I just handed over my four thousand five hundred and forty four rupees with a smile. The painstaking process of writing the receipt began again, and I felt like grabbing it and writing it myself. Finally it was done, handed to me, the money was taken and I headed back towards Mr Surly inside the other room.

He was busy with another foreigner, and I tried to get his attention. Without looking up, he grunted, 'Wait. Next door.' I clearly remembered him telling me to come back again after paying the fine, but I wasn't going to argue with him. I went back and joined Neil. 'All done?' he asked. 'Nope. I've only just managed to pay the fine for being late. Haven't even got to the visa part.'

I sat down again, and pulled out my book, figuring that it was going to be a long wait. Eventually, as the clock crept towards midday (we had arrived in the office at 9.30 a.m. sharp), my name was called again. Surly beckoned me to take a seat, and stroked his moustache thoughtfully. Finally he handed me my passport. 'Go pay, and come back.' Not again.

'Pay?' I asked.

'Pay one hundred rupees for blue book.'

Trying desperately to prevent my eyes rolling and stifling the scream that was threatening to burst from my throat in some maniacal Tourette's fashion, I took the passport and went back to cashier lady. There, I repeated the process of making a payment, received my painstakingly written receipt, and went back inside the room. Thankfully, Surly was waiting for me, which seemed like nothing short of miraculous.

He took the receipt and grunted, 'Come back tomorrow morning.'

'Tomorrow?' I stammered. 'But I thought I would get the book today.'

'I am getting signature from boss. Today not possible. Come tomorrow.'

I breathed another long, deep sigh and forced a smile on my face. I was sure I could bump a few meetings in the morning and come back here again. I went outside to inform Neil of the news. 'I have to come back tomorrow,' I told him, my frustration apparent.

'That's OK,' he told me, patiently. 'At least he's given you a date. Some people are just told to wait until the office contacts them, and that sometimes never happens.'

As we drove back to the office, I wondered how these systems could be so bureaucratic and so unwieldy. Surely there must be lots of foreigners coming to India to work, and although I could appreciate that processes were required to ensure that people weren't just let in willy nilly, at the same time this was the twenty-first century and a touch of efficiency wouldn't have gone amiss.

Though I didn't realize it at the time, my experience was symptomatic of most government offices and organizations in India. These establishments were riven with bureaucracy and were largely administrative nightmares, designed to create complex systems which would in turn create jobs for the masses. At the time though, there was a lot about India I was seeing for the first time, and I hadn't yet started to understand its complexities, though they would in time hit me hard.

**8**

Eventually I received my 'blue book', an archaic looking booklet which actually stated that I would have to inform the government every time I left and re-entered the country, or even the state. I was horrified, but Neil told me with a laugh that no one ever did this, and that it was just some ancient hangover from the past. Now that I was legally a resident here, I felt that I could take on anything India had to throw at me.

I was still seeing Krishna, we'd been out on a couple more dates, and we'd kissed a whole lot more, and I was guessing it was only a matter of time before we took things to the next level. I was enjoying spending time with him, and he made me feel more confident generally about being here. He finally revealed his age—he had just turned thirty, which I was relieved about. Somehow, dating a man in his twenties, even his late twenties, seemed much less palatable than seeing a guy who was thirty. I was dying to gossip to Annabel and Lizzie about Krishna, and gloat over the fact that I'd actually managed to find a man in Mumbai who wasn't sporting inappropriate facial hair or wearing seventies throwback clothing, but I didn't want to tempt fate by telling them about him too early, just in case things didn't end up working out and I came across as being just a little bit desperate.

Meanwhile, things were continuing to go well at work. I'd hired two people to work in my team — Kiran, a sweet girl who'd had a couple of years work experience and who was overjoyed to be part of an international business, and Rohit who was fresh out of college with a postgraduate degree in marketing and advertising communication. Both of them were sent to me by a headhunter, who I had briefed carefully. She asked me what kind of salary I was prepared to pay. 'Two?' she asked me. 'Two point five?' She was talking in lakhs, the Indian equivalent of hundreds of thousands (one lakh was one hundred thousand and a crore was ten million rupees). I quickly did the mental arithmetic. Two lakhs was almost three thousand pounds.

'That's a bit steep,' I told her, conscious that I needed to show some profitability on my business as soon as I could.

'You won't get a college graduate for less than two lakhs a year,' she laughed. 'But let me talk to him.'

A year!! I'd thought she meant a month. I was mortified about my massive faux pas and my western assumptions. 'Well, I'm sure we can stretch to two lakhs, maybe two-and-a-half. If he's really good,' I said, trying to smooth over my confusion.

I couldn't believe that starting salaries for vastly qualified graduates, with postgraduate degrees as well as the regular old graduation and often an MBA or a diploma on top, were so low. Three thousand pounds a year! And yet the salary I was being paid here was higher than I'd expect to get in London. The disparity made me feel uncomfortable, and I was conscious suddenly of my affluence in a country where people had so little.

Of course I'd seen the slums and come face to face with the beggars and the poverty, yet somehow I'd remained unmoved by it. It wasn't part of my world and I couldn't relate to it, and every day I was here I became just a little bit more immune to the harsh reality of so many lives in this country. When it came to taking on a highly qualified young executive at a salary that felt like a pittance, it seemed somehow closer to home. My starting salary, ten years earlier, had been five times higher than these kids were making, and yet they seemed over the moon with the money they were offered.

'They are incredibly excited to be joining a regional team,' the headhunter told me. 'I know they won't get to travel at all, but they'll feel part of something that is international and will look great on their CV.'

'Of course they'll get to travel!' I told her. 'There will be loads of meetings in Bangkok and Singapore and possibly other Asian locations, and there's no reason why they shouldn't attend some of the meetings with me.'

'Really? That's quite unusual. Usually only the senior people get the travel perks.'

'Believe me,' I said, 'travel isn't always a perk. In fact, it can be downright exhausting. Anyway, I'm happy that they are excited about joining me.'

Our small but happy team was formed, and we began the process of bonding with the creative teams in the agency who would be writing the ads for us, many of which would be used across the region. None of them had ever worked on any international business, and they were equally as excited at the prospect of travelling overseas. I was used to working with creative types, I'd done it for years and always enjoyed the banter and faux pas or even genuine aggression that inevitably went with the relationship. These guys were more passionate, more belligerent, more forceful in their views than any of my colleagues back in London. They argued fervently, breaking into Hindi when particularly impassioned, they flung their arms around wildly, used vulgar gesticulations, which at least helped me make sense of the Hindi, and endlessly chain smoked harsh local cigarettes. I was a little scared of them initially, they were all such firebrands, but I soon came to realize that for them this was work and not personal. They teased me, laughed at my English accent, asked me questions about where I was from, whether I had a boyfriend, why I left England, whether I liked Mumbai, where I went out; they fought with me and then invited me out for beers. I was carried away by their enthusiasm and delighted by the passion they showed for their work.

Somehow, I found this kind of exuberance far more appealing than the pseudo intellectual types I'd worked with back in the UK. Here, the energy was almost childlike, genuine and spirited. Back in London's advertising scene the creative teams in particular seemed just a little bit too cool for school, fashion victims trying hard to be non-committal, sneering at those who got excited by briefs and even by advertising. I was reminded of why I got into advertising in the first place—for the sheer joy of creating amazing work, making magic from dull briefs and routine products.

We took a trip to Bangkok for our first ever regional team meeting, where we would meet with other agency groups from the Asian network. We were the creative development team for Asia for our particular product line, a well known shampoo brand, and had to present some ads. I took two creative guys and both of my young account handlers with me. There was a bit of scrabbling around to get passports and visas, we booked our flights (we'd agreed to travel economy class as there were a few of us going) and we left, one big excited group.

I was really excited to be going to Thailand—Mumbai had thus far been my only Asian experience and I was keen to see whether it would be the same, or different, whether I'd love Bangkok as much as I did Mumbai, and whether I would have the same instinctive reaction to the city. I bought a *Lonely Planet Thailand* and did some homework on the country, learning that it was not only a kingdom, but that the Thai people were allegedly peaceful, friendly and welcoming. I wondered whether we foreigners simply stereotyped all Asian nations as 'friendly' (I had read this description more than once during my research into the Asian subcontinent) and I wondered how an entire nation, or continent, could possibly be described as 'friendly'. I supposed that this was just a handy one-size-fits-all depiction favoured by Western copywriters.

Landing into Bangkok's Suvarnabhumi airport, I was surprised by how clean and modern the airport seemed, at least in comparison to Mumbai's international airport, which looked as though it was permanently in a state of disarray, and while impressive in parts, not generally the nicest place to have to wait for a connection. Bangkok's airport looked clean, fairly shiny and smelled of antiseptic. After a long wait for my Indian colleagues to collect their visas on arrival—my UK passport meant that I was automatically entitled to a 30-day stay without a visa—we headed outside to find the cars that would take us to the hotel. The exit from the cool air-conditioned airport interior reminded me of my first landing into Mumbai, although the heat was more humid and the smell more fragrant somehow.

During the journey from the airport to our hotel, I stared out at the considerably flashier cityscape. I found it fascinating that my reference points were all now Mumbai rather than London. To me, Bangkok looked similar to the more commercial areas of London—miles of glittering high rise buildings, clean and sparkling in the sunshine, the air a lot fresher and the sky bluer than Mumbai, and the roads wide and perfectly tarmacked. Rohit and Kiran were wide-eyed and apparently finding the whole experience much more impressive than I was. They looked even younger than their twenty-five-odd years as they literally pressed their noses up to the car window, and marveled at the sights.

'It's amazing,' sighed Kiran. 'So clean, and so many tall buildings.'

'The cars are so cool,' said Rohit, his typically male attention fixed on the traffic and the various models of upmarket vehicles. We were all used to seeing clapped out taxis, rickshaws and the occasional shiny new sedan on Mumbai's roads. Here, every other car was huge and gleaming, there were international models galore and a range of powerful looking SUVs alongside the BMWs and the Audis. I had already learned that the import duties to bring a foreign car into India were massive, and so ownership of the swankier international models was restricted to the very rich. Besides, owning a fast car in Mumbai was somewhat futile given the slovenly, crawling traffic.

That evening, after a fancy and delicious dinner at the hotel, we decided to head out to Khao San Road, the notorious backpacker district, for a shot at the 'real' Bangkok, or at least something approximating it. I stared in amazement as we passed a Boots chemist, its familiar facade looking bizarrely incongruous amidst the stalls selling deep fried beetles and traveller tat. Khao San Road was basically a long road packed with guesthouses, bars, cafes, bookshops and restaurants, with market stalls running its entire length. The road had been closed to cars, and pedestrians wandered along in large groups. I noticed that the vast majority were white, clad in the typical traveller garb of scruffy, flowing often tie-dyed T shirts and baggy trousers, many sporting dreadlocks or shaved heads, even the girls. Everyone looked tanned, relaxed, and many were clearly intoxicated.

'Wow, this is awesome,' breathed Rohit in his limited, teen-speak vocabulary, clearly mesmerized by the sight of so many foreigners and so many bars. Kiran looked a little nervous, and I wondered whether I should have left her behind in the hotel — this was the first time either of them had been abroad and while Rohit was clearly in his element, Kiran was young for her twenty-five years and had clearly led a more sheltered life with her over-protective parents and older brother. I figured though that it couldn't do her any harm to see a bit of the world, as long as I kept my eye on her.

During our stay in Bangkok, we saw a fair amount of sleaze and I picked up on an unpleasant undercurrent, which I couldn't quite put my finger on. I'd heard that Thailand, and Bangkok in particular, was a Mecca for sex tourists, and we saw plenty of fat old men dragging Thai girls (or boys) along behind them, the men throwing their weight around literally and figuratively, and clearly, in my view, exploiting their Thai 'friends'. We visited Pat Pong, where I bought a couple of fake handbags, and we marvelled at the rows of sex shops advertising their sordid interiors with lurid neon signs and blaring trance music. I had no desire to see a live sex show, though clearly there was a huge audience for this kind of stuff. Frankly, it made me feel sick, and I couldn't help but feel sorry for this city and its people, who had been invaded by people who would be considered social outcasts back home, yet were treated like kings here.

Kiran and Rohit spent their free moments between meetings rushing off to the malls, returning with armfuls of shopping bags.

'What are you all buying?' I asked them curiously. I couldn't for the life of me work out what they would find here to get so excited about.

'Everything! Amazing stuff from China...shoes, bags, clothes. We have to take stuff back for our friends and families.'

Apparently the done thing for Indians was to cart vast amounts of gifts back for extended families, and I wasn't talking about a paperweight or a souvenir bookmark here. It seemed as though they were buying entire new wardrobes for everyone they knew, and I was worried about excess baggage at the airport.

In between the shopping trips, during which I lazed around, ordered room service and occasionally wandered down to the hotel gym, we had our meetings. I was very proud of my small team, the creative guys had managed to crack some great work and both Rohit and Kiran were talking passionately about the client's business. It wasn't easy to drum up enthusiasm for shampoo, but these kids managed to do it.

I stayed in touch with Krishna with daily phone calls and messages, some of which started to take on a slightly possessive tone. 'Who were you out with? Having fun?' 'Have you met any nice people?' (i.e. men, I assumed). 'Are you missing me???' It was kind of sweet but at the same time I felt slightly irritated. I was busy trying to focus during meetings, and when I didn't immediately respond to a text, I received another asking if I was OK. Still, it was nice to be wanted and I told myself to stop feeling so ungrateful.

Our four days finally came to an end, and we headed back to the airport, exhausted. I was delighted that the meetings had gone so well. This had been my first exposure as the Regional Business Head, and it was important to make a good impression. Rohit and Kiran were effusive in their gratitude. They could hardly believe they'd been on a trip to Bangkok so soon after joining the agency and I only hoped that they wouldn't become jaded and cynical over time, like the majority of frequent business travellers.

## 9

Back in Bombay, Krishna was delighted to see me. Our relationship had definitely turned a corner, we spent a lot of time together and it was clear that we were committed and 'exclusive', as the Americans put it. Despite his slight possessiveness while I had been in Bangkok, he was generally supportive and interested without being suffocating, and it seemed like a good balance to me. After weeks of his coming to my place to pick me up, he finally took me to his apartment, which it turned out he shared with friends. It was scruffy on the outside, and hardly a palace on the inside, but I figured that at least he was bucking the trend and not living with his parents. I wondered briefly whether he minded that he had to share a place, most of his friends in Mumbai seemed to live with their own parents amidst clear displays of old money, with their own spacious 'quarters' and usually their own servants. My western sensibilities were accustomed to the concept of flat sharing, but I knew that this wasn't common in India—people either lived with their families, their spouses or alone.

'It's not much, but it's home,' said Krishna, as if reading my mind. 'I'm travelling a lot so there's really no point my spending too much on a place but I'm definitely looking out for my own apartment. This is just a stopgap.'

'That's cool,' I told him, eager to sound reassuring and keen to avoid any suggestion that I might be judging him.

After a couple of months of dating, and more kissing, Krishna stayed over at my place and we slept together. Given that we had taken things a little slowly up to now, I felt absolutely ready to take that step. He was loving afterwards, and held me tight, kissing my forehead. I could hardly believe that I'd met such a great guy so soon after arriving, and wondered idly whether we'd get married eventually. I knew I was jumping the gun, and I certainly wouldn't have breathed a word of my innermost thoughts to Krishna, for fear of him running in the opposite direction, but frankly I was tired of being single and fed up of being the only one of my friends who wasn't settled into some cozy twosome. Krishna made me felt great about myself, and he also gave me some weird kind of invisible protection. Somehow, even if he wasn't by my side, I felt the effect of having a man in my life, and one who was local and knew his way around this crazy city was an added bonus. So much for being a feminist. And although I took solace in the fact that I knew I could go it alone if I had to, I wasn't going to resist this if it made my life easier.

I'd arrived in Mumbai at the liveliest time of the year, the pre-Christmas period, which was stuffed chock full of celebrations, culminating in Diwali, the Festival of Light. Diwali was to Hindus what Christmas was to Christians, except that Hindus could generally choose the god or gods who appealed to them most, or whom their families had traditionally worshipped. Krishna asked me to spend Diwali with his parents, in his hometown of Ahmednagar. I was flattered to be asked, and excited to be able to be a part of these important celebrations, though a little nervous at the thought of meeting his parents, and I started wondering what on earth I was going to wear.

'Don't worry,' Krishna told me. 'My parents will insist on buying you two or three outfits for Diwali.'

'I couldn't possibly accept gifts from your parents, I've never even met them before. Surely I should be taking them presents, not the other way round.'

'It's the Indian way,' he laughed, 'they will want to welcome you into the family, and they have to give you a gift. If they don't, it will seem really rude and as though they aren't taking you seriously as a potential member of the family.'

'Er, OK,' I muttered, wondering exactly what he'd told them about me and our relationship. 'We'll have to sleep in separate rooms though, I hope that's OK with you.'

'Of course. Whatever makes them comfortable.' But I couldn't quite believe that at the age of thirty-two I was pretending to my thirty-year-old boyfriend's parents that we didn't have sex. It seemed hypocritical and unnecessary, and made me feel like a teenager, but it was their house and I would of course respect their rules.

The build-up to Diwali was similar to the days that led up to Christmas. Shops and houses were decorated, but instead of Santas and reindeers, the buildings were covered with lights—the more extravagant the better. The entire city took on a magical, fairy tale façade, which served to embellish even the ugliest of exteriors. Entire streets were dressed with swathes of lights, trees started to glitter and twinkle, and every apartment building constructed its own illuminations, which often vied for attention with the décor of the individual flats. As with everything in India, the visual feast was inevitably accompanied by an assault on the ears. Very little was done quietly in this country, and a celebration without noise would be unthinkable. The build-up to Diwali day itself was characterized by a crescendo of firecrackers and blaring music, the former usually thrown randomly in the street, the latter an earsplitting medley of Bollywood tunes that blared from makeshift speakers all across the city. The energy and excitement were palpable, people were frantically shopping for Diwali gifts, stocking up their homes and generally preparing for five days of complete indulgence, with a bit of prayer thrown in for good measure. Not very different from the concept of Christmas, then.

One early morning, Krishna and I took the train to Ahmednagar, my very first train journey in India. It was a seven-hour journey, which amazed me given that it was in the same state, Maharashtra, and hardly looked any distance on the map. I always forgot just how big India was, at least compared to the UK, which was of course miniscule in comparison. We arrived at the Victoria Terminus —a gorgeous building strangely familiar amidst all the pandemonium — hardly surprising given that it had been built by the British in the eighteen hundreds, and bore distinct similarities to St Pancras station in London. The elegant Victorian gothic arched windows and majestic pointed turrets of the station's façade formed a sharp contrast to its scruffy surroundings.

'What on earth is going on here?' I asked Krishna as we entered the station.

At first glance, it seemed to resemble a massive dormitory or open air cafeteria, as the huge concourse was littered with bodies sleeping, eating and even cooking. Entire families seemed to have set up camp in the station's interior and, surrounded by what seemed to be all their worldly possessions, were busy chatting and fighting and arguing and basically going through the usual routine of family life.

'What are all these people doing here?' I asked Krishna. 'They look like they're homeless. It's very strange.'

'They're waiting for their train,' Krishna clarified with a grin.

'But why do they have so much stuff with them? And they are cooking and everything. It looks like they're living here!'

Krishna patiently explained that due to the sheer size of India and the length of the train trips, which entire families would take together, they naturally needed to wait for connecting trains, sometimes for hours and even days. These people were in the middle of a week-long journey from one side of India to the other. I felt slightly embarrassed, as if I'd revealed myself to be the naïve Westerner that I really was. Whereas I would think nothing of jumping onto a plane to cross half the world, there were millions of people for whom travel meant a bus or at best a train, and a journey within one's own country must be calculated on the basis of days rather than hours.

Krishna didn't pick up on my discomfort; I supposed that for him, these kinds of sights were something he was used to—these families were a hindrance rather than a source of fascination, merely bodies to be navigated in search of the correct train.

The train was clean and seemed very efficient, though typically chaotic and noisy, and particularly busy given that everyone was leaving Mumbai to travel back to their hometowns and villages for Diwali. We had no choice but to join in the pushing and shoving on the platform, or we would surely have been left behind. Krishna grabbed me by the hand and pulled me manfully into the train carriage.

Once on the train, I couldn't help but make comparisons to 'back home'. The British Rail trains, with their silent carriages, murmured conversations and buffet cars stocked with miniature gin bottles and hand-cut Kettle chips, seemed a million miles away from the Indian version—carriages packed to the brim, stuffed full of families and their piles of luggage, punctuated with shrill conversations and laughter emanating from every nook and cranny of the compartment—all of this underscored by the repetitive cry of the chai wallah who wandered restlessly back and forth along the carriage. During the journey we were offered various foodstuffs by vendors who pleadingly pressed upon us their wares, which included various fried foodstuffs, sticky sweets that were madly attracting flies, and 'cold drinks'—the Indian ubiquitous term for Coca Cola, Pepsi and Fanta. We fuelled ourselves with endless cups of sugary, spiced chai, absolutely delicious and thoroughly reviving despite the sauna-like heat.

We attracted a fair amount of unselfconscious stares, people were clearly not used to seeing a foreigner with an Indian, and though we were observing all the rules of decorum, and I was pretty well covered in a long sleeved T shirt and jeans, our fellow travellers were still fascinated by us. I was used to the constant staring by now, and I no longer even found it rude or inappropriate. It was largely harmless, and I figured that many Indians, particularly those from more rural areas, had never seen a white person in the flesh before, so I went with it and even occasionally met the wide-eyed stares with a smile.

Ahmednagar turned out to be a dusty, medium-sized

town with little charm and all the noise and dust pollution of Mumbai. We took a rickshaw from the station, Krishna had told his parents not to meet us, as I think he felt that it would be far more comfortable for me to meet them in the house itself. I was a little nervous, and hoped that I looked presentable enough. I had toyed with the idea of wearing a dress, but thought it best to err on the side of modesty in trousers and a formal shirt.

His parents came to meet us as the rickshaw pulled up—his mother was dressed in a gorgeous purple saree, with matching bindi and jewellery, and his father was wearing a loose shirt over formal trousers. They greeted me with broad smiles and a namaste and I made the prayer gesture back, feeling somewhat self-conscious.

'Mum, Dad, this is Julia,' said Krishna.

'Welcome, welcome,' answered his father, with a heavy accent. 'Please come in. Lunch is ready.'

Food, and feeding guests, was at the absolute core of Indian hospitality. I learnt much later that the obsession with food and feeding others was not only a social ritual but also representation of the ability to fend for oneself and take care of others, as well as a symbol of affluence. Krishna had warned me that his parents, like all Indian parents, would try to feed me constantly and suggest that I was undernourished and thin (I was far from it). He told me that I should learn to take very small helpings, and eat little and often in order to avoid interrogation and keep them happy.

His family house was a sprawling bungalow in one of the popular residential districts. Its high ceilings and thick walls provided protection from the blazing sun, and the interior was cool and refreshing. Lunch turned out to be an elaborate and delicious affair—we started with a cool lassi followed by various delicious, spicy treats, which I assumed were the main meal but which turned out to be mere appetizers. I'd followed Krishna's advice of taking small portions, and his mother kept pressing more and more food on me.

'Thank you, Aunty,' I said, using the typical polite address for an older lady. 'This is all delicious, but I don't want to get full too quickly.'

After we'd finished with the starters, the main courses arrived. There were vegetable preparations including my favourite aloo-gobi (spicy cauliflower and potato), a dark green, tangy spinach dish and a smoky tasting glop made from aubergines—normally I hated the spongy texture of the vegetable, but this was delicious, pungent and spicy without being overpowering. There was mutton, or goat curry and the ubiquitous daal. We scooped everything up with freshly made rotis, and there was plenty of mango and mustard pickle in case the food wasn't spicy enough (it was). Lunch was finished off with possibly the most delicious but unhealthy dessert in the world—deep fried condensed milk balls soaked in syrup, or gulab jamun as they were popularly known. Although I was full, they slipped down easily and were absolutely divine and a perfect end to the meal. I was glad I'd heeded Krishna's advice about eating slowly and steadily, and I ate a bit of all of the dishes. His mother was clearly delighted that I had a good appetite. It seemed that she'd cooked only one of the dishes, the mutton curry, but the entire menu was of course her doing and all the food had been cooked by the family help under her supervision.

During lunch, we chatted and Krishna's parents asked about

my life back in England, my work in Mumbai and my family. His father did most of the questioning, his mother wasn't very comfortable speaking English, and my Hindi was basic to say the least. Krishna's first language was Marathi, the language of the Maharastrian state, which was even more complex than the Hindi that I was slowly beginning to pick up. His father asked me what my parents did for a living (this seemed to be important) and I told them that my father was a retired teacher and that my mother didn't work. They asked why I'd come to Mumbai, asked me about my 'designation' and seemed fairly impressed that I was a 'Vice President' (I hadn't the heart to tell them I was one of many in the company) and that I got to travel a lot.

After lunch, Krishna volunteered to show me the sights of Ahmednagar, and his parents retired to take a nap. 'I think they like you,' he said.

'I hope so,' I replied. 'It will certainly make things easier if I have your parents' approval, not that it really matters at the end of the day because this is about us, but I guess that's pretty important in India.'

The next day, Krishna's parents took me shopping. They wanted to buy me some Indian outfits for the Diwali parties that would be happening across the next couple of days. I drew the line at a saree. I'd never worn one and I couldn't imagine that they'd be terribly comfortable, plus I'd heard that they were a nightmare to drape and they'd often reveal a huge expanse of belly. Flashing my wobbling tummy at strangers was not something that appealed, and I suggested that we buy salwar kameezes. The salwar kameez was about the most forgiving outfit on the planet. And what mattered in India was not the fit, but the fabric and the overall bling—like the sari, these outfits could be worn to any function, and were differentiated by the quality of cloth and the number of sequins and the elaborateness of the design. Simple, cloth sarees and salwars were for everyday wear. Silk, particularly heavy silk, sequins and additional sparkly bits were for more formal functions—weddings and the like. It was clear that the parents wanted to dress me up in full finery; I supposed that I would be representing their son and the choice he and they had made to accept me into their family, and here family and reputation was everything.

We entered fantastic shops where fabrics and garments were piled high, treasure troves of richness in rainbows of colour. There was a long glass counter running the length of every shop, behind which men (it was always men, strangely) spread out the garments for the discerning customer to feel, weigh and haggle over. I managed to resist the various neon shades that these men invariably picked for me—somehow they felt, erroneously, that banana yellow and bright orange would complement my pale skin.

'I like dark colours,' I insisted, stubbornly. 'Dark red or green. Purple is good.'

I tried a few on and was impressed by how the material clung to my curves and flattered my figure without being revealing in the slightest. Eventually, we settled on a burgundy number, a green outfit, and, as a concession to the parents, a pale lilac ensemble with silver sequins splattered generously across it. We also bought sparkly Indian style sandals, or chappals, flat comfortable shoes covered in gemstones and more sequins.

The first function we attended was at a family friend's, a

lovely rambling old house in a slightly more rural area, a few kilometres out of town. There were about fifty guests, and I was introduced to most of them. I was glad I was wearing my Indian finery, the women were decked up to the nines, not only were they wearing bright expensive looking sarees and salwars, but they were also exhibiting a range of extremely lavish jewellery—bangles, necklaces, earrings and nose rings. Before stepping out of the house, I'd felt vastly overdressed, wondering if I looked ridiculous in the shiny outfit and matching shoes. Now I felt like the poor relation, bereft of jewellery and bland in the middle of this sea of excess. I was also missing the relative luxury of Mumbai's beauty parlours, which tamed my unruly tresses on a regular basis. My blow dry was a couple of days old, and although I'd smoothed it with some of the serum I'd brought from home, I was aware that I looked scruffy and far from polished.

However, I hadn't factored in the foreign factor. Apparently the fact that I was white and wearing a traditional Indian outfit made me a fabulous creature, or at least it felt that way. Every single woman I met complemented me on my outfit, and oohed and aahed over my look. I was a little embarrassed by all this attention but, as Krishna told me, I was a rarity, especially here, and people thought I was exotic. I thought back to the grubby outfit I'd been wearing when I landed in Mumbai for the first time a couple of months earlier and suppressed a laugh. Me, exotic? I hardly thought so.

The evening's entertainment consisted of drinking, eating, more drinking, more eating, playing cards and finally dinner. I didn't realize that dinner would be served right at the end of the evening, and that it was in fact traditional that everyone would leave once they'd eaten their fill. I avoided eating too many of the snacks that had been circulating from the beginning of the evening, figuring with my newly acquired insight that I shouldn't fill myself up too much and wait instead for the main course. At about 11 p.m., the starters stopped coming round and I assumed it was time for dinner. At this point, however, the serious drinking began, and the card games started up. Diwali was the traditional time for gambling across all of India, and the famous card game teen patti, or 'three cards' (similar to poker but less complicated) was played in homes across the length and breadth of the country.

Krishna and I decided to skip the card games, and sat outside on the veranda chatting. Waiters were circulating and refilling our glasses endlessly, and I suddenly realized that I was a bit drunk.

'What time is dinner?' I asked, squinting at my watch.

'Oh, at about 1 a.m.,' said Krishna, completely seriously.

'You're kidding! Why so late? Is that normal?'

'Of course. Dinner is always served right at the end of a party, and it's the cue for people to leave. If you served it any earlier then people would think you wanted them to go, and they wouldn't know what to do afterwards.'

'So we have to wait another two hours to eat?' I asked.

'Yup. Didn't you eat the snacks earlier?' 'Not really. I was worried I'd get full.'

'Oops. Anyway, keep drinking and you'll be fine.'

By the end of the night I was plastered. I was studiously avoiding his parents, and generally ducking out of any potential conversations with guests. I tried to slow my drinking down, but it was impossible with the over zealous waiters hovering around.

I could feel all the alcohol sloshing around in my empty stomach, and realized, mid conversation with one of Krishna's uncles, that I was actually going to be sick. I made a feeble excuse about needing to look for Krishna, who thankfully was busy making conversation with other family members, and realizing that my urge to vomit was urgent, dived behind a large tree in the garden. Luckily my teenage experiments with alcohol held me in good stead, and I managed to puke quietly and subtly.

As I rejoined the party, wiping my mouth discreetly, Krishna found me. 'All OK?' he asked, wrapping his arm around my waist.

'Fine,' I answered, hoping that I didn't look as green as I felt. 'I was enjoying chatting with your relatives actually.'

Finally dinner was served. Starving hungry, given the recent evacuation of my stomach contents, I ate a vast plate of food. It was delicious but it went down too fast and I realized that I was going to have a very bad case of indigestion the next morning.

The Diwali celebrations continued in more or less the same fashion for the next four days. I was bored after the second evening. It was clear, however, that we had no option but to be part of the festivities, there was no chance of us slipping away for an evening, and I decided to make the most of it.

On the morning of Diwali itself, the family held a puja, a prayer ceremony. This was a fairly complicated ritual consisting of prayers and various symbolic offerings made to a deity. Though my research had told me that pujas could be made to any of the thousands of Hindu gods, on Diwali the puja was always made to the Goddess Laxmi, the goddess of light and also good fortune, beauty and wealth. Before the puja began, the entire house was scrubbed from top to bottom, there was an entire army of

84

maidservants sweeping and brushing, wiping surfaces and sloshing water around. 'It's very important for the house to be pristine before the puja starts,' Krishna told me.

I was intrigued by the upcoming ceremony, and fascinated to be part of it. We all dressed up in our finery and the puja began. Krishna's father recited a Hindi incantation, lit a lamp, or diya, and there was a complicated ritual involving water, rice grains and coins. Each of the family members picked up the golden tray with the diya on it, and made a circular movement with it around the small statue of the goddess. The tray was handed to me, and I self-consciously circled the goddess, feeling like a complete fraud. I had no real knowledge of the Hindu faith, I didn't really know why we were doing this ritual and I wished I'd at least done more research. As a non-Hindu, I wondered if there was some protocol governing my participation in the rites, but everyone seemed happy enough to include me. Finally, everyone touched the forehead of the goddess with a dab of red turmeric powder and we were all given similar marks on our foreheads. I felt a bit silly and wondered whether it would be politically correct to wipe or even wash it off, but decided against it, for fear of offending someone.

The Diwali festivities finally came to an end, and Krishna and I headed back to Mumbai. The firecrackers continued to sound for days after the event was over; it was as though no one could bear to return to reality and instead stretched out the festivities for as long as possible. I carefully hung my new outfits up, proud of the fact that I'd finally acquired 'real' Indian outfits, and used them for a very genuine purpose. I felt slightly smug, superior in the knowledge that I'd delved below the surface.

Back in the office, my co-workers asked me how I'd spent my Diwali, and I regaled them with tales of card playing, drinking and even the puja, which I was inexplicably proud of. It was as though I thought I'd seem more acceptable if I'd participated in some of the local rituals, even though I had felt a bit foolish doing it and I was worried about turning into one of those annoying white people who wanted to immerse themselves in India for spiritual reasons.

## 10

Krishna and I had developed quite an active social life and we were often out and about in the bars and restaurants in Mumbai. We were invited to birthday parties by his gang of friends, to nights out with them and of course to the inevitable after parties. Though the scene was fairly repetitive, I was enjoying myself, feeling part of a social set, and I started developing my own friendships with some of the group, albeit limited only to fairly mundane conversations over drinks, but liberating nonetheless and a development that added to my social confidence. Four months in, and I was feeling happy and fairly settled in this new life. I was glad I had trusted my instinct and moved to Mumbai, and I felt somehow connected to this city of twenty million people.

Krishna and I were of course part of the elite, we were at the very top of the pyramid when it came to India's rather unfair distribution of wealth, or rather failure to distribute wealth. There was a tiny minority of super-affluent families in Mumbai, who seemed to have most of the money shared amongst them and who seemed to own all of the infrastructure, the big corporations and the hotels. Below this level of super-rich, there were people who had more than enough money, and I suppose that included Krishna and I, by the simple definition that we lived in Mumbai's posh area, and had a high disposable income, relatively. I didn't know exactly how much Krishna earned, but he had his own business, drove a decent car and paid for everything, despite my protestations, so I figured he couldn't be badly off despite his slightly shabby accommodation, and certainly he was part of Mumbai's elite social set according to all the party invites he received. Below us there were many levels of social strata, each with its own intricate set of rules and guidelines, many of which were a throwback to the old caste system. I wondered occasionally whether Krishna really felt part of his friends' circle, given that they were clearly all old money and living on inherited wealth, while he was essentially a small town boy who had had to earn his way into that circle. I supposed that India, despite all of its social complexities and difficulties, wasn't as snobbish as England—back home the complex class system meant that breaking into a higher social set would be more or less impossible, though it did of course happen. Here, the fact that Krishna had attended the same university as his friends, though many of them had subsequently gone abroad for their postgraduate degrees, made him part of the gang.

Despite the fact that I was living in a city of millions, I bumped into the same old people with amazing regularity, which just went to show how narrow that pyramid was at the top. I didn't stress too much about the endless number of layers beneath me, nor did I worry that I wasn't connecting with the 'real' India. I was a relatively rich foreigner, and there's no way that I was ever going to be able to truly identify with a poor Indian. Though I appreciated all that I had, and was grateful for it, I didn't think that the slum-dwellers needed my pity, and I focused instead on being grateful for the things that I had.

I decided to go home for Christmas. Even though I had only been away from home for four months, I felt that I needed to spend some time with my friends and family. I missed them terribly and I was dying to be back in an uncomplicated social setting where I could relax and be myself. Besides, I couldn't imagine spending Christmas in the sunshine, and particularly not in a city with a relatively small Christian population, where Christmas would probably be a one-day public holiday and a tree in the five-star hotels, whereas the festive season I was used to meant a month of parties and excitement, in the build-up to the big day. I was lucky enough to get one business class return flight a year with my job, so I booked my ticket and started planning my trip home. I broke the news to Krishna that I would be away for Christmas and New Year and he looked briefly upset.

'It's only for a couple of weeks, and I'll be back at the beginning of January. I really need to see my family.'

'Of course. That's cool. I'll head off to Goa for the holidays with the boys.'

I wondered whether he had been expecting me to take him home with me, especially given that I'd already met his parents, but I wasn't ready for that yet. Besides which, I had no idea if he could afford the airfare. I presumed that he could but I didn't want to invite him and then have him all embarrassed, and I was certainly not going to pay for him. I wondered whether he might suggest that he came along, combining a work trip with a personal visit as I knew that he did some business in the UK, but thankfully he didn't. Also I was secretly and selfishly looking forward to the luxury of my business class trip, and I really didn't want to have to downgrade to keep him company. I did give him my spare set of keys though and asked him if he would keep his eye on the flat, and told him to make himself at home there. I trusted him enough to let him stay at my place without my being there. After all, I'd known him for three months and met his family and friends, and we definitely had a strong connection.

I spent the week before I left Mumbai rushing around picking up gifts for people—silk scarves, Indian style kurta tops, gaudy candlesticks, the ubiquitous mirrored cushion covers and some silver jewellery.

The flight was wonderful, I drank champagne and watched movies until I fell asleep, excited to be returning home again. As I approached London, there was a narrative running non-stop inside my head, which was continually forcing me to compare the two worlds—the crazy, chaotic, adventure filled city that I'd left behind, and the familiar yet strange environment of England that I was returning to. Plane travel always had the tendency to make everything seem strangely disjointed and dreamlike, thanks, I supposed, to crossing through time zones along with the heady rush of free drinks served at 35,000 feet.

I landed in London at 6 a.m. into a blanket of darkness, which surprised me. I'd forgotten about the concept of seasons, and how dawn and dusk times changed during the year, given that I'd been living pretty much on the equator for the past four months. I noticed the smell of London's airport—faintly plasticky, cool and with an undercurrent of cleaning fluid. It was very different from the humid and often foetid warmth of Mumbai airport and the various odours that hit you inside and outside the airport. I made my way wearily off the plane and breezed through customs, flashing my passport smugly—this was a refreshing change from having to fill in immigration forms, stand in a long queue and be interrogated about my purpose in visiting a country.

Suddenly I felt a rush of belonging—this country, though irritating and frustrating in so many ways, was my home. I felt safe and secure here, warmed by the familiarity of systems and processes, people and places that needed no second-guessing nor acclimatization. Having said that, I was completely overwhelmed by my re-entry and overcome with a strange emotion, a mixture of longing for that feeling of belonging as well as simultaneously needing to challenge its comfort and security. I felt like shouting at the top of my voice, yelling to my fellow passengers that I lived in India! I wanted to be recognized for the fact that I had left and that I was successfully forging a life for myself in a foreign and difficult country.

I got on the Heathrow Express and paid an eye watering fifteen pounds for the fifteen minute journey. I couldn't help but compare that to the cost of a taxi ride in Mumbai, or think that that same fifteen pounds would have bought me food for a week in India. I bought trashy magazines, and dived into them on the train—though there were plenty of gossipy papers in India, somehow Bollywood gossip was too sanitized and manufactured for me. I preferred the real McCoy, the scandal and the titillation and the inevitable stories of heartbreak and longing and loneliness and people being reunited and getting pregnant and divorced and remarrying. In India, Bollywood stars, like cricketers, were like gods and they were kept high on their pedestals for the masses to adulate. In the UK, we loved to see successful people falling onto hard times, as a nation we abhorred boasting and the conspicuous ostentation of the newly-moneyed, and we delighted in the inevitable crash that came after a swift rise to the top. It wasn't a particularly pleasant trait, but we did always like to see people put firmly in their places. India was the exact opposite, a country where so many people were struggling to survive in lives that were so difficult and often downright miserable, that they craved the glamour, the success stories and the myth of the superstar who couldn't possibly be toppled from his or her lofty position.

The habit of constantly comparing everything here to my life in Mumbai was annoying me, but I just couldn't help it. I noticed that the atmosphere in London was charged with an undercurrent that I hadn't noticed before. Somehow, it seemed a bit threatening, and certainly less friendly and welcoming than I had previously thought. I imagined how difficult it must be for tourists to arrive here and try to make their way around—though the systems were well established, asking for help from a local was likely to result in a terse response.

I thought a lot about what it meant to be English. I thought about how we refused to tolerate extremes in any form, how we were embarrassed by any overt manifestation of success and how we moderated everything into blandness—from our wonderfully comforting nursery food, to our warm beer and our external air of gentle politeness, which might have masked inner turmoil, but which was always fiercely maintained. The famous British stiff upper lip. I thought about the fact that we could only really deal with our emotions when we consumed alcohol, and how we did that in excess as if to cope with that turmoil and allow it a legitimate avenue for expression. It was vastly different from the way people were in Asia and particularly India, where they delighted in adding spice both literally and figuratively to every facet of life.

From the Heathrow Express, I changed trains at Paddington and got on to the achingly familiar First Great Western train, which would take me to my parents' home in Dorset. I was so excited to be seeing my parents again, we were a small and close-knit family and we loved our Christmases together. The week was spent in the usual manner, there were lots of presents, loads of food and tons of alcohol. From the point of view of over indulgence, it was similar in many ways to my own Diwali experience, though it was much less formal and more about lazing around in slippers watching TV, than dressing up and attending fancy parties.

I visited our local Tesco supermarket and spent literally hours wandering up and down the aisles. I'd become used to Mumbai's tiny, dusty stores where variety was limited and the few imported goods vastly overpriced. Suddenly, I was back in supermarket heaven, and I wandered up and down, fascinated by each and every product category. How come I had forgotten that there were so many different varieties and types of toilet roll? I couldn't believe that so many brands of shower gel actually existed, and I was blown away by the deli section. I fell completely in love with English food, which seemed bizarre given its mainly stodgy and bland repertoire, but it was heaven to my masala saturated taste buds. I ate bacon sandwiches every single day for breakfast, covered with brown sauce and made with wonderful fresh bread—the bread in India was terrible, the brown bread was coloured brown rather than containing wholewheat, and the white bread tasted of nothing at all save a plasticky, faintly sweet blandness. Here, I carved off great chunks of crusty fresh bread, which tasted yeasty and delicious, covered them liberally with butter and wrapped them around sausages, bacon, cheese and anything else that took my fancy. I even had a few fish finger sandwiches, which were glorious. I ate a lot of pies, fish and chips and of course turkey and all the trimmings over Christmas. It was as if my taste buds had died and gone to heaven—I couldn't explain how much I had missed all this stuff; a diet of curry for breakfast, lunch and dinner was a fantastic, exotic novelty but it did wear off after a couple of months.

The other thing I just couldn't get enough of was wine. Wine in India was either disgusting, vastly overpriced, or both. There were a number of Indian vineyards, and the wine industry seemed to be developing fast, but all the local red wines tasted harsh and vinegary to me and the white wines were either too sweet or too sour. Indian wine invariably gave me a terrible hangover and a headache, which could last for days. I had heard that it was made with certain preservatives, which meant it kept longer in warmer climates, but if that meant I was going to have to lie in a darkened room the entire next day, then I'd rather stick to the tried and tested vodka. The wine sold in England's supermarkets, off licences and even pubs was cheap and delicious. I overdosed on gorgeous buttery Chardonnays and rich, luscious bottles of Shiraz and Rioja. By the end of the week, my jeans were beginning to felt the strain and I vowed to join a gym just as soon as I returned to Mumbai.

I spoke to Krishna on the phone every other day, using my parents' landline as the roaming charges on my mobile were horrendous. He was in Goa, partying with his friends and claimed to be missing me terribly, though my phone calls to him felt invariably like a bit of a distraction from what I was doing here in England. He sounded out of it every time we talked, and I put it down to his having consumed a few beers too many, which I supposed was perfectly fine given that it was a holiday. Rather than talk to him on the phone, I preferred to send e-mails to him, I liked to spend time composing my thoughts before putting them down, and I just found that the long distance phone call was sadly lacking in intimacy and any real connection.

While I was at my parents' house, I received a call from my bank in India. I decided to take it, despite the roaming charges, figuring that it might be important.

'Good day, Madam,' came the disembodied, Indian voice. 'I am just ringing to check that you are happy with your new credit card and that you are finding it easy to use.'

'I haven't received my credit card yet,' I told the heavily accented voice. 'In fact I've been waiting for ages for it.'

'We despatched it a week ago and you have used it already,' replied the caller.

'I'm sorry, but I am telling you that I haven't received it and I certainly haven't used it.'

The voice continued. 'The card was used to withdraw thirty thousand rupees from your account last Monday.'

'Listen, I am telling you that not only have I not received the card, but I was in England last Monday and there's no way I have used it. Where was the money supposedly withdrawn?'

'From an ATM in Mumbai, Madam.'

'That settles it then. Your people must have delivered it to the wrong address, or it must have been stolen from my house. I can show you a copy of my passport when I am back, to prove to you that I was out of the country when it was used, but meanwhile please cancel the card and I expect a complete investigation into this, and a refund of my money.'

I was shocked when I put the phone down, thirty thousand rupees was over four hundred pounds—a lot of money here and a small fortune in India. I ran through various scenarios in my head, and concluded that the bank must have delivered the card and the pin number to the wrong address.

That evening I told Krishna what had happened, and he was as shocked as I was.

'That's terrible. You need to get them to give that money back. They've obviously messed up.'

'I know,' I said. 'Don't worry, I will. Anyway, the card was cancelled so I'll just sort it out when I'm back.'

I headed back up to London for New Year and caught up with a few of the old gang of friends including Annabel and Lizzie who were absolutely delighted to have me back. We met in Harvey Nicks wine bar, a fitting location, we thought, for my fleeting re-entry into London's social scene.

'So good to have you back,' exclaimed Lizzie. 'You look really healthy, although I'm surprised you don't have more of a tan.'

'Please tell me you're hating it out there,' said Annabel. 'We were hoping that you might have come to your senses and realized that London is the coolest place in the world.'

'No, we weren't,' Lizzie interjected, flashing our friend a frown. 'We were actually hoping that you're having a wonderful time, made loads of friends and met a hot guy.'

'Well,' I told them, 'I am having an incredible time. Work is great, I've met a lot of people, and I seem to go to parties all the time. It's nothing like London, you don't have to make any effort at all to get invited to parties where the booze and the food is all laid on.' They looked envious and amazed. I supposed that parties wouldn't be the first thing that sprang to mind when you thought of Mumbai.

'And have you met the man of your dreams then?' asked Annabel, gesturing to the waiter to bring us another bottle of wine.

'Well, not exactly. Well, maybe. I don't know. Well, I have met someone,' I answered shyly, not sure quite how much to tell them, but dying to reveal all of the details of my fledgling love affair. In true girl style, and over two more bottles of Pinot Grigio, they squeezed all of the details from me.

'Sounds a bit of a charmer, your Krishna,' said Annabel. 'Shame he's not as rich as his friends though. It would be fun to marry a rich Indian and buy houses all over the world.'

'Shut up,' I told her with a smile, 'it's not always about the money. Anyway, he seems to have enough and he's nothing if not generous.'

'You should marry him and have lots of brown babies. You know that mixed race kids are always adorable,' added Lizzie, ever the optimist.

'Be careful,' intoned Annabel, with a warning note in her voice. 'I'm sure he's lovely, but you hardly know him, and he might just be after you for the wrong things.'

Both Annabel and Lizzie seemed to have done an awful lot in the time I'd been away. Annabel had got through a couple of boyfriends and Lizzie thought that her stable boyfriend might be weeks if not days away from proposing to her. Yet at the same time, their lives seemed to have hardly changed. I supposed I was comparing their lifestyles to the vast transformation that my own life had undergone, and I felt smugly that their news just seemed a little bit dull.

I saw in the New Year with Lizzie, Annabel and a bunch of our closest friends. We threw a sedate but fun party at Annabel's tiny two bedroom flat in Docklands, and reminisced about the crazy New Year we'd all spent together the previous year. It was great to be back, I felt happy and relaxed in their company, we had known each other for a long time and we'd slipped immediately back into the close familiarity that I missed in Mumbai.

I had a day to recover and say my goodbyes and then it was time to head back to the airport. My suitcase was laden with Christmas presents from my friends and family, and I had a couple of gifts for Krishna, along with a few packets of cheese, some bacon and some sausages, which I hoped would survive the journey, and, bizarrely, some English teabags. Bringing tea to India seemed insane given that most of the world's tea came from the subcontinent, but somehow tea bought in the UK tasted better.

I spent the flight back thinking about the year ahead. I'd only just started to scratch Mumbai's surface, and I knew enough about the city to know that I loved it, but I wanted to get deeper, to start forging friendships that were as happy and relaxed as those I had back home, and to start feeling like I really belonged there, rather than feeling perpetually like a visitor. I hoped my relationship with Krishna would continue, I really liked spending time with him and having him in my life certainly made things a lot easier. He was handsome and intelligent and we enjoyed spending time together, and I wondered how things would develop now I was back in Mumbai. Little did I know the turn things were about to take.

## 11

I arrived back into Mumbai's relative coolness, delighted to feel the sun on my face again. January was officially winter in Mumbai, the brief stretch when temperatures dipped to a relatively chilly ten to fifteen degrees at night and in the early morning, and when the peak of the afternoon sun warmed the air to a balmy twenty-five degrees. This was Mumbai at its best, when you could move around the city without collapsing into a heat induced, sweaty stupor, and when your brain felt stimulated and energized rather than heavy and dull. Unfortunately, this window of perfect weather was fleeting — by mid-February the mercury would start to rise, climbing its way inexorably towards the intense late thirties temperatures of the pre-monsoon months.

I jumped into a pre-paid airport taxi — I was still waiting for the car and driver that the company had promised me and which they assured me would be organized this month — and sat back for the long journey home. The distance from my South Mumbai apartment to the international airport was a mere 20 kilometres, but took at least an hour-and-a-half on a good day, thanks to the crowded, winding roads and the circuitous route. Mumbai's public transport system was unfathomable to me, and though it transported millions of passengers a day, I was terrified of the buses, which were all signposted in Hindi and Marathi so I had no clue where they would take me, and local trains, which had no doors so that more people could be crammed into the overcrowded interiors. I'd read that on an average, ten Mumbaikars died every day on the local trains due to accidents — they fell out, got electrocuted when they foolishly rode atop the trains, or died crossing the tracks.

I leant against the window, looking out at the chaos, delighted to be back in the middle of it all again. I'd missed the energy of this city, and though my Christmas holiday had been a very welcome break and an opportunity to recharge flagging batteries, I'd been longing for Mumbai's exhilarating vitality, which was like a drug — you could overdose on too much of it, get burned out, become exhausted, irritable and undergo a severe personality change if you were in the city for too long without a break, but the absence of it created real withdrawal symptoms and depression. I smiled at the goats being led through the Muslim area, presumably on their way to be fattened up for the Eid festival later in the year, at the hordes of women dressed beautifully in vibrant colours, at the bullock carts and the rickshaws, the drivers with no road sense and the pedestrians who avoided being mown down by a whisker.

Finally we arrived home. The taxi driver grumpily helped me unload my bags and received a decent tip for his efforts, and the watchmen, who were permanent fixtures in each and every Mumbai apartment building, smiled cheerily at me. I suspected that they'd missed having someone who came home at all hours of the morning, and who they could gossip and speculate about. I entered my apartment and a foul smell hit me. It was a combination of old grease and stale air, and I saw that everything was covered in a fine layer of dust. The kitchen was filthy, there were dirty plates stacked in the sink, the bed was unmade and there were coffee cups littered around the living room. My heart sank—I had asked Krishna to keep the place tidy, and my maid would be coming later in the day to clean the place, but I really hadn't expected to walk into such a mess, and I had half hoped that Krishna would be here to meet me.

I checked my phone, he hadn't messaged me or called since New Year and I vaguely wondered whether he was OK. Right now though, I was more concerned with cleaning up the mess he'd left behind.

Later that day my phone buzzed, and I answered it.

'Madam, I am calling from Blue Dart Courier company. We delivered a credit card to your apartment two weeks ago, and the bank has asked us to call and verify the delivery'.

'I'm sorry,' I said, 'I've already told the bank that the card was never delivered here, and that they need to refund my money.'

'Madam, your apartment is number 301, Sea View, correct?'

'Yes, that's correct, but the card wasn't delivered here, I've just returned from London and it's impossible that it was sent here.'

'Madam, I am sending my man to discuss this with you.'

I was hot and bothered and now I was extremely irritated. India was renowned for its stubborn bureaucrats, and I wished they'd just take my word for it when I told them I hadn't been here when the card was delivered.

An hour later, the doorbell rang. The Blue Dart man began with a concerned expression, 'See, Madam, we delivered your card on December 23rd and it was signed for.'

I peered at the paper and saw a meaningless scribble. 'That's not my signature and I wasn't here. Do you want me to show you my passport and the exit stamp from Mumbai airport on December 22nd?'

'Madam, was somebody staying in this apartment?'

'My boyfriend may have been here, but he's obviously not going to fake my signature.'

'Do you have a photograph of him, Madam?'

I couldn't believe this man was going to such lengths to disguise his company's incompetence.

'Yes, I do. Why, are you trying to tell me that my boyfriend, whom I trust completely, has faked my signature and used my credit card?'

The man was flustered and uncomfortable. 'No, Madam. I am sorry, Madam. But someone was definitely here. My man is coming now, he delivered the card here, and he will tell us who signed for it.'

I opened my laptop to look for a photo of Krishna. I had a lot, tidied neatly into folders, labeled carefully with dates and locations. The doorbell rang again. 'That will be my colleague.'

Blue Dart Man no 2 came in, and I showed him the photo. 'Yes, Madam, I gave the card to this man. I am sure.'

The penny was slowly dropping in my head, but I fought it. 'How on earth can you have handed my credit card to an Indian man, when it's addressed to an English woman?' I challenged him, my voice raised and slightly wobbly. 'I don't believe you. This is just a very convenient way of hiding the fact that you sent my credit card to the wrong place.'

'Madam, I assure you,' protested the man, unable to meet

my eye. 'This man took your card. Perhaps we should not have allowed him to, but he was very insistent that he was your husband and that you had asked him to collect it on your behalf. He even showed us a photograph of you and him together.'

The truth finally sank in.

'OK, thank you for coming. I'll talk to the bank.' I shooed the two men out, and sank onto the sofa. I could hardly believe what I'd heard, and although the evidence was indisputable, I was still fighting the truth. I ran through a few scenarios in my head. Perhaps Krishna had signed for the card, left it on the side, someone broke into the apartment and stole it. Maybe he'd used it accidentally. Perhaps the Blue Dart Man was lying, to save his skin. I called Krishna, unsure as to how I was going to handle this. My heart was thumping, and my palms were sweaty. A shrill voice informed me in Hindi and then in English that the number was switched off. I checked to see whether he'd left anything in the apartment—there was nothing of his here at all, not even a toothbrush. I called his house in Ahmednagar—he had given me the number when we were staying there, in case anything happened and I needed to call his parents. His father answered the phone.

'Hello, Mr Shinde, kaise hai?' I said, haltingly and somewhat shyly. 'This is Julia, Krishna's friend from Mumbai. I was wondering if he was there with you by any chance.'

'No, he is not here. I thought he was in Mumbai.'

'No, Uncle, I think he went to Goa with his friends and now I can't reach him, but he's probably on the plane on the way home so I'll try his number again later. Thank you for your help and I hope Aunty is well.'

I put the phone down, shaking slightly. I felt sick to my stomach, and I felt a sense of anger surging from deep within me. Though I wished that there was some convenient explanation, the facts were indisputable. My so-called loving boyfriend had been identified and exposed as a fraudster, a liar and a cheat. I wouldn't even have minded if he'd used my card and told me about it. I had more than enough money, and while I would have felt a bit odd about it, I would have been okay with it. The fact that I had called him from London, worried that someone had committed credit card fraud, concerned about the security of my account, and he had pretended to empathize, made things far, far worse. I knew that he wasn't as well off as some of his friends, and wondered whether he had struggled to pay for drinks whenever we went out, but though that softened me slightly, I was still mad as hell. I went to the kitchen and poured myself a large glass from the box of wine that I'd brought back with me from England. It was only 3 p.m. and I'd hardly slept on the plane, but I decided I needed it.

I cleaned up a bit of the mess and took the dirty cups and glasses into the kitchen. While I was wiping down the table I picked up something that looked suspiciously like a 'wrap', the twist of paper that dealers put grams of cocaine into when they sold it on the streets. I had occasionally wondered whether Krishna was dabbling in cocaine: he was always quite hyper and often had that bright-eyed look about him that was typical of coke users. Two glasses of wine later, I'd found two more empty wraps.

I was livid. I was furious with him, of course, but also angry with myself for trusting this man so blindly. I'd entrusted him with my house keys and my personal property after knowing him for barely four months, and I felt like the biggest idiot on earth. To top it all off, I couldn't believe he'd been doing drugs in my house, a company-owned flat, and lied to me about it. Fortified by Chardonnay, I called his number again.

This time, a sleepy voice answered. 'Hey, baby, you're back! How was the flight? I've missed you.'

'I know what you've done, Krishna,' I declared, trying to keep my voice level and fighting to hold the tears back.

'What are you talking about, sweetie?'

'I know you signed for my credit card and used it to withdraw thirty thousand rupees.'

'Don't be ridiculous. Did you have too much to drink on the flight? I would never do that.'

'Krishna, the Blue Dart man saw a photo of you and told me he handed you the card. I know it was you.'

There was a silence.

Finally: 'OK, yes, I did take your card. I was waiting for a payment from the US and needed some cash for a few days, so I borrowed a little bit. I was going to pay you back. I was going to tell you all about it and give you the cash. I was just waiting for someone to pay me for a delivery.'

'I don't believe you,' I answered. 'You lied to me when I called you from London. And you're lying to me now. You used the money to buy drugs, and you left my house in a complete mess, when you said you'd look after it. I never want to see you again, and I want my money back.'

'C'mon babe, this is no big deal. We're great together, you and I, and you know that your life here is a lot easier with me around. I'll give you back the money and we can just carry on.'

'No, Krishna,' I said, trying to sound calm and supportive, yet firm. 'I'm really sorry but I just don't think I can trust you again.'

Suddenly his tone changed. 'You fucking bitch. How dare you think you can just throw me away like that. You white bitches are all the same. I know you've got loads of money, this is nothing to you. Well, you can go screw yourself. I'm not giving you the money back, and I never want to see you again either.'

I was shocked at the vitriol and couldn't believe the sudden change in tone.

'I'll get the money back from you. But that's not the point. You lied to me. You could have just told me the truth.'

'Whatever. Seriously. I can't be bothered with this anymore,' and the phone went dead.

I was livid beyond words, and immediately dialled his father's number.

'Mr Shinde, this is Julia again. I am so sorry to bother you again, but I've spoken to Krishna and I have something very serious to tell you. Your son has stolen my credit card and withdrawn thirty thousand rupees from my account.'

'Impossible,' replied the disembodied, accented voice. 'Krishna is a good boy, there must be some mistake.'

'I can assure you, Uncle, that there is no mistake here. Krishna has admitted it to me.'

'Young lady, you are lying. I don't know why you want to bring dishonour to this family, but it's obvious to me that you've had your fun with my son, used him to settle yourself into the city and now you're discarding him with some made up story to make things easier for yourself.'

He carried on coolly. 'You foreigners are all the same, you

107

come to our country, abuse our hospitality, and lie and cheat and pretend that you are pure. You are all lacking in morals and the West is a nasty, corrupt place.'

I was completely shocked by the way that this man had risen up in defence of his son, attacking me while blindly assuming that Krishna must be in the right. Family in India was of course everything, and family members would close ranks over any stranger, but I was still surprised at the intensity of his attack on me.

'Uncle, I can assure you I am not lying. I have proof that Krishna took my card and my money. I don't want to have to go to the police, but I will if I have to.'

'My son has more than enough money. There is no reason why he would steal from anyone.'

I decided that it was time to take a more direct approach. 'Uncle, I didn't want to have to tell you this, but he used the money to buy drugs. I found the evidence all over my flat. Now I don't care what you do to him, but please get my money back.'

Again, the phone was cut, and I wondered if rudeness was a family trait, but I figured it was a defence mechanism in this case. I called Johann, desperate to hear a friendly voice. 'I've got myself into a bit of trouble,' I told him. I recounted the entire story, feeling foolish and at the same time, relieved to have someone to share the details with.

'I'm so sorry,' Johann said, when my sad tale finally came to an end. 'I did try and warn you at the beginning, I guess I wasn't persistent enough and you seemed to be happy. I never really trusted that guy though, I know that his friends are renowned for being a happy-go-lucky, party lot and I also know that they have a reputation for doing a lot of drugs. Plus, he's always been a hanger-on, never really part of the crowd until you came along. Perhaps you made him seem more interesting.'

'I never even realized,' I said. 'He never did anything in front of me, although come to think of it, he always had ridiculously high energy levels and would party all night after I went to bed.'

'Does he have anything of yours?' asked Johann.

'Only the money, which I intend to get back, even if I have to get the police involved. I know I am being paid well, but I don't think it's ever acceptable to steal money and lie about it, and I assume he never even meant to pay me back.' I could feel tears welling up, and I hoped that I wouldn't break down completely.

'Of course he didn't. Sweetie, you were an easy target, fresh off the boat, trusting and lonely. It happens all the time. Think yourself lucky that you've got away this lightly, it could have been far worse.'

That night, I couldn't sleep for all the thoughts rushing through my head. I couldn't stop beating myself up for having been so blindly trusting and having laid myself open to this entire situation. Half of me felt like packing up, leaving Mumbai and returning to the comfort of my friends and family, but I knew that this was just a knee-jerk reaction to what had happened. I didn't want to give up now, my journey had just begun, but at the same time I didn't want this experience to make me paranoid or have me perpetually looking over my shoulder. I was by nature a trusting person, but I guessed I just needed to avoid falling for any more sob stories or settling for a quick fix for my loneliness.

## 12

I tried to put the Krishna incident behind me, and threw myself into a variety of activities to keep myself busy. A bank transfer of thirty thousand rupees eventually landed in my account from his father, so I felt somewhat vindicated, and I wondered if Krishna had been suitably punished or whether this whole thing had just blown over without further ado. I was sure  Krishna had spun a few lies about me, but I was ready to move on and forget about the whole unfortunate episode and hope that I didn't bump into him in any of the bars and clubs in town. I was still angry, which I figured was a good thing, as my anger was preventing me from lapsing into sentimentality about the time we spent together.

I decided to keep myself busy, and I enrolled in yoga classes and finally looked for a full-time maid and driver to help me survive the rigours of this stressful but wonderful city. I'd been 'borrowing' Johann's maid for the past few months and taking taxis everywhere and now it was finally time for me to start taking responsibility for myself.

My company car finally arrived. I'd been expecting a roomy vehicle, something that I could stretch out a little in, but what finally turned up was a tiny boxlike vehicle that didn't look sturdy enough for Mumbai's bumpy roads.

'It's a great little car,' Neil the office manager told me as he handed me the keys. Clearly the look on my face suggested otherwise.

'Honestly, you'll be glad of a car this size. Much nippier in this traffic, you'll get around a lot faster and the petrol average is fantastic.' By petrol average he meant the number of kilometres you could drive for each litre of petrol, and while the company was paying for my petrol, I preferred to keep my carbon footprint as low as possible, especially given that the city was over polluted as it was.

Neil had arranged for me to meet a driver whom he had shortlisted for me. He was a young Muslim guy, living at home with his parents. He had been a driver for six years and spoke good although broken English. I conducted a short 'interview' with him, which consisted of my asking his name (Hussain) and him staring at his shoes while I smiled past him.

'He's a little intimidated by you,' Neil told me. 'He's never worked for a foreigner before, and while this is the holy grail for drivers, it's also a little bit difficult for them to get used to.'

'Holy grail? What do you mean?'

'There's a very clear pecking order for all these people, the drivers, maids, watchmen and so on. They have very clear levels of hierarchy, so for example if they work for a foreigner, who they assume by definition is wealthy, then they will automatically be higher up in the social structure than someone who works for an Indian. Similarly, if they drive a big car, or work in a big apartment, that adds credibility. And designation is really important, you need to be at least a Vice President to be of value. The icing on the cake of course is to work for an expat family living in a bungalow, with kids. There are a few of those around and they are very lucrative employers.'

My head was reeling. I hadn't even thought about this stuff before. I wondered if he was joking, but one look at his face told me he wasn't.

I wasn't entirely surprised. I knew that Indians were obsessed with the colour of their own and others' skins, and that there was an inherent and in-built racism that existed in every strata of society here. I'd seen the ads for Fair and Lovely, the skin lightening cream, and although you could have argued that white people like to make themselves darker by lying in the sun, somehow those ads, showing fair women succeeding over their darker colleagues, disturbed me.

I wondered what I was supposed to do with Hussain all day after he'd driven me to the office. I ask Neil, who guffawed and told me, 'He'll wait for you, of course. Unless you have any errands you want him to run for you.'

'Wait for me? You mean, all day?'

'Yup, all day.'

'Won't he get bored?'

More laughter. 'Well maybe, but that's his job.'

I couldn't quite wrap my head around the fact that I had someone to drive me around all the time and who would appear on call and take me wherever I wanted to go. This was a far cry from struggling onto crowded tubes and walking from the bus station to home in the pouring rain back in London.

Hussain arrived bright and early the next morning, beaming from ear to ear as he held out his hand for the keys. I got into the car to travel the relatively short distance to the office. I wasn't sure what the correct protocol was—should I sit in the back or in the front next to the driver? In the end I decided that although sitting in the back seemed very impersonal, the car was just too small to sit comfortably up front, so I hopped into the back seat feeling terribly self-conscious. I wasn't at all clear whether I was supposed to make conversation with the driver, or whether I was meant to keep quiet and let him drive. In the end I settled for a compromise—the odd bit of conversation (during which I struggled anyway to understand his accent, though his English was good) interspersed with long breaks of silence. He seemed shy, and with Neil's words ringing in my ears, I realized that he was probably a bit scared of me, given my 'designation', skin colour and apparent status.

We arrived at the office, and I wondered whether he would wait for me, as Neil insisted he would, or whether I should tell him to go home, or whether he would leave the car here and go home anyway. He answered my question himself, 'Madam, I am waiting here, back side of office,' he pointed towards the parking lot behind the office.

'OK, but I will be coming quite late this evening.'

'No problem, madam. This my job.'

'OK, thanks Hussain.'

I also wondered whether I was supposed to give him money for lunch, but Neil had given me explicit instructions here—I didn't need to give him any money during the day, and I just had to give him a small tip if he worked after 8 p.m. The going rate was apparently fifty rupees an hour, approximately sixty pence.

During the day, as I was stuck in endless meetings, I couldn't stop worrying about Hussain being bored, and I was very conscious that he was there, waiting for me. I didn't want to talk to my co-workers about this, as I knew they would scoff at me. I knew this was all just part of the adjustment process, and I just needed to get used to the fact that what seemed to be an enormous luxury to me was simply an everyday occurrence for millions of people. I learned later that my reaction was completely normal. The typical response of Westerners to having maids and drivers was initially disgust that we were participating in what appeared to be oppression on a mass scale, thanks to all our stereotyped principles about exploiting the underclasses. However, most of us soon came to realize that actually we were all supporting families, and that without our rupees, these people would literally be struggling to survive. Once I got used to that fundamental truth, the entire relationship became much more palatable. I was simply an employer, and Hussain was my employee. I was paying him to do a job, he did it well, and I treated him with respect.

I also hired a maid, Deepa, who came every morning at 8 and left at 12. It seemed utterly ridiculous to have a maid come six days a week to clean up after me, but Mumbai's pollution meant that the apartment required a good scrub every single day, thanks to the layers of grey dust that quickly covered the surfaces. I thought back to my life in London, when I used to pay someone seven pounds an hour, the equivalent of what I was paying Deepa to clean for a full week. Again, I felt uncomfortable as Deepa mopped and polished around me, particularly when she was on her knees scrubbing the marble floors. I started off by tidying up before she came, in case she thought I was a complete slut, but soon gave up on this effort, realizing that her incredible efficiency was rendering my efforts pointless. She made me chai in the morning, delicious syrupy spicy tea which woke me far more effectively than my usual instant coffee. We didn't speak very much, but Deepa was always smiling and very cheery, and I wondered what her family life was like. She told me, in halting English, that she was married and had two children aged two and four. She lived a long distance away, in the northern suburbs of the city, and I couldn't help but worry that she had a lot on her plate. She took a train and then a bus to my house, and though I was apparently paying her a good monthly wage, at least by local standards, I felt guilty that I was taking advantage of her good nature.

As well as cleaning the apartment from top to bottom every morning, Deepa washed my clothes in the old fashioned top loading machine, ironed them, and also cooked delicious food for me, which she left in the fridge every day, ready to heat in the microwave when I got back from work. Deepa also offered to do my grocery shopping, so I left an extra thousand rupees a week for her to buy fresh vegetables, fruit, meat and masalas to cook the delicious, simple but spicy curries that she made so well. I couldn't believe how pampered I was—a chauffeur driven ride to work, albeit in a small tin can rather than a limo, my washing, ironing and cleaning done, and dinner cooked for me every day. It was a far cry from my old life, but at the same time I got used to it very quickly, and after a while I couldn't imagine living without this kind of support system.

Mumbai was brutal in many ways, thanks to its chaos, crazy traffic, polluted air and its hectic, constantly on the go regime. Mumbai made London look relatively relaxed in comparison, and though days invariably started earlier in the UK, and finished in the pub, somehow the pace of life there was less frenetic, less madcap and far less spontaneous. Office timings here began and ended late—people started trickling in at 11 a.m., generally arrived by midday, and then sat late into the night, finding last minute solutions for all the problems that had invariably arisen during the day.

'Why do people work so late into the night?' I asked Johann, my fount of knowledge for all things Indian.

'It's actually very simple,' he told me. 'Most people either live with their parents or with their in-laws if they are married women. They generally live in cramped spaces, they will share a TV set and probably a computer with the entire family, and they'll have to pitch in and do chores. In the office, they are free to surf the internet, smoke, drink tea and chat with their colleagues. This is a relative luxury compared to the lives that most of them have at home.'

I'd never really thought about things like this, and again I found my basic western assumptions challenged and exposed for the privileged beliefs that they were. In my world, home was a refuge, a sanctuary from the outside world, a personal space where I could kick back, relax and refresh body and mind. Here in India, home was often an obligation, filled with responsibility and duties. Work, on the other hand, was the place where people could express themselves, adopt alter egos, bully, cajole, bitch and fight and generally enjoy themselves.

I found myself a yoga teacher who came to my apartment three times a week to teach me. I'd taken a couple of yoga classes before, it was very fashionable in London of course, as well as being vastly overpriced. Here, my teacher, Nandini, charged me three hundred rupees, a mere four pounds for an hour's session.

Nandini was in her early thirties and with that particular type of lean agility that the yoga devotee gradually acquires. Her skin shone, her eyes were bright and she was very bendy of course. She made me feel fat and inadequate, but I focused on the bigger picture — if I was going to get fit and lose some of my spare tyres, I was going to need someone who'd cracked it already. We agreed that she would come to my place at 7.30 every morning, which seemed hellishly early to me, especially as I was working fairly late and often ended up sitting up at night, surfing the net and chatting to friends and polishing off a few glasses of horrible local wine, but I guessed that I needed to start somewhere.

I was desperate to get some exercise, I hardly ever set one foot in front of the other in Mumbai. I figured that this must be the worst city ever for pedestrians; for a start there were hardly any pavements to speak of, and my daily exercise consisted of getting into the car in the morning and stepping in and out of the lift. My sedentary lifestyle, combined with all the delicious curries that Deepa left in the fridge for me, the sugary chai and the yummy office snacks, meant that I'd gained at least a stone, or 7 kilos, since arriving here. The lack of exercise combined with the pollution and the chaotic lifestyle were making me lethargic and slow witted, as well as tubby, and I figured that some hardcore yoga sessions would sort me out. Nandini turned out to be an endlessly patient teacher, which was a good job given that I was a complete yoga novice. She demonstrated the basic postures, or asanas, time and time again, adjusting my arms and legs as I struggled to become an eagle, or a lion, or a downward facing dog. My body felt creaky and stiff, and I had to gently coax it to adopt positions that felt very unnatural at first. Nandini instructed me in her calm, sing-song voice, encouraging me to concentrate, to be at one with my body and listen to its needs, and to connect with my inner mind. The only thing my body seemed to need was a break from the contortion, and my mind was an endless whirlwind of lists, plans and racing thoughts, but I tried to heed her words of wisdom.

After a few sessions, I did begin to notice a difference in my energy levels (I no longer found it completely impossible to get out of bed at 7 a.m.) and I did feel slightly more calm amidst Mumbai's whirlwind energy. My burgeoning waistline also seemed to be reducing slightly. After the physical exertion, and a few breathing exercises that were supposed to detox the body and focus the mind, Nandini insisted on chanting Om, an activity that was supposed to create vibrations in the head and aid the attempt to focus and channelize energy. I invariably felt foolish during the long Oh…hhhhhhhhh……..mmmmmmmmm chant, which lasted for an entire breath. I felt like a phony, a wannabe, but I went with it. After all, I was alone in my flat with no one to point fingers at my pretension. Nandini ended every session with an intonation, a combination between a song and a prayer, and as she did so, I focused studiously on my toes, trying to block the laughter that threatened to bubble from deep within me.

Nandini was in demand on the small but burgeoning expat circuit and she invariably began our sessions by gossiping to me about the expats she knew and taught. I couldn't quite reconcile yoga guru with rumourmonger but it was quite fun to hear her stories about who said what and who was seeing whom and who went home with whom. Nandini seemed endlessly fascinated by our world, and though she was clearly from an affluent background, her husband was something big at the Tata group, and she was very well travelled and had spent a few years living in the US, she found us foreigners intriguing. She was keen to know which expats I knew, and what parties I'd attended, and she gave me snippets of delicious gossip that she'd picked up.

One day she told me that it was time to move to the next level of yoga intensity, one that involved a greater commitment in the form of an additional session a week (she currently came three times a week) as well as a new focus towards cleansing my body. She then proceeded to tell me, with a deadly serious expression on her face, that I needed to drink my own urine every night in order to cleanse my body and achieve a perfectly healthy physical and spiritual self. The look on my face clearly said it all, I wasn't sure if she was joking, but she seemed to be completely serious.

'Don't laugh,' she told me sternly. 'Drinking the urine has been practiced for centuries here in India and it will rejuvenate your body and soul. Drink a litre of water before you go to sleep, wake up at 4 a.m. and drink a glassful of your urine. Trust me. It will be highly diluted so it won't taste bad, and you will really feel the benefits.'

Feeling slightly sick, I agreed to try it out that night, figuring that no one need ever know that I'd entered the land of hippy dippy crazies. That night, I forced down an entire litre of water and wondered if I would even last until 4 a.m. without my bladder waking me up. My alarm went off and I stumbled to the bathroom, where according to Nandini I had to drink only the middle section of pee in order to avoid any toxins. I caught the mid-stream in a glass, feeling completely and utterly ridiculous. I blocked my nose and took a cautious sip. There was a faintly dull, metallic taste, otherwise it tasted like water that had been sitting out for too long. I managed a couple of sips before gagging, threw the rest of the glass away, swilled some water around my mouth and cleaned my teeth.

The next morning I was expecting to feel revitalized, fresh and clear of mind. I felt exactly the same as I always did—sleepy, sore eyed and irritable. After a couple of attempts to persevere in this task, I informed Nandini that it wasn't working. She looked at me wryly.

'You have to do this for years, not days. Only then will you see the benefits on your way to attaining a state of blissful Nirvana.'

I looked at her equally sardonically. 'I don't think I can do that, Nandini. It's not for me. And please don't tell any of your other students that I drank my own wee.'

'Tsk, don't worry. I am not gossiping about you, ever.' I wasn't convinced.

Sorting out my household help, drinking my own urine and trying to attain enlightenment, or at the very least more flexible joints, had kept me busy for the best part of a month, and stopped me thinking obsessively about Krishna. The experience had left me bruised, but not beaten, and it certainly hadn't put me off dating Indian men, although I vowed that I'd definitely be more careful in future.

## 13

I decided that it was time for a spot of party hopping. Although my yoga sessions had helped relax and refocus me, I felt the need to meet and make some like-minded friends. India was a welcoming country, full of people who were endlessly hospitable and genuinely friendly, but I was acutely aware of the differences between my culture and background, and theirs. It was rare that I felt completely relaxed in anyone's company here, and I was conscious of being deliberately more cautious after the disaster with Krishna.

I decided to reach out to the expat community, figuring that I could probably learn from others who had been here longer than me. There was a small, but fairly active Expatriates Group whose members sent e-mails and requests for help in finding maids and drivers, bought and sold furniture, cars and other requirements for setting up home in the city, and organized monthly expat events. I joined the group and sent an e-mail introducing myself. I'd been here for eight months now, and considered myself to be pretty experienced at coping with life in Mumbai, although I was keen to learn as much as I could from others.

Mumbai was a fairly complex city, difficult to penetrate and one which certainly wouldn't be the destination of choice for an expat looking for an easy life. The typical expat centres like Singapore and Dubai were far easier for foreigners to navigate, thanks to their systems and their comforts. Even Bangkok, which appeared chaotic, was far easier for Westerners to acclimatize to—local transport was smooth and safe, apartments were swanky and encased within clean, well-kept buildings, and though poverty and hardship existed, they were not as obviously visible as in Mumbai. Living in Mumbai felt like you were permanently on the set of one of those challenging game shows, where obstacles were thrown at contestants in a bid to defeat them mentally and physically, and send them home early. But I liked a challenge and, frankly, I would have been bored stiff in an over-sanitized, bland city like Singapore, a city where everything ran perfectly, yet where you had to search long and hard to find anything that smacked of the authentic. I had friends at home who had lived in Singapore and also Dubai, and who had regaled me with tales of their five-star highly manicured lifestyles. I knew that many of my Indian friends and colleagues longed to leave Mumbai and move to these cities, which in comparison to Mumbai's dirty exterior and anarchic pace, offered a distinctly more ordered and comfortable existence.

I supposed I was looking for something that contrasted with my own safe and comfortable background.

I wondered what kind of expats I would meet in Mumbai. To me, the term expat conjured up connotations of the days of the Raj, leafy colonial homes and fat white army men with moustaches. I hoped this stereotype wouldn't prove to be true, and that I'd meet many different types of people who were here for different reasons, and I wondered whether Indians assumed that all expats were rich and here on fat salaries. I scoured the Bombay expats group site for interesting invitations to events. I started off with a meeting of the European Ladies Group. The name itself was almost enough to put me off, but I decided to persevere and bury my instinctively judgmental attitude for the time being.

I got myself invited to a cocktail event at one of the Ladies' houses. The apartment in question was palatial, and even the exterior of the apartment building was gorgeous, one of those rare Mumbai buildings that was as lovely on the outside as on the inside. There were gold painted railings lining the short driveway and the reception area was immaculate and glossy. The lift doors closed with a muted swish, and the ride up to the tenth floor was smooth and fast. The lift opened right into the apartment, and I could hardly contain my amazement and envy. I entered the apartment, which like many others in the city had an incredible view of Mumbai's skyline, and was greeted by the host, Ilona, who turned out to be a sweet Scottish woman with a reddish bob, wearing a casual kurta and jeans.

'Welcome to the party. So glad you could join us. It's been ages since anyone new came to join our little cocktail evening.'

She steered me over to a huge T-shaped, plush cream sofa scattered with bright silk cushions in various hues of indigo, turquoise and hot pink. 'Let me introduce you to everyone.'

She proceeded to introduce each one of the ten or so ladies in the room, most of whom seemed to be British, French or Swedish. They were all casually, but impeccably, dressed and immaculately polished. Luckily I had also had the foresight to visit my local parlour for a manicure, pedicure and blow-dry, so I was feeling equally glossy and quite presentable, as well as unaccountably nervous, as though I was here for a job interview rather than a casual drink with a bunch of fellow expats. I was relieved therefore when a barman, clad in black bow tie and crisp white shirt offered me a drink.

'Sangria, Mojito or a Kiwi Margarita madam?'

'Er… I'll have a margarita please.'

This was a far cry from the few gatherings I'd had at my place when people were directed to the fridge to grab themselves a cold beer. I perched awkwardly on the edge of the sofa, and struck up conversation with the lady beside me who introduced herself as 'Jennifer from Cheshire'. She asked me whether I was here with my husband, and I told her that no, I wasn't married.

'So you've come over here on your own then? That's brave.'

'Well, I got offered a job and thought it would be a lot of fun, so decided to take it,' I told her.

'So how long do you plan to be here?'

'I hadn't really thought about it actually, but for quite a while I expect. I don't really have any plans to go back.'

'Really? Wow, that's really unusual. So you actually like it here?' she asked, incredulously.

'I love it,' I answered truthfully. 'I mean, I know it can be difficult, and there are lots of things about living here that drive me mad but at the same time it's just so exhilarating and exciting when I compare it to boring old London.'

Her left eyebrow rose almost imperceptibly, and I wondered whether I'd made a faux pas. 'I hate it here,' she said in a confiding tone. 'I think most of us do actually. I can't believe that you'd choose to be here, but it's great that you're enjoying it. I can't wait to go back home. Only another eight months to go.'

'I agree,' added another lady, whose name turned out to be Svenska. 'I just find everything impossible here, and it's just exhausting. I can't wait for my husband's contract to finish.'

It seemed that all the ladies were in agreement, that Mumbai was generally a nightmare, a 'hardship posting', and an agony to be endured for a fat salary before returning to the sanity of home. I tried to put myself in their shoes. None of them seemed to be working, with the exception of the odd bit of volunteer work for various charities, and they all found life here quite unpleasant. They were all obviously missing their friends and families, and I supposed that life must be very different for them—they'd been dragged around the world by presumably ambitious husbands who seemed to spend a lot of time at the office, they were left to manage the maids and the driver and the grocery shopping and the challenges of settling into a world that felt very alien. I figured that it all came down to attitude and life-stage. Though we were roughly the same age, these women were all married and had come to Mumbai as 'trailing spouses', following husbands with lucrative and successful jobs, trying to find ways to keep themselves busy and motivated, and torn from a world in which they had been very content.

I drank a few more cocktails, listened to stories about nightmare maids and difficult drivers, and left. It had been nice meeting these women, and fun to have had a peek into the high-end expat life with all its trimmings, but frankly I much preferred the view from where I was sitting.

I looked for other events, and decided to attend an expat party that appeared to be a free for all—discounted drinks and free appetizers at Olive, one of Mumbai's most popular bars located in the trendy northern suburb of Bandra. Bandra was a cool place, crammed with interesting eateries, bars and tiny boutique style shops, with a laid-back atmosphere that was very different from the old school feel of 'town', as the City's southern financial hub was known. It was a suburb largely populated by Catholic communities, full of beautiful old churches, tiny alleyways populated with white crosses and statues of Jesus and the Virgin Mary, and a vibrant fishing community which lined the sea. It was also a popular area for expats, especially given the sheer number of bars, restaurants and shops that lined the hotch-potch streets. I'd thought about moving there myself, but my apartment was located conveniently close to the office, in the south, and I couldn't be bothered with the endless commute.

I arrived at Olive an hour later than the stipulated time of 9 p.m.; I'd been here long enough to know that people always arrived late to parties and social events, and that many gatherings didn't really get started until after 11 p.m. I walked a little nervously into the bar, which had a cool Mediterranean feel, thanks to its whitewashed walls, cobalt blue tablecloths and pale polished wooden floor. Like Indigo, this was a place to see and be seen, and by all accounts you could regularly spot TV and film stars here if you hung around for long enough. The crowd was outside enjoying the balmy temperatures, cooled by a row of industrial sized fans which were briskly stirring the sultry air. People were wearing short dresses, strappy heels and chinos and smart shirts, and I wondered if there was an element of competitiveness going on here amongst the expats. I took a deep breath, walked up to the nearest group, and introduced myself.

Though I was typically the type who preferred to cling to the wall in the company of strangers, I figured that I'd come here to meet people and there was no point my feeling awkward and self-conscious. The group turned out to be English, they had met here in Mumbai and seemed to have formed close friendships with one another, judging from the banter and the relaxed atmosphere.

'How long have you been in Mumbai?' asked Sarah, a pretty blonde wearing a low-cut halter neck top and sparkling sandals.

'Almost a year,' I exaggerated, figuring that a year suggested that I was a fairly seasoned Mumbaikar.

'We've been here for three months. David and Rebecca have been here for about six months, right guys?' The couple standing next to her nodded vigorously. 'Jonathan has been here for two years.'

'Almost three actually,' interjected a tall, mousy haired guy. 'I plan to stay here as long as I can. I love it here.'

Jonathan had a plummy, public schoolboy accent and he was obviously from a fairly well to do background. It turned out that Sarah and her partner Ben worked for the British Consulate, David and his girlfriend Rebecca were with an investment bank and Jonathan was here working for an NGO, or local charity. I assumed that the two couples were here on a 'hardship posting' and paid a fat salary, which was intended to compensate for the trauma of being yanked from their homeland. Jonathan, on the other hand, looked as though he was supported by some kind of trust fund. I knew I was being judgmental, but we Brits had a habit of sizing each other up, and assigning class labels to strangers in a subconscious attempt to adapt our own behaviour accordingly.

Our class system was complicated and unfathomable to other nationalities, but it was very powerful and deeply entrenched in our collective psyche. I was from a run-of-the-mill, middle class background, but I'd attended a public school, so I could pick up posh, along with wannabe posh, from a mile off, and I'd only recently rid myself of the large chip that had weighed heavily on my shoulder throughout my formative years.

Jonathan continued in his slightly braying voice, 'Yeah, I'm doing some really important work here and I feel like I'm really making a difference and connecting with the locals. It's amazing how rewarding it can be.' I thought he was being terribly patronizing, frankly, but I kept my opinions to myself.

'It can be difficult though,' opined Ben. 'Sometimes I really struggle to know how to approach certain things, I feel overwhelmed by the poverty and the hardship and I feel guilty when I pay for dinner at a fancy place which costs a fortune compared to the amount these people have to live on.'

'I know what you mean,' I replied, 'but you can't go around feeling guilty all the time otherwise you'll just go mad living here.'

'I don't felt guilty at all,' said pompous Jonathan. 'I'm spending most of my time helping these people and I don't see what's wrong with enjoying myself when I can. There's no point pretending that I'm poor, when I'm not, and giving all my money to the poor won't solve their problems.'

Though his tone of voice was irritating, I agreed mentally with some of his points, at least the ones about not pretending to be poor or to have anything in common with those living in poverty. The conversation turned to England and plans for the summer. It seemed that everyone, except for Ben and Sarah who were off to Thailand for a spot of travelling, was headed back to the UK for a long holiday during the monsoon period.

'You have to get out of Mumbai in the monsoon,' said Jonathan, the expert in all things Indian. 'It's grim. Pours buckets for days on end, everything gets damp and mouldy and the skies are grey for weeks. Better to head back to the UK for the summer and then come back to Mumbai in October when the rain has stopped.'

I was actually quite looking forward to the monsoon, particularly now that the weather had heated up and the afternoons and evenings were sticky and humid to the point of being unpleasant. Though I was no fan of the rain, given that England's unpredictable weather had ruined far too many plans for me in the past, I kind of liked the idea of someone just switching on the tap for three whole months and then switching it off again. At least there was a consistency about that.

The conversation meandered back to Mumbai and in particular the difficulty of finding a reliable driver (this seemed to be a common expat topic) and we ordered a few more of the delicious cocktails that Olive was famous for. The place filled up as the night progressed, and I was surprised to see how many foreigners were there. I'd seen a few around in bars and clubs but never been in the company of so many. I swapped numbers with Rebecca and Sarah who mentioned a party the following week at the Embassy.

I spent the rest of the evening hopping between a couple of groups, before spotting my friend Johann and his wife Priyanka. Priyanka was stunning, with a flawless golden brown complexion and thick black wavy hair, which she had tied back with a sparkling clip. Exotic looking rings and bracelets gave her a bohemian look, and she was wearing a trendy fusion outfit—an Indian style top which swept low at the back, over skinny jeans.

She embraced me and kissed my cheeks warmly. 'I heard about your nightmare Indian guy. Sorry to hear it ended so badly,' she said, sounding genuinely concerned. I thought Priyanka and Johann were perfect for each other. I was secretly envious of their glossy looks and of the fact that they seemed to be in a permanently loving state, but I was glad that they had found each other and that Johann was so settled here in Mumbai. I knew that he travelled a fair bit, but Priyanka often accompanied him, and she had her own thriving business as a photographer, so she didn't feel at all threatened by his success. I would have loved to have been in a relationship like that, secure, balanced and happy yet independent and comfortable in my own skin.

After a few drinks, I excused myself and wobbled off in search of the bathroom, which was outside the bar at the end of a long terrace. The room was packed, and as I squeezed through the groups of foreigners deep in conversation, I realized that the door was being blocked by a burly guy who was wearing a striped shirt, similar to those that I'd seen the barmen clad in. Thinking he was a waiter, I tapped him on the shoulder and asked, 'Excuse me, is this the way to the bathroom?'

His head turned slowly, and he looked at me with a look of barely concealed disgust on his face. 'What?' he replied, in an icy tone which didn't fit with my waiter theory.

'Er, sorry, excuse me, can I get past please?' I mumbled, summoning up every ounce of politeness when really I felt like shoving past him.

'Can you get past me?' he repeated, and I wondered if he was on the slow side.

'Yes. I'm looking for the toilets and I think they are outside.' With a cross between a snarl and a smirk, the 'waiter' opened the door for me, and stared hard at me as he gesticulated toward the exterior.

What a weirdo, I thought to myself. As I passed him, I caught sight of his broad shoulders, thick forearms, and a gold chain peeking out from his open necked shirt. Suddenly I realized that his face looked very familiar, and that in fact I'd seen that very face on a thousand billboards across Mumbai. It was Salman Khan, the A list Bollywood actor, not a waiter at all. I was mortified and far too embarrassed to admit my mistake or apologize to him. Besides, I figured that he was only another customer, and that despite being the idol of millions, he should also have been gentlemanly enough to have opened the door for me, or at least given the sarcastic gestures a miss.

I hurried through the door, blushing furiously, hoping he wouldn't recognize me in the future, in the highly unlikely event that we ever met again. I was simultaneously impressed with my first brush with a real life Bollywood star, and mortified that I'd handled it so badly. When I rejoined the group, I told them, excitedly, 'You'll never guess who I've just bumped into. Literally,' I told Priyanka who burst into laughter. 'He's over there by the door. I thought he was a waiter.'

'That's hilarious,' she said. 'He seems sweet but incredibly pompous. Thinks the whole world revolves around him. That sort of star. Quite tedious really.'

'Well. I suppose if the whole of India is falling at their feet

131

then not being recognized by some random foreigner in a bar must be a bit insulting really,' I suggested.

I left Olive that night thinking about the whole expat scene and the people I'd met, read about and observed through the anonymity of an internet connection. There seemed to be two types of Western expats who arrived in India for the long haul: those who had been brought over by a western company, given all the mod cons and luxuries of a western life and who preferred to exist in a bubble wrapped state of false security during their entire posting, living with a sense of detachment and an innate superiority throughout their stay. And there were those who came, driven by a desire to experience a lifestyle that seemed so much more meaningful and spiritual than that which they'd abandoned back home, who actively sought to plunge themselves into each and every Indian experience, cramming each and every local tradition, custom and idiosyncrasy into their days here. I imagined that the former would spend a couple of years here, collecting stories to be used as dinner party conversation material once back home. Perhaps that wouldn't be a bad world to inhabit for a year or two.

One thing the corporate, moneyed expatriate seemed to do really well, according to the mails that flew back and forth on the expat site, was infuriate those who yearned to find India's soul, those who came in their hordes seeking spiritualism and salvation. For this type, living on a meager amount of savings, often volunteering for an NGO, or earning a local (i.e. relatively low) salary, the rich expats with their fat salaries and overpriced housing only drove prices up. I'd witnessed a fair few very heated debates that had foreigners up in arms and attacking each other over who 'did' India better. The purists claimed that eating western food in India was a cop-out and that only the pukka local street food, spicy as hell and served up on grubby plates, would do. Somehow, even the resultant diarrhoea gave them brownie points. They criticized those who ate at five-star restaurants, and accused them of not getting to know the real India. I wondered how I would change and adapt over the years to come, and whether I would become as condescending as Jonathan or as settled as Johann.

## 14

The following weekend, I decided to go to the Consulate party. Johann and Priyanka were also going, along with, it seemed, Mumbai's entire expat crowd. It felt like the party scene in Mumbai was a small one, and I'd already noticed that certain faces kept popping up at the same events.

The security around the consulate building was tight, and we had to show ID and wait for the burly security guards to find our names on the list before we were allowed in. Once inside, we found ourselves in a huge, almost palatial hall dripping with chandeliers and replete with floor-to-ceiling bookcases.

'This is the ballroom,' Johann told us. 'It's where all the foreign diplomats are entertained.'

I was totally impressed, whereas everyone else looked like they did this all of the time, and that it was just another night for them, which in fact it probably was.

We spent the evening drinking wine, which was imported and delicious, and saw a few people whom we recognized from the Olive evening. Even a couple of the European ladies were here, with their husbands, and I waved a cheery hello, filling Johann in quickly about my experience at the Perfect Expatriate Apartment. He laughed as I described the horrified reaction of the ladies to my professed love for the city which they loathed.

Their husbands looked as corporate as I had imagined, fairly buttoned up and stiff, in smart suits and open-necked shirts. It was far too hot for ties.

I was enjoying myself, and I liked the fact that I recognized some faces and that I was beginning to slip into an easy familiarity with a few people. People here were very friendly, and I supposed that we were all in the same boat, far away from home and living without our known creature comforts, and that that in itself was grounds for bonding. I thought back to London, and how difficult it was to make friends once you'd left the convivial, anything goes atmosphere of university. Once you were out in the real world, people tended to form tight cliques, which were pretty impenetrable from the outside. Here, people were open and friendly, everyone needed to make friends; most people arrived here without any, so there was definitely a greater willingness to embrace strangers and make people feel welcome.

Johann and I drank several glasses of wine and then managed a couple of cocktails.

'I haven't had this much fun for ages' he confided. 'Priyanka and I have been so busy and I'd forgotten what fun these people can be.'

I had already picked up quite an undercurrent of competitiveness, though it was well hidden, amongst the expats who were keen to outdo each other with their stories of the city and their slightly condescending attitude to newcomers. I guessed that you needed to be attuned to the subtler signals, which perhaps a non-westerner would miss, particularly because Indian culture seemed so much more open in terms of its direct approach. There was no beating about the bush when it came to asking questions, many of which would have been considered rude or inappropriate back home. Still, the expat crowd certainly believed in throwing a memorable party.

Johann and I filled our bellies with the delicious snacks that were circulating around the room, drank liberally from the free bar, and, emboldened by the copious cocktails, floated around the room dropping into conversations. After a couple of hours I saw Sarah and Ben, the couple I'd met at the Olive expat party, wobbling towards me, clearly slightly worse for wear.

'How'd you fancy getting out of here?' asked Sarah. 'There's a bunch of us headed off to a bar close by. It's a bit grubby, and full of locals but we thought it would make a nice change from all this.'

Sarah and Ben worked for the British High Commission and probably got to go to these kinds of parties all the time, and I'd been enjoying the lavish surroundings, but figured that this was my chance to do a bit of bonding with the crowd.

'Sure,' I said. 'Lead the way.'

We turned up at the bar, a dimly lit, hot and crowded space into which hordes of people were crammed, all shouting to be heard above the blaring soft rock music. In one corner was a small makeshift dance floor, full of people who were clearly enjoying the sounds, judging by the number who were 'air guitaring'. The crowd looked to be mainly Indian, and I hoped that I wouldn't bump into Krishna or any of his cronies. We crammed ourselves into a tiny space near the bar and ordered beers.

'This is fun,' said Sarah, her eyes gleaming.

'So much more down to earth than those expat parties,' added Ben.

'Although I kind of liked the posh food and wine,' I said,

laughing. 'You guys are used to it, but spare a thought for those of us on the other side.'

As we drank our beer and ordered a fresh round, I looked around the room. Most people were deep in intense conversation, and the cacophony of voices combined with the blaring music was almost deafening. As I looked, I saw a pretty girl being dragged onto the dance floor by an over zealous young guy. She was trying to fend him off, but had a smile on her face. For some reason I was fascinated by the girl, she looked both foreign yet Indian at the same time, so I guessed that she might be of mixed parentage. She was very attractive but in a natural way which seemed to owe little to makeup. As I continued to watch her, she disappeared into the crowd and all I saw was her brown ponytail swinging back and forth in the middle of a sea of people.

I turned my attention back to Ben who was holding forth on the topic of the lies people told to get their hands on a visa for the UK. 'I'm just off to the loo,' I said. 'I may be some time.'

As I pushed my way back through the heaving mass, I caught sight of the girl with the ponytail who now seemed to be surrounded by a group of guys. The smile had gone from her face and been replaced with what looked like a mixture of fear and anger. I was shocked to see one of the boys, who couldn't be much older than twenty and with a faint moustache and goatee and open necked shirt, reach out and make a grab for her. Suddenly it was like a free-for-all, and in slow motion I saw that two of the guys had lunged for her and one had picked her up off the floor completely. She was fighting to get free from them, yet no one seemed to be paying any attention to her predicament.

I could see that she was in distress and before I even had

time to think, I dived into the crowd, grabbed the shirt of the guy who had the girl in his grip and yelled, 'Put her down, you pig. How dare you.'

He grinned at me and yelled back in Hindi, I had no idea what he was saying, but from the tone of his voice I didn't think it was particularly complimentary. Dropping her abruptly, he turned and swiftly strode off, pushing his way through the bodies, followed by the rest of his cronies.

'Are you OK?' I asked her, relieved to see that she seemed fairly unaffected by her ordeal.

'I'm fine,' she said, in an accent I couldn't quite place. 'These guys can be a real pain, I'm usually better at avoiding trouble but this time I guess I was a bit careless.' She put out her hand. 'I'm Maya. Can I buy you a drink to say thanks for helping me out of a sticky situation?'

'Sure,' I said, fascinated by this girl who seemed to exude an appealing mixture of confidence and shyness. 'My friends are just over here, why don't you join us?'

I introduced her to the rest of the crowd. 'Where are you from?' I asked her. 'Well I'm actually Indian, my mother is from South India, but my dad is French and I grew up all over the place, so I guess you could say I'm a bit mixed up.' That explained the looks then, children of mixed parentage always seemed to get the best of both worlds when it came to the gene pools. It also accounted for the unplaceable accent.

'Are you married?' I asked, before realizing that this was probably quite a direct question coming from a complete stranger. 'Sorry, none of my business. I'm just so used to being asked that question that it just popped out.'

138

'No, no problem,' she laughed. 'Actually I'm going through a bit of a nasty divorce right now and I just wanted to escape from it all with a few drinks. We're at the final stages and we just can't seem to agree on the last few details, which is completely stressing me out.'

'Oh, I'm so sorry to hear that,' I said, feeling horribly embarrassed at my inappropriate question.

'It's OK,' she replied. 'It's definitely the best thing all round. We got married far too fast, and there was this huge pressure for the marriage to work out. My in-laws hated me from the beginning and we just seemed to be fighting constantly. So it's good that it's being resolved, though of course it is sad when any relationship comes to an end.'

I thought back briefly to my own recent romantic experience. What if I'd actually ended up married to Krishna, in one of those mad impetuous moments, and then discovered that he was only after my money? Nightmare.

She told me that she lived in Juhu, towards the suburbs, an area up the coast away from South Mumbai, a few kilometres north. I asked her whether she enjoyed living in the city.

'I feel like I'm not quite Indian but at the same time I'm not a foreigner either,' she replied, slightly wistfully. 'Sometimes I do feel I have the best of both worlds, but other times when I'm trying to get things done, or fit into my Indian family, I just feel like a complete outsider and it's so frustrating.'

'I know what you mean,' I said, 'though I suppose in some ways its easier for me as I am obviously a foreigner.'

'Plus you have white skin, whereas mine is a bit muddy coloured,' Maya replied with a wry laugh. 'That doesn't work in my favour here, that's for sure.'

Eventually, the barman came over and asked if we'd like to order our last drinks. With a shock, I realized it was almost one in the morning, and that we'd been talking for over an hour. Maya and I exchanged numbers and promised to meet again. I got the feeling that she could use an uncomplicated female friendship, and I was certainly missing a girlfriend to gossip with. Annabel and Lizzie were always there, of course, but it was never the same long distance and the details didn't really translate, so I hoped Maya and I would become friends.

One Sunday I received a call from Johann inviting me to the Breach Candy club, one of Mumbai's most famous institutions. I'd heard about the Breach Candy club, and intended to apply for membership, but I'd not got around to it yet so I was delighted to have an invitation to check the place out. It turned out to be a fabulous old school club made infamous by its refusal to allow Indians (or dogs) through its hallowed doors until the 1960s. We entered the club, Johann signed me in, I received a quick once-over from the doorman, and we walked past an enormous swimming pool to grab ourselves a deckchair in the sun. This was the largest outdoor pool in the country—built in the shape of India so that in one session you could swim down to the southernmost tip of Kerala and back up to the northern foothills of the Himalayas. The club's interior was vast, with a two storey bar and restaurant on one side of the pool, grassy slopes dotted with brightly coloured tables, chairs and sun loungers, and a more informal looking shack on the other side of the pool.

The club was right on the sea, and the expanse of rocks and water lent the place an open and very invigorating feeling, despite the fact that the sea looked filthy and almost black in parts, and the rocks were grubby and covered with detritus and scraps of rubbish. It felt like a haven for anyone craving respite from the insanity of Mumbai's crowded streets, a calm oasis in the middle of chaos. Unlike the majority of these old fashioned clubs, most harking back to the days of the Raj, the Breach Candy Club actually allowed membership to foreigners, though for a maximum period of four years. Indians, on the other hand, had to wait (literally) a lifetime for membership—some locals put their children down for membership when they were born in the hope that by the time they reached adulthood they might have made it to the top of the list. Johann told me that expats were granted membership provided they passed an 'interview' with a member of the Club's Committee, which basically consisted of a few questions designed to ferret out the riff-raff and undesirables.

The Breach Candy Club, along with other club stalwarts such as the Bombay Gymkhana, the Willingdon Club and the Cricket Club of India (CCI), was also well known for its uptight rules and regulations. According to Johann, until recently women were not allowed to become members of the Willingdon Club, and when this rule was relaxed it had caused uproar amongst the male membership who presumably were looking for a place to escape from their wives.

Johann beckoned to a couple of men dressed in khaki uniforms. 'Two deckchairs, please, and a small table.' They disappeared and returned dragging chairs behind them, and set up a makeshift seating area for us. Johann gave them a tip, and they smiled broadly in response, displaying rows of nicotine and paan stained teeth.

I lay back in the chair and stared up at the sky, lazily watching the cloud formations which were drifting in from the sea across the land.

'Pre-monsoon clouds,' murmured Johann, reading my mind. 'It will start raining in less than a week.'

I couldn't imagine rain in Mumbai. I associated the city with hot and dry, and blistering sunshine and dusty streets, not with cool rain and wet roads. Johann called for a menu. 'Let's order some snacks and drinks.'

I took a look at the menu. It was long, and filled with lists of every dish imaginable, from Indian favourites through to spaghetti bolognaise, chicken Kiev, beef burgers and steak sandwiches.

'The continental food here isn't bad at all,' Johann said.

I figured that the club catered for foreigners and for Indians who had travelled a fair bit so they would need to make the dishes fairly authentic, unlike the majority of restaurants here, which localized the international fare. I'd ordered fish and chips a couple of times in Mumbai, only to end up with unappetizing, greasy pieces of thin fish thick with breadcrumbs and dripping with oil, accompanied by stringy french fries which were a far cry from the fluffy-inside-crispy-outside chip shop chips I'd grown up with.

I was delighted to see that alongside the usual chicken and veggie burgers, they had actual beef burgers, which was a rare treat. The cow of course was sacred to Hindus and most places in Mumbai didn't serve beef. It was actually illegal to slaughter or consume beef in most of India, though buffalo was allowed. Even McDonalds only served chicken or goat burgers, slathered in Indian spicy sauces. I'd had buffalo a couple of times here, and I couldn't say that I'd noticed the difference. My tastebuds had been so deprived of real beef that sinking my teeth into a buffalo burger was more than acceptable. I ordered a burger, and they even asked how I would like it cooked, so I guessed that the burger experience here would be fairly authentic. We also ordered a couple of large gin and tonics, and I was shocked at the prices, which were ridiculously low. A large gin with tonic cost the equivalent of less than a pound, and this was a pleasant surprise in comparison to the swankier bars in Mumbai, which pretty much charged western prices for drinks, and then slapped fat local taxes on top of that.

The club was fairly full, there were lots of small groups of people, mainly westerners but with a few locals dotted around, and quite a few children, many of whom were having great fun splashing around in the water or diving off the three diving boards at the sea end of the enormous pool. There didn't appear to be any lifeguards around, but I supposed that people here just kept a close eye on their children, or had nannies or maids to do that for them. We sipped on our cool gin and tonics, nibbled on the delicious starters which Johann had ordered and I thought how perfect my life seemed at this moment.

The next day the monsoon hit the city, earlier than Johann had predicted. As I was on my way home from the office, the skies turned a murky shade of grey and the wind picked up and started to howl. Tree branches were whipped furiously around and leaves and rubbish blew merrily along the streets. The entire city felt tense and tight, as if it would literally explode unless it got some relief. I heard a few drops of rain patter on the roof of the car, and then suddenly it was pouring. It had gone from sunny to a torrential downpour in about ten minutes flat, and I was taken aback by the speed of the transformation.

'Monsoon started,' stated Hussain, with an enormous grin. He slapped on the windscreen wipers, which made a fairly pitiful attempt at slicing through the deluge of water which was pouring down. Suddenly, I felt as though I was in a completely different city. The noise of the rain was deafening, we could hardly see more than a couple of metres ahead of the car, and the traffic had ground to a virtual standstill, all the vehicles honking pointlessly at each other. The water was continuing to pour down, and I could make out that it was already a few centimetres deep, swirling around the wheels of cars in muddy pools.

Suddenly, as abruptly as it had started, the rain stopped. I wound down the window of the car and peered out. Everything was gleaming, shining and looking freshly scrubbed—the pavements looked clean, the trees were dripping and their remaining leaves were fresh looking and bright green. The rain had washed all the dust and grime away. I could make out people who were soaked from head to toe, there wasn't an umbrella in sight, and they were all laughing and screaming with delight.

'They dance in rain,' Hussain told me.

'Why?' I asked him, bemused.

'People love rain. It good for country and for crops. And feels good on body. Clean and fresh.'

Fair enough. I could imagine how good the cool rain must feel against skin that had been baked by the sunshine all year, every year. I had no desire to join the dancing crowds, my aversion to rain and getting wet was inbuilt, thanks to years of shivering in freezing cold downpours. The air was considerably cooler now, and I felt slightly chilly, for the first time in months.

## 15

I was spurred on by my success at breaking into Mumbai's expat party scene, but I soon realized it was full of cozy couples. So far I hadn't met anyone on the scene who interested me, and, honestly, I wasn't really interested in dating a 'foreigner'. My recent dodgy experience had thankfully not put me off the entire Indian male population and I would have loved to meet and settle down with an Indian man. Having seen Johann and Priyanka's relationship, I'd become a little bit obsessed with the idea of finding love here, and I figured it couldn't be that hard to meet a local whom I could actually relate to and who would want me for more than just the obvious.

I decided to try internet dating. Though this had become considerably more popular and less a hunting ground for the sad and lonely in recent years, I knew this was a bit desperate. But I comforted myself with the thought that no one would have any inkling that I was doing it and I only planned to share my idea with Maya, who I'd by now met a few times for coffee and drinks.

She had become quite a good friend, as genuine and down to earth as I had thought she would be on first meeting her. It was good to finally be able to forge a friendship with a girl, and her mixed background meant that she could give me insights into India whilst also identify with me in many ways, unlike Lizzie and Annabel.

I met Maya for a coffee in Bandra one Saturday afternoon, and ran the idea past her.

'Are you sure?' she asked, a look of concern flitting across her face. 'You get a lot of weirdos on those sites, apparently, and you're alone here in the city.'

'I'll definitely be careful,' I said, adding, 'and besides, I'll only meet a guy if I'm sure he's not a freak. Or at least I'll do everything I can to make sure he's OK. Worst case, I can always end the evening early, or meet in the daytime for coffee or something and invent an excuse if he's awful.'

I was sounding much more confident about the whole idea than I was actually feeling inside. I was actually terrified at the thought of meeting a complete stranger and trawling around on the internet chatting to random people but I figured that there was no harm in at least trying.

'You should do it with me,' I told Maya. 'We could double blind date.'

'No chance,' Maya shuddered. 'Besides, I'm still not quite divorced, and I'm too Indian to wrap my head around the concept of dating while I'm still married. I'm so not ready yet. You go for it, and I'll come with you on your dates if you like, or at least sit on the next table and give you my point of view.'

'Brilliant,' I said, feeling instantly more reassured. 'That's a great idea.'

I joined a site called Gofish.com, a place where you exchanged 'nudges' with people whom you were interested in, and where you could scroll through pages of potential suitors. I refused to put my picture up but felt brutally self-conscious every time I logged on. I of course went straight for the men who had posted pictures, which was a bit shallow, but I figured that was a woman's prerogative. I'd only posted a few details — my age (I refused to lie, but I figured that early thirties was nothing to be ashamed of), my location, a brief description of myself, which I liked to think was honest as well as appealing, and of course my username — British India, which Maya and I both figured was a clear clue that I was a foreigner, without being explicit.

Maya came over to my place to check out the results — within an hour I had received my first 'nudge'. And then they came flooding in from men all over India it seemed. I got messages from men in Mumbai, but also from guys in Delhi, Hyderabad and Chennai, as well as a few other places I'd never even heard of. We were both intrigued, and I opened a few of the messages to see what these men were all about. Half of the messages were extremely short, mostly with poor grammar and spelling, with requests for photos of me and questions about my 'interests'. One even went so far as to ask which my favourite position was, the rest were filled with sexual innuendos, but contained within a slightly more subtle turn of phrase.

'Ew, gross,' Maya squirmed in her seat. 'These men are obviously only after one thing. And perhaps the British reference wasn't such a great idea after all. They probably think that white girls are up for it, whereas they wouldn't dream of writing like that to an Indian girl.'

'Well, they don't know that I'm white,' I told her, indignantly. 'I could be a brown British Indian for all they know.'

'They will assume you're white,' she smiled. 'We should have given you a less obvious name.'

'Well, I'd rather weed out the freaks and letches from the start,' I said. 'I've already been lied to by one con artist, and I don't fancy being taken for a ride again.'

The men were a mixed looking bunch, some looked pretty young, perhaps in their early twenties and others were clearly in their late forties or even fifties and looked downright scary. Many of them sported bouffant hairdos, which may or may not have been real, and there were moustaches of all shapes and sizes, many bordering on the luxuriant. Maya and I obsessively trawled through the men and the messages, laughing heartily as we did so, but hoping that we'd eventually come across someone who wasn't interested in sex or 'frandship', and who looked vaguely normal, let alone good looking.

'How about this guy,' said Maya, clicking on the photo of a guy who looked passable. 'Says he's from Mumbai, well travelled, has a good job and is a romantic. He doesn't look too bad, and he writes well. Sounds like he could be an option.'

I looked over her shoulder and read his nudge—'Hey there, I'm Hari, I'm in my early thirties, and looking for friendship and possibly more. I love to read, travel and meet people. I work for an investment bank, I like good wine and I'm a real foodie. Would love to meet for dinner or a coffee whenever you are free.'

He definitely looked passable, even vaguely good looking, and I added him to the 'maybe' list.

'What about this one?' I clicked on a picture of a man with a huge shiny forehead, over which were combed a few strands of black hair. 'Hallo I am Indrajit from Calcutta now residing

Mumbai. I am interested to meet with foreigner and make plans for future happiness and dreams come true. Please reply my massage ASAP.'

'Oh my God, is he for real? He's ticked the box that says 30–35 years, and he looks at least fifty,' I shuddered.

'Oh, go on, meet him,' laughed Maya. 'Please. That would make such an awesome party story.'

'No way,' I told her firmly. 'Not even for a story. I'd have to be out of my mind. Besides, what on earth would we talk about?'

'Your future dreams and happiness of course.'

'Shut up,' I laughed, refilling her wine glass. 'You can't live out all of your twisted desires vicariously, you know! At least find me someone whom I can vaguely relate to.'

After trawling through at least fifty completely bizarre messages, which became funnier and funnier the further down the wine bottle we got, we went back to Hari's message.

'OK,' I said, emboldened by the wine. 'I'll send him a message. Then we'll see what happens.'

We painstakingly composed my response. After a few abandoned attempts, I sent a mail which I thought sounded chatty without being over-friendly, warm without being suggestive.

'Hi, thanks for your message. I've been in Mumbai for over a year, I work in advertising and I am also interested in making friends. I love India and hope to stay here for a while, it's a fascinating country.'

Fifteen minutes later, there was a reply in my mailbox.

'Great to meet you. What brings you to Mumbai? Did you come here for work? This is a great city, there's so much to do here, but it can be a bit overwhelming at times. I hope you are settling in OK. I'd be happy to show you around if you need any help.'

So far so good. Maya and I agreed that this was suitably interesting without being creepy. I decided not to reply immediately so as not to seem too keen, and closed down the laptop for the night, preparing to settle down for a good long girlie gossip.

Maya had already shared some of the details of her marriage with me, and over the course of the next couple of hours, she told me more about what had happened. I got the feeling that she had been keeping a lot of this bottled up for a long time, and I was happy that she felt comfortable enough to be able to share her innermost thoughts with me.

'We met through common friends five years ago,' she said. 'Jayant, or Jay as he is known, was tall and good looking, very confident but also with a sweetness about him that I found really appealing. We started off as friends, I had just moved to Mumbai from Singapore and I was a little lost here, and he kind of took me under his wing.'

'So how did you guys eventually get together romantically?' I asked, always a sucker for a good story.

'We started as friends, I kind of liked him but was a bit wary, and then we started to spend more and more time together. I met his family, who seemed really nice, and then things just started to get more serious. He came to Singapore and met my parents and then he proposed. It all happened pretty quickly.'

'Was it romantic?' I asked.

'Very. He got down on one knee in the middle of a crowded restaurant and popped the question, and whipped out a huge ring. I was completely shocked, but in a good way.'

'So then what happened?' I asked.

'Well, we got married, he's Hindu and so's my mother, so that was straightforward, we had a big wedding in Goa, and then we moved into his parents' house in Juhu.' She paused to take a swig of wine.

'We had a blissful marriage initially, we had a great social life, lots of friends in common, and we really connected as people. I thought life was perfect. We were even talking about having kids.'

'So how did it go from that to divorce?' I asked, conscious that I was being nosey but also dying to know more.

'He started drinking too much,' she answered simply. 'We'd always been the party couple, we went out a lot, and both of us were drinking a fair bit, but his boozing started to get out of control. It was fairly subtle at first, but then by the time we were celebrating our first wedding anniversary it felt like he was always drunk. And then a few months later, he started to get violent.'

'Oh my God,' I breathed, completely shocked.

'It started out fairly innocuously,' she said. 'The first time, we had a fight because he was drunk and he pushed me hard and I fell against a cupboard and bruised myself. I wrote it off as an accident and didn't think much about it. Then it happened again, only this time he actually slapped me and cut my cheek. Then pretty much every time he got really drunk, which was at least once in a month, he'd get angry and aggressive and lash out at me.'

'Didn't you tell anyone?' I asked, horrified.

'Not at first. I was too embarrassed, and I was sure that it was only a phase he was going through. I was so in love with him you see, and I desperately wanted things to work out. Plus he kept telling me that it was my fault, picking fights with me for flirting with other men, wearing sexy clothes and stuff, even though I wasn't. So I ended up kind of thinking that I was somehow to blame.'

I couldn't reconcile this picture of a subservient woman being beaten by her husband with the strong, independent girl I had come to know.

'I know, I know,' she said, catching my look of surprise. 'We read about these victims of domestic violence and wonder how on earth they can let it happen. But I got sucked into it, I was in an emotional state and it was all twisted up in my mind.'

'And what about his parents?' I asked. 'Didn't they notice anything? After all you were living in their apartment.'

'Well, they started to take his side, telling me that I wasn't being a good wife and that it was my duty to keep house for my husband and look after him, and I think deep down they thought that I was too much of a modern woman for their son. His mother used to drop these enormous hints about how her precious son wasn't getting his favourite food and was looking thin, and how miserable he seemed, and how I was taking so long to get pregnant, and it just seemed like they were all against me.'

'That's insane,' I reached for the wine. 'I thought upper class Indian families were supposed to be enlightened in this day and age.'

'Well many are,' Maya said, 'but honestly, the mothers-in-law can be a nightmare. They are more old-fashioned and the relationship between Indian sons and mothers is weirdly close. They are paranoid about their son's wife taking their place in his life, I suppose. I mean, look at all of those TV soap serials. Anyway, there's not much more to tell. The violence got worse, I got more and more depressed, I could hardly work, lost a load of weight, and eventually I guess I came to my senses. He hurt me really badly one night, after coming home shitfaced from a party, and I ended up in the Emergency Room with a broken arm, and a lot of cuts and bruises, and that's when I knew enough was enough. I told him the next day that I wanted a divorce, and ever since then I've been trying to get the whole thing finalized, fighting with his family who are accusing me of bringing shame onto him and the family. I finally got my own place and the divorce is going through, but it's been a long process. And what makes it worse is that he keeps begging me to forgive him, telling me that he loves me, that we are soulmates and that he's changed. But I've heard it all before and, tough as it is, I've hardened myself and I know that I have to move on.'

There were tears glistening in her eyes, and clearly she was having a difficult time dealing with this. I admired her strength, it would have been so easy for her to have given him one last chance, and I knew how hard it was to be single in this town. I felt good about the fact that I was able to offer at least a listening ear, and was glad that we'd met in that packed bar. I wondered whether it would ever really be possible for a foreigner to find happiness with an Indian man. After all, Maya was half Indian, and even she'd struggled to cope with controlling in-laws and unrealistic expectations of domesticity. I guessed I'd cross that bridge if I ever came to it.

## 16

One bright morning, Kiran, the Account Executive whom I'd hired in my first month, approached me shyly in the office.

'Can I talk to you?' she asked.

'Of course,' I replied. 'What's up?'

'I want to put in my papers,' she stated, using that sweet, archaic, only in India phrase.

I was shocked. 'You want to resign? Why? Aren't you happy?'

'I'm very happy,' she said, looking distinctly otherwise. 'I'm getting married and so I need to stop working.'

'You're getting married? Congratulations. I didn't even know you had a boyfriend.'

'My parents have found me a boy and we're getting married in a fortnight.'

I knew that arranged marriages were common in India, but I'd never been up close and personal to anyone who had actually had their partner selected for them.

'So when did you guys meet? That's fantastic news,' I told her, genuinely delighted.

'We met last weekend, our parents prepared everything. He came to my house and we talked for a while.'

'Last weekend! So, you've met him again since then, or just then?'

'Just that one time,' she murmured, looking bashful and slightly embarrassed and not able to look me straight in the eye.

'But if you like him, and you're happy then that's ok, right?'

'He's from a good family. He earns a lot of money. And he seems kind', she said.

'Is he handsome at least?' I asked, trying to inject a lighter note into the conversation.

'He's ok,' she said, smiling a little.

Frankly, I felt Kiran didn't look at all happy about this state of affairs. I knew not to press her too hard; arranged marriages were sacrosanct for many Indians, and they were more about ensuring a happy and prosperous union of two families rather than concerning themselves with trivialities like love and compatibility between the bride and groom to be. It all seemed to have happened breathtakingly fast.

'Are you sure you're OK with all this?' I asked her. 'Wouldn't it be better to get to know him a little better before you get married to him?'

'It has happened quite suddenly, but my parents are very keen that we get married quickly, and the astrologer has told us that there's a very auspicious date coming up in two weeks time, which perfectly matches our charts, so we have to get married on that date.'

'And why do you want to stop working?' I asked her. 'Surely you can get married and then come back to work again?'

'He doesn't want me to work after we're married. He says that he can provide for me, and he wants me to be at home.'

'And are you OK with that?' I asked, hoping that she wouldn't be.

'Yes it's fine. It's his decision and I need to support him. He thinks women shouldn't work after marriage, his mother never did and it's really important to him that I take care of the house.'

I was shocked that such an attitude could exist in this day and age, but there was no point my ranting and raving about an opinion that was appropriate for many in this culture.

'Well, why don't you talk to him? You can take some time off and then come back and work. You'll go crazy sitting at home, you're far too ambitious to be a housewife.'

'Thank you, but I've made my decision,' she said stubbornly, again unable to meet my gaze. Her eyes were shining, and I could see that she was fighting to hold back tears.

'Well as long as you're sure. And if you change your mind, there's always a job for you here.' Kiran was one of my best workers, and I was devastated that she'd chosen to move on. I wished I could persuade her to stay, but I knew it wasn't fair to put too much emotional pressure on her, her family would be doing enough of that, and I didn't want her to feel torn and more confused than she probably was already.

I couldn't help feeling that this whole arranged marriage system seemed pretty unfair and irrelevant in this day and age. I'd read a fair bit about arranged marriages, and many Indians swore that they were an ideal way to create a harmonious state of matrimony, arguing that it was impossible for romantic love to really exist beyond an initial infatuation, and that in fact what mattered more was a deep union, which could only come from ensuring an alignment of values and social status and ambition.

I got where they were coming from, at least in principle, but I thought it was sad. Though I'd had my fair share of disastrous love affairs, and been heartbroken more than once, and of course the details of the breakdown of Maya's romantic, catastrophic marriage were still ringing in my ears, I couldn't imagine someone being selected for me on the basis of their financial stability (which had always been highly irrelevant to me, anyway), meeting them for half an hour and then agreeing to spend the rest of my life with them.

There had been a fair amount of negative publicity about arranged marriages in the UK recently, and several documentaries aired on British TV channels had showed horrific situations involving young British women of South Asian origin being dragged back to their parental homeland, married off to an abusive local, and then forced to live a life of near slavery. Though it was easy to jump on the popular bandwagon, which claimed that all arranged marriages were evil, I had also read stories of men and women finding true love and happiness this way.

I supposed that the majority of 'love' marriages that ended prematurely did so because of compatibility issues. It went without saying, then, that if you at least ascertained a certain degree of compatibility based on similar interests, values and ambition, then the likelihood of that marriage succeeding was higher, as long as both parties were subsequently allowed to let the relationship grow and develop naturally. It was the sheer speed of Kiran's proposed marriage, however, along with the fact that her husband to be refused to let her work, which was making me angry and frustrated on her behalf. It just seemed brutally old fashioned and completely sexist to me.

I had no arranged marriage to fall back on. I'd become immune to the frequent questions about my marital status from my co-workers, my neighbours and even random strangers. 'Sahib kahan hai?' (where is Sir?) they would ask, glancing at my empty ring finger. 'Sahib England main hai,' I always responded—Sir is in England. There was no point trying to explain to the majority of middle class Indians that there was no Sahib. When I'd lapsed sometimes and told people that I was not married, they had looked at me as though I'd grown two heads. 'Not married? Why?' My standard response of 'I haven't met the right person yet,' didn't seem to cut it with most Indians, for whom being single after the age of 25 was unthinkable. Kiran was 26, and her mother had started putting pressure on her to find a suitable boy and get married when she'd turned 20. Maya was my age but at least had been married. I was practically middle aged in their eyes, and should have had a husband and at least a couple of kids under my belt by now and I wondered if I was really past my prime or whether living in India was just making me paranoid.

I hadn't forgotten about Hari, the guy from the internet dating site, and I decided to take the plunge and respond to the last message he'd sent. A few days had passed since his note had dropped into my Gofish.com mailbox and I agonized over the content of my response—I didn't want to appear desperate, nor did I want to come across as vacuous so I eventually settled for something in between. I wrote a lighthearted but friendly response, telling him that I'd been in Mumbai for a while, that I loved travelling, was originally from the UK and was enjoying India. I was aware that it sounded a bit trite, but figured that writing to a complete stranger was a bizarrely contrived thing to do anyway. Almost immediately, a response pinged back. Hari thanked me for my mail, told me that he'd never done this before, that he had recently broken up with a long term girlfriend and that all his friends had told him that he should try internet dating. I wrote back, after leaving a few hours gap so as not to seem too keen, and sent what I hoped was a witty diatribe about the trials and tribulations of living in India. We ended up knocking mails back and forth for a few hours and eventually he wrote asking me to send him a photo of myself.

I instantly felt the butterflies in my stomach. I had a few decent photos, some good ones of me taken during my travels, looking healthy and tanned, but I felt very nervous about sending my picture to a complete stranger, even though he knew my name. While I contemplated it, he wrote me mails telling me more about himself—he was an investment banker for one of the foreign banks in Mumbai, he had studied at the London School of Economics, played squash, kept himself pretty fit, but loved his food and had a particular fondness for good wine. I shared similar snippets of information about myself—including my love for frivolous fiction, my attempts at keeping fit in Mumbai and a bit about my family back in the UK. Finally, I relented to his pleas, and agreed to send him a photo.

I spent ages choosing the right one, I couldn't decide whether I should send him a serious or a lighthearted picture, whether I wanted to come across as bright or breezy. I eventually decided on a compromise and sent him a photo of me taken in London the week before I'd left, holding up a glass of champagne in the garden, with a serious but slightly flirtatious look on my face. The wind had lifted my hair slightly, and I was smiling into the camera but not grinning too inanely. It was a good look and I hoped he liked it, even though I hadn't been blown away by his picture. Female vanity, I supposed. I wrote him a quick e-mail, attached the photo and quickly pressed send before I could change my mind.

I was nervous waiting for his reply, and I couldn't stop thinking about it. If he changed his tone or stopped the mails coming, then I would know that he was disappointed. If he liked me, then I knew that I would feel good but then I would also start getting excited about the possibility of a romance, and he could turn out to be a nightmare in real life. This online dating game was a complete minefield, frankly, and I had nothing to guide me through it, not even Maya, who was away for the week on a shoot.

The next morning, there was a one line e-mail in my inbox. 'Wow! Nice picture. You look great! Sorry for the delay in replying, got caught up with work. Hari xx.'

I looked great!!! And two kisses! Woo hoo. I felt ridiculously pleased, as though I'd passed some kind of test. I urged myself not to think about him too much, and kept reminding myself of my recent experience with Krishna, which had been a result of my trusting a stranger too much. Eventually I decided that rather than prolonging the agony and the banter, I should just agree to his suggestion that we meet. He recommended dinner at Zenzi, an Asian fusion restaurant in Bandra which people raved about and which had received great reviews. I called Maya, who was back in town, and brought her up to date on the developments.

'Oh my God, you've moved fast,' she exclaimed.

'Well, not really,' I replied, feeling slightly defensive. 'You've been away for a week and I haven't even met him yet. Besides, I might as well get the first meeting over with. He seems kind of interesting in his mails, but I still can't wrap my head around the thought of meeting up with a complete stranger.

'Do you want me to come with you?' asked Maya, thoughtfully, 'Or I could lurk around at the bar and jump in if you look like you need rescuing.'

'Not a bad idea,' I pondered, 'but I think maybe I should do this on my own. Worst case, I can always invent some excuse and leave.'

'OK if you're sure,' she said, sounding a little disappointed.

'I'll fill you in on all the gory details,' I promised.

Hari and I had arranged to meet at the bar at 10 p.m., a suitable time for dinner in Mumbai but late enough in my view that I could feign tiredness and leave early if it all turned out to be unbearable. I spotted him immediately, standing at one end of the bar, wearing immaculately pressed chinos and an open necked shirt, which had something vaguely resembling a cravat tucked into it. I had selected a smart but fairly modest wraparound dress, figuring that I didn't want to give off the wrong signals from the beginning and had tied my hair in a demure ponytail.

He leant down to kiss my cheek, and I caught a waft of lemony cologne. He was good looking enough, not as handsome as Krishna, certainly, but appealing in a clean-cut, slightly preppy way. His black hair was cut short, a little too cropped for my liking, his skin was smooth and golden brown, and his features were even, with slightly hooded eyes over a perfectly straight nose. His lips were thin, and his chin was squarish. All in all, he looked like the boy next door—there was nothing offensive about any of his features, yet somehow together they gave him a very ordinary, run of the mill look. He kissed me on both cheeks, European style, which caught me unawares, especially as I was about to hold out my hand for a more formal British style of greeting.

'Good to meet you at last,' he smiled. 'Let's have a drink. What would you like? They have a seriously good wine list here.'

'I'll just have a gin and tonic, please.' I figured I needed something stronger to quell my nerves.

'Bombay Sapphire? Or Gordon's? I am guessing you will be a Gordon's girl.'

'Er, either is fine,' I smiled back, and then wondered if I should have declared a preference. Gin was gin, in my view. As he spoke, chatting comfortably about his week, I tried to place his accent. It definitely sounded British to me, or at least vaguely similar to that of my friends back home.

'You studied in London, didn't you?' I asked. 'You definitely have an accent.'

'Yes, I lived in Highbury for a year while I was studying at the LSE.'

I couldn't help feeling that this was a little phoney. After all, I'd been in Mumbai for over a year and still sounded fresh off the boat. As he spoke, his accent meandered between pure Mumbai, and London's East End, and it was most disconcerting. It was almost as though he was trying too hard, though I tried not to dwell on it too much, figuring that I shouldn't jump to conclusions about him too quickly.

'Shall we eat? I'm starving,' he stated. 'The food here is really good. Their sushi is amazing.' We were seated at one of the low tables in the restaurant area, a dimly lit space with an oriental feel—with bamboo placemats and chopsticks at the table. As he studied the menu, I surreptitiously checked him out trying to work out if I found him attractive or not.

'What would you like to order? Or shall I order for you?' he asked.

Ignoring his attempt to be gentlemanly, I quickly perused the menu, before ordering the crispy salmon with noodles.

'Great choice,' he said. 'May I order the wine?'

'Sure,' I replied, being a girl of fairly simple tastes. There followed a complicated altercation with the waiter, during which Hari asked for recommendations on certain types of wine, which the poor waiter had clearly never heard of. As the waiter became more and more flustered, and looked increasingly uncomfortable, Hari raised his voice.

'What do you mean, you can't recommend a wine to accompany this main course? This isn't acceptable. Please send the manager over.'

His voice was loud enough to carry across the restaurant, and I began to feel embarrassed. I wondered if this show was for my benefit, or whether he was always like this.

'It's impossible to get good staff here in Mumbai,' he hissed loudly, again too stridently for my liking. 'It's nothing like London here. I'm sure you're used to far better service in restaurants.'

'Actually I've got used to Mumbai,' I murmured, feeling rather defensive of my adopted city. 'The problem is that staff are cheap, and they don't get trained properly. So it's not really their fault.'

'Well I much prefer London restaurants,' he replied, with a pompous tone.

This whole interaction was beginning to make me squirm, and I guessed that he was putting it on for my benefit, when I'd have been happy with a glass of local wine or even a beer. The manager scurried over, and Hari continued to interrogate him. Finally he found a bottle of wine that suited his palate, and I drank thankfully from the glass that was poured before me, readying myself to answer the questions that I knew were buzzing around his brain. Sure enough, they began to flow thick and fast.

'So tell me about yourself. What did you do in London? And what made you leave?'

I told him that I had been offered the job here and had accepted it gladly. He looked as though I was completely mad to have swapped the comforts of London for Mumbai.

'I hate India,' he said. 'I plan to go back to the UK as soon as I can. I'm just waiting for the right job to come up, and then I'll be gone. It's so filthy here, and the people are so backward. London is far more civilized.'

I bit my tongue, wanting to jump to the defence of India's masses, yet not wanting to get into an argument with this guy who clearly had an over romanticized view of my hometown, and a very different view of Mumbai from my own.

'But don't you find this an incredibly energizing city?' I asked. 'There's so much potential here, and it's so exciting.'

'Not at all,' he replied with a smirk. 'India will never get anywhere in the world. It is too corrupt, too backward, and too poor. The only way to get anywhere in life is to leave.'

I was shocked at his words. I knew that many Indians wanted to travel, but couldn't understand how anyone could be so dismissive of their country of origin, however difficult it might be to live and work there, and so condescending about one's fellow citizens. I knew that I was often critical about England, but I always managed to take a balanced view, and could see both the pros and cons of living in each country. Hari, it seemed, was on a complete mission to discredit his own country and had been seduced by the apparent superiority of the West and its glittering exterior.

As the evening continued, and our main courses arrived, his vitriol for India, the waiters and even the crowd around us increased. He seemed to automatically assume that I would share his opinions, given my nationality, and I found this more and more offensive the further down the bottle of wine we got. As we drank, his faux English accent became further pronounced, until he ended up sounding like he was auditioning for a role in the British soap opera Eastenders. I had already guessed that he had been attracted to me thanks to my British India screen name, and wished that I'd had the foresight to think of a name that sounded less obviously foreign.

The evening was dragging, I was finding him more and more of a caricature, and his opinions progressively more tedious. When Hari clicked his fingers at the waiter and made the universally naff air squiggle which translated as 'bring the bill please', I knew it was my cue to leave.

'I'm so sorry, but I need to head off. I have a big meeting tomorrow morning and I really need to get some rest.'

'On a Saturday?' he asked, with a frown. 'I thought we'd catch a nightcap somewhere. It's been wonderful sharing an evening with someone who understands where I'm coming from.'

I cringed inside. 'Yes, we have a business planning meeting in the morning. You know how it is at this time of the year.'

I had no idea whether this was a difficult time of the year or not, but Hari seemed to buy my lame excuse.

'OK but let's meet again soon, I had such a good evening.'

I couldn't believe that he hadn't picked up my obvious discomfort at his brashness, but I could see that subtlety wasn't his strong point.

'Sure,' I said, chickening out of the chance to tell him that I wasn't interested. I waved goodbye to him and ducked into my car in case he tried to kiss me goodbye. On the way back home I called Maya to fill her in on the gory details.

'He was dreadful. It was awful. Never again, I'm done with internet dating.'

She howled with laughter as I aped Hari's whiny faux English accent and his obsession with all things British.

'You poor thing. Ah, well, you live and learn.'

I decided there and then to stop hunting for love, and hoped that it might eventually creep up on me unnoticed.

## 17

A few weeks later, the office decided to throw a party to celebrate winning a new big piece of business. They had booked one of the kitschy, all-American theme bars that seemed to be suddenly springing up all over Mumbai, with their over enthusiastic waiters, ridiculously calorific deep fried starters smothered with cheese and sour cream, and faux Americana décor. They served enormous cocktails, which came in vast glasses that were so heavy that you could hardly lift them with two hands. I decided to throw caution to the wind, relax and enjoy myself. I was in good company, I'd spent months bonding with my colleagues and I just felt like taking a night off from being continually on my guard.

The bar was packed and our little team was huddled around a table piled high with an assortment of greasy delicious items, which were all the more tasty given that none of them were flavoured with masala or Indian spices. Though I loved Indian food, I also craved bland, cheesy, creamy food that hadn't been near a chilli in its entire life. I dived into the plates of towering nachos, glued together with warm fake cheese, sour cream, and something vaguely resembling guacamole. I ate greasy potato skins, loaded with more cheese and bacon. I devoured prawns fried in crispy golden batter and dipped them in Thousand Island dressing. It was all sinful, but went fantastically well with the enormous vats of alcohol that we were all guzzling.

I ordered another lime margarita, loving the way the salty rim around the glass contrasted with the sour, icy drink, and enjoying the warm buzz that was starting to hit my system. My colleagues were busy gossiping about the client who was allegedly dating his boss, and the production company that only hired gay men. I felt relaxed, happy and part of the crowd. I was squeezed in between a pretty Account Director, Jill, and a copywriter, Anees, who had always been friendly and occasionally even a little bit flirtatious with me in the office. He was handsome, in a slightly quirky way, with a small goatee beard, a long fringe and sharp cheekbones. He was on the short side, but had an impish charm and an infectious good humour.

'Come on, let's order another round,' he said. We called the waiter over, who rushed up with a beam, pen poised to take our order. I was sure I could hear a bit of an American twang in his accent and guessed this place took its branding pretty seriously. We ordered another round of drinks for the table, and the music cranked up a notch. I wondered whether I should be sociable and move around the other tables, but I was feeling a little too tipsy to get up at this point, and I was quite comfortable wedged in between Jill and Anees.

Anees turned to me. 'So, you're enjoying life in Mumbai then? You've been here a while.'

'Almost eighteen months already,' I told him. 'I can't believe how fast the time has flown. And yes, I'm loving it here.'

'What is it about Mumbai that you firangs like so much?' he asked me, using the local, colloquial expression for 'foreigners'.

'Well, I suppose that for us, it's just so different and exciting. I mean, back home everything is so ordered and proper, and logical, and planned. Which does make life easier, for sure, but it's also really boring. When I go back home to England to visit my family, I just feel bored stiff after the first couple of days. I mean it's lovely to see everyone, and of course there are certain things that I miss, but I just find it hard work. Harder work than Mumbai.'

'Really? Wow, that's certainly a different way to look at things. We Indians are obsessed with going abroad, of course, and we really can't understand why you people would choose to leave a clean, organized, beautiful country to come and live here. But I do get what you mean about Mumbai. I'm originally from Pune but I find Mumbai completely intoxicating and totally addictive. Plus for a creative person, it really gets my juices flowing, if you know what I mean.'

We talked on and on about Mumbai and what it meant to live here. I'd never really got this deep into talking about my adopted homeland with an Indian before, and I was finding the exchange fascinating, helped by the buckets of margarita that we were pouring down our throats. Suddenly I realized that I was actually already quite drunk. I stood up to go to the toilet, and the room spun slightly.

'Are you OK?' asked Anees.

'Yup, I'm fine' I replied, weakly. He stood up to let me pass, and I brushed past him in a bid to squeeze out of the tiny space. I thought I felt his arms come around me, possibly to help me balance, but his steadying hands lingered for a little longer than they needed to and I wondered if he was interested in me.

'Hurry back,' he grinned. 'I'm enjoying talking to you.'

I bumped into several people on the way to and from the bathroom, got engrossed in a couple of conversations and then headed back towards my table, realizing that most of its former occupants had in fact shifted to the makeshift dance floor and were strutting their stuff to a series of predictable Bollywood tunes. Anees was sitting at the table nursing the dregs of a drink. His face lit up when he saw me.

'There you are. I thought you'd got lost. Come on, let's dance.'

He pulled me onto the dance floor, and I was drunk enough to acquiesce. We shimmied and shuffled along to the catchy track, and before I knew it he was giving it the whole Bollywood boy seduction moves. I responded with suggestive hip movements, fluttering eyelashes and pouty expressions. I was loving this, I felt relaxed and comfortable, despite the fact that I was surrounded by work people. In fact I was oblivious to everyone else, focused only on Anees and his gaze, which in turn was locked on to me. I realized that I was flirting shamelessly, and the thought that this behaviour was inappropriate flitted briefly through my mind, but I shut it out, figuring that I deserved to let my hair down. We danced for a while, increasing the intensity of the intimacy with each number, until Anees finally grabbed me, and whispered in my ear.

'How about we get out of here?'

My head was telling me that this was a very bad idea, but I shoved the thoughts away, and, fuelled by the alcohol and the fact that I was attracted to Anees and hadn't let down my guard and enjoyed myself for months, agreed to leave. I glanced furtively around me, realized that most people were deep in their own conversations or flirtations, and we headed for the door. Once outside, the warm air hit me and I realized that I would have to go through with this now.

'How about one last drink?' asked Anees. We headed to a grungy bar in South Mumbai which was something of a local institution, its walls covered in years of graffiti scribbles and with a rather unflattering neon lit interior. We ordered large vodkas and huddled in a corner.

'I've always liked you,' said Anees, any inhibitions completely forgotten. 'I thought you were hot the first time I saw you.'

'Nothing to do with me being a foreigner, I hope?' I asked him.

'Of course not. You just seemed like a lot of fun, though you're always busy and very serious about things. It's good to see you let your hair down and enjoy yourself.'

'Well, it's fun to relax and stop worrying about things,' I smiled. 'Life's too short, right?'

We finished our drinks, and he looked expectantly at me. 'So, what next?'

Fired up by a bellyful of spirits, and intoxicated by the rare sensation of throwing caution to the wind, I suggested that we head to my place for another drink. It was walking distance from the bar, I had left the place tidy, and I had some decent wine in the fridge. We walked up the hill to my apartment, and Anees grabbed my hand. I felt a little self-conscious about walking past the ever-observant doormen with my hand in his, and so I let go as we approached the gate, on the pretence of searching for my key. Despite that, the watchman's eyes were on stalks as we walked towards the lift.

We entered the apartment, and before I even had time to close the door behind me, Anees had grabbed me and was kissing me. The kiss was vigorous and I suppose passionate, though I would have preferred a little more small talk before getting down to things. I decided to go with the flow, I was still drunk, I found him really attractive, and thoughts of the office were very far from my mind. He pulled me down on the sofa, and we made out like teenagers. Our clothes came off, and I offered a silent prayer of thanks that I'd actually had the foresight to wear my decent underwear. His kisses were good, though slightly slobbery, and I restrained myself from actually wiping my mouth at any point, resorting to furtively rubbing my cheek against the cushion. Somehow I couldn't quite allow myself to get down and dirty in the living room, so I stood up and pulled him into the bedroom. He was all over me, his breathing was raspy and he was obviously very turned on, and the last remnants of our clothing were off. I was enjoying this, although it was all moving a bit fast for my liking, but I figured that we'd gone too far to stop now, so I decided to go with the flow. I hadn't had sex with anyone since Krishna, which was a good few months ago now, and I really didn't care at this point if I felt bad in the morning. I deserved to have a good time and this was a natural culmination of a fun and flirtatious evening. Things got more steamy, and it was clear that we were going to do the deed. I reached for a condom, luckily I had a store in my bedside cabinet, and though I briefly wondered whether that made me look like I did this all the time, I decided that it would be better to be safe than worry about my virtue at this stage.

I was amazed, frankly, that he was able to perform, given all the drinks we'd had. I was feeling pretty numb all over, but I was enjoying the intimacy nonetheless. He rolled the condom

172

on, entered me at the first attempt and began to move back and forth. He hadn't exactly turned me on with foreplay, but I was too drunk to notice whether it hurt or not. Thankfully he seemed happy enough with the missionary position, which suited me just fine as I didn't think I had the energy or inclination for sexual acrobatics at this point. He lasted for about a minute, and then came with a huge groan, before falling heavily onto me. He was a dead weight, and I was finding it hard to breathe, but thankfully he pulled out, grabbing the condom as he did so, rolled over and immediately fell asleep.

I don't know what else I was expecting, especially given that he was drunk and that the last of his energy had clearly been sapped with his ejaculation, but a hug wouldn't have gone amiss. I wasn't naïve enough to think that men enjoyed pillow talk, particularly after what was likely to be a one-night stand, but I wouldn't have minded laying my head on his chest and sharing a moment of faux intimacy.

He was flat on his back and snoring like a train and I took the opportunity to look at his body. He was fairly muscular without being buff, his body was trim but not skinny, and his chest was hairy but looked as though it had been shaved at some point. His skin was pale brown, and lighter where the sun hadn't touched it, but his forearms, shins and face were darker. His penis was small and shriveled, but it had seemed adequately sized during our lovemaking so I didn't dwell too much on that. Besides, it was only men who were really obsessed by the size of their penises.

After what seemed like an age of lying awake intermittently staring at him and the ceiling, which had only recently stopped spinning, I fell into a restless sleep. I was in the middle of a dream in which I was predictably running naked through the office, when I felt a shifting beside me. Anees had got out of bed and was pulling his clothing on. I turned over and asked him, 'Are you OK? Can't you sleep?'

'I need to get home,' he mumbled. 'I told my folks I'd be home hours ago, and my Mum will only worry.'

Of course. I'd reckoned without Indian Mummy fretting over her precious thirty-year-old son.

'Why don't you send her a message and come back to bed?' I asked, hoping that I wasn't appearing sad and desperate for a warm body in my bed. 'You've only slept for a couple of hours.'

'No, its OK, I really should get going. Thanks anyway for a great evening. I'll see you in the office.'

And with that, he pulled on his shoes and was gone, banging the front door loudly behind him. His final words rang in my ears. I couldn't believe that I'd actually gone and slept with a work colleague, and what had seemed like a fun way to end the evening now felt like a big mistake, and one that would return to haunt me.

The next morning was thankfully a Saturday, and so I had two whole days to avoid seeing my office colleagues, or coming face to face with my shameful encounter. I just knew that he wouldn't call me for a friendly chat or a 'how are you, I loved spending the evening with you'. Our brief affair had had all the hallmarks of a one-night stand, and it had left me feeling irritated and slutty, rather than satiated or content. I didn't suppose he was feeling the same way, and I wondered for the hundredth time why women always always felt compelled to put themselves through this process of self flagellation and guilt trips.

I decided to put the whole thing out of my mind, and spend the weekend reading, watching trashy TV shows and visiting the gym in an attempt to make myself feel at least physically better. Monday morning came, and I dragged myself to the office, determined to act as though nothing had happened. I was sure I spotted a couple of my co-workers giving me sneaky sideways looks, and I knew that I was blushing, a trait that Indians found endearing because most darker skinned people didn't blush as red and embarrassingly as we fairer types did. I didn't see Anees all day, and I studiously avoided going anywhere near his cabin. When I did meet him, a couple of days later, in passing, he avoided my gaze and gave me a kind of shifty half grin. I felt really bad about the entire incident, and spent days afterwards deconstructing the entire chain of events and wishing that I hadn't had so much to drink and acted so rashly but I managed to bury the whole experience deep in the recesses of my subconscious.

Christmas was again approaching fast, and I decided that I didn't want to go back to England for the festive season, as I'd done previously. By now I was settling into the rhythm of life in Mumbai, had crossed the two-year point and felt more and more settled as the months passed. I almost felt now as though London was more foreign to me than Mumbai was and I had managed to condense the things I missed about my homeland down to a short list — my friends and family of course still featured prominently, although the friends list had dwindled significantly as I realized that many of my so-called fair-weather friends had dropped off the radar completely. The other things that remained on the list were the fat wedge of Sunday papers, which would typically occupy the entire day and the rest of the week, pints of warm, frothy English beer and of course the food staples—the blander the better. Bacon, sausages, and cheese in particular. I still woke on Sunday mornings dreaming of crispy bacon sandwiches on fluffy white bread with HP sauce. In the grand scheme of things, though, I felt that these were small trifles to have given up for the life I was living in Mumbai, and the constant, mesmerising high that drove me from week to week.

I still missed Annabel and Lizzie, though the pain of being away from them was easing as the months passed. We were still close, and we still spoke often on the phone, but somehow I found myself turning more and more often to Maya, or to the friends with whom I had developed closer ties in recent months—both Rebecca and Sarah, the English girls I had met all those months ago at the Olive expat party had become friends rather than acquaintances, and even pompous Jonathan, who had turned out to be a sweet person underneath all the posturing. Of course I still saw a lot of Johann and Priyanka, and I was also friendly with a few of the people from the office and so the void that I'd felt initially had been largely filled. I had made three trips back to London since leaving, and had slipped back into an easy camaraderie with the girls back home, and there was something very satisfying about our connection and our closeness. However, I no longer felt the ache of not having them in my life on a daily basis, and found myself enjoying the challenge of forging new friendships, which I hoped would deepen as time went on. I did, however, miss my parents a lot, and even occasionally yearned for my sister Louise's endless domestic dramas, her tales about trying to conceive, false pregnancy alarms and her constant fights with her boyfriend who was now her fiancé.

After a long discussion with Maya about the pros and cons of opening up my apartment to the masses, I decided to throw a Christmas party at my place. I felt as though it was about time that I invited people to my home for a change. I'd received many invitations to parties and events in recent months and I figured that I should return the favour. Besides, I'd always been the type to organize social events back home in London, and I loved to introduce people to each other. I'd been here long enough now, and attended enough parties and gatherings to have amassed a decent list of people who I could count on to attend, although I was a little bit nervous about inviting people in case they didn't turn up.

My social life in Mumbai had recently taken off though, and I had developed quite a long list of contacts, although I wouldn't have called them good friends. Mumbai's party scene was notoriously fickle, if fun, and it was difficult to forge deep or more meaningful friendships—everyone seemed to be permanently busy and preoccupied with their own lives, and, given the continual challenge of keeping one's head above water in a city that bombarded you constantly with obstacles, this wasn't surprising. Thankfully, Maya and I had become closer than ever in recent weeks, and I also spent time with Johann and Priyanka whenever we could find the time in our busy schedules. I was still enjoying the relative novelty of a city where invitations to events and parties flowed thick and fast, though I was aware that I was overdoing the partying a little bit, drinking too much and eating too many of the rich snacks that invariably circulated. I was beginning to get just a little bored of having the same conversations with the same people, and although I had adjusted well to my new life, I would occasionally lapse into a fit of homesickness, which I always successfully managed to push to the back of my mind with a night out on the town and a few stiff drinks. Since sleeping with Anees, I'd been very wary of letting my guard down, and I'd built a pretty solid wall around myself when it came to intimacy, so my casual social life suited me well and acted even as a kind of protection.

I planned my party carefully and decided to make it a big event. This was my first real party, and I wanted to put a lot of effort into making sure that it went with a bang. I spent the next few days finalizing the guest list, booking bartenders, dreaming up imaginative cocktails and decorating the place with cheap and cheerful Christmas decorations which I picked up from tiny market stalls in Bandra's Catholic areas. I even planned to serve food, though my British roots typically had me focused only on the alcohol. I'd been in India long enough to know that a few bowls of crisps and peanuts wouldn't do, and that people expected food to be served, even if they didn't eat it. I ordered some starters from my local kebab shop, succulent chicken tikka, paneer tikka for the vegetarians, and two huge pots of biryani, a veg and a non-veg version. I also stocked up on expensive imported crisps and picked up some extortionate but delicious dips from the local expat deli, which charged a small fortune for delicacies that could be picked up for peanuts back home. I sent a mass SMS inviting a mix of people mainly from the office and the expat crowd as well as a few Indian friends whom I'd met through Maya, figuring that it would be fun to mix everyone up, and hoping that everyone drank enough to loosen up and talk to each other rather than staying in their cliques.

By 10 p.m. on party night, there were six people sitting in my living room looking rather lost, listening to Christmas carols and being served mojitos and sangria by the two barmen who were hovering and refilling glasses as soon as they were empty. Maya was on her way, having got stuck at a shoot which had overrun. I'd invited people for 9 p.m., knowing that no one would arrive until 9.30 p.m., but as usual I underestimated the Mumbaikar's inbuilt inability for punctuality. Most people here didn't bother to confirm their attendance to an event in case something better turned up, and they were notorious for being fickle and keeping their options open. It was frustrating when it came to organizing anything, but it was best to go with the flow and I was fairly confident that my social circle was robust enough to make this party a success.

By 11 p.m. the occupants in the room had swelled to twenty, there was one group of work people standing at the far end of the room and another from the expat crowd sitting around on the sofas. Johann and Priyanka had arrived, and were deep in conversation with Rebecca and  David, Rohit and Kiran were trying not to look too wide-eyed in the presence of so many foreigners, and I was on my fourth mojito, desperately trying to will the time to pass faster. Maya rushed into the room in a fluster, red in the face carrying a bag full of clanking wine bottles.

'I'm so sorry I'm late', she exclaimed. 'I meant to be here an hour ago but the traffic was insane.'

'Yes I figured', I hugged her. 'I guess everyone else got caught up in it too.'

Half-an-hour later, at precisely 11.25 p.m., the doorbell rang and then kept ringing as people poured through the door.

It seemed that everyone I'd invited had come, and brought their friends, and before too long my small apartment was absolutely packed, with no room for anyone to move around, let alone refill their glasses. I flitted from group to group, noticing that people were clinging to their social cliques, and although I tried to play the party hostess and introduce groups of people to each other, they kept pinging back to their own kind and so I eventually gave up. My work colleagues drank beer and sat on the floor looking relaxed and enjoying themselves while the majority of the foreigners perched on sofas and stood around drinking wine and cocktails. I eventually decided to stop worrying about whether people were having a good time, let them all talk to who they wanted, and started drinking mojitos mixed by the cheery barman who seemed determined to make me relax and enjoy myself. As soon as the last person had left at 3 a.m., Maya and I collapsed onto the sofa and analysed the evening.

'What a great party,' she said. 'I think everyone who you invited turned up.'

'And a few more,' I giggled. 'Who were those people who arrived right at the end? The ones wearing the fancy dress costumes.'

'No idea,' she replied with a smirk. 'Never seen them before. I guess they were gatecrashers.'

I was relieved the evening had gone well, thankful that I'd done my bit as party host for the next few months and hoped this meant that I'd finally become part of Mumbai's social scene.

## 18

The New Year began with an attempt to compose a list of resolutions. I made these every year, they usually revolved around various ambitions involving losing weight, drinking less or at least drinking only on weekends and resisting the temptation to smoke socially. This time, I made a more focused promise to myself—if I didn't stop burying my loneliness beneath parties and boozing, and if I hadn't met someone who could be relationship potential in the foreseeable future, then I'd seriously think about leaving India. I didn't want to be alone forever, and I was beginning to become paranoid about ending up sad, lonely and watching all my friends tripping down the aisle and producing babies. I was also brutally conscious of not wanting to give off the vibes of the thirty-plus woman desperate to settle down. There was nothing which would guarantee that a man would turn tail and run more than a woman of a certain age fretting over time running out, subconsciously sending signals of wanting to settle down. That would kill any budding relationship, however casual, and I knew that men could sense these signs from a thousand paces. I decided instead to focus on my work, to stop actively looking for love, but at the same time to give myself a deadline and see how fate played itself out.

Unfortunately I managed to break my traditional New Year resolution of cutting down on the alcohol with an indulgent, party filled January. It was as though everyone was in collective denial about the time of year and refusing to accept that the festive season was over. I attended two or three huge parties and a few smaller events, and I drank myself into a stupor at most of them. Just as I was about to embark on a complete detox, Maya called me to invite me to a 'huge' fashion event, which she claimed that anyone who was anyone would be attending.

'You have to come,' she said. 'I have VIP passes, and the whole of Bollywood will be there. I only managed to get passes because of the last styling job I did on that Shah Rukh Khan movie, and I made friends with his makeup girl who fluttered her eyelashes at his designer who had some spare tickets.'

'Nooo, Maya,' I groaned. 'I've been overdoing it for the entire month of January, and that's after deciding to detox from January 1. I have no willpower at the best of times, without you being around.'

'OK, make this the last blowout,' she said with an evil grin. 'I promise that after this one, I'll leave you alone completely to your carrot juice and your yoghurt and your early nights. But please please come with me to this one. I promise we'll have a brilliant time.'

Maya was her usual persuasive self, and frankly my resolve was weak. I usually made my resolutions on New Year's Eve, followed them rigidly for about five days, before falling off the wagon into a vat of vodka, and this year was proving to be no exception. This year, I felt like I'd almost made a pact—send me a man, and I'll give up boozing and socializing. It was sad, but I did almost feel the need to bargain for what I wanted, figuring that it might at least result in some sympathy from whatever higher being had decided to throw me a bum deal on the romance front during my time in Mumbai.

Thursday evening, I poured myself a glass of Chardonnay, poured myself into a dress, which I hoped didn't show off too much of the Christmas weight gain, applied dark, smoky eyeshadow to accentuate my grey eyes and a slick of dark red lipstick, and set off for the swanky five-star hotel where the event was being held. The sweeping driveway that led up to the hotel's entrance was lit with garlands of tiny twinkling lights in blue and white, and the security at the gate was fierce. The long line of fancy cars suggested that this was indeed an event for the crème de la crème of Mumbai's society, and I marveled for the thousandth time to myself that I actually had access to these kinds of affairs. In London I'd never have had the slightest sniff at such exclusive parties, despite having a good job in a fairly cool industry; there, these kinds of events were reserved for the rich and famous. I'd gatecrashed my fair share of such events in Mumbai, and knew that I and the rest of my expat friends wouldn't have too much difficulty blagging our way into a society party, whereas most Indians, unless they were famous, would probably struggle. It felt unfair, but then again, Mumbai was riven with injustice and inequality, and I didn't feel badly enough about it to refuse to attend these parties.

Maya was waiting for me in the lobby and as usual she looked divine, her long hair styled into an exotic looking topknot, and her lean body shown off to maximum effect in a long, emerald dress, which looked amazing against her brown skin. Maya had finally managed to get her divorce papers signed, and had moved completely out of her ex-husband's apartment and into a tiny but beautifully furnished apartment in Andheri, a busy northern suburb close to Juhu and an area filled with wannabe TV stars and starlets, small-time actors and the odd real celebrity. It was a vibrant, lively area, lacking Bandra's charm but significantly cheaper and with a fun atmosphere. She had already embarked on another relationship, a fairly casual romance with a small-time actor.

'Be careful,' I warned her. 'You've just come out of a nightmare situation. Don't jump into something else too quickly.'

'Don't worry,' she reassured me. 'I'm not looking for a serious relationship. Rishi and I are just having fun, he's younger than me and obsessed with his career and becoming a serious actor and, besides, he's far too vain for me. I'm just enjoying the attention and the flirtation. It's exactly what I need after Jay. Plus, Rishi keeps my mind off the events of the past, which suits me perfectly.'

I admired her resilience, and marveled at how opposite our life stages were. She had been though a terrible marriage, and was now looking for nothing but a lighthearted fling, with a few added benefits. I was searching for a far more meaningful connection, though trying hard not to let this show.

'No Rishi tonight?' I asked her, half expecting her chiseled toyboy to be hanging off her arm.

She shook her head. 'He's working. Plus, he's so star struck, he'd only embarrass me by trying to strike up conversations with the Bollywood people, and try to get parts in their films, and I'd be mortified, frankly. Better he's not here. Anyway you and I need a proper girlie night out together.'

We walked down the sweeping staircase and into the glittering ballroom, where a long ramp had been set up surrounded by rows of chairs decked with white silk covers and jaunty blue bows. We were still relatively early so we decided to head to the bar for a drink.

'So what's tonight's occasion?' I asked Maya, sipping from an interesting vibrant blue cocktail which the barman had insisted we try.

'There are a couple of young designers showing their new collections. They are the protégés of two of the biggest names in Indian fashion, so they're likely to go far.'

'So how come they are being sponsored by the big guys?' I asked.

'A family connection, of course,' Maya said. 'You know how Mumbai is. Bollywood is one big family and the industry has its connections throughout all of the other businesses associated with films. You know, the fashion designers, the makeup artists, the production crews. Most of the Bollywood wives design jewellery or clothes, I mean some of their stuff is awful but of course their launches get write-ups on Page 3 and they get the celebrities turning out to their events en masse.'

I knew about Bollywood and its tightly knit community and its control over Page 3, the highly sought after gossip page of the Bombay Times newspaper. Most of the A list actors seemed to have the same surname and I was sure that couldn't be a coincidence. I had read occasional success stories of wannabe actors who had made it big on their own merit, and I guessed that these tales fuelled the ambitions of the thousands of aspiring actors who poured into Mumbai every year, many of whom ended up spending a fortune on auditions and bribes to get into auditions, and taking bit parts in TV commercials to survive.

'OK, let's go star spotting,' said Maya, grabbing my arm excitedly.

'I thought you worked with these people every day,' I smiled back.

'Well, I've worked on a lot of these films but I don't really get near the big stars,' she said. 'Like every Indian girl, I'm obsessed with Bollywood.'

We wandered around the room, checking out the hordes — the women were mainly dressed in Indian formal wear, sarees and fancy salwar-kameezes, and were dripping with the usual heavy jewellery, preening like peacocks. The men were clad in a mix of Indian and western clothing, some were in gorgeously ornate sherwanis and others wore beautifully tailored two- or three-piece suits with bright ties. This was the absolute upper crust of Mumbai's society: I vaguely recognized a few faces from the society pages, and I guessed that this room represented a few million pounds worth of wealth.

'Ooo, there's Hrithik. And Suzanne!' hissed Maya in my ear. I turned to see the Bollywood megastar with his wife. Having embraced Bollywood in a big way when I first arrived in Mumbai, I had soon become bored of the identikit plotlines and characters who would burst into song at the drop of a hat. I would occasionally watch one for the sheer spectacle and to pass the time, but I lacked the Indian ability to totally suspend disbelief and enter into the worlds of the jilted hero, wronged heroine or feuding family. Still, I had always thought that Hrithik was one of the more attractive male stars, with his green eyes, longish curling hair and fine features. Certainly he was streets ahead of the other buff heroes, with their six packs and their pouting, doe eyed expressions. He could really shake his stuff too, and he made those complicated dance routines look completely effortless. I stared at him and his entourage, and more critically at his wife who, I thought bitchily, was quite a plain looking girl to have snared such a star.

People started to drift in the direction of the banqueting hall, which had begun to pump out loud music, presumably a signal that the main event was about to begin.

'Quick, let's grab another drink,' I said. 'We may need one, if this goes on too long.' Clutching our newly-filled cocktails, we finally headed into the hall to find ourselves a seat. The entire place was completely packed, every seat occupied by incredibly glamorous types, with frenzied paparazzi jostling for space at the end of the ramp, trying to zoom into the expressions on the faces of the front row A listers. I squinted from our back row seats and tried to work out who was who.

Our star spotting was interrupted by the dimming of the lights and the start of the show. The event was an extravaganza, beautifully choreographed and showcasing gorgeous but impossible clothes. I'd never been to a real live fashion show before, and it was fascinating to see the gorgeous, angular models strut down the catwalk and execute lightning fast outfit changes to reappear in a matter of minutes. The styling was exquisite, although like the clothes, more suited to the ramp than to real life. I doubted whether I'd have been able to squeeze my big toe into most of the trousers, and there was no way that any of the dresses would have flattered or even fitted real women.

The show came to a deafening crescendo and the models poured out, dragging the two newbie fashion designers onto the stage. They both looked incredibly trendy but young and overwhelmed, not surprising, given the pedigree of the audience. As they blushed and fought to retain their composure they were joined by the big guys—the famous fashion duo that had taken India and now the world by storm. The front row gave a standing ovation, quickly followed by the rest of the audience, and the flashbulbs went crazy. When they'd left the stage, and the madness had subsided, we went back into the bar to carry on taking advantage of the free flowing alcohol.

'Let's get completely drunk,' said Maya. 'This is the last real bender before you go on your silly detox thing. Let's make the most of it.'

'Maya, I really don't want to drink too much,' I protested. 'I've been feeling terrible all month about my pathetic willpower, I've been drinking and partying far too much the whole of last year and I think it's time I got back into shape and I always feel so depressed after a big blowout. Plus I've got to work tomorrow.'

'I hear you,' she said, trying to empathize but not really understanding why I was making such a big deal about this. 'But let's just go nuts tonight and then I promise that I'll help you with your clean living lifestyle, OK?'

As usual, my ability to say no was weakened in the face of temptation. 'OK, just one more night then. And then I swear, I am back on the wagon.'

'Great,' Maya said happily. She turned to the barman. 'Two large vodka and diet cokes, please,' she asked him.

I took a big sip from the deliciously refreshing drink, felt the vodka hit the back of my throat and took a look around the room. The young designers were in one corner, surrounded by well-wishers and hangers-on. The A listers were in another corner, protected from the masses by their security guards and their hangers-on, and the normal people were at the bar or milling around checking out the contents of the lavish buffet and trying not to ogle the stars too conspicuously.

We finished our drinks quickly and ordered another round. I'd already decided that I might as well make the most of my last night on the town, and although I knew that I'd feel the worse for wear the next morning, and it was a working day, I'd be able to get through the day and then recover with a rigid detox over the weekend. That was the trouble with the free bar concept, what seemed like a brilliant thing during the party turned out to be a terrible curse the morning after. Unlimited drinks meant unlimited headaches, in my experience, and a relentless amount of day-after blues.

We quickly got drunk, and struggled to retain our composure. At some point in the evening, I decided that it would be a good idea to eat something, and came back from the buffet with a plate piled high with desserts. The main courses were too complicated to navigate after a few drinks, while puddings were always appealing. Buoyed up by a sugar high, we started talking animatedly to random strangers, who as always were overwhelmed by Maya's beauty and fascinated by my background. I dodged the usual set of questions about what had brought me to Mumbai and why I loved India so much. These enquiries had seemed charming when I first arrived, and I had enjoyed sharing my thoughts about Mumbai with strangers, but after more than three years of the same line of interrogation, I had become really bored of it.

Tonight Maya and I were in a mischievous mood. We decided to make up an entire story about our origins—tonight we were entrepreneurs looking to invest in business in India on behalf of our rich husbands. Business cards came flying thick and fast in our direction, and I felt vaguely guilty about misleading people, though we were having a lot of fun with our tales of global domination. One particularly repulsive man placed a sweaty arm around my shoulder and I tried not to recoil at the sight of the wet patch under his armpit. He licked his rubbery lips in a gesture that I think he thought was sexy, and which I found plain revolting. I noticed a bling encrusted wedding ring glinting on his ring finger, and tried to extricate myself politely. Maya and I now decided that a loo break was in order, and collapsed into giggles in the washroom.

'Did you see that man?' she gasped, trying to catch her breath. 'How foul was he?'

'Did I see him? Maya, he practically had his tongue down my throat. How could I miss him?' I answered, shuddering.

We spent the rest of the evening dodging the fat married man and making up more and more extravagant tales about our origins. We were both on a high, spurred on by each other's confidence, and loving the attention. I was vaguely aware that I had to be up for work in a few hours, but drunk enough not to care. At the end of the evening, we ordered one more drink for the road and then I decided that enough was enough.

'Thatsh it,' I said, in a voice which I hoped sounded determined and not just drunk. 'No more vodka for me. I'm detoxshing.'

'Sure you are,' grinned Maya. 'Come on, drop me home. I'm too drunk to take a taxi or a rickshaw now. God knows where I'll land up.'

I located my car and the ever-patient Hussain, dropped Maya, and rested my head against the cool glass. Would I ever learn, I wondered? I could already feel myself sobering up and I knew that I would really feel this the next morning.

As the alarm sounded a few hours later, I grabbed it, silenced the shrill ring and opened my eyes, feeling as though I'd hardly slept. I was completely wrapped up in my sheets, I was sweating profusely, and felt awful. My head was pounding, and I had that familiar sinking feeling inside me as the memories of the previous evening came gradually back to me, I felt disgusted with myself and my inability to say no to a night of drinking, and I felt as though I was about to fall headlong into a bottomless pit of depression.

'That's it,' I thought to myself. 'I've managed to completely screw things up. I can't stick to my resolutions even for a month, let alone a year. If I can't control myself then there's no hope for me.'

As the day progressed, and I struggled to retain my composure, and my breakfast, in the office, I reconsidered my decision to wait for a while to see if Mr Right would come to my rescue. That seemed the stuff of fiction and so I decided that it was time to think seriously about leaving the city and moving on. I'd been living the expatriate dream for more than two years, and though I'd had a lot of fun, I felt that I'd achieved very little, and that I no longer had time to waste. I would throw myself into work, and formulate an exit plan.

## 19

Work was the only thing that was going well for me now, and I figured that it would be a shame to abandon my career in Mumbai now, but knew that I had to focus on the bigger picture and ultimately my own personal happiness. My job had settled into a steady pace, it was stressful on occasion, with the usual inevitable deadlines and pressure, but nothing I couldn't handle. My love life, or lack of it, was causing me far more stress; in comparison, my work felt like a breeze. I had replaced Kiran, who had had a glamorous engagement party soon after resigning, and who was now busy planning her wedding and presumably learning to be a good housewife, with Lata, a girl who was already married, slightly older than Kiran, but whose husband also worked in the advertising industry and who seemed to be slightly more progressive in his outlook than Kiran's traditional husband-to-be. We were embarking on a new advertising campaign for the client to build the brand of shampoo that I was ultimately responsible for. I decided that this would be my last big campaign before handing in my notice and looking for a job back home. The creative team had developed scripts, the client had approved most of them, we'd gone backwards and forwards on the budgets and finally we were all set to shoot. I told Lizzie all about it as we caught up on a long overdue phone call.

'It sounds amazing,' she said, enviously.

'It sounds great,' I said, 'but it will be really hard work. Shoots are long and really tedious. The client will be there, which means that I have to babysit him, and keep him out of the way of the director who will freak if the client tries to interfere.'

'Who's the director?' asked Lizzie who pretended to be interested in these things, for my sake.

'Not sure,' I said. 'I think it's some guy from Delhi but I don't know exactly. He's bound to be a pompous egotist though, these directors all are.' I wondered whether I should tell the girls that I was thinking about leaving India, but figured that I should probably keep my news to myself, at least until I had more concrete plans.

As we prepared for the mammoth shoot, the creative team told me that the director had been selected and was flying in from Delhi to meet the team and to attend the pre-production meeting—the session where everyone came together to discuss final details for the shoot, including casting, wardrobe, location, and timelines. We all sat in the crowded meeting room, waiting for him to arrive. After fifteen minutes of making small talk and pouring coffee, the Creative Director's phone rang. 'It's Vikrant Kumar, the director,' he said. 'I need to take this. Hi Vicky. Cool, you're on your way. No, we haven't started. OK see you in ten.'

'Typical,' I thought. I bet this guy has a huge ego. He can't even be on time for his own pre-production meeting, and I bet he's being paid a fortune for this. After a further twenty-minute wait, the door flew open and in burst a slightly dishevelled figure, his shoulder length black curly hair fighting to escape the band that was attempting to hold it back, an Apple Mac laptop tucked under one arm, and a take-away coffee cup in the other hand. I looked at him, and was hit by a jolt of surprise. I knew I'd never worked with him before, but he looked strangely familiar.

'Hi, Vicky, welcome,' the Creative Director said. 'Let me introduce you to the team.' He went around the table, introducing the clients, the creative people, and finally me. Vicky gave me a curt nod, and I supposed that in his oh-so-creative world, us lowly account directors didn't really figure. The meeting started, and Vicky began to talk in a surprisingly eloquent and powerful voice. He sounded authoritative without being over opinionated, and he managed to capture the attention of the entire room with his vision for the advertisement and how he planned to shoot it. This was always my favourite part of the whole process — though I enjoyed the initial strategizing, writing the briefs and getting the creative teams excited enough to produce great scripts, I loved to see the magic happen as their work was brought to life by the director's vision. I'd worked with enough directors in India to know that the shoot itself would likely be difficult and filled with endless drama and tantrums, but I adored hearing how the pictures and words on the storyboard, the simple visual representation of the script, would look through the camera lens and eventually on TV screens in millions of households.

The meeting went well, the client confident that this Vikrant would turn his investment of several millions of rupees into a film that would encourage women to buy his range of shampoos, the details were finalized and I began to get excited about the upcoming project.

The meeting ended, everyone got up to leave, and I stood up, dropping my meeting notes as I did so. I was about to pick them up, when Vikrant, who was just in front of me, bent over and collected them into a tidy pile before handing them back to me.

'There you go,' he said in a low voice, which seemed to me to be just the right side of sexy.

'Thanks,' I said, wondering again why he seemed so familiar. I wondered whether I was just reacting to his obviously attractive looks, but I was definitely having a very strange reaction to this man, who would no doubt turn out to be as arrogant as all the rest of the directors I'd come across in my career.

I couldn't contain my excitement when I received my itinerary from the production company. I felt this was exactly what I needed to lift me from the depression that I'd sunk into after the fashion show, and I even wondered whether it might be enough to persuade me to stay on in India for a while longer. I wasn't just reacting to Mumbai, I knew that deep down my body clock, or something similar, was yelling at me to get out of this place where I'd end up some lonely old spinster.

I knew Maya was also worried about me. We had become extremely close over the past few months and I knew that she relied on me as her confidante and best friend. But more than that, I knew that she wanted me to be happy. She couldn't understand why I was stressing so much about meeting someone.

'Don't worry, you'll find someone,' she told me, over and over again. 'Besides, marriage isn't all that it's cracked up to be. Life is far better when you're single, trust me.'

I couldn't help but smile at that. 'It's OK for you, Maya, you've been married. And even though it didn't work out, and you're more or less single now, you've still been there.'

I was beginning to feel as though I had a big sign on my forehead screaming that I was desperate. The more I tried not to think about it, the more I ended up thinking about it. I couldn't help think that I'd be better off back in my own country where at least I understood the men, at least as far as any woman can understand the male psyche.

'I know what you mean. At least I think I do. Anyway, you never know, you might meet the love of your life before you leave,' she said, trying to boost my spirits.

'I doubt that very much, Maya,' I said with a laugh. I tried to explain how I felt, after being here for two long years, with no sniff of Mr Right. 'It's been disaster after disaster, and besides, I don't know if mixed marriages can even work. I know that Priyanka and Johann have a fantastic relationship, but it must be so difficult when culturally there are so many differences.'

I still felt like an outsider even though everyone tried so hard to make me feel like part of the place. I wasn't sure that Maya could really understand how I was feeling. She was at least half Indian.

I met the creative team, Siddharth and Vanita, and the client, Elmo, a Dutch expat who was responsible for the brand for the entire Asian region. He was a highly-strung, nervy man, who took his job and his responsibilities very seriously, yet he had a sweetness that showed when he let his guard down. My job during the fortnight ahead was to handle him and ensure that he didn't get too close to the director and at the same time felt that his money was being well spent. It was a difficult job, and although I'd done it many times before, I always felt like I was walking a tightrope in having to manage a complex set of egos.

The next morning I woke up bright and early, Vanita and Siddharth had left at the crack of dawn for the shoot, but cameras were only scheduled to start rolling at 9 a.m., so we had enough time for breakfast and a catch-up. Elmo was a fairly humourless type—it was my job to make sure that he remained relaxed throughout the shoot, and that he didn't try to interfere too much. Most clients failed to understand the complexities of the shooting process and didn't realize that what they saw being shot on set would look completely different once it had been edited, graded and put through the complex post-production process. Some clients fancied themselves as budding directors and those were always the most difficult to manage. Elmo had been trained well by the multinational corporation he worked for, and generally respected the roles of the agency and the production company, though it could still be extremely frustrating trying to explain certain creative fundamentals to him. I knew that I had a tough few days ahead of me, and so I ate well from the lavish buffet, knowing I'd need the energy.

'So what is this director like?' asked Elmo as we ploughed through our omelettes.

'I don't know much about him, to be honest,' I answered. 'I know he's done a lot of great work, and the creative team has been raving about him. He's just starting to make a name for himself in India and he seemed very organized in the pre-production meeting. I'm sure he'll do a great job with the script.'

We arrived on the set bang on time, to find the cameras ready to roll. I was a little surprised that the shoot would start on time, my experience of most shoots in India was that they would inevitably start a couple of hours late, particularly if celebrities were involved, as they invariably liked to throw their weight around and show how important they were by turning up late or keeping everyone waiting by taking ages in hair and makeup. I found a spot for Elmo and me to watch without getting in the way of the action, and we settled down, storyboards and Blackberries in hand.

The complexity and cost of a shoot for a TV advertisement never ceased to amaze me. Everyone on set had a very specific role and responsibility, there was always a vast number of people running around lifting and fetching and carrying cameras and setting up equipment, and the director would sit right in the middle of the action, like the conductor of a huge orchestra. I could see Vicky, our director, sitting in his chair, scrutinizing the opening shots on a small TV set, which would play back the action for him to review. His long hair was again fighting to escape from the band he'd carelessly tied it with, and he was wearing a long-sleeved white T-shirt and jeans.

The morning passed slowly, like all shoots, as the same action sequences were repeated time and time again until the director was completely happy, and his shout of 'cut' was heard. Finally, we broke for lunch, and I took Elmo to the makeshift area that had been set up with a mobile canteen, tables and chairs. Catering on set was usually incredibly good, the theory being that you needed to endlessly feed cast and crew to get the best out of them. The shoots themselves were so boring to watch that I usually found myself picking endlessly at the goodies provided between meals, and invariably ended the day overfull.

As we sat down, Vikrant walked towards us, carrying a full tray. 'Do you mind if I join you guys? I have to run through the afternoon's sequences with the team once I've finished lunch, but I have ten minutes or so to eat.'

'Sure,' I said, thinking how remarkable it was that a director should actually choose to sit with the client and the agency suit. We were usually the uncool guys, left on the outside while the creative types bonded over in-jokes. As we chatted about how the morning had gone, I scrutinized Vikrant, or Vicky as he preferred to be called, from behind the safety of my sunglasses. He had a kind, open face, with smooth skin that crinkled slightly around the eyes and mouth when he talked. His eyes were the darkest brown, almost black, and his gaze, when it fell upon you, was direct, as though he were focusing his attention completely. His nose was straight, his face longish with chiseled cheekbones which gave him a slightly distinguished look, and which contrasted with his mass of hair and his thrown-together look. I liked the curly long black hair. His teeth were white and straight, and his lips surprisingly soft and full. I caught myself staring at his mouth and pulled myself back with a jerk. I hoped that my sunglasses were dark enough to hide the fact that I'd been studying his face, and paying particular attention to his mouth.

I felt myself blushing and turned my head to look at Elmo, who was in the middle of describing the way his latest shampoo product was flying off the shelves. Vicky was giving Elmo his full attention, and I appreciated his efforts, especially as I knew that it would help my often uptight client relax, safe in the knowledge that his marketing budget and his precious brand were in good hands. After a few more minutes had passed, Vicky pushed aside his half-eaten plateful of noodles. 'Right, no rest for the wicked. I'd better get going, we need to set up for the afternoon's shots.

See you guys later.' I guessed that he'd forgotten my name, and tried not to feel bad about it, though that small omission left me feeling ridiculously disappointed.

The shoot went exactly as planned, and even Elmo was happy. My job there had been relatively relaxed, with an organized crew, a friendly director, and a calm client, my work had been straightforward. On the final evening, we all met for dinner at a hotel—a relaxed affair, we all had a couple of drinks but were careful not to overdo it—that would come at the end of the shoot when our work was finished. I sat next to Elmo with Siddharth on the other side, and we made polite and relaxed conversation. I could see Vicky across the other side of the table, deep in conversation for most of the evening with the producer, whose job it was to ensure that everything happened on time and on budget. I definitely found him attractive, but I didn't dwell on that. Now that I'd decided to leave India, it was pointless chasing after a man who anyway lived between Delhi and Mumbai when I'd be thousands of miles away. Besides, I had no more energy for the inevitable cultural clashes, even if he did find me attractive in turn, which I figured was highly unlikely.

## 20

As we wrapped the final shot, and the crew began to dismantle the heavy equipment, which had cost a small fortune to rent, Vicky hugged the creative team and shook the client's hand.

'I can't wait to see the finished product,' Elmo said, as animated as I'd ever seen him. Even his typically taut, conservative and sceptical nature had been replaced by an uncharacteristic enthusiasm. I hoped that the rest of the process would go as smoothly—the difficulties with creating any ad film invariably came at the post-production stage, when the film was being edited and the hours of laboriously shot footage were condensed into a mere minute, if you were lucky to have a client who was prepared to pay that much for a longer spot and had bigger budgets to fund more media time. Most insisted on thirty-second edits, which rendered the agency's job almost impossible—condensing hours of footage into a few seconds and keeping everyone happy meant inevitable differences of opinion and arguments. For the time being though, I didn't think about the difficulties ahead but focused on enjoying this moment, watching the sun set slowly over a beautiful landscape, surrounded by happy people who were celebrating a job, my job, well done.

That evening, it was clear that we were celebrating. The

production manager booked a huge table at a relaxed local restaurant overlooking the sea, which served delicious Goan food. By fate or perhaps my subconscious design, I ended up sitting next to Vicky, which I was ridiculously pleased about. I hadn't really spoken to him since our brief meeting and although I was still feeling uncharacteristically star struck by him, and slightly overwhelmed in his presence, I had the strangest sense of wanting to connect with him somehow.

'Hey,' he murmured in his low and strangely sexy voice as we sat down at the table laden with snacks and glasses, 'I haven't seen you for a while. What have you been up to?'

'Keeping my client away from you, mainly,' I answered with a grin. 'I know you were having some problems on set, so I thought it better that we stay out of your way.'

'Thanks for that,' he smiled. 'The last thing I needed was an agitated client to deal with on top of all the other problems.'

'So has it gone well so far?' I asked.

'It's actually gone brilliantly,' he smiled. 'I mean it's a great script with a decent budget, so we are starting from a fantastic place for a change, but so far the shoot has gone to plan and we've got some great footage.'

'So how many shoots have you worked on?' I asked, aware that I was sounding like a fan. 'Hundreds,' he said, with a laugh, 'but this is one of the most complicated given the number of sets and the different countries that we have to shoot in.'

Suddenly, I was fascinated to know more about this man, who seemed such a paradox. He was friendly without being overbearing, warm without being gushing and completely at odds with the uptight and egotistic directors who I'd encountered previously.

'Would you like something to drink?' he asked.

'I'd love some wine if they have any, or if not I'll just have a beer,' I replied, dying for something to take the edge of the nervousness I inexplicably felt. With my glass topped up with wine, which turned out to be surprisingly delicious, I felt myself relax. As he filled his own glass, Vikrant turned to me for a 'cheers' with a cheeky look in his eye.

'We've met before, you know. Before this job I mean.'

'We have?' I asked, trying to sound calm and collected, hoping that he couldn't tell that I was inexplicably nervous.

'On the dance floor at the Taj. You were with a rather possessive young man, and I rescued you from almost certain embarrassment.'

'Oh my god,' I breathed. 'You were the guy who caught me when I was about to fall flat on my face? I knew you looked familiar the first time I saw you.'

I stopped abruptly, feeling the heat rise in my cheeks. 'I can't believe you remembered me. It was dark and I was ...'

'Drunk?' said Vicky, with a smile.

'Well yes, I suppose so,' I said sheepishly.

'Don't worry, you were fine. I thought it was kind of cute. So how is the boyfriend these days?'

'No longer my boyfriend, I'm pleased to say. It all ended rather badly, but let me not bore you with all that.'

I desperately wanted to ask about his girlfriend, the long legged model type who'd been hanging possessively onto his arm, but thought it might seem a bit obvious.

'So, tell me more about yourself,' asked Vikrant. Now that we'd broken the ice, I felt comfortable in sharing more about my life. 'Well, I'm from the UK, I worked in advertising for a few years before I was offered this job in Mumbai and I leapt at the chance to try something new. I moved here over two years ago and I've loved it.'

'Really? And did you know people here before you came?' he asked, sounding genuinely interested.

'No, I didn't know a soul when I got here. I've made friends of course, but I think that's helped me really make the most of my experience.'

'Wow, that's brave. Mumbai is tough for us locals, let alone for foreigners who come here without friends and family.'

'Well I've made quite a lot of friends,' I said, keen to correct the impression that I might be coming across as a sad, lonely figure. 'Mumbai is a very sociable place, and it's been fairly easy to fit in.'

'I bet you get asked this all the time, but what's your favourite thing about India?' he asked.

I thought for a while. 'I suppose if you get beyond all the clichés about the colours and the sights and sounds, my favourite thing has to be the fact that everyone here just seems so positive,' I said.

'And they're not back in England?' he asked with a smile.

'Well, we do have a reputation of being a nation of whiners and I think to a certain extent that is justified,' I replied. 'When I go back to visit, it just seems that everyone is completely wrapped up in their own issues and problems and making a huge deal about how difficult life is, and then I come back here and I see people who genuinely have a lot to moan about but who persistently look on the bright side.'

'I know what you mean. People here just refuse to take no for an answer, but, believe me, that can be exhausting as well.'

'Well, neither extreme is perfect,' I said, 'but I know which I'd rather be surrounded by. I hate negativity and I think that was one of the things that drove me away from England in the first place. Even when I read some of the English newspapers now, they seem to be filled with doom and gloom, whereas the Mumbai press seems to put a more happier spin on things. Even a few people dying in a road accident is described as a mishap, as though life has to go on despite death and destruction, which of course it does. People here are not fickle about life and death, they're just realistic. And I honestly find that refreshing.'

I wondered if he'd think I was mad, banging on about death and mishaps.

'But most Westerners come here for completely opposite reasons,' he said with a smile. 'They come here to find themselves, to seek spiritual answers to deep questions, to discover the meaning of life.'

'That's true,' I replied, 'and there is a lot of depth to Indian tradition and belief, but Indians don't all spend their days meditating and making deep and meaningful connections. They are preoccupied with the minutiae of life, just as we all are, and ironically are perhaps more self-obsessed and money-orientated than any Westerner, I guess because their world lacks that fundamental safety net called the welfare state which we enjoy back home. So, it's dog eat dog, and the spiritual stuff has to wait.'

'That's a very interesting interpretation,' came the response, and I wondered whether I'd gone too far in suggesting that his country was somehow lacking in values and beliefs. I struggled to correct myself.

'I don't mean that people are shallow, don't get me wrong. Just that unlike the stereotyped beliefs that many Westerners have, and all of the books that bang on about finding the answers in yoga and meditation and the ancient rituals, actually people here are driven by materialism and the present and the need to succeed and of course to feed their families, and they just get on and do all of that without whining about how crappy life is, and that's kind of refreshing.'

'You've obviously got to know India pretty well,' Vikrant said in what I hoped was an admiring tone. 'And what about all of the things that most Westerners can't handle — the dirt and the poverty and the crowded streets and the traffic and the lack of queuing?'

'Well I'd be lying if I said that that didn't get to me, especially after being here for a while. But I've developed my own systems to cope with all of those things, and of course I'm lucky enough that I live in a quietish area with air-conditioning in my apartment, and I live on my own so I can always close the door on all that.'

We talked on as the wine flowed and the food kept arriving, and I realized that I was opening up to Vikrant and letting my defences down. He had an uncanny ability to cut through any pretence or formality and I felt very relaxed and comfortable with him, as though we'd been friends for a long time. I wanted to ask him about his life, particularly about his personal life, and wondered whether he was married. He wasn't wearing a ring, though that didn't necessarily mean anything in India, and he hadn't talked about a girlfriend or wife, but there was no way I was going to ask him and risk coming across as though I was interested in him. I wasn't, and anyway I was leaving India and so getting into a relationship or even a flirtation was the last thing on my mind.

We talked about Delhi versus Mumbai, he told me that he'd been born and brought up in Delhi, that his family were all still based in the North but that he pretty much lived between Delhi and Mumbai where most of his work was based. He was thinking about moving permanently to Mumbai but hadn't had the time to look for a place to live, so invariably ended up staying with friends or living out of cheap hotels. He had travelled extensively, had studied in the US for a couple of years, though I was relieved to note than unlike my disastrous internet date Hari, hadn't picked up the local accent, nor did he give the impression of being star-struck by the West. In fact, he seemed more and more down to earth as we talked, and I wondered whether we'd become friends and stay in touch after the shoot was over.

Eventually dessert was served, and the producer came up and tugged on Vicky's arm. 'I need to talk to you about the final production timing plan.'

'Can't it wait?' asked Vikrant with a smile. 'I was in the middle of an interesting conversation.'

'Actually, I need to get back to the team with the final plan, and we need to book some stuff so it kind of has to be now so I can get the schedule locked.'

'No rest for the wicked,' sighed Vikrant with a smile which I thought was tinged with regret. 'OK Julia, it was lovely talking to you. I guess I'll see you again when we come to present the final film to the agency.'

'Sure,' I smiled, disappointed that our conversation had come to an end, though simultaneously basking in the knowledge that we'd spent the best part of two hours talking. I had enjoyed every moment of our discussion and had loved the fact that it had been so relaxed and that the conversation had flowed.

That night in bed, I tried not to dwell obsessively on the memories of Vikrant's curly, almost springy long hair and the way his eyebrows bunched together when he asked a question. I completely avoided thinking about his animated smile, and the way his dark eyes had locked onto mine as he'd asked me intently about my life and about my plans. Obviously he was being friendly, but there was no reason why I should start obsessing about him, or reading more into our interaction than a desire to make polite conversation, a superficial attention which he'd have paid to anyone else on the set.

## 21

Back to my regular routine following the shoot, I carefully composed an e-mail to my former boss James, who thankfully was still in London and whom I'd been in touch with sporadically during the past three years with chatty, optimistic updates on my life and on my work. I wrote asking whether he had any openings back in the London office and explained that I'd actually spent a year longer than I'd initially planned in Mumbai, that I'd had a wonderful experience and done some great work for the client whom I'd been sent to handle, but that it was time for me to think about coming home and getting back on track in London.

I hoped that my Mumbai experience would mean that I'd be given a promotion and more money back in London, but honestly I wasn't really bothered. I'd decided that as long as my work stayed on track, I'd focus on trying to sort out my disastrous love life before it became too late. Somehow, I imagined myself landing back in London to a bevvy of eligible men, eager to hear my exotic tales from the Orient. I knew deep down that it wouldn't be like that, I had heard enough stories from Annabel in particular to know that the pool of eligible men dwindled significantly after the age of thirty and I wondered for the hundredth time whether

I'd done the right thing by leaving at that critical age, and missing out on those important years on the dating scene.

James wrote back telling me that there might be a position coming up in three to four months time, that I would need to let him know within a month whether I was definitely interested so that he could hold it open for me. Part of me recoiled from returning to London and my old life. I knew that many of my friends had moved on in the past couple of years, some of them had become distant and uncommunicative, some, like Annabel and Lizzie, had worked hard to stay in touch, others I'd be able to pick up contact with once I arrived back.

I wondered whether the office would be the same or whether it would feel different. I'd become used to a more aggressive working culture, a style where feelings were voiced openly and where arguments and disagreements were commonplace and tempers were lost quickly. Though there were frequent flare-ups, these were quickly calmed, and fights would turn to friendship in the blink of an eye. India was a country where resentment and anger rarely seemed to simmer for long, although I had heard of family feuds that lasted for years. Office politics, for the most part, were more about letting off steam and venting the frustration caused by intensely stressful living conditions. England was the opposite. Though London wasn't easy to navigate, and travelling could be as stressful as Mumbai if you got caught on the tube at rush hour, people kept their irritations to themselves, bottling up their feelings until they festered and became toxic. Looking back with a fresh perspective, I realized how bitter many people in my home country actually were. Somehow, there existed a collective sense that life wasn't fair, and this manifested itself in many ways, from the more obvious whinging about life's hardships, to the more subtle office politics and complex games that played themselves out in workplaces across the country. I wondered whether I'd now be seen as too brash, too argumentative and too loud—I'd had to adapt myself to Mumbai or risk my voice being lost in the commotion which never seemed to calm. I still retained a great deal of my English reserve, but I'd learned how to push to get to the front, how to take on the queue jumpers and how to shout at the top of my voice, literally, to be heard during raucous meetings. I guessed that I'd eventually adapt back again; just as I'd acclimatized to Mumbai, I'd learn to live back in London again. The question remained, did I really want to?

I was tempted to tell James immediately that I was definitely interested in the job, but decided to make myself wait a month, to let my thoughts settle a little and my head to clear. The last thing I wanted was to make a commitment that I'd end up backing out of, and I wondered whether finally I'd end up pitting my heart against my head in making my big decision. I also needed to tell the office in Mumbai that I'd be heading back and I figured that they'd need some time to find a replacement, but I didn't want to get them started on that task as yet. For the time being I needed to focus on the immediate task on hand—ensuring that the post-production for the advertisement went smoothly, and that Elmo was happy with the final product which had cost him the best part of a quarter of a million pounds, if you counted all the versions and edits that were required.

Siddharth and Vanita huddled up with the producer and Vicky for a fortnight working on the edits and adding the special effects that would bring the film to life. I wasn't allowed anywhere near the studio, and my job was to manage the timelines and keep Elmo ready for the presentation of the film and handle any differences of opinion on the edits. Meanwhile, there was a fair amount of work to be done on the day-to-day business, and I also scheduled a catch-up with Maya over dinner at Indigo.

As I waited at the bar for her to turn up, I couldn't help but think back to that evening almost three years earlier, when I'd come here with Johann and ended up meeting the disastrously intentioned Krishna. I'd come to the bar, knowing virtually no one in town and feeling like an outsider. These days, it seemed like I knew everyone, and I felt as though I belonged here, for the most part. Now that I was seriously thinking about leaving the city, I couldn't help obsessing over the past, and over the life that I'd created for myself. I wondered whether that first drink in Indigo years back had set a pattern for me, perhaps I should have been more selective and not jumped for the first guy who had shown any interest in me. Perhaps I should have refused all advances, got to learn more about the city and the way it worked, and then started dating. Maybe I had just been hanging out in all the wrong places, perhaps I had just been trying too hard. My mind was in a whirl, and I couldn't sort through the complex feelings that were rushing through it. I decided that one of the barman's famous mango mojitos would do the trick in settling some of the angst, so I ordered two, one each for Maya and me, and went to wait at the table I'd booked.

'So, tell me all about the shoot,' she said animatedly, as she sat down a few minutes later. I gave her a rundown of how well everything had gone and how satisfied the client was.

'That's it? That's all you have to tell me?' she asked in mock surprise. 'I think you've missed out the important stuff. Come on, dish the gossip.'

I must have blushed, as she pounced on me. 'I knew it. There is gossip. Tell, tell.'

'There's nothing to tell, honestly. We were all working really hard, there was hardly any socializing, my client behaved himself, and the crew were sweet.'

'No, I don't believe you,' she said with a wicked look in her eye. 'Something else happened. You look kind of different. Weird. Hopeful. Happy. Something.'

I knew that I couldn't fool my perceptive friend for long, plus I was dying to talk about Vicky. 'OK, well, I did get to know the director a little bit and he was fun and kind of interesting.'

'Interesting? You mean you fancied him? I'm not surprised, directors always have that whole power thing going on during a shoot and everyone is flapping around them and they're the centre of attention. Very appealing.'

'No, he wasn't like that at all,' I said, feeling strangely defensive of Vikrant. 'He was actually really sweet and quite gentle and considerate, despite the fact that he's obviously pretty successful in his field. So we chatted a couple of times and I sat next to him at dinner. That's all.'

'Are you sure?' she asked, mischievously.

'Completely sure. Anyway, you know that I've decided to leave so it would be completely pointless getting into something else now. Plus, with all of my experience in dating Indian men, I can tell you that the whole thing would be a disaster. I just don't think different cultures mix very well when it comes to relationships.'

'What about Johann and Priyanka?' she asked.

'Well, they are an exception. I mean, for a German guy he's super chilled and she's a total international babe, and perhaps it's easier when the woman is Indian and the guy is European. I don't know, something just tells me that Indian men and European women spell disaster together.'

'Well, never say never,' she grinned, taking a huge slurp of the margarita. 'Look at my parents for a start. They've been together forever. Besides, they always say that love creeps up on you when you stop looking.'

I changed the subject and we started gossiping about friends we had in common and the whole Bombay party scene. I couldn't help thinking about what she'd said, though, and I realized that I was becoming a teeny bit obsessed with Vicky.

The next week I was called to the studio for the first reveal of the film. Though I was at the bottom of the agency pecking order when it came to seeing the creative product, I was the one who would have to reassure the client that it was a great ad, and manage any nervousness or doubts on his part, so eventually they had to show it to me. Siddharth smiled broadly as I pushed open the heavy door to the claustrophobic editing suite. I looked around the darkened room — Vanita was sitting on the sofa chewing her nails, and Vicky was on the edge of the editing table, looking relaxed and happy, with his long hair down around his shoulders. I tried not to stare at him.

'Hey there,' he smiled up at me. 'It's the person whose opinion really counts. If you like the film, then I'm sure the client will. This is an important one.'

I was used to being treated like the poorest relation by the director and I felt stupidly flattered by his words. 'Well, I'm sure it will be fantastic and the client will love it. I've been waiting for this moment for ages. Come on, let's see it.'

The editor hit a button, and the film started to roll on the enormous flatscreen in front of me.

The scenes were mesmerizing in their depth and colour, and the attention to detail was astounding. The film ran for a mere sixty seconds, and when the final super or title appeared, I felt the excitement that always comes with a great first cut, and realized that I was a little lost for words.

'Well?' asked Vicky, clearly impatient to hear my opinion.

'It's fantastic,' I said, my heart beating and my body rushing with adrenalin. 'Honestly. It's not only gorgeous, but the product is right in there, and not in a clumsy way. I'm sure the client will love it!'

I could hear everyone breathing a metaphorical sigh of relief and I was thankful that I wouldn't have to get into a fight at this early stage about packshots and product—the client's agenda of course was always to make sure that his product was seen as much as possible; after all, that was what he was paying for. The creative team and director usually wanted to keep the product out as much as possible, figuring that it compromised on creativity and too many shots of the packaging would lose the viewer. The team had done a fantastic job with this ad though, there seemed to be just the right balance between product and emotion, and even the brief demo sequence, was mandatory for all ads for this particular brand, didn't seem to get in the way.

'Are you sure you're not just saying that?' Vicky asked.

'No,' said Sid. 'You can trust Julia to speak her mind. She's as Indian as all of us when it comes to being direct, there's no polite

Brit left in her.' I smiled inwardly at what seemed like a bizarre but genuine compliment.

'OK then,' said Vicky. 'Next step, client. Hope it goes well. Good luck!'

With that, I realized I was being dismissed and felt stupidly disappointed. I felt as though this was the last chance I'd have to see Vicky again, we had no more meetings scheduled and it wouldn't be as though we'd get the chance to work on another project together now that I was leaving.

I called Elmo to let him know that the film was finished, and set up a date and time for the presentation. Sid and Vanita would attend with me, but it would be my job to 'sell' the film, to do the setup and to take comments and feedback. This was the part that I was good at, managing the client's nerves, reassuring him about minor changes, persuading him to be brave when he needed to be, and knowing when to concede and agree to changes when they were required. I often felt like I was walking a tightrope, trying to maintain the delicate balance between keeping the client and the creative team happy, but I'd always been good at communicating and smoothing over problems, and I enjoyed the challenge.

The meeting date arrived and Vanita, Sid and I sat nervously waiting for Elmo to arrive. This was by far the biggest film I had ever presented, and I desperately wanted to avoid the need for endless re-edits and re-work, which would totally demoralize the team and take the joy out of the project. I knew that Elmo was a conservative client, but I figured that having him along on the shoot had helped to manage his expectations, besides which the edit I'd seen was fabulous and I couldn't see how he'd be able to pick holes in it. As I concluded my opening summary, reminding Elmo about the campaign objectives and strategy, and the way we'd agreed that we wanted the film to look and feel, I stood back, pressed play and tried not to stare at his face for signs for a reaction. Sixty seconds passed quickly, and Elmo's expression remained impassive.

'One more time please,' he requested curtly in his heavily accented English. I shot a look at Sid, trying to beam waves of reassurance and 'don't stress, he's always like this' vibes in his direction.

Once again, Elmo's face remained blankly impassive. As I pressed stop on the machine, he started to clap, slowly at first and then more animatedly.

'Bravo!' he smiled. 'It is simply outstanding. Of course we will need to increase the length of the packshots in a couple of the scenes, but overall I love it.'

I could hardly believe that Elmo was actually gushing. My teutonic, uptight anally retentive client was actually pouring praise on our efforts and, though I had hoped for a positive response, I was overwhelmed by this reaction. Sid and Vanita broke into broad smiles, Vanita looking happier than I'd seen her in weeks.

'That's great,' I sighed, offering a silent vote of heartfelt thanks to whichever gods had smiled upon us. 'So, I'm sure we can work out the specifics of a little extra time on the packshots, right guys? But it looks like we're good to go.'

'I'd better go and call Vicky,' said Sid. 'He's dying to know how the presentation went.'

At the mention of his name, I felt my stomach flipping and

217

was hit by the realization that I really liked this man. Not only did I find him attractive, but I also found him warm, witty and mesmerizing. It was a good job that our paths wouldn't cross again and that I'd be able to get him out of my thoughts soon enough. I tried to yank my thoughts from Vicky and his dark, intelligent eyes and the smile that played across his lips from time to time, back to the matter at hand. This was the culmination of months of hard work and it was a great way to end my time in Mumbai.

## 22

I decided to break the news of my impending return to Annabel and Lizzie, knowing that that would make everything seem more real, and give me something to focus on. I called Lizzie first, she was the more sensible one of the two and I knew that I could rely on her for an honest and sensible opinion.

'Hi, Lizzie. It's me.'

'Jules! How lovely to hear your voice. I was just thinking about you, it's been a while since we chatted.'

'I know,' I said, feeling guilty that I'd let a few weeks pass since my last call. 'How are things? How is that lovely boyfriend of yours?'

Lizzie and her boyfriend Richard had been together since university. He was a sweet, if slightly reserved cerebral type, who seemed perpetually amazed that he'd landed this smart, sassy girl who'd gone on to become a successful lawyer. Despite their obvious differences, their relationship had gone from strength to strength, and I was more than a little envious that they'd found each other so effortlessly, and avoided all of the pitfalls of the dating scene.

'He's as awesome as ever,' said Lizzie. 'He's been really busy with work but as always he still manages to find time to pay me attention. I can't believe how lucky I am to have him sometimes.

I know people say that I'm boring for still being with my first ever serious boyfriend, but so what?'

'Well, I'm sure they're just jealous,' I said, feeling a pang of envy course through me.

'So what about you?' she asked. 'Any romance in your life? Have you been whisked off your feet by that tall dark handsome Indian man yet?'

'No, nothing like that,' I said. 'To be honest Lizzie, my experiences with men here have been pretty disastrous. So much so, in fact, I'm thinking about coming back home.'

'Really? That's amazing. It would be fantastic to have you back here, but are you sure you're making the right decision? It can't be all about the lack of available men, surely.' I heard echoes of Maya's words in her voice.

'It's not just about the fact that I've not managed to meet anyone here, Lizzie,' I said. 'It's more the feeling I've got that I'm wasting my time here, throwing away those important years when I should be out and about on the dating scene, and I've kind of given up thinking I'll ever meet anyone here. I mean, I didn't come here with the intention of getting into a relationship, but I've had a couple of bad experiences with men, and I think I've just come to realize, finally, that although I think I'm really settled here and connected and treated like I belong, when it comes down to it I'll always be the outsider and I don't want to sit on the sidelines waiting and watching while everyone else I know gets settled into cosy couples. It's also hard here, constantly being on my guard, continually having to translate not only what people say but what they really mean. Plus I miss you guys like mad.'

'But coming back here to London doesn't mean you'll meet someone, necessarily,' replied the ever practical Lizzie.

'I know that, but at least it feels as though I'll have a fighting chance, that I won't be butting my head against the inevitable cultural issues. I mean, I think I know enough about Indian society now to know that even if some lovely man decides that he likes me, his mother certainly won't, and the family for sure won't welcome a foreigner into their midst. It's all very well having white friends and we're great for dropping into conversations when there are people to be impressed, but when it comes to marriage, that's kind of sacred and we foreigners don't really get a look in. Even if I met someone who didn't care what their parents thought, and that's highly unlikely, it would still be an uphill battle.'

I guessed that she could hear the resignation in my voice. 'Well that's sad in a way, but I suppose you've been out there for a while and it will be great for you to reconnect with people back here again. Can't wait to have you back.'

'Thanks Lizzie,' I said, feeling a whole lot better and grateful to have such genuine friends with whom I could just pick up the pieces and move on, even after a long physical separation. I wondered how many of my Mumbai friends would stay in touch; I guessed Maya and I would be friends forever but most of the rest would probably fall by the wayside once I was out of sight.

Annabel was similarly concerned for me, yet delighted with my news. As always, she didn't hold back when it came to telling me what she thought.

'I told you from the beginning that going after Indian men would be a disaster. I mean, come on. I've seen enough Bollywood movies to know that the guy always marries the good girl, and I don't think they count English women on their list of possible matrimonial targets. Besides, though I thought that Krishna wasn't bad looking, at least from the photos, they'll all revert to type after a few years, as the moustaches and pot bellies come out.'

'Annabel stop it,' I laughed despite myself. 'That's so mean. There are loads of handsome older Indian guys. Look at Amitabh Bachchan for one. Or Shah Rukh Khan.'

'They are movie stars,' she said firmly. 'Therefore an exception to the rule.'

Both calls made me feel better. I started thinking about my imminent return home, trying to get excited about summer afternoons in the park, wine that didn't cost me a fortune or taste like it had been blended with vinegar, meetings that were polite and conversations that were gentle and wouldn't leave me feeling exhausted and aggressive.

A couple of days later, my phone rang with an unknown number. Thinking it would probably be a spam call from a bank or someone trying to get me to sign up for a health insurance policy, I answered the phone with a curt 'Yes?' I heard a familiar voice which I couldn't place.

'Are you always this pleased to hear from people?'

'Er, who's this?'

'This is Vikrant, Vicky. Your director and creator of the shampoo masterpiece that has brought fame and glory on your agency.' I could hear the laughter in his voice as I almost dropped my coffee in surprise.

'Oh, hi Vicky, I'm so sorry…I didn't recognize the number…I thought it was a spam call. Anyway, how are you? Are you calling about the film? I'm sure you heard that the client loved it.' I was aware that I was babbling like an idiot, but I'd been caught completely unawares.

'No, I'm actually calling to see if you'd like to meet for a coffee or maybe lunch if you're free. I'm in Mumbai for a couple of days and thought it would be fun to hang out and carry on that conversation.'

I could feel myself blushing dark red and was thankful that I was alone at home. 'Er, sure, why not?' I answered, trying to recover my composure.

'Great. So save my number and I'll buzz you when I arrive. Let's tentatively say coffee on Saturday afternoon, after my meeting gets done.'

'OK, sounds great,' I said weakly. As he cut the call I found myself wondering why on earth he'd called in the first place but strangely excited that he had. I wondered whether he was interested in me, or whether he just had some time to kill and thought it might be fun to meet. Trying not to think too much into things, I put Vicky, Saturday, coffee into my electronic diary and started to wonder what to wear.

He called again on Friday afternoon and we arranged to meet for a late afternoon coffee at The Taj Lands End hotel in Bandra, the sister concern of the Taj Mahal Hotel, which had seen the horrific terrorist attack a few years earlier. The Taj hotels were a little grander than my usual hangouts but he was here for meetings with another agency team and was being put up at their expense, presumably they were trying to woo him to direct an ad for them—an expensive hotel was considered a suitably appropriate means of helping snag a highly sought after director.

I dressed carefully in what I hoped was the right balance of casual and cool, and set out to meet him, my palms strangely clammy and hoping that we'd find something to talk about without any awkward silences. He was already waiting for me in the busy bar area, and was looking even more attractive than I'd remembered. I couldn't put my finger on what I found so interesting about him, looks-wise. All that long, slightly unruly hair gave him a wild, creative look which appealed, and there was something about his face that made me feel like confiding in him. I wasn't sure whether it was his eyes, which had a gentle look about them suggesting hidden depth, the not quite chiseled look of his cheekbones, or the fact that it was all thrown together and just seemed to work. I'd sneaked the odd cheeky look at the rest of him when he hadn't been looking, and had noted that he had a good body, slim but not skinny and with no sign of the paunchy belly that I'd come to associate with many Indian men.

I couldn't help but think that he was out of my league. Though I'd been told I was cute looking, I thought that my looks were pretty average, certainly when I compared myself to all the exotic beauties I seemed to come across in Mumbai. He greeted me with the European double kiss and we sat down.

'How are you?' he asked. 'I hope you don't mind me calling on you like this?'

'Not at all,' I replied, wondering if he had a specific agenda in mind for our meeting, or whether it was genuinely a casual catch-up. 'It's nice to see you again.'

'So, what have you been up to?' he asked. I played along, wondering if he would eventually turn to the reason for our meeting.

'Not a lot actually,' I said. 'Pretty busy with work, but of course the fact that your film was such a success has made things a little easier all round. We're busy planning for next year's activity and you know how these clients like to endlessly make schedules and budgets, which invariably end up changing, but which keep us on our toes.'

'So how long have you been in advertising?' he asked.

'About nine years now,' I answered. 'Long enough to start wondering if I'll get stuck doing this forever but not long enough to have got bored of it yet.'

'And what made you come out to India to work?' he asked. I trotted out the usual spiel about being offered a job here. 'I felt like I'd hit an early mid-life crisis, somehow. I mean I was happy enough, and life was pretty good by most people's standards, but something was missing. I don't know what it was, and I still don't really know, but I do know that I've come closer here to being happy and fulfilled than I was in London.'

'So you're not completely happy here then?' he asked. I hesitated, not wanting to come across as moany or as a stereotypically whinging foreigner.

'Well, I love it here. I've made some good friends and I think Mumbai is the most incredible city. But somehow, I just feel that it might be time to think about moving back. I guess I'm missing my friends and family back home.'

I left it there, not wanting to go into the details of my deeper loneliness or my feelings that I was missing out on finding love and settling down. I didn't want to make him think that I was lonely or desperate, preferring instead to paint a picture of myself as a curious world traveller who wanted to return home for a while.

'That's a shame,' he said, with what I thought was a touch of regret in his voice. 'Mumbai needs more sorted people, and I love the international feel that is being created by all the foreigners who are coming here to work. India certainly isn't for everyone but it's great if you can manage to find your way here.'

'That's true. Anyway I haven't made up my mind completely but I have a couple of weeks to decide. So what about you, have you travelled much?'

'Well, like all good Indian parents, mine wanted to send me abroad to study. My father is in the army so I was a bit of an army brat, dragged all over the country, so I was very used to moving around. I graduated from Delhi University and then went to New York to study film at NYU. My parents wanted me to be a doctor or an engineer of course, but I desperately wanted to get into filmmaking, so after a bit of a fight, and a few tears from my Mum, they agreed to let me pursue my dream. I took a loan from them to study and I paid them back in five years.'

I knew how hard Indian parents pushed their children to study 'traditional' courses and pursue safe careers, and I was impressed that he'd followed his dream, and that he had obviously made a success of what he'd done so far.

'So how was it coming back to India after you finished studying?' I asked. 'Didn't you want to stay in New York? Most Indians seem to want to leave India.'

'Not really,' he answered. 'I could always see the potential in India, and things were starting to really change here a decade ago. There was, and still is, energy and an incredible entrepreneurial spirit as well as a can-do attitude here. I love Europe and some parts of the US but I just find things easier and more comfortable here, which is ironic really.'

'I know exactly how you feel,' I said excitedly. ' It's like you can do anything if you put your mind to it. And the usual things that would faze people back home, like a bit of dirt, a lot of poverty and the absence of systems, seem to be minor impediments here.'

I realized that I was sounding a bit like a spoiled expat, so I added, 'Of course these are things that do cause misery to millions. But somehow, despite all that, there's a just get on with it kind of attitude. There's no time to moan about hardship, people don't have the luxury of feeling sorry for themselves, and so they just get on with things, turning negatives into positives. At least that's the way I see things.'

'Interesting. So you still want to leave, despite feeling like that?'

I was aware that I was sounding like a bit of a hypocrite but I wasn't willing to share my real reasons for wanting to leave.

'Yes, I think so,' I told him. 'At least for a while, anyway. And then, let's see what happens.'

We carried on talking for another couple of hours, the conversation was flowing and there were few silences. The backdrop was gorgeous—the hotel looked right out over the sea and the sun was beginning to set, casting a romantic hue across the room. Vicky told me that his parents were strict but caring, traditional yet modern in some ways, that they were Hindus but not terribly devout, and that he had a younger brother and sister as well an older sister. His sister Aparna was married with two children and his brother Ashwin was meandering through a series of jobs, while his youngest sister Sangeeta was still at college. As we talked, I was aware of the fact that he genuinely seemed to want to share some of the details of his life with me, and he also seemed interested in me and my background. I wondered whether he was another Indian guy who wanted a trophy white girl, an international notch on his bedpost, but decided to give him the benefit of the doubt. There was something that seemed quite genuine about him, although, as I thought wistfully, I'd thought the same thing about Krishna when we'd first met, and look how that had ended.

Eventually, after a couple of cups of coffee each, he said, 'I have to get going, I have a couple of meetings this evening. I'm in town for a week, though, would you like to get together again, perhaps for dinner this time? I really enjoyed talking to you.'

I found his polite, slightly formal approach almost endearing, and the fact that he didn't seem to want to play games was a refreshing change. I was still persisting in the belief that he just wanted to be friends, but something inside me was telling me that it was more than that. And although I wanted to believe it, I was thinking about my plans to leave and how this was absolutely the wrong time to meet anyone new. I told myself that worst case, I'd have one last fling before leaving Mumbai, that I wouldn't anyway have the time or inclination to get into anything serious, and that worst case I'd spend an interesting evening or two with someone who I could talk to.

'Sure,' I said, 'let me know when. I'm pretty free this week.' Just as I wasn't going to delude myself into thinking that this was going to turn into some great romance, neither was I going to be bothered to play the usual games and feign indifference or invent a packed diary to make myself seem more interesting. We parted with another kiss on the cheeks and this time a hug, and I spent the rest of the weekend feeling unaccountably happy and excited at the prospect of seeing him again.

## 23

I was sufficiently curious to do a little bit of research into Vicky's background, and probed Vanita for details about him, without giving away my reasons for doing so. Vanita wasn't the gossipy type, and coolly told me, when I dropped the topic into conversation, that Vicky was a serious kind of guy, he'd dated a pretty well-known model for a few years but they had recently broken up and she got the feeling that he was licking his wounds a little bit.

'I did wonder,' I told her, as we sat in the agency canteen drinking chai. 'I mean, it's none of my business but we spent a fair bit of time talking and I got the impression that he's quite sad inside somehow. He's certainly not the flamboyant, bossy type that I've come to expect, most of these directors are arrogant idiots.'

I quickly changed the subject and googled him when I got home. Indeed he had dated a particularly stunning model from Delhi for a few years, and I read various accounts of his long love affair, written mainly by the entertainment and gossip columns, which took great delight in revealing the eventual downfall of his relationship. I felt sorry for him; though he wasn't a celebrity by any means, he was well known enough for his personal life to have been written about, or perhaps she was the more famous one of the two and had merited those column inches. She certainly seemed to be everywhere, and though she was gorgeous to look at, there was something flinty and hard in her eyes. I couldn't imagine that he would possibly be interested in me after dating such an incredibly hot woman, and I figured that possibly he was looking for rebound sex, which I definitely wasn't up for.

When he called me in the middle of the week, however, my heart jumped and I felt the familiar butterflies in the pit of my stomach.

'Hey, how are you?' he asked me.

'I'm good thanks. Another busy week, but nothing I can't handle.'

'So do you fancy meeting for dinner?' he asked. 'I'm starved of company here, and most of my friends seem to be out of town.'

I felt slightly put out at the implication that I was a last resort, but I didn't think that he meant that he was literally scraping the barrel. We arranged to meet at Busaba, a quietish and unpretentious bar located in one of the recently-developed midtown mills. Bars and restaurants were springing up in these areas, which had been grabbed by eager property developers following the closure of the old textile mills. I arrived a little early and made my way upstairs to the table he'd thoughtfully booked. For some reason, my nerves had disappeared. I wasn't reading anything into this dinner. Since finding out that he'd recently come out of a long term, serious relationship, I guessed that he was just looking for a bit of fun, and I'd decided to enjoy the attention, though I told myself to be strong and not give in if he suggested we spend the night together. I was used to fending off amorous desires, and though this one, if it happened, would be more difficult to resist, I didn't want to end up as a trophy shag, or worse, a sympathy shag.

'Hi, you look lovely,' he smiled as he sat down, admiring my freshly blow dried, shiny hair and my new top, which I hoped said sexy but not slutty. I felt confident and in control, the butterflies that had kept appearing earlier now banished by my resolve. Dinner was delicious, and we ordered extensively from the Asian menu.

'I'm glad you're not a vegetarian,' he grinned, as I tucked into my barbecued pork ribs.

'Far from it,' I replied. 'I eat everything, although I'm a bit sick of curry frankly.'

'I don't blame you,' he said. 'Where I'm from, the diet gets pretty boring after a while, it's all tandoori meat, rich gravies and naan. And daal of course. The food up north is really heavy and gives me terrible indigestion.'

'So which do you prefer, Delhi or Mumbai?' I asked.

'Well, Delhi has been home for a while, but I prefer the buzz here. People in the north tend to be more aggressive, and people say it's not a very friendly place, particularly for outsiders.'

'Yes I've heard that.' I said, recalling stories I'd heard from expat friends who had lived in Delhi. 'I've never been, but I suppose I should make a trip there some time. In fact, I need to visit a whole load of places before I leave India.'

'So you're really serious about leaving then?' he asked.

'I think so,' I replied, before deciding to open up about my reasons for leaving. 'To be honest I'm in a bit of a dilemma,' I said. I wasn't trying to impress him, and so I figured that being honest about my desire to meet a man wouldn't make any difference.

'I've been on my own here, pretty much since I arrived. And while I love my freedom, and the fact that I can do whatever I want, when I want to, I suppose I'm a little bit lonely and I'd love to meet someone and settle down, so I don't think I have much of a choice but to go home.'

'You don't think you'll meet anyone here then?' he asked, genuinely interested.

'Well, I haven't done so far, and I've been here for getting on for three years. I mean, I have dated but it's all been a bit disastrous and I just kind of get the feeling that I'm chasing something that just isn't meant to be. And although being in a relationship isn't the be all and end all, it's something I miss and I think I need now.'

I stopped, hoping that I hadn't made him feel bad about his recent breakup, or come across as sad, lonely or desperate. I made a joke to ease my own self-consciousness. 'I suppose alternatively I could always go off in search of enlightenment or fulfillment with some yogi in the hills. That seems to be a particularly popular choice for us lost westerners.'

He laughed, 'Yes I know a few people like that. But you don't strike me as that type. You seem to have your feet firmly on the ground, and I can't see you being seduced by the promise of Nirvana.' I took that as a compliment.

'So, what about you? Are you religious?' I asked.

'Not really. I mean I was raised Hindu but my family aren't that strict, and I've never been able to work out what it all means. I guess I do believe in God in a way, but Hinduism seems fairly forgiving so I don't worry about it too much. I think my parents are secretly hoping that I marry a nice Hindu girl, but I think they've given up on me now. Luckily, I have an older sister who's given them a couple of grandchildren, so I'm off the hook, although there's a lot of pressure for the sons to produce heirs for the family. Hopefully my brother will be the one to do that eventually.'

'So you don't want kids?' I asked, hoping my question sounded as innocuous as I intended it to be.

'I do, definitely,' he said. 'One day. All depends on meeting the right person I suppose, and that is the most important thing.' His tone was far from flirtatious, and I liked the fact that he was confiding in me.

'Me, too. I mean, I've never wanted kids. To be honest, I think I'm terrified of the responsibility, but you never know. I just want to meet someone who I feel comfortable with, and who I can build a life with, and then I'll take it from there.'

I felt strangely liberated by our conversation, as though we had abandoned any pretence of flirtation and were just connecting as friends, potentially good friends. At the end of the evening, after he'd paid the bill, he turned to me and said, slightly nervously, 'Listen, I really want to talk to you about something. Can you come back to my hotel for a drink, and I promise this is not as sleazy as it sounds.'

'Well I don't mind having another drink,' I said, intrigued by his tone and somehow trusting him completely. We grabbed a taxi and headed to his hotel and made our way to the bar. I had hoped that he wouldn't suggest that we go to his room for drinks, and he didn't. We ordered our drinks, beer for him and wine for me, and after the waiter had finished fussing around us, he turned to me, looking slightly bashful.

'So Julia, the thing is, and I don't quite know how to say this, I actually really like you, and I was kind of hoping that this would turn into something more. But I don't want you to feel that I'm after you for one thing, and I know that you're planning to leave, and I don't know how much time I have, so I thought I'd come right out and tell you.' He stopped abruptly, clearly embarrassed by his revelation.

I was surprised and a little shocked by the directness of his disclosure. I was used to games and to flirtation but I wasn't accustomed to attractive men putting their cards on the table like this. He noticed my hesitation, and put two and two together.

'Listen, I'm sorry. I didn't mean to ambush you like this. But I'm only in town for another day and I just needed to tell you how I feel before you send me an e-mail telling me you're already back in London. I don't want to influence your decision, but if you do decide to stay, then I'd like to see if we can make something work.'

'OK,' I said, stalling for time, not sure how to react to this very upfront admission.

My mind was in turmoil, I found him attractive, interesting, and I had loved our conversations and I was tempted to see whether we could make a go of things. On the other hand, this was all moving very quickly, we hadn't even kissed, I had made up my mind to leave and I was still convinced that any cross-cultural relationship would be doomed to failure. I decided to go with my heart, which by now was beating insanely fast.

'Well, if we're being totally honest here, I really like you as well. But I'm really confused. I've had a couple of pretty bad experiences, and I'm not sure if I can really ever be in a relationship with an Indian guy. I mean, I don't have anything against you at all, I find you really attractive and interesting, but

I'm scared that things wouldn't work out long term, and I am looking for something long term, not just a quick fling.'

I had decided to be completely honest, given that he had put his cards on the table. We weren't playing games, there was no flirtation happening, we were just two adults having a conversation about what might or might not be.

'Well, do you think you could give it a go?' he asked. 'If the answer is no, then we'll stay friends and forget this conversation ever happened, though I might be a bit embarrassed. If the answer is yes, then maybe you can stay here for another few months and we'll see what happens.'

I sat quietly for a moment, thinking things through. Although I'd reached out to the London office and to James my former boss, I hadn't yet resigned from the Indian company, and there was no reason why I couldn't carry on in Mumbai for another few months. I knew instinctively that if I rejected this man I would regret it forever.

'Well this is crazy,' I said. 'But why don't we see what happens. I can stay for a few months for sure, and we can date I guess. But you're in Delhi and I'm in Mumbai, so how is that going to work?'

'Well, we can start with you coming to Delhi next weekend,' he grinned. 'I'm serious. Come to Delhi, let me show you my city, and you can meet my friends, and we'll take it from there. No pressure, no drama. Just promise me you won't make your final decision to resign for a little while.'

'OK, I can do that. And yes, I can come to Delhi next weekend. I've been dying to go there for ages.'

'I'll book you a nice hotel room,' he said. 'And it's on me. No arguments, if I'm dragging you to Delhi, I insist on paying for it.'

It felt like we'd made a business arrangement, but I was excited and I couldn't help hoping that this would turn into something meaningful. We finished our drinks and I decided to leave. I needed to put some space between us, to allow myself time to reflect on what had happened, and I didn't want to push things too fast now, or end up doing something I'd regret. I couldn't help thinking about what might be, and I wondered whether this would be the start of something really exciting or just another disastrous experience.

I booked my flight to Delhi, and did my usual pre-reading, determined not to come across as a tourist. I'd heard that Delhi was very different to Mumbai, that it was difficult, aggressive and that Indians from the north were quite different to those from other parts of the country. As the country's capital, it housed the main Parliament building, as well as World Heritage sites and of course the ubiquitous markets and arts and crafts areas. I wasn't sure of the religious or cultural background of the area, and read that like Mumbai, Delhi was a melting pot of religions.

Maya called me one evening to invite me to a party at the weekend.

'I'm actually going to Delhi,' I told her.

'Oh, really? Client meeting?'

'No, actually, it's a personal trip.'

'Who do you know in Delhi?' she asked.

'No one really,' I said. 'Well, that's not quite true. You remember Vikrant, the director? He's asked me up for the weekend.'

'Er, what?' she said, a tone of disbelief in her voice. 'Has something happened between you guys? Have you seen him? How come I don't know about all this?'

'We had dinner and he kind of told me he liked me and asked me to go to Delhi and so I said I would and well there we are,' I mumbled, aware how ridiculous it sounded.

'You are seriously going all the way to Delhi to meet this guy?' she asked. 'Whatever happened to your plans to leave India?'

'Well, I haven't quite made up my mind about that yet,' I muttered, aware that I was sounding horribly flaky.

'Well, I hope you know what you're doing,' she replied, and I detected a note of something in her voice—perhaps criticism, or maybe disappointment.

'Maya, listen, I am just really confused at the moment. I don't know which way this is all going to go, and I don't want to get my hopes up, but he did tell me he likes me and we've spent a bit of time together, so let's see. I still think I need to leave India but I might just delay my departure a little bit. After all, I don't really have anything to go back for, job-wise, and I'm the one who decided to leave. This might all be a crazy wild goose chase, but I don't intend to fall in love with the guy so I think it will all be just fine, whatever happens.'

'OK, well, just be careful,' she said. 'You're the one who's been telling me how it's impossible to date an Indian guy, now don't go and make yet another mistake and then get even more miserable and end up leaving on a bad note.'

'I promise I won't,' I said, sounding more confident than I felt. 'I really will just see how the weekend goes and then I'll decide when to go.'

'And you promise you'll tell me everything?' she asked.

'Every single detail,' I vowed. 'I'll bore you rigid, but you'll know everything.'

# 24

I landed in a smoggy Delhi late on Friday evening, the sprawling city looking similar to Mumbai as the plane landed, but with a distinctly foggier skyline. Vicky was there to meet me at the airport, as he had promised. He was carrying a bunch of yellow roses, a cheesy but sweet gesture.

'How was the flight?' he asked.

'Fine,' I said, keen to have something to talk about to break the ice. 'Longer than I expected actually. This country is so huge. If I took a two-hour plane ride from London, I'd end up two countries away at least.'

'Come on, let's get you to the hotel and then you can take a shower before we go out. We're meeting a few of my friends for a drink.'

Noticing the look of panic that must have flitted across my face, he added, 'Don't worry, it's all very casual. I've just told them you're a friend visiting from Mumbai.'

I was relieved that he hadn't alluded to a potential relationship. After all, I hardly knew what we were doing, and I certainly didn't have any expectations for the weekend, though deep down I was hoping for a bit of old fashioned romance. The flowers were a good start, and I guessed that he'd opted for yellow rather than red roses to avoid being too obvious.

We climbed into the back of a huge old Ambassador taxi, and Vicky gave directions to the driver—though he spoke in Hindi, it sounded very different to the language I heard every day in Mumbai. He had booked me into the Park Hotel, a trendy but comfortable boutique hotel which was less intimidating than a more traditional five star.

'I'll leave you to shower and change if you need to, and I'll be waiting in the bar.'

'Are you sure?' I asked, 'I mean you can come up if you want, er, I mean, you can wait in the room and I'll shower and …'

'I know what you meant,' he laughed. 'It's OK, really. I'll just grab a drink and I have a couple of calls to make so you take your time.' I appreciated the formality, I wasn't sure I was ready to be placed in an uncompromising position so early on in the trip, and I wanted to relax and shower without the feeling that he was right on the other side of the door.

'OK, that's cool. I won't be long.'

The room was lovely and it came with a bathtub, a luxury that I sorely missed in my apartment in Mumbai. Showers were fine, but I missed the luxury of being able to wallow in hot, bubbly water. I decided to take a quick bath to energize myself and wash away the aeroplane grime, and threw in half of the dinky bottle of bubble bath thoughtfully provided by the hotel. If nothing else happened this weekend, I'd make sure that I made the most of the hotel's luxurious environment.

Conscious that Vicky was waiting for me downstairs, I didn't linger for too long in the warm fragrant water, and quickly changed into a clean top and what I thought would pass for sexy underwear, just in case. I left my long hair loose in what I hoped were sexy blonde waves, as I'd recently had my mousy locks highlighted.

'So who are these friends we're meeting?' I asked him, as the barman set our cocktails in front of us.

'A bunch of people who I work with on a regular basis. There's Adi who composes music for some of the films I've worked on, and his wife Tania. Then there are a couple of sweet girls who model, and one who's a stylist and Sunny who is a photographer. And probably a few others. It's a very casual group.'

I wondered about the models and hoped that they wouldn't end up being friends of his ex-girlfriend. I was curious about how his friends would react to me, and, recalling the night long back when I'd received a frosty reception from Krishna's female entourage, hoped that they would be friendly and that I wouldn't feel that I was being scrutinized. As it turned out, they were a completely different type from Krishna's friends. His gang had all been college mates, and they had bonded together with a ferocity that made them appear insular and almost clannish, and they were rarely apart from one another socially. But Vicky's friends were quite obviously different. As he introduced me to Adi and Tania, and Natasha and Priya the models, I received warm smiles and handshakes from them all.

'So you're from the UK?' asked Adi.

'Yes I am, and now I'm living in Mumbai, I answered.

'How did you guys meet?' asked Tania.

'We worked together on that shoot,' Vikrant said. 'You know, the one that drove me completely mad for weeks.' His explanation was convincing and the conversation switched to Mumbai.

'I love it there,' said Tania, slightly wistfully. 'I moved here when I married Adi, but I still miss it. Delhi is OK, but it's hard work. The people are so snobby and really judgmental sometimes. And so competitive.'

'Shut up,' Adi gave her a playful nudge. 'You love it here. And you love me, so you really love it here.'

'No, she's right,' smiled Vikrant. 'It can be a tough place to live. And it's not as safe as Mumbai, that's for sure, especially for women. You hear a lot of terrible things about eve teasing and worse.' He was referring to the unpleasant euphemism for women being harassed and even physically abused, which happened all too often in India, apparently.

Although India was in many ways a modern and progressive society, I often forgot that Mumbai was the very tip of the iceberg in terms of India's population and that it was hardly representative of the country at large. Over seventy per cent of India's billion plus population lived in rural areas, in villages that often had limited or no electricity and were often fiercely traditional as far as the roles of men and women were concerned. I'd read horror stories in the papers about the abuse of women, and though primitive practices such as sati, the horrific practice of widows throwing themselves onto their husband's burning funeral pyre, and the tradition of demanding enormous dowries from girls for marriages were outlawed, occasional stories in the paper made me realize that there was a lot of this still going on.

'Well, I'm looking forward to seeing Delhi for the first time,' I said, keen to focus the conversation on a more positive note. 'I've heard that the food is amazing, that the streets are green and clean and that the Parliament buildings are definitely worth seeing.'

'Well, lots of Delhi is choked with traffic and filthy dirty but, yes, the areas around Parliament are where all the taxpayer's money gets spent and that is definitely worth seeing,' said Vicky with a laugh.

The evening passed very sociably and then we moved on to have dinner at a nearby restaurant which specialized in Delhi's famous northern cuisine. It was similar to the tandoori food I'd eaten in Mumbai, but much heavier, and we drank pints of chilled Kingfisher beer to wash it all down.

'Who fancies clubbing?' asked Natasha, a stunning girl wearing a short skirt and high heels. I looked at Vicky, not wanting to come across as a killjoy, but not really up for carrying on the evening at a loud, flashy nightclub. Although I liked clubbing and loved to dance, I was also enjoying the opportunity to relax and get to know Vicky in the context of his friends. So far, I hadn't seen any deviation from the man I'd met a few weeks earlier in Mumbai. He was effortlessly charming without being phony, clearly the centre of this social group without being overbearing. He was confident and conscious of including me in conversations, and I appreciated his efforts to make me feel welcome and relaxed.

'I think we should call it a night,' Vicky glanced at me. 'I'll take Julia back to her hotel and she can get some sleep. I want to take her out sightseeing tomorrow and she's only here for a couple of days.'

'Thanks Vicky,' I sighed gratefully. 'I've had a lovely time but I'm exhausted and I want to have some energy to see the city tomorrow.'

As we drove back to the hotel, I looked out at the sights around me. On the outside, everything looked very similar to Mumbai, with the usual dusty, dirty streets and traffic that never seemed to stop crowding the streets. The air generally just seemed filthier, I could taste the acrid tang of diesel at the back of my throat, and I supposed that Mumbai's proximity to the sea meant that much of its pollution got blown away.

'Did you have a good time tonight?' asked Vicky, glancing across at me as the taxi driver navigated the cars in front, which were hogging the fast lane. 'I had a lovely time,' I said truthfully. 'I really liked your friends, they were very down to earth and very welcoming.'

'Yeah, they're good guys. They've been there for me recently when I went through some tough times, and I owe them a lot.' I guessed that he was referring to his recent breakup, but didn't want to probe further, figuring he'd tell me if and when he was ready.

He dropped me outside my hotel and I clambered out of the car, grateful that he hadn't tried to kiss me, or worse still, tried to invite himself in. In fact, his behaviour to date had been immaculate, and though I appreciated his softly-softly approach, I almost wondered whether the revelation that he liked me and wanted us to take things further had just been a figment of my imagination. I told myself not to be so silly, that I was here in Delhi and that we'd see how things panned out over the weekend.

I slept soundly, and woke rested and ready for the day. Vicky was waiting for me in the lobby at 11 a.m., with another huge old white Ambassador car waiting for us, complete with driver wearing an off-white uniform with a peaked cap.

'I hired him for a couple of days.' He laughed. 'Isn't he great? He takes his job very seriously.'

'He's brilliant. And I love these old Ambys.'

'All foreigners are obsessed with these cars. We Indians can't understand it. They are old fashioned, unwieldy, terrible to drive and they guzzle fuel. But the firangs go crazy over them. Some even buy themselves one and paint it in crazy colours.'

'They are adorable cars,' I said. 'I mean, look at this one, it's a classic.'

'Like the British Raj and old movies, you mean?' he replied with a chuckle.

'Well, at least this car has character, unlike all the rest,' I said. 'I expect some fat paunchy man with a briefcase to step out of most of them, and try to sell me something.'

'You're hilarious,' said Vicky, laughing even harder. 'Seriously. I don't know if you know how funny you are.'

He seemed genuinely amused by my words, and though I hadn't thought that I was being particularly witty or humorous, his reaction made me feel good.

The driver, whose name was Raj, took us to a few tourist sites, including the Qutub Minar, a red sandstone and marble tower covered with ornate carvings set in a peaceful green park, and India Gate, the national monument of India, which was apparently inspired by the Arc de Triomphe in Paris. We also drove past the Parliament buildings, which were of course impeccably maintained, with tidy lawns and carefully clipped trees surrounding the beautifully constructed dome that formed the centrepiece of the Hall of Parliament. It was all very different to Mumbai, where the ancient buildings and temples nestled alongside shanty homes and apartment buildings billowing drying washing from their tiny windows. Here, the sense of space gave an impression of a very different kind of India. I felt like a tourist, but enjoyed Vicky's narrative as he explained the stories behind the buildings and ensured that he brought some of the city's history to life.

After a delicious lunch of succulent chicken tandoori and mutton kebabs, washed down with cool lassis, he took me to see the livelier part of town, which was more like the India I had come to know and love. We attempted to navigate the tiny lanes of the crowded Chandni Chowk marketplace area, drove around the enormous, congested Connaught Place, and finally, and at my insistence, took a quick tour of the backpacker district Paharganj, which was jam packed with teeming crowds, lots of foreign backpackers in their typically scruffy tie-dye attire, and tiny shops selling bangles, scarves, glittering bags and jewellery, nestled between hotels and hostels, many of which looked filthy but which boasted rock bottom accommodation prices.

'Now, this is more like the India I know,' I stated.

'These foreigners all love this stuff,' Vicky laughed at my statement. 'I swear, they all want to find the cheapest deals and half of these people look like they are completely penniless. They're so scruffy, and what's with all the baggy clothes and the tie-dye?'

'It's a backpacker thing I guess,' I told him, defensively. 'We don't all come here and want to look like this.'

'Of course not,' he replied, 'but there are so many who do. Ironically, when most Indians travel they wear their best clothes, look smart and the trip is a big adventure for most of them. Indians can't really understand why Westerners would come here looking so unwashed and unclean. It's bizarre if you think about it.'

'I suppose it's kind of like a role reversal,' I said. 'Back home, everything is relatively clean and tidy and ordered and people have to look smart for work. Here, people can come and relax and be themselves and dress differently. I think also that some of these backpackers think that they will blend in wearing all this stuff, when actually they stick out like a sore thumb.'

'They look dirty and slovenly, frankly,' said Vikrant, with a note of real disgust in his voice. 'It just annoys me a little bit when I see people letting their standards slip.' I must have shot him a surprised look, as he went on to add, 'I mean it's entirely their decision of course but I just think it's weird. There are millions here struggling to get out of lives filled with dirt and poverty, and the rich Westerners who have led sheltered lives feel that they have to run around here looking like beggars. No offence but it's just really strange.'

'I'm not offended,' I stated, diplomatically. 'I know what you mean, and since I've been living here I've started to find these people quite irritating as well. But they don't really get in my way, and I suppose in some way they are spending money here, however hard they try to scrimp and save and bargain.'

During this conversation, I had caught a glimpse of a more opinionated Vicky, and I found that I liked it. I'd seen his polite, friendly and charming side and I was reassured to know that there was an edge to him, which I guessed I'd see more of.

That evening, after another bath and a change of outfit, we headed to Hauz Khas, a small, rapidly growing area within the city that had recently become a mecca for Delhi's vibrant arts scene. Originally a village, the small space had evolved into a lively creative hub, with fashion designers, musicians and artists setting up shop there, and restaurateurs opening small atmospheric eateries and bars. Vicky had booked a table at a tiny restaurant which apparently served incredible vegetarian food.

'I thought you might fancy a break from Delhi's carnivorous overload. It can get a little tough on the digestive system.'

As we sat down at an outside table situated under gently whirring fans, the waiter lit a candle for us. The entire tiny space was bathed in a warm glow, and fairy lights twinkled all around us, adding a magical air to the scene. It was without doubt an incredibly romantic environment, and I felt relaxed, happy and excited about the future. Though I didn't want to tempt fate, I had a great feeling about the evening and Vicky, and I could feel his magnetic presence and felt deeply attracted to him.

'So, what do you think? Kind of romantic, huh?' His voice had a distinctly teasing tone.

'Yes, very,' I smiled. 'I guess you're wining and dining me, right? Seducing me into thinking that Delhi is a romantic, cool place to be?'

'Absolutely. I need you to love my city. You might end up moving here one day.'

'Or you might end up moving to Mumbai,' I suggested, in an equally flirtatious tone. He reached across the table and took my hand in his, a serious look flitting across his face. The candlelight was gently lighting the bones in his face and reflecting in his almost black eyes and he looked gorgeous. His touch was light and cool, and his fingers gently caressed mine.

'You're lovely,' he said simply. 'I'm so glad we met.'

'Me too. I just hope that the timing isn't all wrong.'

'The timing is in your hands,' he replied, with indisputable logic. 'Come on, let's order. Then I am coming back with you to your hotel. No arguments.'

His words were thrilling and suddenly I couldn't wait to be alone with him. He'd put all his cards on the table and so had I, and there seemed no need to play games. I was almost tempted to suggest that we skip dinner, as my appetite had completely disappeared, but decided that prolonging the romance and the atmosphere would mean that the final event, assuming it happened, would be even more meaningful. I hardly tasted the food, and wasn't particularly interested in the exotic dishes. There was a palpable tension in the air, but it was a positive feeling, an anticipation of things to come. He continued to caress my hand throughout dinner, and I revelled in the feeling of his touch. I looked deep into his eyes, saw the candlelight reflected in the black depths, and felt as though I was being completely carried away by the moment and by my attraction to him.

I was aware that I was standing on the brink of a precipice and though I didn't want to over-dramatize the moment, I also knew that if this backfired on me, I'd be done with India for good. I didn't want to start making plans for the future, but I'd shared enough of my hopes and dreams with him, and been searingly honest about the fact that I was looking for a serious relationship, and I was sure that he wouldn't trifle with me if he wasn't looking for the same thing. Our relationship was new, bright, shiny and exciting, but at the same time, we'd built a friendship over a few weeks, and I really felt that we'd got to know each other and that it was time to take things to the next level. Besides, he'd done all of the chasing, and I didn't feel that this was a mere flirtation on his part. He had taken pains to explain his feelings for me, he'd exposed himself to potential rejection and he had also invited me to his city and introduced me to his friends. It all felt reassuring and comfortable, and at the same time exciting and full of promise.

We finished dinner quickly and neither of us wanted dessert. He paid the bill despite my protestations, but I gave in as I was used to this typically Indian behaviour by now. I'd learned that there was no way that an Indian man would ever allow his date to pay the bill, and I figured that I might as well drop the habit of a lifetime and accept this graciously. As we rolled around in the back of the huge old Ambassador, sliding around on the smooth seats as the car jerked its way through the traffic, he slipped his arm around me. I felt safe, secure and happy, loving the way his hand was resting protectively around my shoulder and conscious of his smell—a mix of fresh, sharp cologne and the scent of him, slightly earthy and deliciously masculine.

We arrived at the hotel and he led me straight to the lift. I could feel the usual butterflies in my stomach, but these were more due to anticipation rather than fear. Somehow this man knew exactly how to put me at ease, to make me feel comfortable and secure. I opened the door with my key card, and just about managed to turn on the lights before he pushed me up against the wall and kissed me hard. It was a passionate, no holds barred kiss, the kind that comes from the final release of a serious amount of pent up tension and suppressed attraction. He was gentle but insistent, and I responded equally enthusiastically.

'I've been waiting for a long time for this,' he said, breathing into my hair, which he was stroking. I silenced him with another kiss, and he pushed me down onto the bed. Part of me wanted to slow things down, to play coy and suggest we took things step by step. The rest of me figured that we'd had plenty of time to get to know each other and that if this was meant to be, it would be, regardless of how physical we got on this particular occasion. Deep down, I sensed that this was the start of something, and the usual paranoia that invariably lurked inside me was strangely and pleasingly absent.

He undid my shirt buttons feverishly and I helped him by pulling the shirt over my head and wriggling out of my trousers. His shirt and jeans quickly followed, and I admired his firm, lean body. He was slim without being skinny, and his skin was a beautiful shade of brown, the parts that didn't see the sun more olive in tone. His penis stood up enthusiastically from the mass of springy black hair at its base. He had come prepared, and as he ripped open the condom, I could feel that I was already wet and dying to feel him inside me, and I felt simultaneously slutty and turned on, but in a good way. I wasn't completely unselfconscious, this was no Mills and Boon novel, but I was surprisingly relaxed and enjoying every moment. There were no fireworks or crashing waves of orgasm, but the sex was surprisingly good, and more because I felt a connection than due to any physical reaction. He was both tender and strong, pushing me down hard on the bed, but gentle when he entered me and moved slowly inside me. The last man I had made love to was the one night stand office guy, Anees, and although I shivered with disgust at the memory, this was vastly different. It felt good to be with someone who I cared about and whom I had spent time with and I felt that this was a natural and inevitable part of the journey that we were embarking on together, as cheesy as that sounded in my mind. Unlike Anees,

Vicky didn't roll over and start snoring after the event, but slid gently out of me, wrapped his arms around me, and kissed my forehead. It was a small and gentle gesture which made me feel warm, secure and special.

'That was amazing,' he said. 'For a first time. You know how awkward these things can be.'

It was as though he had read my mind. 'I know exactly what you mean. It's been quite a while for me, and I was a little bit nervous.'

'Well I've had sex with the same person for almost five years,' he told me shyly, 'so I was very nervous. Now we've got the first time over, let's do it a few times more before you leave. But first, a glass of wine to celebrate.'

'What are we celebrating?' I asked, flirting with him and wanting to hear his reassuring words.

'Our meeting and our first sexual encounter,' he smiled. 'Or bonk, or shag or however you Brits like to put it.'

I laughed out loud as I heard those familiar colloquial terms coming from his mouth. He found a half bottle of chilled white wine in the minibar, opened it and poured us a glass each.

'It should be champagne, but wine will do,' he said. 'Here's to us.'

'To us,' I echoed, hoping that this would be the start of something new and exciting and wondering whether I could tell the girls at home about this, or whether I should hold off just a little bit longer.

## 25

We made love twice more that night, and though I was sore in the morning, I was happier than I could remember being for a very long time.

'We're meeting the gang for brunch,' he said, caressing my cheek. 'Wear something nice, brunch is a pretty formal occasion here.'

I'd packed a couple of smartish dresses and heels, so I was all set to go.

'So what time do we meet them? Eleven?' I asked. 'It's already ten.'

'No, this is brunch Indian style, which basically means lunchtime. We'll meet them at one. I'm warning you, though, these brunches are a big affair with unlimited food and booze so be prepared to go a little crazy.'

'Well, my flight isn't until 8 p.m.,' I said, 'so I guess I can stagger onto the plane and sleep it off, right?'

'Definitely,' he grinned. 'You need to make the most of the free-flowing champagne.'

He left me to have a bath and get ready, and went back to his parents' place to change. Like most unmarried Indian men, he lived with his parents, but in his case it was more for convenience than anything else; he had explained the previous evening that he spent so much time travelling that it really didn't make sense for him to pay rent on an apartment, and he was vaguely planning to buy something in the city. I wondered whether I'd get to meet his parents, and figured that it was a little early for that. I ran the bath and lay soaking in the deep, bubbly hot water. I ached all over and I was bone tired but I was ridiculously happy, and couldn't stop grinning as I recalled the events of the previous evening. Whenever I thought about him kissing me, my stomach lurched but this feeling wasn't accompanied by the usual insecurities, worries or concerns. I had plenty of time to wallow in the water, and I made the most of it, knowing that it would be a while until I could enjoy a deep soak again.

I dressed carefully, wanting to look as good on the outside as I felt on the inside, put my hair up into what I hoped was an elegant chignon, and chose a pretty knee-length smock dress with a funky pattern, along with heels and some chunky jewellery. We were meeting for brunch at a fancy five-star hotel in the city, where I'd arranged to meet Vicky in the lobby. He was already waiting for me when I arrived, looking fresh and relaxed in a pair of cream linen trousers, sandals and a flowing, comfortable shirt. His hair looked freshly washed and was bouncing on his shoulders like something out of a shampoo advert. He saw me and his face lit up.

'Hi gorgeous,' he sighed, pulling me into a hug and planting a kiss on my lips. 'Looking good enough to eat. I love that dress.'

I felt warmed inside by his compliments, and by his touch as he pulled my hand into his. It felt as though he was preparing himself to announce our brand new, shiny relationship to his friends. We were joined for brunch by Adi and Tania and by a short guy who introduced himself, with an endearingly camp lisp, as Tarun, a hairstylist who was also apparently one of the inner circle but who had been working on Friday night. Tarun was clearly gay and proud of it and I admired his confidence in a country that was still largely homophobic and where homosexuality had only recently been legalized.

'So,' Vicky said, 'The deal here is that you basically start with a cocktail, and then start attacking the food in any order you want, and order another drink every time you go up for a refill. We'll be here for a good four hours so pace yourself.'

'Sounds amazing. I'll start with a Bloody Mary.' My drink arrived, it was deliciously spicy and I could taste the generous slug of vodka.

'So have you guys had a good weekend then?' asked Tania.

'We've had a great time,' Vicky told her, squeezing my hand.

'We went sightseeing yesterday,' I said, 'and then for dinner at Hauz Khas.'

'And what do you think of Delhi?' asked Adi. 'Do you find it as aggressive and as intimidating as some of these Mumbaiwallahs say?' he added, throwing a cheeky look in his wife Tania's direction.

'Not really, although it's very different to Mumbai. It seems much more sprawling, the pollution seems worse and I can't seem to get my bearings. I haven't really noticed much of a difference with the people here, but then again I've only met you guys so it's hard to tell.'

'Good answer,' laughed Adi. I was hungry and we got up to check out the buffet. It was an exceedingly lavish spread, with a sushi bar, hot and cold dim sum, a Teppanyaki counter, salads, a Thai food area, various hot dishes and an incredible array of what looked like extremely calorific desserts. I started with a plate of sushi and my tastebuds went crazy; I hadn't had sushi since leaving England, it was very hard to find in Mumbai or ridiculously expensive. We spent a relaxed, fun afternoon eating and chatting, the conversation was light but interesting and I felt that I made a connection with Vicky's friends. It was clear to them that we had become a couple — he held my hand, referred to 'us' a lot and laid his arm along the back of my chair once we had finished eating.

The strong cocktails went to my head, and I felt giddy and intoxicated both by the alcohol and by the feelings that were swelling inside me. I was trying not to get too carried away but I couldn't help but envisage various scenarios in my mind, mainly involving taking him to England and him meeting Annabel and Lizzie and my family. I felt that Adi, Tania and I had connected, and felt relaxed and comfortable in their company. Tarun was hilarious, keeping us entertained with tales of his clients and their particular whims, and he brought them to life beautifully, imitating their whiny accents with a touch of camp thrown in. By the time the waiter came to inform us that the buffet was closing and to take our last orders for drinks, we were all slightly sleepy and completely stuffed.

'I'll have one more mojito for the road,' said Adi.

'I'll have a coffee. Espresso please.' I smiled regretfully. 'I've got a flight to catch.'

'Oh you're not leaving us already are you?' asked Tania. 'How sad. When will you be back again?'

'I have no idea,' I glanced at Vicky. 'Let's see how it goes.'

I hugged Vicky's friends goodbye, and he took me back to the hotel to pack.

'I'll drop you at the airport,' he said. 'Now let's talk about when we'll meet again. I hope you don't think that I'm not already making plans to meet you again.'

'I wasn't sure,' I said. 'But I kind of hoped that you would want to hang out again soon.'

'Well, I was thinking next weekend,' he smiled, 'but I do have some work to finish up. How about I come to Mumbai in a couple of weeks time? I can combine it with some work stuff. Can I stay at your place, or would you prefer that I stay at a hotel?'

'Don't be silly. Please come and stay with me. If you're really uncomfortable, you can sleep in the spare room,' I smiled.

'With you in the next room? Are you mad or what?' he asked, laughing. As we said goodbye at the airport, I held onto him tight. Though all the signs were good, and although I couldn't imagine that he would suddenly start playing games, I'd had enough experiences of men saying one thing and doing another and I vowed to try and keep calm and rational about all this, although I knew that it would be easier said than done.

'See you in a couple of weeks, lovely girl,' he kissed my forehead.

'See you then. Let me know when your flight is arriving and I'll try and meet you at the airport.'

On the flight home, I obsessed over all the details of the weekend. I could hardly believe how well things had gone. I thought about the future and decided to see how our next meeting went, before making any decisions about whether to leave India or not. In a way, I wished I'd met Vicky when I'd first arrived from England, but on the other hand I was glad that I'd had the opportunity to live independently, make friends and learn my way around the city. I had had to push myself hard and, in the absence of a partner to lean on, I'd had to take matters into my own hands, which I felt had given me valuable insights and also toughened me up. It hadn't been easy being a single girl in Mumbai, and in fact the deep down loneliness had almost driven me away.

The next two weeks passed agonizingly slowly. Maya of course was dying to hear all about my trip to Delhi, and she even came all the way to my place to share a bottle of wine with me after work one evening to hear the gossip. I had decided to tell her everything, I was desperate to relive the experience and I knew that she would give me her honest opinion of the events and of my budding romance.

I filled her in on everything, from the time I landed in the capital city, to the moment we kissed goodbye at the airport.

'Well, it sounds promising,' she stated, taking a swig of wine. 'Has he contacted you since you left?'

'He's sent me sweet text messages every day. Just asking how I am, telling me he's thinking of me. I don't want to get overexcited, Maya, but I really think that he could be the one.'

'Well that's what I thought when I met Jay,' she said. 'I don't want to put a dampener on your excitement, but just remember that he's an Indian man and they all tend to be similar when it comes to relationships. Possessive, egotistic Mummies' boys. I hope this one turns out to be different, but it runs pretty deep. I've yet to meet an Indian guy who isn't a chauvinist deep down.'

I sighed. 'Well, I think Vicky may be different. At least I hope he is. He's travelled a lot, and he only lives with his parents because it's easier. He seems to have a fairly progressive approach to life. Besides, he's sexy and he seems to enjoy taking care of me. I don't mind the idea of a bit of old fashioned romance.'

'Well, as long as he doesn't end up suffocating you,' Maya stated with a serious look on her face. 'These Indian guys are also crazy jealous and some of them can be very controlling. Just make sure you get to know him before you jump into anything.'

We finished the bottle of wine, her words ringing in my ears. I supposed it was useful advice, but I really didn't worry about it too much, figuring that she'd been through a recent bad experience and was probably still a little bit shell-shocked and paranoid. I decided to introduce her to him when he came the following weekend. After all, I'd met his friends and I didn't see why he shouldn't meet mine.

Vicky arrived as promised on the Friday evening. I sent Hussain to meet him at the airport as I had to finish up a couple of work projects, and I hoped that he wouldn't mind too much. I had planned to get back to the house before he arrived, ensure everything was spotlessly tidy and that the place smelled fragrant. I was conscious that he was coming to my home for the first time, and whilst I was proud of the space I'd created, and the homely touches that I'd added, I hoped that he'd like it and feel comfortable there and, frankly, I wanted to impress him. I arrived in time to plump the cushions and ensure that Deepa had changed the sheets, and artfully placed a couple of bunches of flowers around the room.

The doorbell rang, and I jumped up, checking my reflection in the mirror one last time and trying to banish the butterflies which had appeared again.

'Well, hello again,' he grinned, leaning against the doorpost and looking sexy and remarkably unruffled from his trip.

'I'm so sorry that I didn't come and meet you,' I smiled back. 'I just wanted to get some stuff finished off at work, so that I could have some peace over the weekend and not get disturbed by the office.

'No problem. I wouldn't have been able to resist ravishing you at the airport anyway, so maybe its better this way.'

'Would you like a glass of wine?' I asked him, feeling very much the self-conscious host, as he sat on my slightly threadbare sofa looking around.

'I would, but first I'd like a tour of your flat, then I'd like to kiss you, and only then would I like a glass of wine,' he replied.

'Sure,' I blushed, feeling an absurdly warm glow. That sounds good. There's not much to show you though, it's a small flat,' I said, feeling a little as though I and my possessions were on display. As I showed him my bedroom and the tiny attached bathroom, the spare room and finally the kitchen, he scrutinized everything, even picking up the photos that I had scattered around the place in bright frames.

'Who is this?' he asked.

'That's my sister Louise,' I replied, 'and those are my parents. And these two are my best friends Annabel and Lizzie, who live in London.'

'They look like fun,' he replied, studying the picture. He stopped at my bookcase and I hoped that my books, with their proliferation of chicklit titles would pass his scrutiny.

'Nice place,' he said finally, 'You've made it very homely.'

'Thanks. I like it. And it's a good area of town, although I hear

259

that the suburbs are the coolest places to be these days.'

'Well maybe we can look for a place there, if I move to Mumbai,' he stated, confidently. I smiled, not knowing whether he was joking or not.

'Now for that kiss,' he embraced me and pushed me down on the sofa. We kissed for a good twenty minutes before he released me. The kisses were as intense and delicious as I remembered.

'So, what's the plan for the weekend?' he asked.

'We're meeting a friend of mine for drinks tonight,' I told him, 'and then tomorrow we can chill at home, or watch a movie or go shopping or whatever you fancy. And then tomorrow evening there's a party at one of the expat's houses, which might be fun.'

'Sounds perfect. Let's see how we feel tomorrow morning.'

That evening, I'd arranged for us to meet Maya at Indigo, a safe bet for a relaxed evening, a delicious dinner, yummy cocktails and great service. I wanted to impress Vicky, but at the same time I didn't want to come across as one of those foreigners living in an expat bubble and I planned to go somewhere a little more informal the next day for lunch to balance the Indigo five-star experience. Vicky took a shower in my little bathroom, which was spotless but hardly luxurious. He emerged with his hair wet and his chest glistening with water, a towel wrapped around his slim waist. His body wasn't particularly hairy, but his chest was lightly covered with coarse black hair though thankfully his back was hairless and smooth. I was tempted to grab him there and then, but didn't want us to be late for the restaurant booking.

Maya was already waiting for us, and she'd brought along a friend, Adnan, to balance the numbers. Rishi, the actor who she'd been dating had bitten the dust, she'd found him too petulant and had ditched him unceremoniously. Adnan was a sweet guy who I suspected had a crush on her, and she played along a little bit, enjoying the attention. I had frequently told her that she should put the poor guy out of his misery, but she continued to dangle him on a piece of string and used him to boost her ego when she needed it. He was good company though, and I was glad he had come.

'Hi, I've heard lots about you,' said Maya, as I flashed her a glance which said—play it cool.

'All good I hope?' replied Vicky, smiling at her.

'All good. Let's hope you can live up to the hype,' she bantered back.

'Stop it, you guys,' I smiled. 'Enough already. Let's get some drinks.'

'How have you been Julia?' asked Adnan.

'Good actually. Kind of busy. Did a bit of travelling with work, and now all the usual stuff back at the office.'

'No plans to visit England again?' he asked.

'Well, I thought I might go back in summer for a weekend when the weather's better, and when I've had enough of Mumbai's monsoon.' I was already making plans in my head to invite Vicky to London with me. We carried on chatting over dinner, Adnan and Vicky bonded over a mutual love of photography and travelling, and Maya and I gossiped about mutual friends in Mumbai. After dinner, we excused ourselves and went to the toilet.

'He's gorgeous,' she sighed. 'I can see why you're so nuts about him. That hair is amazing. And he seems really sweet. And totally into you.'

'Yes he's lovely isn't he?' I replied, thankful for her glowing feedback. 'I'm so glad you like him.'

'I think he's a keeper. Just don't forget what I said. Be a little careful. And I want to be a bridesmaid, don't forget.'

'Maya, please! Don't get me married off already. I've only just met the guy.'

'Well, I'm just saying. Don't forget that I want to choose my own dress, and I'll style the whole wedding for you if you like.'

'OK, that's enough,' I laughed. 'Come on, they'll wonder where we've got to.'

Later that night, after we'd made love slowly and gently, I lay cuddled into the crook of his arm, playing with the hair that spilled across the pillow.

'What are you thinking?' he asked.

'Not much,' I said, truthfully. 'I just kind of zoned out.'

Usually I hated it when men asked me that question, but this time I didn't mind. It didn't sound cheesy coming from him, and I knew that he was genuinely interested in what was inside my head rather than relying on the scripted one-liners that I'd heard so many times before.

The next day we got up late, after a lazy morning lying in bed, talking and drinking coffee. I felt incredibly comfortable and relaxed with him, and our conversation felt effortless. I took him to Britannia for lunch, a legendary Parsi restaurant that had been around for years and served delicious berry pulau, a sweet-sour biryani type dish with plump chunks of mutton mixed with fluffy, fragrant rice. The place was a Mumbai institution, down to earth and elegant with a gorgeous old fashioned interior, which looked like something straight out of the history books.

We spent the afternoon wandering up and down the streets of Colaba, which were lined with market stalls selling a mix of touristy tat and naval artifacts. We strolled along hand in hand, dodging the hawkers and the beggars. I felt sorry for them but I knew that if I stopped to give money to one, we'd be hounded by crowds. I bought chocolates and handed them to the grubby street children, my heart breaking as always at the sight of their tiny, filthy faces and bright, hopeful eyes.

'You know the begging is all part of a scam,' Vicky stated coolly.

'I've heard that, yes, but I just feel so sorry for the kids,' I said. 'It's not their fault that they were born poor, and I've heard horrific tales of their being beaten and mutilated to get sympathy donations. It's horrible.'

'That's India for you,' he replied, matter of factly. 'It exists, our society is corrupt in so many ways, and we all turn a blind eye to a lot of shit.'

I didn't want to come across as the naïve foreigner, and I knew how endemic the corruption and the poverty were here. At the same time, I found it impossible not to be moved by the plight of some of these people, and though handing out a few chocolates to street kids did little to ease my conscience, it was better than nothing.

That evening we headed to Bandra for a house party being hosted by Bill, a plump, good humoured British expat whom I had met on several occasions. We had arranged to travel up to the suburbs with Johann and Priyanka who lived close to my place and who had also heard rumours of my new mystery man — Maya and Priyanka occasionally met each other for coffee, as neither of them worked regular office hours and Maya had filled Priyanka in on Vicky. Though I was glad that I'd introduced them to each other, I also knew that it made it impossible to stem the gossip. We pulled up outside their building, and Priyanka climbed into the back of the car.

'Hi there,' she held out a perfectly manicured hand for Vicky to shake. 'I'm Priyanka. Johann is just coming down.'

'This is Vikrant.' I felt a surge of pride as I said his name.

'But please call me Vicky,' he told her, shaking her hand.

Johann arrived and got into the front seat, leaning back to introduce himself.

'Should be a fun evening tonight,' said Priyanka. 'Bill's parties are quite legendary, he seems to have pots of money and he always throws the most lavish dos.'

As the car navigated the constricted streets of the largely Muslim area of Mahim, past the beautiful white mosque and narrowly missing the goats that were running rampant across the road, I glanced over at Vicky, whose features were profiled against the streetlights. His expression was calm and content, his straight nose and defined cheekbones smooth and almost sculpted in the low light. I wanted to pull his face towards mine and kiss him there and then, but figured that I'd better not shock my friends or embarrass my driver.

After a forty-five minute drive, we arrived at Bill's apartment, another palatial place with imposing gates and glass fronted floors with carefully cultivated plants hanging from the balconies. Though I knew that some expats earned a small fortune and were paying, or rather their companies were paying, crazy amounts of money for their swanky apartments, I somehow liked the fact that

---

my place was a little more down to earth, less flashy and certainly not imposing. I knew that I would have felt awkward living in a place where the monthly rent equaled the annual salaries of my junior team members, for example, and though I certainly didn't want to live in squalor, I knew that my apartment wasn't particularly extravagant, though I supposed that for many Indian families, particularly those living with innumerable relatives, my two bedroom-two bathroom space would have been considered an absolute luxury.

Bill, a swarthy plump man wearing cotton trousers with sharp creases in them and an immaculate tailored shirt, greeted us at the door.

'Hello, hello my lovelies,' he exclaimed, ushering us in. 'Welcome to my humble abode.'

'Bill, this is Vikrant,' I said. 'My, er, friend from Delhi.'

Vicky shot me an almost imperceptible look, and I was pretty sure that I read disappointment on his face.

As we walked through into the living room, I felt Vicky's hand on my arm, clasping me tightly. 'Are you going to introduce me to all your friends like that?' he asked.

I looked up, expecting to see a smile on his face, but his expression was serious. 'You mean describing you as my friend?' I asked.

'I thought we were more than that,' he said, his eyes flashing anger as he spoke.

'Well... I... er, yes, well I mean, I... er... well, I wasn't sure,' I stammered, not knowing quite how to express myself. In truth, I didn't know what we were and had no clue how to introduce him. Announcing him as my boyfriend seemed presumptuous

265

given that we hadn't had the whole conversation about whether we were exclusive or not, to use the American term. Friend seemed a bit too casual, but then there was really nothing in between.

'Do you have some kind of history with that guy?' asked Vicky.

I assumed that he was joking. 'With Bill? Yeah, right,' I laughed. He didn't laugh back, and I realized that he was serious.

'Vicky, I have no history as you put it with anyone here, so please relax. I would have introduced you as my boyfriend but honestly I didn't know if you would be comfortable with that. But I'd love us to be boyfriend and girlfriend proper, if that's what you're worried about.' I was aware that I was sounding like a teenager, but this seemed important to him.

His expression relaxed slightly. 'OK sorry. I overreacted. It's just that you know how much I like you and that I'm serious about this.'

'OK, boyfriend it is then,' I said, putting my arm around his waist and squeezing him hard.

I introduced him to the small groups of expats who were dotted around the room.

I spotted Rebecca and Simon in the corner. 'Hey Becky, long time no see,' I hugged her hello. 'This is Vicky, my boyfriend.' The words felt really strange coming from my mouth, it had been so long since I'd had a boyfriend, and in Krishna's case I'd taken a while to get used to the idea, and by the time I had, it had been all over.

We spent the evening chatting with various people and sampling the delicious snacks that Bill had had catered from one of the restaurants in town. Vicky kept an arm around my waist most of the evening, and although I found the feeling of being with someone a complete novelty, I liked the pressure of his arm around me, and felt secure and happy. It had been a long time since I'd been out with anyone officially, and been part of a couple, and I liked the feeling.

Later that night, Vicky and I lay in bed and analysed the evening. 'I had a good time,' he said, 'but I thought some of those expats were complete idiots.'

'What do you mean?' I asked.

'Well, they seemed friendly enough but I got the impression that they were judging me. I could just tell from the way they looked at me when you introduced me.'

I didn't quite know how to react. I wanted to tell him that he was being ridiculous, that everyone had been friendly and chatty, but I didn't want him to think that I was taking their side against his, and he seemed quite sensitive about the whole thing.

'I think they were probably just a bit surprised to see me with someone,' I said. 'I told you that I've been more or less single since arriving here, and suddenly there you are, so they are bound to be a little bit surprised. But I am sure they are all happy for us.'

He didn't answer, and I got the distinct impression that he was sulking just a little bit. Though we hadn't argued by any means, I got the impression that the atmosphere between us had changed, I could feel a tension, which I tried to ignore, and hoped that things would be lighter in the morning.

## 26

I woke suddenly, reaching for my phone, which was charging by my bedside. It was 10 a.m., and I realized that the bed was empty. My blood ran cold, and I sat up in a panic. Had Vicky left already? Had I made the mistake of not finishing our conversation properly? Maybe he had decided that this wasn't right and had gone to the airport. My mind was full of a thousand panicked scenarios and I jumped out of bed, detangling myself from the sheet and almost fell over as I tried to stand up. I pushed open the door to the front room, and saw that the cushions were plumped on the sofa and that the coffee table had been cleared of the glasses and the empty wine bottle that had been there earlier. It was Sunday and I knew that Deepa wasn't due to come and clean the place until Monday morning. I went through to the kitchen and found Vicky, in boxer shorts and a T-shirt, making toast and brewing a pot of coffee.

'Hi, gorgeous,' he said, his face breaking into a huge smile. 'You're up. You were sleeping so peacefully that I didn't want to disturb you. I've made us some breakfast and coffee. Do you want some of that revolting Marmite that you Brits are so fond of? I found some in the cupboard.'

Vicky was being charming and his mood was light and

happy. I guessed that he'd got over his slight sulkiness from the evening before, and I was relieved that the drama had passed and evaporated with the new day.

'I'll have some toast and jam please,' I asked, not wanting to ruin my breath with the delicious but strongly flavoured Marmite, a favourite of most British people but generally loathed by most other nationalities and with a taste that unfortunately tended to linger long after it had been consumed. I decided to take him to the Breach Candy club for lunch and a swim. Though I wasn't particularly proud of my bikini body, I figured that we were past the being coy part of our newly emerging relationship, and if we were in boyfriend-girlfriend space already, then I certainly shouldn't worry about a few lumps and bumps on my thoroughly imperfect body.

'The Breach Candy Club,' whistled Vicky, when I suggested it to him. 'Wow, we are going up in the world. I've never actually been there, although I've heard stories about how great it is. Isn't there like a hundred-year waiting list?'

'Well, expats get immediate membership.' I felt slightly embarrassed about the preferential treatment that I enjoyed. 'Although there's a four-year limit on membership and life memberships are only open to Indians.'

'Which are impossible to get,' suggested Vicky, with a sardonic smile.

'Well, yes, that's true,' I said, not wanting to give the impression that I was a spoiled expat taking advantage of the colour of my skin.

'Well, I suppose most foreigners are only here for a short while, so it kind of makes sense. What if you're an Indian expat though? Born in India but moved abroad and then back here again?'

'I think they go on foreign passports,' I said. 'So even if you're Indian origin you can get an expat membership as long as you have a foreign passport.'

'Hmm. And what about Indians who marry expats?' he asked, with a teasing note in his voice. 'Are they also then entitled to join as expats or are they banished onto the sidelines along with their fellow countrymen?' He smiled, but it was a sensitive subject, and one which I really wasn't ready to get into just yet.

'I have no idea, but at least it's not a complete expat haven,' I replied. 'There are all sorts of people there, well, mostly rich people I suppose, but it's a good mixed crowd. Plus the food is amazing and the drinks are crazy cheap, and the pool is huge.'

'What are we waiting for then?' he asked. 'Ah, I know. There's one important thing we have to do before we have breakfast and get ready.' And with that he put down the coffee cups, put his arms around me and pushed me hard against the kitchen wall. I knew that the neighbours from the opposite building had a habit of peeking into the kitchen, so I pulled him into the living room.

'I don't want to get even more of a reputation for myself,' I said, jokingly. 'At least I can close the curtains in the living room.' Our lovemaking was fast and urgent, it seemed as though he wanted to clear the air between us somehow, and there was an intensity that I hadn't experienced with him before. Afterwards, he clung to me, our bodies running rivulets of sweat, which mingled together and dripped onto the couch.

'Sorry, I'm sweating all over your sofa,' he said, pulling me tight to him.

'We're both dripping, and it's really OK. This is lovely. Deepa can always wash the sofa covers.

It was indeed lovely. A lazy Sunday morning, a passionate lovemaking session, and the prospect of an afternoon swimming, eating, drinking and looking out to sea, contented and happy in my new relationship.

Vikrant was impressed with the well-tended environs of the Breach Candy club, by the immaculate clubhouse and the huge pool. He changed into a pair of stylish shorts and I briefly offered a silent thank you for his taste in swimwear and the absence of speedos or tight fitting trunks. We arranged our deckchairs carefully, mine out in the sunshine, ensuring that the sun's rays hit my carefully lotioned body, his under the shade of an umbrella.

'I'm dark enough as it is,' he laughed. 'I go really black the moment the sun hits me.'

'I love your colour,' I said. 'At least you don't go bright pink and peel like I do. My skin is a curse in this country.'

'It's far from a curse. I bet it opens a fair few doors for you.' The last thing I wanted was to get into a debate about the benefits of being white in India, and so I quickly changed the subject. Though I was prepared for the inevitable discussions and even disputes given our very different perspectives and our obviously different backgrounds, I didn't feel like a serious conversation when the sun was shining and the pool was beckoning, its bright blue water lapping invitingly against the footpath, in stark contrast to the dark, muddy brown sea churning against the rocks a couple of hundred metres away. We spent the afternoon swimming and relaxing, chatting and eating the delicious snacks that the club was famous for.

Vicky looked great in his swimming shorts, his body was athletic enough, and his hair hung in loose, damp tendrils around his shoulders. He hadn't shaved for at least a couple of days, and he had a slight stubble, which gave him an edgy, sexy look.

We lay in companionable silence, relaxed and happy, without the need to make polite conversation. I saw a few people I knew, and waved lazily at them from the comfort of my sun lounger. I didn't have the energy to get up and be sociable, and I knew the club was the kind of place where people came to relax and be with their friends and families, and there was no pressure to socialize necessarily.

'What time is your flight again?' I asked.

'Actually, I have a surprise for you,' he said. 'It's not until tomorrow morning. I changed my plans at the last minute, and I hoped you wouldn't mind if I stayed an extra night.'

'Of course, I don't mind,' I smiled, genuinely pleased that we had another entire evening to spend together.

'As long as you don't mind if Hussain drops you to the airport again tomorrow morning, as I need to be in the office bright and early.'

'I'll take a taxi,' he said. 'Honestly, I'll be fine. There's a number I use all the time, I'll give them a call.'

'I'm so happy you're staying.' I reached over and squeezed his thigh, which was resting gently against mine. 'The time seems to pass so quickly, every time we meet.'

'I know,' he told me, 'I wish we lived in the same city. Seriously though, do you think you could ever move to Delhi?'

I thought carefully before answering. 'I honestly don't know,' I said. 'It's not like I hated the place when I came to visit, but I have become really fond of Bombay, and if I'm going to stay in India then this is really the place I'd want to be, in an ideal world.

Besides, my job is here and there aren't so many opportunities for foreigners in Delhi, unless you work for the Embassy or an NGO.'

'So you've decided to stay in India then?' he asked, a slightly more serious look on his face.

'I thought I'd make a decision this weekend,' I replied.

'And have you?' he asked.

I paused before replying. 'This seems to be going really well, though to be honest I really hadn't expected to meet someone at this point, so it's thrown me a bit, Vicky. I had pretty much made up my mind to leave, but I think I should stay and see how things work out between us. I'd hate to walk away from this. We'd never survive a long distance relationship, plus the irony of the whole thing is that I decided to leave because I thought I'd never meet anyone here and now that I have, or at least I think I have, I'd be mad to leave.' My words had spilled out of me in a tumble of sentences.

'I'm so glad you feel that way,' he said. 'I was so scared you'd leave India. I don't want to rush things or get too heavy too fast but you know how much I like you and I want us to get into a more serious relationship. I had a fairly bad experience when my last relationship ended but I think that enough time has passed now for me to move on. And I want to move on with you.'

His words warmed me, and I felt genuinely moved by his honesty. Apart from a flash of another side of his personality over this weekend, one which was a little more jealous and perhaps possessive than the Vicky I thought I knew, I felt that he was perfect for me, and that the timing was immaculate. Perhaps, I wondered, he'd been sent to keep me in India by some divine force, goodness knows I was surrounded by enough idols and gods and religions, although my own beliefs remained squarely on the fence.

We spent the evening at home, watching a DVD and eating takeaway Chinese food. The DVD was some futuristic action thriller, which we'd selected on the basis that it was not a Bollywood movie and nothing too heavy or too romantic. Though he claimed to enjoy the odd Bollywood movie, I was by now sick of their seemingly identical plotlines and bizarre scenery shifts. Besides, the tiny amount of Hindi I'd picked up was of course woefully inadequate when it came to entire dialogues and I didn't fancy squinting at the screen to read subtitles. The food was typically Indian Chinese style, or 'Chindian' as many people referred to it. It had a taste all of its own, the typical Chinese flavours blended with a touch of local masala and spice, it was greasy, and utterly delicious.

'So, when do we meet next?' he asked me as we lay entwined on the sofa, dirty plates and glasses strewn around us.

'I don't know. Soon I hope,' I said.

'I think I can swing some work here so why don't I try to do that?' Vicky said. 'Then I can stay for longer, rather than having to rush back. To be honest, there's tons of work here in Mumbai, it's just that I've never really had any reason to be here for long before, and I preferred to be where my parents and my family were. Now, I have a great reason to be here, so why don't I take advantage of the fact that my work is flexible.'

I loved the thought that Vicky could be here in Mumbai for longer periods of time. I was finding the effort of fitting things into a single weekend quite stressful, and I was aware that we were both constantly on our best behaviour given the brevity of the time we had to spend together whenever we met, and I wanted us to get into a space where we could relax and behave like a normal couple and see how things went.

'That sounds perfect. And of course you can stay at my place whenever you're in town, there's plenty of room.'

The conversation left us both in positive, happy spirits, and the atmosphere in the room was charged with a great energy. I now decided to throw myself entirely into this relationship, and I was looking forward to getting completely under the skin of this fascinating man.

## 27

As promised, Vicky started to spend more time in Mumbai, staying with me in the evenings and going off for meetings during the day. He'd lined up a few jobs with advertising agencies in the city, though we managed to avoid working directly together, which I was relieved about given the one and only disastrous attempt I'd made at mixing work with pleasure. I didn't really want my two worlds to collide—Vicky was becoming a huge part of my life. I certainly wanted him to spend time with my friends and I hoped that he'd meet my family in the not too distant future, but work was work and for now I wanted to keep that separate from my life with him. We started spending whole weeks together, and suddenly it felt as though he was with me all the time. I even cleared out one drawer of my cupboard for him, and he kept some clothes there, his toothbrush and body spray taking up permanent residence in my bathroom. We slipped into a familiar and yet still charged relationship, physically things went from good to better as we began to know each other's bodies and lost our initial shyness. He liked to be in control in the bedroom, but it was nothing I couldn't handle, he was gentle but firm and I enjoyed the feeling of being manipulated in a spirited and sexy way. We became closer and closer as we spent more and more time together. Now that he was practically living with me, Vicky seemed to have abandoned all signs of the fleeting insecurity that I'd caught a glimpse of at Bill's party. We hadn't really talked about our pasts, nor had we mentioned previous relationships, but it was clear that what was behind us would stay there, and I knew that we were both working hard to make each other feel secure and confident. It certainly wasn't a perfect union, I knew that deep down we were both struggling with the inevitable fear and uncertainty that accompanied the early development of any close relationship, and we were plagued by the same nagging inner voices which occasionally threatened our happiness. Did we both feel the same way about each other? Were our pasts completely done with? Were we risking inevitable heartbreak if we succumbed to our feelings? I knew that he was feeling the same way as I was, as occasionally he would become quiet, pensive and a little moody. When that happened, he claimed that he had work on his mind and needed to sit quietly with his laptop. I gave him his space, knowing that he would re-emerge in a few hours his old, bubbly self.

The row came out of nowhere. It was the middle of the week, I'd had a long day with my client Elmo being difficult about the budgets that I'd sent him for the upcoming campaign, and I was exhausted. As I put my key in the door, I could hear sounds of movement from within, and I guessed that Vicky had returned before me, and hoped that he was warming some of the food in the fridge.

'Hey, you're back,' he said, wiping his hands on his jeans. 'What do you fancy doing for dinner tonight?'

'I'm so tired. Can we just heat up whatever Deepa's left us, and have an early night?'

'Sure,' he replied, a look of what I thought was disappointment flitting across his face. 'Why don't you take a shower, it'll make you feel better, and then we can eat.'

As I brought plates through from the kitchen whilst Deepa's amazing curry was heating in the microwave, I heard my phone ping with the sound of a text message. 'Someone's messaged you. Do you want me to read it for you?' Vicky asked from the other room.

'Er, no, that's OK,' I said. 'I'm right here.' Somehow I felt really awkward about someone else reading my messages, even if it was the man I was falling for and practically living with. Whilst we'd been open with each other about most things, I felt that a certain degree of privacy was important in any relationship.

I picked up the phone and saw a message from an unfamiliar number. 'Hey, long time. Was just thinking of you. Wondered if you wanted to meet some time. Take care, Hari.' It was my disastrous internet date guy from months earlier. I'd successfully managed to avoid his calls and I'd thought that my terse messages back to him shortly after we'd met and then again after he'd sent me a Christmas greeting had been suitably off-putting.

'Anything important?' asked Vicky.

'No, just Maya wondering what we're up to tonight,' I told him. I don't know why I didn't tell him the truth but somehow it just seemed easier not to bring up the subject of another man, even one as innocuous as Hari.

'Don't you want to call her back? We can meet her for a drink if you like. Or you girls can catch up on your own.'

'No, no its OK, really,' I said, wondering if I should just call her and hope that she'd fall into line. As I held onto the phone, it rang suddenly. It was Hari. I looked at the handset in a panic, not knowing what to do. The fact that I'd told a bit of a lie about the text message was making me jittery. I pressed the call stop button.

'Some number I don't recognize. I can't be bothered to talk to anyone tonight.'

I must have looked as guilty as I felt. 'Julia, what's going on? You seem really strange. Who was that on the phone? And who was the message from?'

'Actually, it was some guy I used to know,' I said weakly. As soon as the words were out of my mouth, I regretted them.

'Some guy? Really? So he sent the message and then called you?' he asked, coolly, and I could feel his hackles rise.

'Yes, just someone I met a long time ago. Nothing happened. He was just asking how I was and then I guess he called because I didn't message him back,' I answered, feeling ridiculously guilty, even though I had absolutely nothing to feel bad about.

'So, is this guy still part of your life then?' he asked, his voice dangerously calm and his tone low.

I felt suddenly sick, even though I'd done nothing wrong. 'Vicky, he was never part of my life. I met him once, for a drink, and then never saw him again. I have no idea why he's suddenly texted and called me now, out of the blue.'

'So how come you met him once? What was that all about? And why did you lie to me about the message?' I felt as though I was being interrogated, and I didn't like the feeling at all. I felt hot and suddenly the flat seemed unbearably stuffy and claustrophobic. I decided to be completely honest, and just tell it how it was.

'I met him on a dating site. We met once, I didn't like him, and I never spoke to him again. And as I said, I have no idea why he has messaged me again.'

'So was this one of many guys that you met on the internet? I thought you told me you hadn't really dated much in Mumbai. In fact that was one of the reasons I liked you. I thought you were special. I thought you were different from all the other white girls who come over here and jump into bed with the local guys.'

I looked at him, unable to believe what I was hearing. The words coming from his mouth were so irrational, and so out of character that I almost felt like giggling. I swallowed hard, and instead of laughing, my hysteria turned into tears, which threatened to spill down my cheeks. I could feel my throat tensing and constricting as I battled to calm myself.

'Vicky this is really ridiculous. This was the only time I ever tried internet dating, I was lonely and Maya put me up to it, I met this one guy and then nothing happened and I never did it again.'

'So, you never did anything physical with him?'

'Hardly. I met him in the restaurant, we had dinner and I left. That's all.'

He stood up and started pacing the length of the room, his fists clenched and held tight against his sides. Suddenly, he had turned from my peaceful, calm boyfriend into some kind of jealous monster. Half of me wanted to scream at him, to tell him that though I'd not been a saint, I hadn't exactly been a slut in the past three years that I'd been here, and besides, it was all in the past. I wanted to tell him to get out, to stop making me feel like this. More than anything, I wanted the loving, sweet Vicky back, the man who made me feel cherished and secure, not anxious and sick to my stomach.

'So there was no one else then? No one until you met me? Or were there other men? And are they all still sending you text messages at night?'

My insides flipped over as I remembered Anees, the office one-night stand, and Krishna, my three month long relationship that had ended so disastrously.

'I did date another guy, the one you saw me with when we first met at the Taj, but I don't really want to talk about all this now, Vicky. Please. It's completely irrelevant. I haven't exactly been a nun since I've been here, but I've hardly dated anyone, and I've fallen for you now and this relationship is all that matters. Besides, I'm sure you were in relationships before you met me, and honestly I don't care.'

'Well, I do,' he said, his eyes flashing dangerously, and his voice rising. 'I care that my girlfriend has random men texting her at night, and I care that she hasn't been honest with me. In fact, I'm not even sure that I want her to be my girlfriend any more.' As he uttered those words, he picked up his phone and his wallet, and left the apartment, slamming the door behind him.

I stood in the middle of the living room, completely shell-shocked, unable to comprehend what had just happened. I felt a mixture of emotions, I was angry that someone had the power to make me feel so bad, and livid that I had been portrayed as a woman with questionable morals by someone who knew nothing of my past. I was scared that I'd lost the man whom I was beginning to fall in love with. I was mad with myself for having even read that text message, and for saying that it was from Maya. And most of all I was disappointed, in myself for having allowed myself to become so happy so quickly, and in Vicky for treating me so unfairly and making me feel so bad. I deleted the message from Hari, angrily erased his number from my phone, and immediately wished I'd written back telling him that I was in a relationship and not to message me again. I composed a message to Vicky, in what I hoped was a conciliatory but firm tone, 'Hey, listen I'm sorry about what just happened. Please know that whatever has happened in the past is irrelevant. It's you I care about. Let's talk this over when you're ready'. I wanted to fling myself at his feet, to apologize and tell him that life had had no meaning until I had met him, but at the same time I knew deep down that he was the one being irrational, and my old stubborn self held me back from completely abandoning my self-respect. I decided to pop a Valium and try to sleep. I had a stash of sleeping pills that I'd picked up in one of Mumbai's more flexible no questions asked pharmacies to help me sleep during long flights, and I knew that that was the only way that I'd be able to achieve the dreamless oblivion that I craved.

I woke the next morning feeling groggy and spaced out. The Valium had certainly knocked me out and given me some blessed relief from the traumatic rollercoaster of thoughts streaming through my head, but it had also left me bleary eyed and with a thumping headache. As I reached for the glass of water that I'd kept beside my bed, I checked my phone for messages. Nothing. I decided not to panic, but to get ready for work and to carry on as normally as possible, which would require superhuman self-control but which I knew had to be done. Luckily, my day was quiet and I managed to get through it in a zombie state. I knew that my team members could sense that something was up, but the last thing I wanted to do was talk about it. I was tempted to message Vicky again, or to call him, but I figured that the ball was in his court and that whatever happened he'd have to come back to the flat to collect his things, and we'd talk it through at some point, unless he had decided that things really were over, in which case I'd have to lick my wounds, admit defeat and carry on with my original plan to return home. Banishing all scenarios from my mind, I focused on the dull but mind-numbing task of clearing out my jammed inbox, and tried not to think about what might happen later.

I heard nothing more from Vicky that day, and I knew that I wouldn't be able to sleep unless we talked things through, and decided on a plan of action either way. I was the kind of person who liked to talk things out, and his silence was nothing short of torture. Finally, as I sat nursing a large glass of wine, trying to distract myself with mindless television shows, the phone rang. It was Vicky.

'Vicky! Are you OK? Where did you sleep last night? I was so worried about you.'

The words tumbled out of my mouth before I had time to think about trying to act cool, or even a little bit offended that he'd stormed out of the place in a rage.

'I'm sorry Julia. I know that today must have been really difficult for you,' came the disembodied voice, so familiar but at the same time so very distant. 'I know I behaved badly by leaving but I'm not sure I can handle this. I didn't realize how much I cared about you and I'm finding it quite difficult to accept that there are guys here in Mumbai who might come back into your life at any time.'

I could hardly believe that we were having this conversation.

'Vicky, as I told you last night, I haven't been a saint, but I've hardly been a slut either. I'm sorry that guy messaged me, but it meant nothing and anyway nothing ever happened.'

'That's not the point, Julia,' he said, sounding sadder than I'd ever heard him before. 'The point is that you lied to me. And that's the thing I find hardest to forgive. Maybe I'm overreacting, but I'm not sure that I can imagine a future where I can trust you again.'

Maya's words about Indian men and their controlling tendencies were ringing in my head, along with Vicky's harsh accusations about white girls being easy. I tried to banish them both from my mind and focus on calming him down. 'Vicky, please. This meant nothing, it means nothing, and I only evaded the truth about the text message because I was scared that it might upset you. It was nothing and I wish I'd just been honest with you.'

'So do I, Julia. I'm sorry, but I don't think this is going to work out. There are just too many differences between us. I hope we can be friends one day.'

With that, he disconnected the call and I was left with only the sound of my sobbing for company.

## 28

I woke the next morning with red, swollen eyes and a sadness that began somewhere deep inside me and reached into every fibre of my being. I was confused, exhausted and on an emotional rollercoaster, alternating between desperate sadness and regret, anger that I'd been unfairly treated, and fury with myself at having been burned yet again by a cultural divide which even Maya had warned me about. I couldn't believe that Vicky had overreacted to what seemed to me to be such a trivial matter and tortured myself mentally, obsessively running through the events of that night in my mind, blaming myself for my stupid lie.

I called Maya that evening, desperate for some insight on Vicky's reaction, my fingers trembling as I dialed the familiar number. 'Hey hun, what's up?' she asked, cheery as always. 'How's love's young dream?'

My throat had tightened with the effort of trying not to cry, and it was all I could do to form a sentence. 'Maya. Something awful has happened.'

'Oh my God, you sound terrible,' she said, immediately reacting to the tone in my voice. 'What happened?'

I told her the entire story, crying throughout. 'I'm coming over,' she said immediately.

Over large glasses of wine and a box of tissues, she tried to comfort me.

'Bloody Indian men,' she said. 'I did try to warn you. They're all the same. As soon as they feel threatened, or they think you're not the Virgin bloody Mary, they'll get vicious and make you feel like a slut. For fuck's sake, you've hardly dated at all since you've been here, in over three years. Where does he get off on making you feel bad? I bet he's not been a saint. But he's a man so it doesn't count, right?' Her rage was diffusing a little of my own anger, and I could feel myself softening.

'Maya, I caught him off guard. We haven't even really had the conversation about our pasts, let alone laid them to rest, and suddenly there's this random guy texting me and then to add insult to injury, I lied about it. I'd probably feel the same if he got a message from some girl late at night.'

'Yeah, but you'd have kept it to yourself, right? You wouldn't have acted like some jealous psycho and stormed out of the flat and then ended the relationship.'

'Well, no. But Vicky is a creative guy, and these types are prone to emotional outbursts. Plus he's Indian. I guess they take these things more seriously.'

'Nonsense,' she said dismissively. 'He's just being a control freak. Don't tell me that he hasn't overreacted.'

'To be honest, I'm hoping he'll call me and tell me its all been a terrible mistake,' I said. 'I do love him, Maya, and I am still really hoping we can work through this. But I need him to make the first move.'

I threw myself into work, which helped take the edge of the pain, and decided that I needed to put some physical space between myself and everything that reminded me of Vicky. His things were still strewn around my flat, and I hadn't had the heart to tidy anything away, clinging on to the hope that he'd eventually return. I sent him a text message asking if he wanted to come and pick his things up, in the hope that seeing me in person might persuade him to rethink his actions. Though I was still angry with the way he'd left, I knew that I would jump at the chance to rebuild our relationship. He replied with a short, to the point message in which he said that he was in Delhi for work but would be in touch when he returned. I tried not to read into that, and decided that I needed some space back home with Lizzie, Annabel and my Mum and Dad. I wasn't sure how much I'd tell them about what had happened, but I knew that I needed to be in some uncomplicated, undemanding familiar company. I called Maya and told her that I'd be away for a couple of weeks.

'I think you need a breather,' she agreed with me. 'Mumbai is crazy enough if you're feeling strong and in control of things, and unbearable if you're unhappy.'

As I headed for Mumbai's international airport on a dark and smoggy evening, I sighed and looked out at the now-familiar surroundings. I had so wanted to take Vicky home to meet my friends and family, and could hardly believe that I was making this trip alone. Landing into London Heathrow airport was strange and slightly disconcerting. I found my pre-booked taxi and moved towards the queues of traffic heading into central London. I had arranged to stay with Lizzie at her flat in London's trendy Clapham, a sensible investment that she'd made a few years earlier with her boyfriend Richard, and as always I found myself admiring her ability to plan her life and be sensible without being dull. I had always felt that I had charged rather recklessly through life, taking each day as it came. I had no pension plan, no savings and no idea where I'd be in the next few years, and now that Vicky was no longer in my life I wasn't even sure where I'd end up next.

The minicab finally pulled up outside Lizzie's place—a top-floor flat in a typical row of sweet, terraced Victorian houses. It was a fairly small two-bedroom place with a tiny boxroom, which could arguably be called a third bedroom, or could even be turned into a nursery if she and Richard decided to take that step, which I instinctively felt that they soon would. The street looked identical to millions across London and England—indistinguishable red brick houses, with miniscule patches of grass masquerading as gardens at the front, bay windows on top and bottom and slightly larger gardens at the back, separated by neat wooden fences. I paid the taxi driver the seemingly exorbitant price of forty pounds for the trip, trying hard not to convert it to Indian rupees, put my finger to the doorbell, which I'd pressed so many times in the past, and tried to calm the tension that bubbled in the pit of my stomach. I knew that Lizzie would know that something was wrong with me, and though I'd told her on the phone that I simply wanted a break from Mumbai and work, she was the more perceptive of my two best friends, and I knew that she'd sense my sadness. We were going to Annabel's later that evening and I knew we'd dissect the events of the previous few weeks in detail, but for now I was grateful that Lizzie and I would have the chance to talk calmly about the matter, and I knew that she'd be able to put things into perspective for me.

Lizzie flew down the stairs and opened the door breathlessly. 'At last, you're here!' she cried, enveloping me in a huge hug.

'How was the journey? Is it good to be back? It's been too long.'

I smiled at her barrage of questions. 'Lizzie, I'm desperate for a cup of your builders tea. Nice and strong with a couple of sugars.'

Over huge mugs of tea, I haltingly told Lizzie about what had happened between Vicky and me. 'You mean he dumped you because you got a text message from another guy?' she said, incredulously.

'No, he ended it because I lied to him,' I said. 'I do think it was a bit extreme, but Lizzie, these Indian guys are different from English men, they are a lot more intense in many ways and I'm beginning to think that jealousy is a national characteristic.'

'Well, I think you should just forget about him and move on. Maybe back to London.'

'I guess so,' I said, wearily. 'I mean, I don't suppose there's any point hanging onto something that just isn't meant to be. Anyway, how are you and Richard doing? I hope you're as happy as always?'

'Well, I think he might be up to something actually,' said Lizzie excitedly, her voice dropping to a near whisper. 'He's been acting very mysteriously, and I think he's been shopping for a ring. I just have this weird feeling. And even though we've talked about it and we're obviously planning it in the long term, it's still really exciting.'

She stopped abruptly, a look of distress on her face. 'I'm so sorry Jules, I didn't think. Here's me going on and on about how happy I am and you've just had a horrible breakup.'

'Don't be silly Lizzie, I'm so happy for you. Just because I'm in a pickle doesn't mean that I can't be excited for my best friend when she tells me that she's finally going to get that ring on her finger,' I said, hoping I sounded less wobbly than I felt inside. 'You deserve a big, fat, frilly wedding dress and a wedding with all the trimmings and I can't wait to see you walk down the aisle finally.'

We continued to chat about our lives, and I tried to explain my fascination with India to her. 'I don't know, Jules,' she said. 'Don't you miss home? You're so very far away from us all. And judging from what you've told me, it's a terribly difficult place to feel comfortable. Wouldn't you be happier back here?'

'Honestly, Lizzie,' I replied, feeling a deep sense of sadness, 'I feel completely torn. I guess I'm still hanging on to the romantic dream, and there's a lot I love about Mumbai but I just need to give it some time and make my decision when I'm over this. I don't want to leave just because I'm reacting to the breakup. I've already been through the entire cycle of deciding to leave and preparing myself mentally for that, and then I met Vicky. I can't keep changing my mind. This time it has to be for good.'

That evening, Lizzie and I headed to Annabel's trendy flat in London's emerging Docklands area. Her flat was the opposite of Lizzie's—whereas Lizzie had created a warm, cozy space, which she and Richard had carefully decorated in muted hues, with casual but comfortable ancient furniture and bright velvet cushions dotted around the place, Annabel's home exuded trendy, single-girl-about-town vibes. The wooden floor was new, the kitchen was all chrome and grey and filled with expensive looking appliances which didn't look as though they got much use, and the sofas were clearly expensive but not built for comfort. Everything matched perfectly and Annabel had ensured that her eye for detail, and her perfect taste, were represented in her living space. I rang the doorbell and she buzzed us up.

'Oh my God, it's been too long,' she said, clasping me in a

typically rib shattering hug. 'Why the sudden visit? I mean it's wonderful to see you, but you don't normally just drop in like this.

'I know,' I said. 'I just wanted to see you guys and I guess I was feeling a little homesick.' Over large gin and tonics I relayed the details of the breakup to Annabel.

'You're kidding me,' she spat, in her typically dismissive way. 'He dumped you because you got a text message from some other guy who you hadn't even kissed, let alone had a relationship with? What the hell is that all about? You're better off without him.'

'Annabel, it's a bit more complicated than that,' I protested. As I tried to explain the events of the past couple of weeks, I realized how feeble my words sounded. Buoyed up by the strength of my friends and their logical convictions, I could feel my sadness slowly turning to anger.

'Then again, perhaps you're right. It does seem like an extreme reaction, and the implication is that I was in the wrong and have somehow behaved badly, even though I think I've actually been pretty good during my entire time in Mumbai, at least by our standards.'

'Of course you have,' said Annabel. 'You've had, what, two relationships and a couple of flings? That's pretty reserved compared to some people.'

'The problem is that Indian men expect their wives to be virgins,' said Lizzie. I looked up, surprised at the angry tone of her voice. Annabel was typically the more outspoken one of my two friends, whereas Lizzie normally tried to see the best in every situation.

'Well, that may be the case in some parts of India, but it's different in the cities. Vicky definitely had no illusions about me, but I guess at the end of the day, he just couldn't handle it.'

'More like he couldn't handle himself,' chipped in Annabel. 'Honestly, Jules, you're better off without him. Now, let's order pizza.'

Later that week, I took the train down to Dorset, a picturesque and languid journey that I'd made a thousand times before leaving home. This time I was returning home with a heavy heart.

As the train made its way through the London suburbs, and the landscape slowly metamorphosed from the grey monotony of houses crammed tightly together with their rows upon rows of tiny box-like gardens, into an altogether more spacious, rural environment, I sat back and contemplated the traditional English, chocolate box views of swathes of green fields dotted with black and white cows and fluffy white sheep. The sense of openness and space was remarkable after London and of course compared to Mumbai's tightly packed streets and alleys. I spent the journey thinking about my past and wondering where my future would take me.

The train pulled slowly into Dorchester station, and I looked out at the familiar sights, at the platforms that I'd stood on so many times before, waiting for trains that would whisk me away to a brighter, more exciting life and at the formerly shabby cafeteria, which had now been revamped by one of the ubiquitous coffee chains, in which I'd spent hours smoking cigarettes, reading magazines and planning my future. As I stepped onto the platform, I felt a sudden rush of emotion as I peered through the clusters of people, looking for my parents. I saw them from a distance, Mum wearing her usual faded pinkish coat, Dad in what looked like a new anorak. Behind them was Louise, her dark hair swinging around her shoulders and her cheeks reddening in the wind. 'Mum, Dad,' I shouted, dropping my bags and waving enthusiastically in their direction. They saw me, and their faces lit up.

'I thought you'd never get here,' said Mum, engulfing me in a hug, her gentle Dorset accent making my heart ache. My Dad gave me his usual awkward kiss on the cheek and Louise grabbed me enthusiastically. 'Great to see you, sis,' she exclaimed.

We spent the rest of the afternoon drinking endless cups of tea, as Mum fussed around me with homemade cake and biscuits, gossiping about the events in the village. I hadn't told them the real reason behind my return, only that I had some holidays left to take and felt like a break. Louise had gone back to her house to run a few errands, and I let Mum's conversation wash over me gently, feeling comforted by the easy familiarity of my surroundings. The home that I'd grown up in was overstuffed and the furnishings were on the shabby side, but it exuded a warmth that always made me feel relaxed and calm. There was no standing on ceremony in my parents' house, no formality and none of the polite rigmarole that some of my schoolfriends' parents had demonstrated with their rigid timetables for meals and frosty hospitality. Here, the atmosphere was warm and slightly chaotic, more English eccentric than stiff upper lip, and I thanked my lucky stars again that my family were so normal, so down to earth and so non-judgemental. I knew that that even if I decided to tell them that I was coming back to England to live, they would simply be happy for me.

## 29

That evening, as we sat around the table polishing off the remains of Mum's incredible shepherd's pie, my phone rang. It was a UK number which I didn't recognize and I assumed it was one of my friends from home calling to catch up.

'Hello,' I said brightly, hoping that it was someone I could have a good natter with.

There was a short silence and then a deep male voice said, 'Julia?' before the call abruptly disconnected.

My entire body went numb and I knew that I must have looked as though I had seen a ghost. 'I'll be right back,' I said, scraping my chair back from the table and rushing out into the living room. I took a deep breath and sat down heavily on the sagging sofa which ran the length of one wall. The voice on the other end of the line had sounded exactly like Vicky's, and I wondered if I'd been hearing things. My head was spinning and I felt almost as though I was going to pass out. The phone rang again. It was the same number.

'Hello,' I said, breathlessly, desperate to hear that voice again. 'Jules? It's me, Vikrant.'

'Vicky? Is that really you?' I gabbled, aware that I was sounding like a complete idiot. 'Where are you? Why are you calling me?'

'Jules, I'm here, in England. In fact I'm in your parents' village, at the train station.'

This was too much for my confused mind to comprehend. 'You're where? I don't understand.'

'Jules, I'm here in Bridcombe. I've come to talk to you.'

I could hardly believe what I was hearing, and I felt the tears threaten to cascade down my cheeks.

'How can you be here? You're in India.'

I heard him chuckle. 'Jules, I flew to London yesterday and then got on a train to Bridcombe. Maya told me you were here and I need to see you. Anyway, it's freezing, can you come and pick me up from the station?'

'OK, I'll be there in twenty minutes,' I said, my befuddled brain swinging back into action. I took a deep breath and walked back into the kitchen, putting on what I hoped was a normal sounding voice.

'Mum, Dad, a friend has just turned up unexpectedly at the station and I need to go and pick him up. I've only had one glass of wine so I should be fine to drive.'

'Who is it love?' said Mum. 'Anyone we know?'

'No, it's a friend from India actually.'

Louise looked up at me in disbelief. 'From India? And they've just landed on your doorstep? Just like that?'

'Yes, just like that. Anyway, I'll explain later. He's a nice guy, you'll like him.'

As I drove to the station in Dad's ancient Vauxhall Nova, I tried to calm down, and stay focused. I wanted to give the impression that I was in control, and knew that I'd need to battle to keep my feelings from showing. I didn't want to second guess the reason for Vicky's sudden appearance, and though I hoped deep down that he'd come to patch things up, I didn't want to reopen all the old wounds I'd been working so hard to heal. As I pulled up at the station, I saw him standing by the exit, his familiar, lithe body illuminated by the light from the nearby convenience store. His hair was longer than ever, scraped back into its trademark ponytail, and as I stopped the car and flashed the headlights, I could see that his achingly familiar face looked tired and drawn.

He got into the car, and I was relieved that I wouldn't have to decide whether to hug him or not. 'Julia,' he said simply, sinking into the seat.

'Hi, how are you, I can't believe you're here,' I babbled, trying perversely to act as though nothing had happened.

'Julia, stop,' he said. 'Let me look at you.'

I took a deep breath and tightened my hands around the steering wheel, turning to look at him as I did so.

'Julia, I missed you so very much,' he said, his familiar deep tones washing over me and making me tremble. 'I realized that I'd overreacted and I wanted to apologize and see if we could try and work things out. Your phone was off and Maya told me that you'd gone to England, to your parents' place so I decided to just come here and talk to you.'

'Yes, I don't use my Indian number here, roaming costs are too expensive,' I said foolishly, wondering why I was having trouble processing his words. I felt as though I was dreaming. 'Vicky, let's go home and we can talk properly.'

'Are you sure? I can go to a hotel and we can talk tomorrow, or talk there. I don't want to be any trouble.'

I laughed wryly. 'It's no trouble. I've already told my parents that a friend has come to visit, and I'd rather you stayed with us anyway. I can make up a spare bed for you.'

We arrived home and I opened the front door, taking a deep breath to steel myself. 'Mum, Dad, Louise, this is Vikrant. He's a friend from Mumbai.'

I saw Louise's eyebrows shoot up as she looked at Vicky's tall, imposing figure. 'Wow, hi Vikrant,' she grinned, and I hoped desperately that she wouldn't ask any embarrassing questions.

'Hello there,' said Dad, standing up with his hand outstretched. 'Nice to meet you.'

'I'm so sorry to have landed on your doorstep like this,' said Vicky politely, his accented English sounding strangely out of place amongst the gentle Dorset tones. 'I wanted to see Julia and I couldn't reach her on the phone, so I thought I'd just turn up and hope that I wasn't interrupting anything.'

'You came all the way from Mumbai to meet Jules?' asked my nosy sister, her curiosity getting the better of her.

'We'll chat later,' I said firmly, steering Vicky in the direction of the stairs. 'I'm sure Vicky wants to use the bathroom and then I'll show him where he's going to sleep. The guest room bed has clean sheets, right Mum?'

'Yes love, I made the bed today,' Mum answered, and for once I was pleased at her fastidiousness.

Vicky picked up his bag, a small rucksack that he'd carried everywhere with him when we'd first met. It's simple familiarity filled my heart with a mixture of sadness and longing.

'I'll just show Vicky where the bathroom is and let him freshen up and then we'll be down,' I said, hoping that we'd be able to get our story straight in that time.

I led Vicky into the small but charming guestroom, and he sat heavily on the narrow single bed. 'Come, sit. Let's talk,' he said, patting the space beside him.

'Don't you want to take a shower first?' I said, trying to prolong the inevitable. 'I mean, you've come all the way from Mumbai. You must be dying to shower.'

'I'm dying to talk to you,' he said with a sad grin. 'I've plucked up the courage to land on your doorstep and now I think the suspense is going to kill me. I have a few things I need to say, and even if you've decided you're better off without me, I need you to hear them.'

I took a deep breath to steady my nerves and sat down gingerly beside him. Half of me wanted to throw my arms around him and tell him that I'd missed him desperately, but I managed to hold myself back, wanting to hear what he'd come all this way to say.

'Jules, I'm sorry about what happened,' he said, haltingly. 'I know that I completely overreacted, and I had no right to make you feel bad about something that was completely innocent. I can't explain why I behaved like I did. I guess I was scared of losing you.'

'So you pushed me away and lost me anyway,' I said, trying not to sound bitter or aggressive. I knew that taking my pent up frustration out on Vicky wouldn't solve anything, although it was tempting to get it all off my chest and make him suffer just as I had.

'Well, I've come here to see if we can try to salvage the relationship,' he said, looking deep into my eyes. 'I've realized over the past couple of weeks how much I care about you, Julia, and I can't imagine a life without you.'

I swallowed, willing myself to be strong. 'Well, if you want me, Vicky, you'll have to accept my past as well, and you have to learn to trust me completely. I'll never lie to you again, not even a teeny lie, and in return you need to stop with the jealousy. I don't have many ghosts from the past, and if they do ever pop up then we have to deal with them calmly. Just as we'd deal with any of your exes.'

I ended my short speech abruptly, my heart hammering in my ears and my insides turning somersaults at the thought that I hadn't lost this man after all.

'Come here you,' he said, pulling me towards him. I let myself sink into that familiar sharp, spicy smell, feeling the firm contours of his chest beneath his fitted jumper. 'I'm sorry. I'll keep saying it until you believe it, and you also need to trust me in return. I'm never going to behave so irrationally again. If you want, we can tell each other all about our pasts, and then there'll be nothing to surprise us.'

'No, I don't think that's a very good idea,' I said, flinching at the thought of having to explain my disastrous past love life and hearing all about his model girlfriends. 'Let's just agree to focus on the future and we'll deal with any ghosts if and when they come up.'

I looked into his deep brown eyes and knew that I needed to take this slowly. 'Now that we've got all that sorted, let's go down and get you some of my Mum's famous shepherd's pie. It's an English specialty.'

As we entered the kitchen, my parents and Louise looked up expectantly. 'So, have you settled in okay, Vicky?' asked Mum.

'Yes, thank you, Mrs Robinson,' he said, sounding like the perfect gentleman. 'You have a lovely home by the way.'

Mum blushed like a teenager and giggled. I could see Louise dying to ask what was between Vicky and me, and I decided to prolong her agony just a while longer. My world had turned upside down again since Vicky's phone call, and I needed time for everything to sink in and to convince myself that we were really back together again. Everything was too new and too raw for me to begin telling my family that we were in a relationship.

After Vicky had eaten, he started yawning. 'I'm sorry, that was incredibly delicious but I just can't keep my eyes open. I guess the jetlag has hit me, finally.'

With Vicky safely installed in the saggy but comfortable guest bed, I sat on my bed, breathing deeply and trying to digest what had just happened. My room was filled with memories from my childhood, Mum had hung on to them all, and although I had told her dozens of times to throw all the junk away, right now the soft toys piled on the shelf in the corner of the room, the annual school photographs pinned to the wall and even the curling posters of various lookalike boy bands seemed to provide a reassuring familiarity when I needed it most. I felt as though my world had been ripped apart and then glued suddenly together again, and I fell asleep hoping desperately that it wouldn't shatter once more.

The next morning, I knocked at Vicky's door with a cup of tea. To my surprise, he was already up and dressed.

'I woke really early,' he said, slightly sheepishly. 'I guess I'm still on Mumbai time.'

'Do you fancy a walk down to the local post office to grab the newspaper?' I asked. 'I can show you all the sights of our glamorous village.'

'Sure,' he said, laughing at my words.

The post office doubled up as a corner shop, its shelves stacked with what looked like antique tins of vegetables, spam and tuna, and a whole range of jars filled with the wonderful old fashioned sweets that I'd spent my childhood munching. I recognized the lady behind the post office window.

'Hello, Mrs Pitt, how are you?' I asked as she peered at me from behind thick, wire rimmed glasses.

'That's never Julia,' she said, in a high pitched, birdlike voice. 'You're back again then? Your Mum told me you'd gone away. Somewhere hot isn't it? In the Middle East?'

'India,' I smiled, 'I moved to Mumbai a few years ago. This is my friend Vikrant. He's visiting from Mumbai.'

Clearly this was too interesting an introduction to pass up, and Mrs Pitt clambered down from her stool and came out from behind the window to take a closer look at this rare specimen.

'Oooh, what a handsome one,' she said. 'Does he speak English? Or only Indian?'

I was more amused than embarrassed by this gaffe, and replied, 'He speaks perfect English actually. Don't you Vicky?'

'Yep, I suppose I do,' he replied, with a mischievous look in his eye. 'English is actually my first language, though I do speak a few other Indian languages.'

Mrs Pitt's poorly plucked eyebrows were by now hovering around the top of her head, as she struggled to equate the sight of a dark skinned man, fresh off the boat from India, with the stream of almost perfect English coming from his mouth.

'So do you like it there, then?' she asked me, clearly more comfortable conversing with me for the time being.

'I love it. It's a really interesting place, and the people are very friendly.' The look on her face suggested that she was struggling to deal with the concept that people thousands of miles away could be anything but hostile, but I didn't hold it against her, knowing how parochial English people could be in some of the rural areas. England as a country was highly multicultural and indeed there were areas of London and the Northern cities where you'd see more brown faces than white, but the South West in particular, especially the rural areas, were much less racially mixed. I supposed that it was similar to the stares I had by now grown accustomed to in Mumbai—there I was different, and I stood out, just as a dark skinned Indian stood out in a village which to my knowledge had never housed a non-white resident.

'I don't fancy India much,' she continued. 'I've been to Tenerife once and that was OK but it was too hot for me.'

'Well, it's certainly not everyone's cup of tea,' I told her, 'but it's a really interesting place, full of history and culture and of course lots of sunshine.'

'Well you have fun while you're home. Your mum has been talking non-stop about you, I know how much she misses you.'

I felt the familiar tug of guilt deep inside me, and pushed it away. 'Thank you, Mrs Pitt. See you again soon. I'll just take some lemon sherbets before I go.'

Sucking on the sour but delicious sweets, we ambled slowly along the road, breathing in the sights and smells of the countryside. The sweet smell of manure was pervasive, it wasn't unpleasant like the foul whiff of sewage that pervaded many of Mumbai's areas, but rather earthy and rich, and somehow very comforting. There was something warmly reassuring about being able to return to a world that had almost stood still in time.

Vicky took my hand in his. 'Jules, I know it's early days, but I just want to tell you how happy I am, and how relieved I am that we can move on with our lives, together. I was terrified that you'd send me packing, actually.'

I squeezed his hand, 'I suppose I should have done really,' I told him, a grin playing about my lips. 'You deserved to be sent away, frankly.'

'I know, I know. You're an angel and I'm the devil but I'm a devil who's in love with you, Julia. Madly, passionately in love with you.'

I was embarrassed but overjoyed at his words, words that I'd longed to hear for so long. 'I love you, too,' I said, shyly, squeezing his hand and wondering why I felt so tongue-tied.

We spent the rest of our week rebuilding our relationship, relaxing and enjoying the quiet tranquility of the village. I had decided to tell my parents and Louise that Vicky and I were an item, and they took the news surprisingly well, given that it would probably mean that I would be prolonging my stay in India.

'He seems like a nice lad,' Dad said in his typically understated fashion.

My sister was slightly more vocal about the revelation. 'Oh my god, I knew it. He's so handsome, I can't believe you've gone and snagged some sexy Bollywood bloke.'

'Louise, he has nothing to do with Bollywood,' I laughed, 'but yes, I suppose he is quite sexy.'

'He's gorgeous,' she said. 'And charming with it. I just hope he treats you well. I know what those Indian men can be like.' I had no idea what random piece of tabloid journalism Louise had been reading, but let her comment pass.

'He's lovely to me and I'm really happy Louise.'

The rest of our week passed quickly as we learned to relax again in one another's company. We talked about the past and about the future, trying to lay the insecurities of the past to rest while focusing on the long term. The stares in the village and even in the nearest decently sized town continued, but they were more curious than hostile, and we learned to ignore them. I took pleasure in holding Vicky's hand tightly as we walked through the streets, and I was tempted to kiss him in public to give the more curious types something to look at, but I'd never really been one for public displays of affection. Vicky seemed to relax completely into the whole experience of being in this part of the world. Though he'd spend a couple of hours a day checking his Blackberry and phone, he focused on me, on us and our surroundings, as I took him the length and breadth of the small county and showed him the few tourist sites, which largely consisted of ancient ruins and old castles.

After a week of spending time with the family and making the most of the uncharacteristically good weather, I knew both of us were dying to get back to Mumbai, now that we'd made the decision to build a life together. As we said goodbye to mum and dad on the station platform, I felt the usual rush of emotion as my throat choked and tears threatened to spill. Our farewell seemed particularly poignant this time round, given the sad state I'd arrived in and the euphoria in which I was leaving.

'Bye, love,' whispered Mum, hugging me tightly and trying to fight off the tears which I knew weren't far away. We'd been through this ritual ever since I had left Dorset for my northern university town, and, even after almost fifteen years, I still felt

Becoming Mrs Kumar

emotional parting from my parents. Louise had said goodbye to
us earlier that morning, in her characteristically cool way.

'Hope it works out for you,' she'd whispered into my ear as
we had hugged each other goodbye, and I'd smiled, knowing that
that was praise indeed coming from my critical, insecure sister.

'Don't cry, Mum,' I told her, hoping that I wouldn't break
down as I'd done so often in the past. 'We'll be back soon.'

'I just wish you'd both come and live back here,' she grabbed
me even tighter. 'India is so far away.'

'It's only half a day away, Mum,' I said, laughing, 'and I
promise we'll come back lots.'

She turned to Vicky, pulling him into an equally tight
embrace. 'Look after her,' she instructed. 'I know Mumbai is safe
enough, but I worry about her.'

'Mum!' I laughed with embarrassment, 'I'm all grown up now.
Honestly, you don't need to worry about me. We'll see you soon.'

I hugged my Dad who was fiddling slightly self-consciously
with the strings of his anorak, and pushed Vicky in the direction
of the train, which had just pulled up on the platform. 'Come
on, it will leave without us if we're not careful,' I said.

'Well, at least that's your family met,' said Vicky on the plane
home. 'They're really lovely, by the way. I hope you like my lot
as much, I'm sure you will.'

I was a little nervous about meeting Vicky's parents, and
worried that they might not find me suitable for their only son,
but decided to cross that bridge when we came to it, safe in the
knowledge that as long as we were together, we could handle
anything.

# 30

Meeting Vicky's family came more quickly than I'd imagined. A week after returning to Mumbai, he casually dropped into conversation news that we had been summoned to their home.

'So my parents are throwing a small party in Delhi for their fortieth wedding anniversary,' he told me as we were both getting ready for work, 'and they really want us to go. I've told them all about you and they've asked me to invite you as well.'

'Um, OK,' I said, trying to sound happy and positive about news that actually filled me with dread. Later that evening, I rifled through my wardrobe, looking for a suitable outfit to impress the parents.

'When my Mother says "small", she actually means around two to three hundred people, so you'd better wear something fancy,' Vicky said, laughing.

'Are you serious? Really? For a party? How will they cope with all those people? Do your parents live in a mansion, or what?' I asked, my mind reeling.

'No silly, they'll hire a venue,' he said. 'No one has parties at home these days. They'll probably have it at some fancy five-star hotel, knowing my mother.'

'But that will cost …'

'… a small fortune,' he finished my sentence with a knowing look. 'Yep, my parents, well my mother at least, is all about impressing the great and the good. She likes to feel that she's "someone" in society so she goes all out to show off whenever she can.'

'You don't sound like you enjoy that very much?' I asked, wanting to get the lowdown on Vicky's feelings about his family, and in particular his mother, before meeting them.

'I hate it,' he replied, simply. 'I love her, of course, but I can't stand the way she always has to be at the centre of attention. It's exhausting.'

'What have you told them about me? I assume they know we're living together?' I asked him.

'Kind of. Well, not exactly. Well, I haven't really talked about it. But I assume they know.'

'So they actually don't know that we are sharing an apartment? And a bed?' I asked, incredulously.

'Well, I haven't lied to them. I've just kind of avoided the subject. Living together isn't really the done thing in India, at least not until you're married, so they don't need to know the gory details. I guess they think I'm staying in a guesthouse or with friends, as I normally do.'

I bit my tongue, determined to control the invective that threatened to spill from my lips. I knew that India and Indian parents were different when it came to co-habiting and sex before marriage and all those things that we in the more liberal West took for granted, but at the same time I wanted Vicky to take my side over his parents, and be honest with them about our relationship.

'Well, I guess you know how best to handle them,' I said

grouchily, trying not to sound like a petulant child. I knew that this was an area that we'd never completely see eye to eye on, and so I decided to let it slide, figuring that it was one of those things in our relationship that we'd just have to agree to differ on.

After rejecting the entire contents of my wardrobe as 'too slutty', 'too casual' or 'too cheap looking', I went shopping for an outfit that would pass muster at a fancy society party. I settled for a pretty salwar kameez, with a flattering cut. It was sufficiently sparkly to be acceptable for a party, yet modest—as far as I was concerned, meeting the family for the first time was an important event and I wanted to make sure I made the right impression. The embarrassing vomiting incident from the party at Krishna's parents' place was still fresh in my mind, and although I'd managed to avoid public humiliation then, the memory of being drunk and ill wasn't a pleasant one.

Vicky was a lot more laid back about the whole thing. 'Just chill, wear whatever you want. My parents have to accept you anyways, I'm not exactly waiting for their seal of approval, so just be yourself.'

'I know, Vicky, and that's sweet of you to say, but I want to make sure that everything goes well. It's a bit nerve wracking, honestly.'

Vicky's parents seemed so different to my own, and the cream of Delhi society so far from Mum and Dad's sleepy Dorset village, that I was beginning to feel overwhelmed before I'd even met them.

'Just relax,' he smiled, squeezing my hand. 'Everyone will love you.'

'I'm fine really,' I said, trying to shrug off the tension which, despite his words of reassurance, was refusing to leave me. I wished I hadn't spent so much time listening to Maya's words of doom and gloom about her in-laws, and decided to be as positive as I possibly could. After all, what was the worst that could happen? Even if they didn't like me very much, Vicky had told me repeatedly that his feelings for me were the only ones that really mattered.

I decided to meet Maya to tell her all about my happy reunion with Vicky, and to get some tips on dealing with the in-laws, deciding that even if she was scarred from a bad experience, she'd at least be able to provide me with some insights about how I should behave.

'Hey, it's me,' I said as I called her the following day, conscious that the last conversation we'd had had been all about the breakup and that I'd been in an extremely fragile emotional state.

'I got your text message,' she said. 'So you guys are really back together again? He turned up on your doorstep, just like that?'

'Yep, just like that,' I laughed. 'It was pretty insane actually. If I hadn't been so traumatized at the time, I'd have found the whole brown-man-turns-up-in-sleepy-Dorset-village thing quite hilarious. But I wasn't finding much very amusing back then.'

'I know,' she murmured sympathetically. 'You were in a right old state, and I'm not surprised. Are you sure you're OK now? And more importantly, do you think you'll be able to trust him again? I mean what if he loses it again over some trivial matter?'

'I honestly don't think he will,' I told her confidently. 'Maya, we've done nothing but talk for the past few days and, unless I'm the biggest fool on the planet, I really think we've put all that behind us now.'

We arranged to meet a couple of days later and I hung up

the phone, feeling much more confident about the impending meet-the-in-laws session, determined that it would be a success and that they'd embrace me with open arms.

Maya and I met in one of our favourite restaurants, a dingy but relaxed place which served cheap spirits and delicious Indian snacks. Over crunchy samosas, succulent tandoori chicken, and large vodka-tonics, we caught up on the events of the past few weeks.

'So how did your family react to Vicky turning up on their doorstep?' she asked.

'Actually, they loved him,' I answered truthfully. 'He was charming without being sleazy, he made a real effort, and even Louise thought he was awesome.'

'Wow, sounds like he made a real hit,' she said. 'He really sounds like he's turned over a new leaf.' I wondered if I could detect a note of cynicism in her voice.

'Well, no relationship is ever perfect,' I told her, 'and I know he's kind of jealous deep down, but I think now that we've decided to move on, together, this one is definitely a long term thing. I think we can work out our differences, or at least agree to have different opinions on certain things.'

'Well, one piece of advice I would give you is to get everything clear and upfront before you get married, if you do,' said Maya, looking serious suddenly. 'You need to talk about where you both stand on the religious part, especially if you plan to have kids. What kind of schools you intend to enrol your kids in, where you want to live in the future, what part both your parents will play in your lives, and how you're going to split your finances, etc. Make sure that he's cool with you working after marriage, especially if you have kids. A lot of Indian men expect their wives to turn into housewives after marriage, and many of them will even expect you to live with their parents, and cook and clean for everyone.'

My face must have looked as horrified as I felt, as she squeezed my hand and added, 'I mean, don't get paranoid, I'm just saying that you need to talk about all this stuff. Hopefully he's the more liberal, modern type. I'm sure he is, but just to be on the safe side.'

'Well, let me get his parents over with first,' I said, with a weak smile. 'Any tips on how I should behave with them?'

'Just relax and be yourself. Delhi people are notoriously shallow, sorry to generalize but they're often easily impressed by material wealth and appearance.'

'But I'm not particularly rich,' I protested, thinking of my salary which, while fairly generous, was certainly not enough to throw me into the rich list.

'Ah, but you're white,' she said, 'so they'll assume you're rich, and also that you come from a "good" family. Those are two major obstacles for any Indian parents looking for a match for their child.'

'Child? Vicky's thirty-six.'

'Ah, but he'll always be a baby in his mother's eyes,' she replied with a grin. 'Trust me, the relationship between the Indian Mummy and her beloved son is a complex and almost incestuous one. She'll treat him as her baby his entire life, and woe betide any daughter-in-law who tries to take her place.'

She stopped abruptly, realizing that she was supposed to be encouraging me, not filling me with dread and paranoia. 'But you'll be fine,' she said. 'As long as you and Vicky decide on the boundaries, you'll be fine.'

'So why are Indian mothers so obsessed with their sons?' I asked.

Maya had several theories on the subject, most of which centred around the premise that boys would provide for the family, whereas girls were seen as a financial burden. I left the restaurant with my head spinning, a little overwhelmed by the concept of controlling in-laws but confident that Vicky and I had the kind of relationship that would allow us to create our own small unit, tied to, but not dependent on parents or their advice.

The weekend of the party came around quickly, and before I knew it, we were sitting in the back of a luxurious sedan car, which smelt of brand new leather, sent to the airport by his parents. I was a little surprised that no one had come to meet us, but I figured that they must all be busy with the party preparations. We pulled up to an enormous, colonial looking house, and the gates swung open smoothly.

'Wow, this looks amazing,' I said nervously, my throat drying up.

'It's home,' said Vicky wryly. 'Or at least, their home.'

It had been a long time since I'd actually been in a proper house, as opposed to an apartment. Mumbai people, even the richest, all lived in flats, unless they were lucky enough to own one of the old, gorgeous looking bungalows which were few and far between now that ambitious property developers were seizing them to build more high-rises. Delhi was a far more spacious city than Mumbai; whereas Mumbai's inhabitants were crammed onto what was effectively a small set of islands glued together with reclaimed land, Delhi was a huge, circular metropolis, which sprawled in every direction. Moreover, it was India's political capital, and consequently the place where funds for development were diverted. Whereas Mumbai's roads were riddled with potholes, and its sewage, water supply and transport systems ancient and often falling apart, Delhi received the lion's share of investment for new roads, swanky metro systems and sanitation.

As we entered the pretty two storeyed house, my eyes widened at the glittering chandelier atop the vast hall, a sweeping staircase completing the luxurious feel. I was so used to cramped spaces, that the sheer size of this room was making me reel. A very chic looking lady was waiting at the bottom of the staircase, accompanied by a man who had clearly once been very handsome, and from whom Vicky had obviously inherited his good looks. His mother was wearing a beautiful, shimmering, emerald green saree with matching, though subtle jewellery, which looked expensive and classy, and I immediately felt underdressed despite the fact that it was the middle of the day and I was dressed appropriately in a calf-length linen shift dress and low heels.

'Darling,' she said, embracing Vicky in a gentle hug. 'I'm so glad you made it. And this must be Julia.'

She took my hand and squeezed it gently, her head turned slightly as if appraising me, but with a smile which looked genuine enough.

'Very nice to meet you,' I smiled, in what I hoped was a confident manner.

Mrs Kumar looked pretty high maintenance to me, her makeup was subtle but impeccable, and her hair looked freshly blow dried, falling in soft waves around her face. She smelt gorgeous, and I caught a waft of expensive smelling perfume as she took my hand. Mr Kumar was clad in an open necked shirt and smart trousers, and as he leaned over to shake my hand, I caught sight of a large gold watch on his wrist. I wondered whether these people even knew how to dress casually.

Besides telling me a little bit about his parents, Vicky had briefed me earlier on his sisters and brother. 'Aparna's the eldest,' he'd told me, as I frantically tried to memorize the details. 'She's pretty uptight, a typical over achiever and honestly I think her life is really dull. She's the sensible one of all of us.'

'So she's married, right?'

'Yep, married for the past ten years and the mother of twin boys. They're only eight years old but they seem to be enrolled in every extra curricular class going.'

'Ouch, that sounds horrific,' I said, recalling my own laid back childhood.

'Yep. They're turning into right little brats,' he said, with a chuckle. 'Then there's me, and then comes Ashwin. He's cool and lots of fun but very lazy,' he told me. 'I think he's hoping that Dad hands him a fat inheritance and he can live off that for the rest of his days.'

'What about girlfriends?' I asked him. 'Maybe he just needs a good woman to kick him into touch?'

'Fat chance,' Vicky said with a resigned smile. 'He's too lazy to run after a girl. I think he's happy being on his own, and jumping from one hare-brained scheme to another.'

'What about your younger sister?'

'Sangeeta? She's sweet actually,' Vicky said. 'She's probably the most responsible one of all of us, ironically. Probably something to do with the fact that she's the youngest, and was kind of overlooked by my parents as a result, although we kids all doted on her. I'm sure she was an accident, and my parents were tired of raising kids by the time she came along. She hasn't had it easy, but she's always very positive about things.'

'How old is she?' I asked.

'She's in the last year of college, just turned twenty-one.'

Ashwin and Sangeeta both joined us for lunch, which was a long and languid affair seated around a long table on the sweeping patio behind the house. Vicky's two younger siblings were both living at home, of course, as was the custom before marriage. I thanked my lucky stars that Vicky had broken free from that particular norm, I wasn't sure that I could handle dating a man who was still living with his parents, however liberated he might be. Aparna apparently was tied up with some important meeting at her kids' school so was absent from the table.

'So how did you end up agreeing to go out with Vicky?' asked Ashwin, mischievously. 'Did he pester you for ages?'

'Well, er, no not really.' I looked at Vicky for help.

'Take no notice of my younger and infinitely less wise brother,' Vicky cut in. 'He'll tease you endlessly if he knows he can get the upper hand.'

'Even I'm curious, though,' said Sangeeta, her curly brown hair bobbing in the gentle breeze. 'How did you two meet?'

I launched into an abbreviated version of how our working relationship gradually turned into something more serious, keeping my tone suitably light and I hoped, witty.

'Well, our Vicky is a charmer, that's for sure,' said Ashwin, with a wink in my direction. I gulped and focused on my plate, not wanting to find myself caught in the middle of sibling one-upmanship.

'Julia do tell us more about yourself,' Mr Kumar said. 'What made you come to India in the first place?' As I launched into the by now familiar script about leaving London I wondered whether they would find it odd that I'd left my friends and family behind to move to a foreign country.

'But you must miss London?' his mother asked. 'It's such a lovely city. Daddy and I have so many happy memories of it.'

'Well, I do enjoy going back, but honestly, I'm loving Mumbai,' I replied, truthfully.

'And what do your parents do? Are they in London proper?' she asked.

'We're from Dorset. My parents are both retired now but my dad used to be a teacher and my mum stayed at home and brought my sister and me up.'

I wasn't sure that my dad's profession really cut it in terms of Indian aspiration, and I couldn't tell from their expression whether they found this to be suitably respectable.

'This is really delicious,' I said, changing the subject and spearing another piece of succulent lamb kebab.

'I have the best servants in India,' said Mrs Kumar. 'It's so difficult to find good help, and even more difficult to make them work, wouldn't you agree?'

'Er, well I wouldn't really know,' I spluttered, thinking of Deepa who was an absolute delight to have around the house, and very hardworking.

'Well, you'll have to get used to managing the help when you are married,' said his mother, delicately wiping the sides of her mouth with a pristine linen napkin.

I tried not to look as though her comment had fazed me, taking a deep drink from the water glass which had just been filled by one of the helpful 'servants'. I snuck a look at Vicky and saw that he was taking the comment in his stride.

'Mum, seriously,' he said laughing. 'Let Jules get used to the idea of this family before she decides whether she wants to jump into it permanently.'

'But there's no harm in being prepared,' started his mother, before Vicky's 'Don't mess with me' look halted her. 'OK, OK, I'll change the subject,' she said, with a smile that looked ever so slightly forced. I wondered why she was so keen on the topic, after all, it wasn't as though Vicky and I had been dating for years, in fact relatively speaking, this was still a fairly new relationship.

'She's desperate to get me married off,' he told me later.

'But why?' I asked, genuinely bemused.

'Well, I'm the oldest son and therefore it's important that I have kids to pass down the family name.'

'Like there aren't millions of Kumars in India and all over the world,' I said with a laugh.

'Well, there are, it's a fairly common name but there's this obsession with producing heirs, and they only count if they're the sons of sons.'

'So no pressure, then,' I said, sarcastically. 'So not only do I have to marry you, but I have to give you sons. What if I don't want to marry you, or have your children?' I hoped that my voice conveyed a lightness of tone, but whilst I wasn't against the idea of either marriage or children in principle, I did object to being put under what I considered to be unrealistic and somewhat sexist pressure. Still, as always, I took a deep breath and told myself that this was India, that I needed to adapt and be patient.

'Well, I am assuming that you love me enough to want to marry me,' he said, with a grin. 'And as for kids, well, let's cross that bridge when we come to it. I'm not sure we've done having fun ourselves yet.'

I didn't know how to react to this 'kind of but not really' proposal and I certainly didn't want to look as though I was the kind of woman who was desperately wanting to snare a husband. I gave him what I hoped was a winning smile and changed the subject, keen to keep the pace of our relationship on an even keel. Little did I know that the matter was about to be taken out of my hands entirely.

The party was every bit as glamorous as I'd imagined. The venue was an exceptionally fancy five-star hotel in the exclusive Diplomatic Enclave, Delhi's political centre where all the embassies, monuments and government buildings lined vast, pristine streets. It was a far cry from the shabbier side of town and indeed from Mumbai's claustrophobically crammed thoroughfares. I dressed carefully, wishing that I had real diamonds rather than the set of obviously fake (to my mind) cubic zirconia studs which were twinkling in my ears.

'You look gorgeous,' said Vicky, as he swung by my room after I'd finished dressing. 'Suitably desi, and at the same time irresistibly firang.'

I smiled at his choice of colloquialisms. 'Well, as long as I fit in,' I said. 'Anyway, what are you doing in my room? Isn't it forbidden to be in a girl's room before you're married to her?'

'Ha bloody ha,' he said, grinning. 'I know my parents are super traditional, but frankly, most Indian parents would stop short of allowing their son or daughter to share a bed before they were married. It's just not the done thing.'

'I know, I know,' I said, thinking of the times I'd brought boyfriends home without my parents batting an eyelid when they'd slept in my bedroom. Vicky was wearing a gorgeous dark gold Indian sherwani, which looked incredible on his dark skin.

'You look like an Indian prince, seriously,' I told him, admiring the way the heavy fabric sat on his broad shoulders. I'd never seen Vicky looking so formal, and I thought he looked incredible. His long hair hung half-way down his back in a sheet of glossy black, the outfit looked regal and exotic, and I couldn't believe he was all mine.

The evening passed in a blur of champagne and innumerable guests who all looked the same—the men portly and wearing tuxedos or smart suits, the ladies dressed as though to outdo each other, in bright jewel coloured sarees and the requisite diamonds. I drank enough to relax, but not enough to lose my senses. I wanted to remain firmly in the present. Mr and Mrs Kumar were clearly well connected; Vicky pointed out a number of important people who were apparently big in the media, business and even politics.

'How come your parents know so many people?' I asked, trying not to feel overwhelmed.

'They are unbelievable networkers,' he whispered. 'It's all a bit shallow in my opinion, but it makes them happy.'

His elder sister Aparna joined us, with her husband Rajeev in tow. He looked exhausted, and had a slightly bashful air about

319

him. I wondered if he was as hen pecked as he looked, battered into submission by his domineering wife.

'So glad you could join us, Julia,' said Aparna, in a strident voice. You must come and spend time with the boys. Adoo and Vivoo are such fun, and you'd be amazed at how smart they are.'

'I'm sure I would be,' I murmured, trying to keep a straight face. As she launched into a story about how her darlings had recently topped their class, Vicky interrupted her, 'I'm so sorry, Aparna, but I promised to introduce Jules to the Guptas. You know how Sanju Aunty is always asking why I haven't settled down.' He pulled me away gently, and I gave her an apologetic smile.

'What was that all about?' I asked him as he steered me in the direction of the luxurious gardens. 'And who is Sanju Aunty?'

'Some old and irrelevant friend of my mother's,' he answered with a smile. 'But that's not the real reason I wanted to get you to myself. I've had a couple of glasses of champagne and so I think I'm brave enough to do this.'

'Do what?' I asked him, perplexed by his sudden odd behaviour.

'Sit down,' he said, as we approached a gorgeous fountain encircled by wrought iron benches.

'OK,' I said, slightly bemused by his tone of voice, which seemed to be veering between authoritarian and nervous.

'Julia Robinson,' he said, taking my hand in his and clearing his throat, 'Um. I well. I suppose I should do this properly.' As he gazed deep into my eyes, he dropped to the floor, on one knee. I felt an enormous blush spread through my body. My heart was racing. This was really it. A marriage proposal.

'Will you marry me, Julia?' came those fateful words,

accompanied by a small box that appeared miraculously before me, which he opened to reveal a gorgeous solitaire in a Tiffany style setting. I was completely lost for words, and could only stare at his beautiful, deep brown eyes, which suddenly seemed mysterious and hard to read in the moonlight.

'Well?' he asked, as I gazed at him, my mouth practically dropping open. A thousand thoughts were flashing through my mind. Would we be able to make it together, given our different backgrounds and possibly even expectations? It struck me that we hadn't had any of the serious conversations, the 'where will we live?', the 'do we want to have kids?', the 'what religion will our kids follow?' questions remained unanswered. And yet, despite the rational part of my brain, which was rendering me dumbstruck, lost in the contemplation of a future that even now seemed uncertain, my heart was swelling, overwhelmed with the feelings of love and elation that were flooding through me. I found my voice.

'Yes, yes I will. I will marry you, Vicky.'

'Thank goodness,' he said, catching me in a tight embrace. 'I thought for a horrible moment there that you were actually going to turn me down.'

'Aren't you supposed to put the ring on my finger?' I asked, laughing. 'Of course, how stupid of me. Here.' And with that he slid the glittering jewel onto my ring finger where it sat sparkling fire and glinting under the moonlight.

'Wow, it fits perfectly!' I said. 'How did you manage that? And when did you buy the ring? Have you been planning this all along?'

'Enough of the questions,' he replied, laughing. 'Let's just say that I've been trying to pluck up the courage to ask you for a while, and with all this talk of marriage and us being with my family, I just felt that it was the right time. And now we can go and announce it and make my mother happy.'

## 31

The Kumars, it seemed, were delighted at the news of our engagement. From Ashwin's 'cool' to his mother's more exuberant 'what wonderful news', I was pleased at their reaction. I hadn't expected to be welcomed into their family so spontaneously, and had suspected I'd have to work a little harder for them to accept me as a future daughter- or sister-in-law, but they seemed genuine enough. I wasn't sure how to break the news to my friends and family back home, and ended up calling them all after a couple of glasses of wine for fortitude.

Lizzie and Annabel were brilliantly supportive, despite the fact that the last time they'd seen me, I'd been literally crying on their shoulders.

'I'm delighted for you, darling,' Lizzie said. 'I'm sure you're making the right decision, and it all sounds terribly romantic.'

Annabel was of course slightly more cynical, but she tried her best to be positive. 'As long as you're sure, then I'm thrilled for you, of course. Can't wait for the wedding! And to meet this dreamboat.'

Her words took me aback, although of course I knew that a wedding was imminent, I hadn't really wrapped my head around the concept, nor considered its potential complexities.

'Will his parents want you to get married over there?' asked Mum, as accommodating as always.

'I don't really know,' I said. 'We haven't really talked about the details, to be honest. I think we're just trying to enjoy the being engaged feeling, which is quite enough to get used to for the time being.' I felt a sudden pang of guilt that my parents might be denied the chance to organize their eldest daughter's wedding and stun the local parish with a colourfully international affair. I knew, though, that practically speaking, it would be far easier for my friends and family to make the journey to India than for Vicky's typically extended Indian family to travel to Dorset or even London.

After fending off countless questions from my workmates, friends and family about the wedding date, I decided to take matters into my own hands and start the ball rolling. Suddenly, I'd transitioned from paranoid potential bunny boiler to bride to be and wedding planner. It was a strange although not entirely unpleasant feeling.

That evening, I took a deep breath and asked Vicky, 'So, do you think we should start thinking about wedding dates? Or would you prefer a long engagement?'

'Actually, I'd like us to get married quickly,' he said, pensively. 'I mean, after almost losing you, and then plucking up the courage to propose, I think we should just get on with it. I'm dying for you to be Mrs Kumar.' The name Julia Kumar sounded surreal to my ears but I couldn't wait either. We talked about locations, discussing the merits of England over India.

'To be honest,' I told him, 'England is beautiful for a wedding but only if the weather behaves itself. If not, it can be awful. Think shivering guests and sodden canapés. Plus, I'm assuming that your family, at least the extended family, is a lot larger than mine.'

'Well, that's true. I can't see my mother wanting to invite fewer than a thousand people.'

'A thousand!' I spluttered. 'Are you serious?'

'Well, believe it or not, that's actually considered a smallish wedding in India. My cousin Vivek had a wedding with three-and-a-half thousand guests. Basically, this is a chance for my parents to show off to the world. Although if you'd prefer it, we could have a tiny wedding, just the two of us and close friends.'

I juggled mental images of an idyllic beach setting with only our best friends and immediate family on the one hand and a big fat Indian wedding on the other. The extravaganza won hands down, despite my lifelong romantic leaning towards the former. If I was going to marry an Indian and presumably live in India, then I wanted to do things properly.

'No, bring on the excess,' I said, hoping I sounded more confident than I felt. 'But isn't it going to be terribly expensive? And don't the girl's parents usually pay for the wedding? I'm not sure my parents are going to be able to afford that.'

'Well, traditionally yes, but we're not exactly conventional and I already know that my parents want to organize and pay for this. It means that Mum will try to railroad us into a few decisions, but I'll make sure you're OK with everything first.'

I couldn't imagine trying to take on the indomitable Mrs Kumar and emerge unscathed, but a part of me liked the idea of going with the flow, with allowing someone else to take care of the preparations, the organizing, and the hard work.

That weekend, we discussed the plans with his parents over the phone.

'I'm thinking one of the better hotels in town,' said Mrs Kumar, delighted that we'd decided to get married quickly.

'Or we could rent a venue and decorate it how we want it,' said Vicky. 'All the weddings are at fancy five-star hotels and honestly, they are really boring.'

I could almost hear the wheels turning in Mrs Kumar's mind as she weighed the options, considering which would have more impact amongst her society friends. 'Perhaps you're right darling,' she said. 'Hotel weddings are done to death. I've been to five already this year. Let's find a spectacular venue and I'll hire the very best decorators to work their magic.'

'Can I at least choose the colour scheme?' I asked Vicky later. 'I've got my heart set on a dark turquoise colour. Kind of a sea green. It always brings out my eyes, and I guess I need to look my best for the big day, right?'

'Darling, you can have any colour you want,' Vicky said, laughing and shaking his head. 'Except I guess your saree will need to be red, that's kind of traditional.'

'I can handle that,' I said. 'As long as I look the part.'

We had fixed the wedding for November, which gave us a few months to plan things. I immediately sent 'hold the date' e-mails to my friends. I phoned Mum to tell her that we'd decided to get married in Delhi, knowing that it would be a big deal for them to come out to India. While I knew that they were excited and happy for me, I knew that they'd be nervous about such a long journey, especially to a country which they termed 'third world' and imagined as being filled with potential disasters and the inevitable hygiene issues. My parents had taken several holidays to France and Spain, usually opting for the package trips, which came with all inclusive perks and nice hotels. They had occasionally veered outside their comfort zone and had even done a now notorious camping trip through northern France, but they'd never been outside Europe before. My sister's reaction was equally uncertain. She told me bluntly that she and Matthew were worried about the dirt and the bugs and the diseases. I tried to put her mind at rest.

'Lou, listen to me. It's true that there is dirt and poverty here, but there is also lots of other stuff. It's very westernized here in most places, there are plenty of nice hotels and bars and restaurants which have amazing food and it's a lot cheaper than London. Plus, it's going to be a really big, fancy wedding. It's not every day that you get invited to a genuine big fat Indian wedding.'

'Yes, I know. I'm pleased for you Jules, really I am. But it's just so far away and it won't be cheap.'

'Louise, just pay for your flights and the rest will be taken care of,' I said, wondering why, for my sister, practical considerations always had to come in the way of enjoying.

Over the next few weeks, we flew to Delhi a couple of times and finalized the venue with Vicky's parents, shopped and shopped and shopped some more for sarees and other outfits for all the various parties that would make up the big event, and sampled the wares of endless caterers, all of which tasted similar to me. We met a designer who took our brief for the transformation of the venue, promising to work miracles on the decidedly barren looking space, which was apparently one of the most sought after locations for society weddings.

'You should really see it when there's a wedding going on,'

said Mrs Kumar, sensing my nervousness as I gazed at the huge bare grassy area and what looked like an enormous pile of rubbish in the corner.

'I'll take your word for it,' I murmured, knowing that at least given my future mother-in-law's predilection for impressing the great and the good, the wedding would end up being spectacular. I also knew that India was great at transformations—what often looked awful initially ended up looking incredible, even if it was only temporary. I soon realized that what I had thought would be a single day's celebration was actually turning into a week-long affair.

'So first there's the haldi ceremony, then the sangeet, then the mehndi and then the wedding itself,' said Aparna, who had joined us for an afternoon of wedding talk. Seeing my look of bemusement, she went on to explain, 'you'll get covered in turmeric paste at the haldi ceremony. That's to brighten your skin. Then we'll all dance at the sangeet. Then you'll have your hands and feet covered in henna designs at the mehndi. You have to be prepared for the big event. There are loads of other traditional ceremonies but we might skip some of those, as we only have a week.'

I decided to go with the flow. 'You tell me where to be and when. And I'll make sure my guests from England and Mumbai block their diaries for a week.'

I wondered whether it was OK for me as a non-Hindu to get married in a traditional Hindu wedding ceremony.

'We'll have to register the marriage after so it's legally binding, but actually Hinduism is a very tolerant religion,' Vicky told me. 'Anyway, neither you nor I are particularly religious so I don't think it matters. I wouldn't even mind a church wedding if you preferred that. And our children will make up their own minds about which religion they prefer, when they're old enough.'

'Well, I suppose that we should have the Hindu ceremony as your parents are organizing the wedding,' I said. 'And if my parents want, we can go to church with them when we're next home and see if the vicar will give us a blessing. That way everyone will be happy.'

The wedding week approached far more quickly than I'd imagined. Vicky and I had had fairly low key hen and stag nights, which had been fun. Maya had organized mine, and although I'd missed my English girlfriends, I enjoyed playing silly games and drinking complicated cocktails with the Mumbai girls. My Mum and Dad, along with Louise and Matthew flew into Mumbai a fortnight before the wedding to spend a few days at our home before we all travelled to Delhi together. Lizzie and Richard were flying directly into Delhi, as was Annabel, who was bringing some new boyfriend along with her. I waited anxiously at the airport to meet my family, jostling for a position with the drivers and the hotel staff, friends and relatives all eager to catch sight of their guests. Eventually I caught sight of them—Louise striding ahead, visibly taken aback at the wall of heat that hit her on exiting the airport, and Mum, Dad and Matthew trailing behind, a look of blind panic on Mum's face.

'Louise! Mum, Dad!' I shouted, waving frantically in their direction. They spotted me and I caught the relief on their faces. Mum caught me in a tight hug, clearly reassured that I had actually turned up at the end of the long flight.

'Come on, let's get to the car,' I attempted to steer them in the direction of the waiting vehicle. I had rented a larger car for the week, a Toyota Innova, which would easily seat all of us plus our luggage, had air conditioning units in pristine condition, and gave Hussain a feel-good boost for the short time he'd be driving it.

'Oh my God, it's so hot,' sighed Louise, after grabbing me in an uncharacteristically close bear hug.

'This is nothing,' I said. 'This is the cooler time of the year, it's much worse in the summer.'

We piled into the car and drove back to the apartment, which Deepa and I had spent the morning scrubbing. I watched their faces as we drove through the streets, and the emotions that played out on them as they struggled to interpret the sights before them. I'd of course experienced identical reactions myself, but it was fascinating to watch my family marvel at things that by now seemed so very ordinary to me.

'Don't think much of their driving skills,' exclaimed Matthew, never one for subtlety.

'Ssshhh,' I whispered. 'Hussain's actually an excellent driver.'

'Look at the way those cars are veering all over the road,' said my Dad, his eyes on stalks. 'I can hardly believe there aren't more accidents.'

'There's a cow wandering along the road,' came my Mum's faint voice.

'No, actually, there's a whole cow family wandering along the road, Mum,' I smiled. 'See, there's the Mummy cow, the Daddy cow and the baby cows.'

'I can't believe it.'

'Cows are sacred here,' I told her, 'so they wander around the place freely. They hold up traffic and they're a complete nuisance in rush hour but kind of sweet I suppose.'

As we journeyed the twenty or so miles home, there were similar exclamations over the beggars, the dirt, the piles of rubbish adorning some of the street corners and the general chaos.

'Oh look! They sell Pepsi in India,' said Louise, pointing to an advertising hoarding.

'Yes they do,' I told her, trying to keep the sarcasm out of my voice. 'And they have McDonalds and KFC too.'

'And Burger King?' asked Matthew, hopefully.

'No, no Burger King. And no beef burgers, for that matter.'

Matthew looked as though he might not be able to last a fortnight in India without a Big Mac. 'What will we eat?' he asked, plaintively.

'Curry for breakfast, lunch and dinner,' I told him wickedly, finally succumbing to the temptation to wind up my stick-in-the-mud, conservative, brother-in-law to be.

We finally arrived at the apartment, where Vicky was waiting anxiously to greet us.

'Hello, Mr and Mrs Robinson,' he said, embracing Mum in a warm hug, and shaking Dad's hand. Louise received an equally enthusiastic welcome, and both she and Mum were all smiles and blushes.

I showed them around the small space.

'It's a bit poky isn't it?' said Louise. 'I thought you lived in a posh place out here.'

'Well, believe it or not, this is considered quite posh,' I told her. 'Apartments are expensive to rent here, and exorbitant to buy and this is a really upmarket area so this is really quite a coup for me, this flat.'

Louise eyed me suspiciously, clearly unsure as to whether I was teasing her, as I'd done so often throughout our childhood. Clearly, she and probably my parents had imagined that I was living in some colonial palace, with a slew of servants at my beck and call, wafting around in linens and sipping G&Ts. While I did a fair amount of the latter, I certainly wasn't spoilt, and I think my apartment and the ride through Mumbai's crowded streets had dealt them a dose of reality. I knew, though, that my future in-laws' house would certainly impress them.

'It's lovely,' Mum said loyally. 'You've made the place really cosy.'

I showed them to their rooms, where they were suitably impressed by the en suite bathrooms, which were fairly standard here. I'd long forgotten the days of queuing for the bathroom in my shared London flat and the endless race to claim the hot water before it ran out every morning. The Indians I knew who had been to the UK found it a constant source of amazement that each house had one or maybe two bathrooms on average, that we all sat for hours in our own dirty water, and that we only had the option of scalding or freezing our hands, given that there were always two separate taps in the sinks. These were all things that I had taken for granted back at home, but they did seem a little ridiculous seen through a different lens. In the same way, I now expected every bedroom to come with its own bathroom, most rooms to contain air conditioning, and the entire house to become filthy in a matter of hours, thanks to Mumbai's pollution.

We spent the next couple of days acclimatizing and touring

Mumbai. The city had little for tourists to see, apart from the Gateway of India and the gorgeous architecture of the old British buildings of South Mumbai, but we managed to occupy ourselves shopping in the tourist markets and eating at Mumbai's more international restaurants. Even Matthew was impressed with the food, and though he studiously avoided anything even vaguely spicy, he tucked into the dishes at the upmarket, westernized eateries that I took them to. Matthew seemed to think that all of the locals were somehow after his money, and he took great pride in driving a hard bargain at the market stalls. He'd obviously read the section in the *Lonely Planet* that talked about the art of haggling, and he rubbed his hands with glee as he counted up how much money he'd saved at the end of the day.

Though I didn't like to be ripped off, and understood the innate need of the traders to enter into complex negotiations, which were as much about social etiquette than the money, I still couldn't help but feel that a few rupees here and there was nothing to us, but a lot to many of these people. The same logic applied for me with rickshaws and taxis—I hated being blatantly ripped off, which did occasionally happen thanks to the colour of my skin, and being charged two or three times the regular fare by drivers looking to make a quick buck infuriated me. On the other hand, haggling over a few rupees seemed pointless and mean spirited to me. Matthew, on the other hand, took great delight in driving the shopkeepers and market stall owners down to the very lowest prices, crowing over how cheap everything was in pounds. I didn't really see the point of arguing with him, frankly, or entering into a philosophical discussion, which could go round and round in circles for hours and one that I'd frequently had during my time in Mumbai.

Louise and Matthew started snapping at each other a little bit during the third day, nothing unusual for a couple who had been together for years and who were now overwhelmed by the heat, smells and the sheer cacophony of a new city. As we sat in my living room after the particularly busy day, I asked 'So, are you enjoying yourselves?'

'Lovely,' smiled Mum and Dad. 'Very different,' said Louise. Matthew was silent.

'What about you, Matt?' I asked. 'I hope you're having fun.'

Matthew gave me a look that suggested otherwise. 'Yeah, it's OK.'

'Honestly, Matthew,' Louise said with a note of exasperation in her voice. 'You can never be grateful for anything can you?'

Matthew glowered at her. 'I'm sick of you always telling me how to feel and how to behave,' he replied tightly.

'OK calm down,' I said, trying to smooth over the troubled waters. 'I'm sure he's had a lovely time, it's just that Mumbai's pretty intense and it's probably getting to him.'

'Don't you tell me what I need. Honestly, I'm sick of you lot.' With that, Matthew set his beer bottle down on the table and stomped off to the bedroom. I looked at his retreating back with dismay. Louise started to cry.

'He's being impossible at the moment. He hates it here in India and he's really fed up that I've dragged him out here.'

'Well, it's only a fortnight,' I said. 'And you're here for my wedding. If he's really not enjoying himself, well, it's not as though he has to be here forever.'

I was disappointed but not entirely surprised by Matthew's

reaction. I'd imagined that both he and Louise would find it hard to adjust, but I'd gone out of my way to ensure that everything would be perfect for them, and I tried not to see his outburst as a personal attack. Louise followed him into the bedroom presumably to try and placate him, and we heard raised voices for the next hour or so. I turned the music up on the iPod dock and hoped that it would drown out the sound of their fighting.

'All couples have their moments,' murmured Mum. 'They're ever so close really.'

'Yeah, I suppose so. I guess he's written India off completely, which is sad.'

'Well, it's not for everyone, love,' said Dad. 'We're having a lovely time, but to be honest, it's more about being here for your big day than about coming to India. I'm glad we've done that and I really admire you for sticking it out here.'

I supposed it was pointless to try to tell them again that I was here because I loved it. No amount of my gushing about my adopted country would convince them that I would willingly have exchanged my comfortable life in London for an alternate reality. I couldn't explain that my ties to Mumbai were emotional, that I'd lost my heart to the city the moment I'd landed here and that I felt a connection to the place and its people which I couldn't rationalize.

The next morning, Louise and Matthew got up as though nothing had happened. I had wondered whether Matthew might apologize for his behaviour, but he didn't mention the previous night and I guessed he was embarrassed.

As we sat on the runway later on, waiting for the Delhi bound plane to take off, I thought I'd better brief everyone, gently, on the Kumar family. I didn't want Mum and Dad to feel out of their depth, and I knew that the combination of Mrs Kumar's confidence and 'in your face' personality, mixed with their obvious wealth and ostentation, might make my far meeker parents feel uncomfortable.

'Vicky's Mum and Dad are lovely,' I told them, 'they're quite rich and you know Indians have this thing about wanting to flaunt their wealth. It can be a bit embarrassing for us Brits, you know how shy we are when it comes to talking about money, so just take it all in your stride. And the wedding will be quite a big event.'

'I hope my dress will be Ok for the wedding,' Mum said nervously. 'It's only Designers at Debenhams but it's really lovely.'

'Mum, you'll look amazing,' I said. 'You all will. There's no need to be nervous. Imagine how I feel! I'll be the centre of attention, and that won't be easy.'

'Well, we'll all be there for you,' said Dad with an uncharacteristically emotional squeeze of my hand. 'The wedding will be a little different too,' I told them. 'There's no church, no white dress, and no walking down the aisle'. 'So what will you do then?' asked Louise. 'I'll be dressed in a saree and there will be some blessings and then we have to walk around a fire. Or something,' I answered, still fairly unclear as to the details. I hoped that Dad in particular wouldn't mind that he was being denied the chance to walk his eldest daughter down the aisle, in time honoured tradition.

We entered the now familiar grandiose driveway and I heard Mum's intake of breath, which she quickly tried to cover. I had booked my friends and family into a small but comfortable boutique hotel close to the wedding venue, but I wanted to get the parental introductions over before moving them there. The Kumars were, as always, dressed impeccably. Mrs Kumar was relatively soberly attired, by her standards, although she'd clearly made an effort to impress, with her carefully ironed slacks and pretty printed blouse. As we sat drinking chai in the gorgeously furnished living room, they all made polite small talk. I could see Louise looking around the room, her eyes wide at the sight of the opulence.

'Julia tells us that you're from a lovely part of England,' Mrs Kumar said, beckoning the maid to pour more tea.

'Yes, we certainly are,' Mum answered, grateful for the chance to speak on a familiar topic. 'It's right in the middle of the countryside, very pretty, and we've been living there since before the children were born.'

As my parents exchanged pleasantries I lost myself in the contemplation of the days ahead, looking forward to the arrival of my best friends the following day.

Lizzie, Richard, Annabel and her new boyfriend Dexter were on the same flight. Annabel had told me all about Dexter, or Dex, in an enthusiastic e-mail. Although I couldn't help thinking that he had a ridiculous name, I was dying to meet him. Now that Lizzie and I were settled and on our way to becoming married women, I didn't want Annabel to feel left out.

I spotted them easily in the midst of Delhi's busy airport. As Annabel dropped her bags and ran to embrace me, I couldn't help thinking how bizarre it was to have my two best friends, who were completely part of my London life, here in India. Dex turned out to be a buff but surprisingly intelligent guy, a little younger than Annabel but clearly besotted with her. Maya was the next to arrive, with the long suffering Adnan. I wondered how she would get on with Annabel and Lizzie; though we were all close, Annabel and Lizzie had known me for years, and we had that comfortable friendship that time brings. Maya and I had become close quickly, but we were still getting to know each other.

Vicky had come to the airport with me, and I could hardly believe that I was introducing him to my best friends for the first time, a week before our wedding. Annabel's eyes widened imperceptibly as she took in his broad physique and long, curly locks, which he'd left loose.

'It's so good to meet you, finally,' she breathed.

Lizzie was much more practical, of course. 'Great to meet you, Vikrant,' she said. 'Make sure you look after this girl, or you'll have us to answer to.'

Though her words were said in jest, I knew that she was deadly serious. When it came to protecting her nearest and dearest, Lizzie was a professional.

Everyone had the chance to meet each other properly at the sangeet, the first function of the wedding and the event where everyone, including bride and groom, let their hair down, and danced into the night. My English contingent was wearing a mix of outfits which fused East and West. Annabel was in a gorgeous, but slightly risqué lehenga, a two piece Indian outfit which sat low on her hips and emphasized her slim figure. The dupatta, or scarf, which was supposed to be worn across the chest for modesty, was instead wrapped around her neck, drawing attention to her equally low cut blouse. Lizzie was wearing a short and flattering flared dress which had accents of Indian styling, and my parents were clad in Western outfits with a nod to India—Mum had found a pretty scarf at the local market, which she wore with a wraparound dress, and Dad was wearing a short kurta over casual trousers. Maya of course was in her full Indian regalia, shimmering in a beautiful saree.

'It's from my wedding trousseau,' she confided. 'Might as well get some wear out of it.'

The evening was filled with laughter, music and food, as was to be expected from any Indian function. The music was mainly Hindi pop, and a fair amount of bhangra, which everyone danced to enthusiastically. The bar remained open all night, and everyone drank a lot as was apparently the tradition at Punjabi weddings.

I thanked my lucky stars that I was marrying a man from a community that embraced the drinking culture. Many Indians followed more restrictive guidelines when it came to the consumption of alcohol and even meat, which would have certainly been difficult for me to adapt to. I was pleased to see that Maya, Lizzie and Annabel were making an effort to get along with each other. I knew that while Lizzie was happy that I had made a good female friend in Mumbai, Annabel was a little jealous, although she covered it well as she oohed and aahed over Maya's brilliant blue saree.

The entire Kumar family was on the dance floor moving enthusiastically to the catchy tunes. Maya needed no prompting of course and even Lizzie and Annabel dragged their partners onto the dance floor. From the corner of my eye, I saw Mum down the contents of her glass of wine, and take Dad's hand. Before long, they were also in the middle of the thronging mass of dancers, and although their moves were initially a little self conscious, they soon became more confident, Dad even attempting the bhangra 'arms in the air' dance.

The haldi ceremony came next in the lineup of pre-wedding events. Traditionally held at the bride's home, we decided to buck convention and make this a joint event. Mrs Kumar had kindly offered to host the haldi in her sprawling garden, and was busy distributing plain white kurta pyjamas to the guests, who were mainly friends and family.

'Why do we need to wear these?' Annabel asked me.

'You'll be glad that you're not wearing your own clothes,' Maya told her with a smile. 'This is one of the messiest rituals we have, and you'll all be covered in gloopy yellow paste by the end of it.'

As I donned my bright yellow bride-to-be saree, which clashed horribly with my freckles but was also a part of the tradition, I smiled to myself, thinking how far I'd come since leaving London. As I took my place next to Vicky, who was also wearing the requisite plain white kurta, I looked nervously at the huge vat of mustard yellow sludge which was waiting to be applied to our faces and bodies by the enthusiastic guests. The bright yellow haldi, or turmeric powder, was supposed to brighten the skin of the bride and groom before the wedding. I hoped that it wouldn't stain my fair skin; the last thing I wanted to do was resemble a banana at my own wedding. The guests lined up to take their turn at applying the sticky mixture. Before long, they were rubbing it enthusiastically into our hair, slapping it onto our faces, and massaging it into our arms and legs. By the end of the ceremony, Vicky and I were bright yellow from head to toe.

'Leave that on your face and hands for an hour,' Mrs Kumar told me. 'You'll look gorgeous and glowing at the wedding.'

I had arranged to meet Annabel and Lizzie at their hotel that evening, for a catch up and a brief respite from the elaborate celebrations. I hadn't really had the chance to talk to them since they had arrived and was craving some quality girl time. They sent their respective partners out for dinner, I booked a table at a nearby restaurant for my family who had also invited Vicky to join them, and Annabel, Lizzie and I headed out for drinks.

'Crazy huh?' I asked as we sat down to order from the extensive cocktail list.

'It's certainly different,' said Annabel. 'But I really like Vicky, he seems genuine and down to earth and he's really handsome.'

'I can't believe I'm actually getting married. Here in India. It all seems mad,' I said, deciding finally on an exotically named mango cocktail.

'Well, you left London to pursue your dream, and you've really done it. You've got the swanky job and now you've landed the sexy man.'

'Well, I suppose it's all worked out well but it was a pretty rough ride along the way,' I said, laughing.

Vicky joined us after dinner, a broad smile on his face. 'Your parents are super sweet,' he said. 'Even your sister is lovely, though I swear she was flirting with me all through dinner and Matthew didn't seem very pleased about it.'

'I'm not surprised,' I said, with a smile. 'He's grumpy enough at the best of times, and Louise takes a perverse pleasure in winding him up.'

The mehndi was the next on our packed schedule. This was

one for the ladies, and basically saw us all lying prone on soft pillows whilst elaborate henna designs were painted onto our hands and, in my case, feet. The mehndi application took hours, the designs were intricate and painstakingly applied and so we were rendered immobile for most of the day as the henna dried. It smelled terrible, and looked bizarre, until finally the dried goo was washed away to reveal gorgeous orangey brown shapes and swirls. My own designs went all the way up to my elbows and over my feet, in the bridal fashion.

'This is so exotic,' sighed Lizzie, as she tried to pick up her chai without smudging the pattern.

'Exotic and messy,' I said, wondering how long it would take me to scrub the dried henna off my hands and feet.

The day passed in a pleasant haze of gentle conversation, chai, endless sugary snacks and finally a glass of wine.

'I ordered this specially for our English guests,' Mrs Kumar said, summoning a bottle of Pinot Grigio from the fridge. 'I know how the English love their wine.' I caught Annabel's eye and stifled a grin. After hours of small talk we were all dying for a large glass of wine.

With mehndi designs adorning my hands and feet, and my skin brightened with the liberal application of turmeric, I was now ready for the big day.

Mrs Kumar had arranged for me to have my hair and makeup done professionally, and one of the many 'aunties' was coming to tie my saree. I had worn a saree before on a couple of occasions and didn't think I'd ever be able to get the hang of the complicated draping. My bridal saree was a traditional deep red, adorned with typically rich embroidery with gold detailing. Thanks to the extent of the embellishment, the saree and the pallu were heavy, and I wondered whether I'd be able to last the entire day without flagging. The ceremony itself was scheduled for the supposedly auspicious hour of 2.01 p.m., after which I'd change into a (thankfully) lighter saree for the extravagant party that would follow. I hadn't seen the party venue in all its transformed glory, but Mrs Kumar assured me that it looked spectacular, and that the decorators were indeed delivering on their promises.

By noon I was ready, my saree tied, the pallu draped over my head in the traditional bridal style, colourful bangles jangling prettily on each wrist, silver chains around my ankles, and heavy, expensive looking gold jewellery glinting at my throat and ears. An ornate bindi sat between my eyebrows, topping off my transformation into Indian princess. I could hardly believe my eyes as I gazed at my reflection in the long mirror. I looked like a bona fide Indian and, although my white skin belied my origins, the smoky makeup around my eyes and bright lipstick gave me an exotic look.

Maya, Annabel and Lizzie entered the room, gasping as they did so.

'Oh my god, you Maharani,' exclaimed Maya.

'You look amazing,' Lizzie said, pausing to take a small fold of the saree material between her finger and thumb. 'Oh my god, this is so heavy. How are you going to be able to wear that all afternoon?'

'I know Delhi's on the chilly side at the moment, but you'll be sweltering in that, sitting around the fire,' said Maya. She was referring to the 'phera' or traditional fire that the bride and groom had to walk around a total of seven times to legitimize the marriage.

'I'll manage,' I said excitedly. 'I'm more worried about my makeup slipping down my face than I am about feeling tired.'

My family was equally amazed when they caught sight of my wedding attire.

'You look so different,' Mum said with what I thought was a tinge of regret in her voice.

'I'm still the same old me, under all this,' I said, laughing.

As I was led towards the wedding venue, I heard the deafening sounds of a traditional band playing, complete with what sounded like trumpets, trombones and drums, all creating the most incredible cacophony. As we approached, I saw that the street was filled with people dancing with their hands held aloft, cheering and whooping.

'That'll be the groom's lot,' Maya said, steering me into the middle of the chaos. 'You have to join in and dance.'

'Where's Vicky?' I asked, keen to catch my first glimpse of my husband to be in all his wedding finery.

'He'll arrive in a few minutes on a white horse,' Maya said, as if this was the most normal thing in the world.

'Ah, OK,' I said, stifling a grin at the extent of the exuberance of the dancers.

As always, I mentally compared my surroundings to England. The sombre, still church wedding wasn't a patch on all this noise and energy. Everyone here seemed to be having a wonderful time, dancing and celebrating, and that was before the wedding had even started. Back home, people only let their hair down once the wedding ceremony and the dinner were over.

Right on cue, I heard the clattering of hooves, and Vicky arrived atop a beautiful white horse. He looked every inch the Indian prince and I could hardly believe that he was about to be mine. As he slid off the horse, he slipped his arms around me.

As I looked up at him, my heart stopped. I'd come a long way since leaving my home, experienced amazing adventures, and now I, was finally here.

'You look gorgeous,' he whispered to me, 'Absolutely stunning. Come on, Miss Robinson, let's go and get married.'

# Acknowledgements

Thanks to everyone who supported me in turning my lifelong desire to write a book into reality.

My sister Julie with whom I navigated India for the very first time, in 2000. Those first sights, sounds and smells of Mumbai were overwhelming, and it was so much easier to handle the insanity with her by my side.

My Mum and Dad, who have always blindly supported my ambition and provided me a respite whenever I've needed it.

My Granny, who sadly passed away before meeting my husband-to-be, and who never got to see her longed for great grandchildren, and my Grandad who inspired my love of books from a very early age.

My husband Vivek and my Indian family—Papaji, Mummy and my four sisters in law Bharati, Suman, Jyoti and Karuna who welcomed me into their midst without flinching, despite my tendency to be glued to my laptop during family events. My adorable sons Jake and Noah who I hope will grow up to discover the best of all that is Indian and British.

My two best friends Sarah and Justine, who have stuck with me through thick and thin, since we met as student politicians two decades ago.

## Acknowledgements

My colleagues and friends who have made this ten year adventure in Mumbai an absolute delight. Especially those who helped me settle into what seemed to be a world teetering on the brink of insanity. To Meera and Natasha, my partners in crime on the party scene. To Ali, who has made sense of my late night incoherent mumblings and driven me home safely for the past six years.

To Meru and Faiza at Random House India who saw potential in my story and who have patiently structured my ramblings and focused my thinking.

And finally, to India, where anything can happen.

# A Note on the Author

Heather Saville Gupta worked in London's top advertising agencies before fleeing England for a backpacking trip in 2000. She was seduced by the thrill of Asia and took up an advertising job in Bangkok before moving to India. She now lives in Mumbai with her husband and two children.